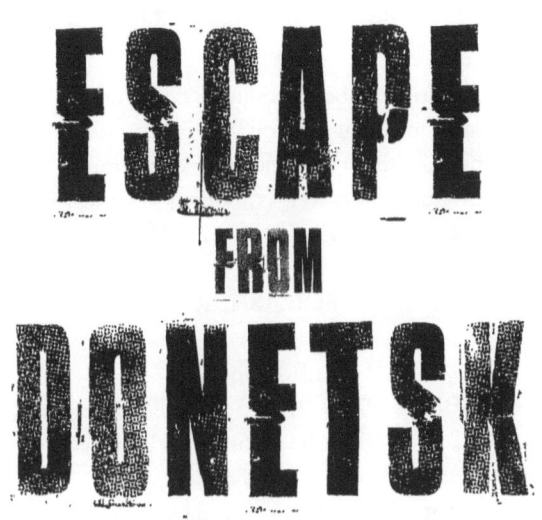

ESCAPE FROM DONETSK

A JON SMITH NOVEL

BOB ASHER

BOB ASHER

First Edition 2024
ISBN-13: 978-1-958115-04-6 (Paperback)
ISBN-13: 978-1-958115-05-3 (Hardcover)

This is a story of fiction. The names, characters, organizations, places, events, and incidents are either products of my imagination or are used fictitiously.

Books by Bob Asher
Jon Smith Military/Espionage Thrillers
BEAR TRAP
SMOKE SIGNALS (a Jon Smith Short Story)
FLASH OVERRIDE (Coming soon)

Zack Goodson Crime Thrillers
HOPE IS DEAD

Please join my Newsletter using the link below for updates on future Jon Smith novels and short stories and I will give you a FREE copy of my Jon Smith Short Story, SMOKE SIGNALS. I promise I won't sell or share your email address with others.
Bob Asher Books Newsletter

Book Cover Design and Interior Formatting by 100Covers.

DEDICATION

Once again, thank you, Sierra Kilo, for your patience and unwavering support while I locked myself up in my office at night to write this story.

CHAPTER 1

22052 (0105HR LOCAL)
FARMHOUSE OUTSIDE
DNIPRO, UKRAINE

Jon was the fourth man in a tight stack of six standing along the back wall of a secluded stone and brick farmhouse on the outskirts of Dnipro, Ukraine. It was a little after 0100hr local time and even though it was a pleasant 70°F this July morning, he was sweating under his helmet and plate carrier. The team and he were wearing Ukrainian Army uniforms tonight and carrying suppressed HK416 carbines with IR lasers. The rest of their gear was also obviously of American origin but since the United States and most of NATO were sending weapons and equipment to help the war effort it didn't matter as long as the administration could say no American combat soldiers were operating in Ukraine. That was technically true. Jon's team was not from the US military, although most were retired from American military special mission units. They fell under the often-used euphemism OGA or other government agencies.

He tried to focus on the op but couldn't help flashing back to two years earlier when he had been in a similar stack in Mosul, Iraq when he saw an explosively formed penetrator explode through a cinder block wall, vaporizing, his best friend, Clint's head as he stood just a foot in front of him. Even now, he could smell the burnt flesh and taste the brain matter that he almost swallowed. Jon tried to shake off the memory. *Get your head out of your ass and focus,* he thought. He had experienced bouts of PTSD ever since, though he refused to acknowledge his diagnosis from his personal civilian doctor, whom he paid in cash. His doctor had transitioned into calling it PTS to hopefully alleviate any stigma attached to the word disorder. There was no way in Hell he would use his military retiree Tricare health insurance to pay for the counseling. He didn't want it popping up in his medical records so to be sure, he used another alias. *Fuck you, PTSD. You can't stop me. I'll operate until I die.* On occasion, he had numbness and tingling in his hands and an annoying twitch in the corner of his right eyelid but only when he was safely in the rear, never while he was on an operation.

Through his Ground Panoramic Night Vision Goggles or GPNVGs, he could see the stack and his team leader, Charlie One, although the team just called him Boss. The four-tubed goggles aka four bangers were a giant leap forward from the dual-tubed goggles he had used in Iraq. Boss was standing at the front of the line facing his team as he began counting down from five with his gloved fingers. When Boss signaled three, Charlie Six cut the electricity to the house. On two the breacher let go of his carbine to let it hang from its sling as he reached back, bringing the duckbilled Mossberg 590A1 shotgun into action. He pressed the end of the barrel against the door between the doorjamb and the deadbolt, before squeezing the trigger. The wood exploded, leaving a four-inch hole. Boss kicked the door open, tossed an M84 stun grenade into the kitchen, and stepped back. After the grenade exploded, he rushed into the darkened room followed by the stack. Instantly, six IR lasers were darting across the room hunting for targets.

They were looking for a Russian SVR officer named Fyodor Nikolaev who had expressed his desire to defect to a CIA case officer. He was sharing this safe house with three other SVR officers who without prior notice or legal process evicted the Ukrainian owners at gunpoint. Jon thought they were no better than the mercenary Hessian troops the Redcoats employed during the American Revolution. The Hessians were infamous for their brutal treatment of the colonists. No one was safe from their outright thievery and physical brutality. The defector was to be identified by his red tracksuit top and excessively submissive posture on the floor with his empty hands on his head. The plan hit a momentary snag when the team encountered four men staggering around the first floor in varying stages of undress, none wearing the required red tracksuit top and all holding handguns. A man wearing a white wife beater and boxers ran into the darkened kitchen. He was looking down while trying to load a magazine into his pistol. Boss shot him with three rounds to his chest from his suppressed carbine.

"Drop your weapons! You are under arrest!" Charlie Five yelled in Russian as loud as he could amongst the chaos, hoping the Russians would stop resisting and make themselves easier targets. Only one Russian was going to leave this house alive. Charlie Two engaged an SVR officer in the family room as he dove behind the overstuffed couch in front of the fireplace. Charlie Two saw half of a bare foot sticking out from the end of the couch. He blew the toes off and was rewarded with a loud yelp, encouraging him to empty half a mag into the couch, instantly killing the man. Charlie Three shot the third SVR officer in the back as he ran for the front door. Jon and Charlie Five saw a man's naked legs disappear up the stairs to the second floor. Charlie Five was Jon's friend Angus "Angie" Hawkins recently retired from the Australian Special Air Service Regiment or SASR. He had been hired as a contractor for this mission thanks to Jon's recommendation and his fluency in Russian and Ukrainian. They followed the naked legs cautiously upstairs, no reason to rush to your death. *Slow is smooth, smooth is fast*, Jon thought.

"Surrender and you will not be harmed!" Angie yelled in Russian.

From the far bedroom, a voice replied in thickly Russian-accented English, "Do not shoot! I surrender, I am Fyodor Nikolaev."

Jon took a quick peek into the room with his NVGs, then carefully entered ready to fire followed immediately by Angie. They saw the man sans trousers face down on the rug, his hands on his head, and his legs bent upward at the knees and crossed at the ankles. His tracksuit top had been hastily draped across his back like Superman's cape. Jon yelled out, "We have the package! Don't move motherfucker." He covered the man while Angie searched him.

"You idiot! Why didn't you have the red tracksuit jacket on as agreed? We almost killed you!" Angie scolded him in perfect Russian.

"It was hot up here in bed and you weren't supposed to be here for another hour. I thought I had plenty of time to get ready," SVR Officer Nikolaev slurred his words. Too much vodka.

4

Arriving early was a smart way to reduce the team's ambush risk. Jon grabbed Nikolaev's trousers off the chair next to the bed, checked the pockets, and tossed them to him. "Put your pants on," he said.

Boss entered the room as Nikolaev rolled back and forth on the floor trying to get his skinny jeans over his hips. "Damn, he looks like Gru from that movie, *Despicable Me*," Boss said after laughing. "Fyodor, what are you doing? We told you what to do when we got here."

"The others wanted to drink vodka, so I had to drink with them. It would have been odd for me not to drink. They all know how much I love vodka," Nikolaev replied in slurred English.

"You don't seem very upset over us killing your friends," Boss said.

"They are not my friends. I never worked with them before we came here for the war. We would have all been dead within a few weeks anyway. Our operational security is shit. We are dying every day. Take me to America. I will tell you everything I know," Nikolaev replied.

"Why didn't you just resign and go back to Russia?" Boss asked.

"I am SVR. Is like Bratva. My country is run by criminals now. The only way you leave SVR is to die," Nikolaev explained. The Bratva was the Russian version of the American Mafia, except much more brutal and effective.

Three transmitted over the team radio, "Boss, Six and I went to get the vehicles, but the Russians are already there. They're setting up an ambush for us. We're coming back to the house now."

"Negative, Three, disregard coming back to the house. We're moving to the secondary exfil site. Go ahead of us, and secure the

LZ," Boss transmitted back. He switched radios and transmitted, "Ghost 21, Charlie 1."

"Go for Ghost 21," the agency pilot and air mission commander of the MH-60 Direct-Action Penetrator or DAP Black Hawk responded as he and his wingman, Ghost 22, randomly orbited about five minutes to the northwest. Ghost 21 was a retired Army CW5 who had served over twenty years in the 160th Special Operations Aviation Regiment known as the Night Stalkers.

"Ghost 21, our ground exfil has been compromised. We are moving to the secondary exfil site," Boss replied.

"Roger that, Ghost 21 five mikes out. Advise when the LZ is secure," the pilot replied.

Boss turned to Angie and said, "Five, zip him up and we'll head out," and then yelled downstairs, "We're coming down."

Angie zip-tied Nikolaev's hands behind his back and led him out of the room to the stairs. He said in Russian, "Be careful. We don't want you breaking your neck on the stairs after we went to all this trouble coming for you."

"Do not worry about me. I have been drinking vodka since I am nine," Nikolaev replied as he effortlessly sauntered down the stairs. He was happy to be leaving the war behind him.

They followed Boss down the stairs and stepped over the bodies as they made their way through the kitchen to the back door. Boss cracked the door open and listened for a few seconds.

Two transmitted from the far side of the backyard, "It's all quiet, you're clear."

Boss checked for himself. "Let's go," he said quietly before he led Jon, Nikolaev, and Angie quickly across the yard where they disappeared into the trees and thick brush.

Two took point and signaled for the group to follow in single-file formation. They fell in behind him at five-meter intervals except for Angie who kept one hand on the Russian. A hundred yards into their trek something growled nearby. Two threw up his left fist to signal the group to freeze. He listened for a few seconds. The group heard something large hurrying away through the brush. Two gave the dog signal with his hand and then motioned for them to follow him. They carefully but swiftly made their way through the woods for about another half mile to the secondary exfil site, a small elementary school playground, where they linked up with Three and Six. The others spread out and covered Angie as he pulled a harness out of his three-day pack.

"Raise your left leg," Angie whispered to Nikolaev.

Nikolaev was confused but complied. "What are you doing? Why do I need a climbing harness? We are flying out in a helicopter, yes?" he asked.

"Sort of, yeah. Right leg," Angie replied as he tugged at his right leg.

Nikolaev raised his leg, but he still didn't understand. He asked, "What? What is sort of?" as the whine of turbine engines grew to an ear-splitting volume just before a large black mass blocked out the stars to hover above him at treetop level. The rotor downwash enveloped them in an invisible cyclone of dirt and debris. Anything not anchored to the ground was flying. The team ran to the center of the playground and grabbed the thick rope that dangled from the bottom of the helicopter. Individually they attached the large D-rings on their harnesses to the rope. Angie finished tightening Nikolaev's harness, and he and Jon pulled the confused Nikolaev along with them. Angie connected Nikolaev's primary D-ring and secondary safety D-ring to the rope before attaching his own.

"Wait, this no good. What is this? Why am I, wait!" Nikolaev shouted as Boss signaled the Black Hawk's crew chief that they were ready. The helicopter leaped toward the stars yanking the team along beneath it. Nikolaev screamed in terror, the sound lost in the roar of the helicopter. The climb was so severe he thought his shoes would come off. He watched wide-eyed as the trees and buildings fell away from him as he rose to sixty meters above the ground before quickly accelerating away in an unknown direction. This high-risk extraction technique was called the Special Patrol Insertion/Extraction or SPIE system. It was not for those with a fear of heights.

"I, I think I will be sick," Nikolaev shouted.

Jon reached above his head and slapped Nikolaev's shoe. "Like fuck, you are! If you puke on me, I'm gonna climb up there and cut you loose! If you throw up, do it inside your shirt!" Jon yelled.

Angie was hanging above Nikolaev laughing. "Relax mate! A little vodka and half-digested Borsch won't hurt you!" Angie shouted to Jon between laughs. A string of green tracers interrupted his laugh and tightened his sphincter as they zipped across the sky toward the helicopter from a road intersection about 500 meters to the east. The helicopter was briefly silhouetted against the lights in the distance.

The crew chief on the right side returned fire with devastating effect from his window-mounted M134 minigun, silencing the machine gun. The M134 was a six-barreled 7.62mm Gatling gun capable of firing up to an incredible 6,000 rounds per minute or

100 rounds per second. The well-disciplined Night Stalker pilot continued on course without any abrupt evasive maneuvers.

"Charlie 1 are you boys still in one piece down there?" the pilot of Ghost 21 calmly transmitted.

"Roger that, looks like we're all here and no one's leaking. I hope that shithead didn't nick our rope," Boss replied.

"Well, if he did you won't have to worry about it very long," Ghost 21 said.

"Three, two, one," Three transmitted on the team radio before he and Six pressed send on their MK152 - remote radio detonators. Almost three miles away, the tree line erupted in spectacular orange and red flashes as the team's SUVs exploded, taking a platoon of Russian Airborne Infantry off the board, and sending large chunks of steel skyward. The SUVs carried an abundance of exotic weapons and ammo. Three and Six shared satisfied smiles and an exploding fist bump. The crew chief sitting behind the right minigun nodded his approval.

CHAPTER 2

2330Z (0230HR LOCAL)
ST. MICHAEL'S CATHOLIC CHURCH,
DONETSK, UKRAINE

Sister Joan was so pissed off she wanted to punch someone in the throat just as her father had taught her when she was thirteen years old. She stood in the kitchen pantry looking at empty shelves that, hours earlier, had been overloaded with food. Only a small fraction remained. She locked the door and hurried away to find the father. She stormed into the large classroom in the basement of the church. It had been hastily converted into a nursery and playroom. Rows of old army cots filled the room. In the two weeks she had been at the church Father Del Toro, and she had taken in almost a hundred children ranging from newborn infants to young teenagers. Some were displaced kids whose parents were fighting the Russians, but most were orphaned by the war.

Father Del Toro, the Spanish priest, was sitting on a tiny red chair between their cots, entertaining them with a spirited reading of a story from a book of Ukrainian folktales. They laughed at the story and his difficulty reading Ukrainian. Sister Joan waved from across the room to get his attention.

"Oh, yes, sister," he said quietly as he waved back. "Excuse me, boys and girls, Sister Joan needs my help," Father Del Toro said as he stood. He handed the book to an older girl. "Katya, please, finish the story for the children." The children moaned their disappointment. "Oh, please, don't upset Katya. She is much better at reading Ukrainian than I am." She sat down and delivered a spirited reading of the fairytale. As he crossed the room, he could see the concern on Sister Joan's face. He placed his hand on her shoulder and whispered in English, "Don't be cross sister. I know it is late but one of the children woke up crying from a nightmare which caused several others to wake up."

Sister Joan shook her head and led him out of the room so the children couldn't hear her.

"What is wrong, sister?" the father asked.

"Food is missing from the pantry, a lot of food. We have maybe a day's worth left," she said quietly as she struggled to control herself.

Father Del Toro was shocked. "How is this possible? We keep the pantry door locked. We should have food for five days," he said.

She rolled her eyes. "Please, Father, you know who took it, it's obvious. There's only you, me, and Yurochka here," she replied. "He stole it while we were busy with the kids." Yurochka Yecoshenko was the church gardener and handyman. He lived in a small cottage behind the church next to the barn and cemetery. He had become more and more unreliable as the days passed under Russian occupation. They walked through the kitchen at the other end of the large basement. The pantry was in the rear of the kitchen. Sister Joan unlocked the pantry door, and they walked inside.

Father Del Toro slowly surveyed the empty shelves, his anger quickly surpassing Sister Joan's. It had been very difficult to keep the pantry stocked as every day more and more hungry children were placed in his care. On his last foraging trip, he had to trade everything of value the church possessed. "He must have worked for hours moving the food out of here. If only he worked this hard at his daily duties, the church would be pristine. I will speak to him to give him a chance to explain his actions and then we will bring the food back to the pantry," Father Del Toro said. He wasn't afraid of confronting the thuggish, Yurochka. Father Del Toro had earned his green beret in the Unidad de Operaciones Especiales or Spanish Army Special Forces before entering the priesthood.

"Father we should change the padlock. Only the two of us should have keys," Sister Joan said.

"I am sorry to say you are right. I have another lock in my desk. Come with me, we'll get it now," Father Del Toro replied, "While I'm there I will try to call the bishop and ask him to evacuate the children again."

"It's late. He's probably sleeping," Sister Joan warned.

"My children are awake and soon they may be hungry. He can be awake too," Father Del Toro said. He wasn't afraid of bishops either. The father kept an Armor of God challenge coin in his pocket to remind him of what was important. He knew who he answered to.

They walked up the stairs and as they passed the church's front doors, they heard the rumble of trucks coming up the long gravel driveway. They shared concerned looks and Father Del Toro cracked the door open to peek into the darkness. The streetlights at the entrance to the church property had stopped working weeks before. He saw a convoy of headlights coming toward the church. "They must be military trucks, Russian or Chechen, I'm not sure. Stay in here and I will go out to talk to them," he said. He walked outside, closing the massive wooden doors behind him. He stood on the edge of the driveway as three large green military cargo trucks came to a stop. Twenty Chechen soldiers climbed out of the trucks and stood in a semicircle around the priest. Their commander stepped forward. He was a tall, overweight man with a long graying beard.

He smiled and said in English, "Father, I am Colonel Marvan Sultanovich of the Chechen Special Forces." He offered his hand to the Father.

Father Del Toro smiled back politely, shook his hand, and said in English, "It is good to meet you, Colonel. I am Father Domingo Del Toro. How may I help you tonight?" as he scanned the soldiers arrayed in front of him.

"Father, I have received reports that many children are being housed in your church. This is a war zone, and they are not safe here. I am concerned for their well-being. I am responsible for all civilians living in my sector. I am here to evacuate them to a safe area where they can be properly protected," Sultanovich replied.

"Thank you for your concern but there is no need for worry, Colonel. This is God's house," Father Del Toro said as he motioned to the sturdy brick and stone church behind him, "The children will always be safe here under God's protection."

Sultanovich nodded and said, "I have also been told you are running out of food to feed them. There are no stores left in this sector for you to get more food. It will be much better for the children if they come with me." His men stepped toward the doors and the priest stepped in front of them.

Now the father smelled a rat. How could the Colonel know the food was gone unless he was working with Yurochka? "Colonel, I assure you we have plenty of food for the children," Father Del Toro said as he backed up to the doors and grasped the handles behind his back to keep them closed. He knew what the Chechen had planned for his children, and he would not permit it. There were numerous reports of Ukrainian children being rounded up by the Russians and Chechens only to be taken out of the country never to be seen again.

The Colonel took a deep breath and expelled it quickly in exasperation. "Very well, I grow tired of this charade, teach the priest a lesson in exchange for his insolence," Colonel Sultanovich said with a smile. The soldiers moved forward sensing fresh meat. Father Del Toro dropped the first man with a swift kick to his groin and the second with a left jab that destroyed his nose. The soldiers swarmed Father Del Toro, two grabbing his arms. Father Del Toro headbutted the one on the left and drove his right heel into the other's knee. He was rewarded with a satisfying crack as it bent unnaturally sideways, and the soldier fell to the ground. More arms grabbed him, and he was able to elbow a soldier in the temple causing him to collapse unconscious. The rest of the swarm enveloped the father, taking him to the ground. They pummeled the priest with their fists and kicked him back onto the driveway.

They took turns stomping and kicking the poor priest in the head and torso like a bunch of drunken soccer hooligans. He was hopelessly outmatched against so many men. *I must stay alive for the children*, he thought. He cried out, "Por favor, no se detenga más no más!" in his native tongue. His eyes were swelling shut and he couldn't breathe through his broken nose. A gash on the back of his head where his skull was cracked covered his neck with blood and spinal fluid. *Father, forgive them for what they do,* was his last thought before he died.

Sister Joan cried helplessly as she watched the beating from the window. Tears ran across her hands as she covered her mouth, hoping they wouldn't hear her. She was frozen in terror. She prayed for a miracle to save the good father, but none came. In her young life, she had never witnessed anything so callous and brutal, totally devoid of humanity. It was akin to a pride of lions eating a baby impala while it was still alive. The soldiers were laughing, except for the five that required medical attention. Then she thought of the children, she didn't worry about herself. How could she save the children? She prayed again, then looked around for something she could use as a weapon.

"Bring out the children!" Sultanovich bellowed to his men as he rubbed his hands together while stepping over the dead priest's body. He was already imagining the huge stacks of euros he would be depositing in his Zurich safety deposit box.

Sister Joan stood just inside the doors with a sturdy five-foot-long oak coat rack held above her head. She would make the fat colonel pay for his sins.

But before he could step inside the threshold a young baby-faced captain yelled to the colonel from the cab of the second truck, "Colonel, the Ukrainians have mounted a counterattack on the airport. The base is in danger of being overrun."

Sultanovich stopped three feet short of having his skull caved in, turned to look at the captain for a moment, and then back to the church lobby. He weighed his options and finally turned toward his truck and said, "Very well, our retirement plan will have to wait. Mount up. We will come back for them later." The trucks roared to life and the lead truck made a hard left turn, plowing deep furrows in the manicured lawn with its massive offroad tires quickly followed by the others. He would never know the Ukrainian Army saved his life.

Sister Joan remained frozen with the coat rack above her head. She was stunned by what had just happened. She had been given the reprieve she asked for. Why would the Lord save her but not his faithful servant, Father Del Toro? There was so much she didn't understand. She needed help, so she would call the one person in the world who had always fixed her problems. She ran to the church's office and sat down behind the father's desk. She looked at the phone and made another silent prayer. Telephone service had been intermittent for weeks. She picked up the receiver and got a dial tone. She called her mom in Norfolk, Virginia.

"Please, answer! Please, answer! Please, answer!" she begged.

"Hello," her mom said.

Sister Joan was so excited she tried to say everything all at once. She sounded like a scared thirteen-year-old girl, "Momma, it's Kimmie! I need help! Chechen soldiers came to the church and killed Father Del Toro! They beat him to death, Mom. We're trapped behind the Russian lines!" And then the phone went dead again. "No! No! No! Please, Lord, help me!" Sister Joan cried as she prayed aloud with her head bowed, "Oh Jesus, our beloved Lord and Savior, please, help me protect these innocent children. I ask this through Christ, our Lord, Amen." She tried the phone again but there was no dial tone. She tapped the plunger several times, but the line was dead. At least her mom had heard her. She knew Kimmie needed help. Now she thought of her immediate problem. She had to bury Father Del Toro.

CHAPTER 3

The two passengers observed the scene below through their NVGs as their Mi-2 transport helicopter flew low and slow over the smoldering remains of the two Agency Chevy Suburbans. The SUVs' white-hot metal framework glowed bright green in their goggles. A platoon of soldiers moved about in the darkness retrieving the bodies and body parts of their comrades to stuff into rubberized bags. The Mi-2, NATO codename – Hoplite, landed a kilometer down the gravel road near the farmhouse where Jon's team had collected their defector only an hour and a half before. The two men jumped from the Hoplite and hunched over as they hurried out from under the rotor arc. They walked with purpose as they passed the soldiers forming a loose perimeter around the house. No one dared confront them. They raised their NVGs out of the way as they entered the brightly lit interior of the farmhouse through the front door. Three body bags were lined up on the floor. A lieutenant colonel, the battalion commander, was standing beyond the bodies near the kitchen with his back to the men as he gave orders to his officers. The older, taller man bent over and unzipped the first bag to see the occupant's face. He quickly zipped it up and moved to the second bag. He zipped that bag up and moved to the final bag. He unzipped the third bag and froze for a moment. He dropped to one knee and took his glove off to touch his younger brother's bloody face. His partner knelt next to him and put his arm around his shoulder. Tears fell from the older man's face as he closed his brother's dead eyes. He wiped his tears away, approached the colonel, and asked, "Colonel, where is the fourth SVR officer, Fyodor Nikolaev?"

The colonel looked over his shoulder and said, "I will talk to you in a moment. I'm issuing orders to my officers," before turning back to his men.

The man grabbed the colonel by his arm and spun him around, "You will talk to me now, Colonel. Where is SVR Officer Nikolaev? We need to determine if he has been abducted or is a traitor."

"Get your hands off of me! Who do you think you are? This is my AOR. What is your authority here?" the battalion commander demanded to know as he looked down on the man.

The man looked up at the colonel and punched him in the face with his right fist sending him to the floor. The colonel's officers moved to defend him. The man's partner raised his rifle and shouted, "Stop or you will join these men in the bags!"

"Who are you? What is your rank?" the colonel asked loudly as he held his bloody nose between his fingers.

The man straddled the colonel's waist and bent over. He pointed to the embroidered patch stuck to the side of his MICH helmet that read M22. "I am SVR Zaslon Officer M22." He pointed to his partner behind him and said, "He is Zaslon Officer M29. We have been ordered here to track down a hostage or a traitor. I can kill you if it is my wish without any concern. I can remove any trace that your wife and children ever existed. That is my authority. Now, where is SVR Officer Nikolaev?" Zaslon was Russia's most secretive special-purpose or Spetsnaz unit within the Russian external security service, Sluzhba Vneshney Razvedki or SVR.

"He was taken by a team of American Spetsnaz. They flew away in a Black Hawk helicopter," the colonel replied.

"We need transportation. Where is your car?" M22 asked.

"Fuck you! You can't have my car!" the colonel yelled. He had stolen the Ultimate Black Metallic Land Rover Defender 110 fair and square from a Ukrainian bank president.

M22 shot him in the face with his rifle. The colonel's young officers recoiled in horror, frozen by the violence. "Who is the executive officer?" M22 asked the men. The two lieutenants pointed to the man standing between them. "Come with us, Major, and bring his key fob."

Minutes later, M22 drove past the soldiers manning the perimeter around the burned-out Suburbans. M29 sat next to him, and the major sat in the backseat. M22 left the headlights off and relied on his NVGs to navigate along the road. He slowed to 40 KPH and said, "Thank you for the escort, Major. You may go now."

"What? The car is still moving!" the major complained.

"You are the mighty Airborne Infantry. Jump," M22 said.

M29 turned in his seat, displayed his pistol over the seatback, and said, "It will only get faster from here," before he motioned with his pistol for the major to jump. The major reluctantly opened his door and launched himself out of the vehicle. He tried to protect his head as he hit the gravel.

M29 watched him roll to a stop and stagger to his feet through the back window before he turned back around to speak to M22, "I don't mind throwing an occasional major out of a moving vehicle, but you must stop executing battalion commanders. Eventually, someone will complain."

CHAPTER 4

After an uncomfortable fifteen minutes of being dragged along behind Ghost 21, it finally landed in a clearing long enough for everyone to climb inside. Jon was sitting in the right rear seat. Nikolaev sat next to him in the middle seat with sound-suppressing headphones over his ears under a black hood. Nikolaev spread his legs wide and complained loudly, "My balls are on fire! I think the harness strangled them! I have been castrated! Tell the medic to check my testicles!"

Jon pulled the sound-suppressing cup about three inches from Nikolaev's ear and yelled, "Shut the fuck up or I'll cut'em off for real!" Jon let go, allowing the cup to slam into his head. The startled defector shut up immediately.

Angie sat on the other side of Nikolaev. He was chugging some local imitation of Red Bull that Jon knew from personal experience tasted like artificially sweetened tiger piss. He choked on his drink as he laughed after hearing Jon's threat. Boss and the rest of the team were sipping coffee provided by the aircrew. Jon was looking out of his window trying not to fall asleep when his satellite phone vibrated. He had turned it back on after getting inside the helicopter. He disconnected the comm cord from his team radio and plugged it into the sat phone. He answered, "Hello."

"Jon, it's Carol! I need your help! Kimmie called me about an hour and a half ago. She's in danger! You have to help her! Please, Jon!" she cried out.

Jon sat up straight in his seat. "Whoa! Slow down, Carol, take a breath! What's wrong?" Jon asked. He was wide awake now.

She took several deep breaths and said slowly, "Don't tell me to calm down. Kimmie needs help. You know she's a nun now, right? She's called Sister Joan. She volunteered to leave her church in Austria two weeks ago to help with the humanitarian relief efforts in Ukraine. They sent her to St. Michael's Church in Donetsk. It's behind the Russian lines now. She said the Chechens came to the church and murdered her priest. They beat him to death, Jon. She is scared to death. She needs help getting out. Jon, please, help her."

"Jesus Christ, Carol! Why did you let her go to Ukraine? It's a damned war zone! Are you fucking stupid?" Jon yelled into the phone. Angie and Boss heard him over the roar of the helicopter and turned to look. Even Nikolaev moved his head around under the hood like Stevie Wonder searching for the origin of the phantom sound. Angie and Boss had never seen Jon that pissed off, even in combat.

"Don't yell at me, dammit! She's an adult! I didn't let her do anything! She gets to decide what she does now! She was in Donetsk before she even told me! Now, stop yelling and help me! You're the only person I know that can get her out of there!" She started crying again.

Jon was on the verge of hyperventilating. He followed his own advice and took several long deep breaths to calm himself.

"Jon? Hello? Are you still there?" she asked between sobs. She sounded weak and small now. Like her only hope of saving her daughter had faded away.

"Yeah, I'm here, Carol. I'm sorry I blew up at you. I know this isn't your fault. I happen to be less than a day away from Donetsk. I'll get her out," he replied.

Relief rushed over her. She could breathe again. Carol worked to regain her composure. "She was terrified, Jon. She said she needed help. She didn't actually say she wanted out. What if she won't leave?" Carol asked.

Jon looked at the phone like it must be malfunctioning. "Carol, are you serious? When I find her, she's coming out! There's no question about that!" Jon replied, "Give me the number to the church. I'll try to call her." She read off the number and Jon wrote it on his left forearm, before programming it into his sat phone. "Try not to worry. I'll get her. Hey, why did you wait to call me?"

"I couldn't find the number for your damn sat phone. I've been turning the house upside down," she replied.

"I left it on the front of the fridge, remember?" Jon said.

"Yes, that's where I found it," she replied.

"Okay, I better go," Jon said.

"Thank you, Jon, and Jon, be careful," she said like she was going to cry again.

24

"I will. No worries," he replied.

"I love you, Jon," she said quietly.

"I love you too. Talk to you soon. Say hi to the kids," he disconnected the call and wiped his eyes. He started shaking his head and cursing out loud to himself.

Boss leaned over and touched Jon's knee to get his attention. He tapped his ear signaling Jon he wanted to talk. He waited until Jon reconnected his radio. "What the fuck was that?" Boss asked Jon over the team radio.

Now everyone on the team would hear about Jon's private business but he really didn't care. They were all good people. After training together for four months and then operating together for six more they had become like brothers. "That was my old swim buddy Clint's widow. She said my goddaughter, Kimmie, who now happens to be a Catholic nun named Sister Joan called her and said she's trapped behind enemy lines at her church in Donetsk. The Chechens came to the church tonight. She saw them beat her priest to death," Jon explained.

Boss shook his head and said, "Those shitheads are savages. I've seen them skin people alive."

"Boss, I'm sorry about this, but I have to go after her," Jon said as a matter of fact. He wasn't asking for permission.

Boss nodded. "No shit. Of course, you do. You do anything for family. I'd drop this SVR asshole off at the Polish border and go with you, but I know the Agency would have a shitfit. They'll say some bullshit about the Russians already threatening to go nuclear if there is any American intervention in Ukraine and forbid me from helping you. But as I remember, you have a bunch of use or lose leave on the books. So, if you want to go on vacation for a couple of weeks, I'll approve it," Boss replied.

"Thanks, Boss," Jon said.

Boss waved his hand in the air to signal no thanks was warranted. He wrote down an address in his notebook and ripped the page out. He handed it over to Jon. "This is the address to our cache house in Lviv. We'll drop you off nearby. You'll find a black Chevy Suburban there and all the weapons and equipment you'll need."

"Boss, if it's all the same to you, I'd like to go with Jon," Angie said.

Boss turned to Angie and said, "Well Hawkins, you did a fine job with us on your first contract. I hope we'll be able to work together again." He held out his hand and they shook. "I think we'll be able to manage the rest of the way to Poland without you guys," Boss replied.

Jon reconnected his sat phone to his headset and called the church's number. *Come on, Kimmie, answer the phone,* he thought. He tried several times, but the call never went through. *Lord, please, let her be safe until I can get her out of there,* he prayed silently.

CHAPTER 5

0100Z (0400HR LOCAL)
ST. MICHAEL'S CATHOLIC CHURCH,
DONETSK, UKRAINE

Sister Joan quietly walked between the cots until she got to the girl she was looking for. "Katya, wake up." The girl looked up at the sister. "Please, wake up the six oldest children. Tell them to get dressed and meet us outside the nursery," Sister Joan whispered. Katya spoke English and was able to translate for the sister. Five minutes later she led the group upstairs. "Katya, please tell everyone to sit in the last pew," Sister Joan said. Katya translated the message into Ukrainian for her.

"I'm sorry but I have terrible news. Chechen soldiers came to the church tonight. They intended to take all of you away to Chechnya where your families would never see you again. Father Del Toro fought them for us and hurt many of them before they killed him," Sister Joan said. Katya translated as she cried. She was quickly joined by the others. Sister Joan gave them time to compose themselves.

"When will they come back? We should run away before they come back," a frightened boy said.

"Calm down. We must be strong for the little ones. I will ask Sister Joan," Katya said in Ukrainian before switching to English for the sister. "He is scared. He wants to run before they come back to get us."

"Tell him not to worry. Father Del Toro told the bishop to send people to evacuate us and I called home to get help. Have faith. Help will come for us," Sister Joan said in her most confident voice. Katya relayed the message.

"Now, we have to bury the father before the children wake up. They can't be allowed to see his body," she said. She handed out the shovels she retrieved from the barn and said, "Follow me."

CHAPTER 6

A portly, balding man hurried down the empty hall as fast as his short legs could carry him toward the White House Chief of Staff's office. Flop sweat flowed from every pore. His damp bowtie was about to strangle him. He pounded rapidly on the office door and then entered before receiving a response. He flipped on the light switch. "Harold, we have a problem!" he said near panic while trying to catch his breath. Harold was Harold Lamb, White House Chief of Staff, the President's right-hand man.

"Of course, we do, Pres, it's," he squinted in the bright light as he looked at his watch, "another early Tuesday morning in the White House," Lamb replied unimpressed from underneath his Harvard University fleece blanket. He sat up on his couch and rubbed his eyes. "Well?" he asked.

Pres took his glasses off and cleaned them with his handkerchief. "A CIA paramilitary officer, with the cover name, Jon Smith, is on an unsanctioned mission in Ukraine to rescue his goddaughter. She's a Catholic nun at St. Michael's Church in Donetsk," said the National Security Advisor, Preston Alexander.

"So what? Who gives a fuck? Wait! That's under Russian control, right?" Lamb asked.

"Yes, and if we don't get him out of there, he could ruin Wynken's trip to Belarus," Alexander replied. Wynken was Secretary of State Anton Wynken. His trip to Belarus was scheduled to occur in two days. He would meet with the Russians to discuss a peaceful resolution to the illegal invasion of Ukraine. Oddly, the Ukrainians weren't invited to the peace talks that could very well determine their nation's future.

"Wait a minute. Let's think this through. He's just one guy. How much damage can he do?" Lamb asked, "He'll probably get killed before he can cause any problems."

"Actually, there are two of them. His teammate, a contractor from Australia named Angus Hawkins went with him," Alexander said.

"Okay, two guys. Big fucking deal. I'm tired of everybody acting like these special operations guys are supermen. They're a bunch of knuckle-dragging gun monkeys. They're expendable like toilet paper or MREs. There's always another dumbass farm boy dying to take their place.

"Make sure the DNI and DOD are told not to help them under any circumstance. If they go to Donetsk, they're fucked. They'll never get out alive." Lamb scratched his scruffy gray beard. "Track their progress and report back if they stir up any shit that might cause a problem. I have to be up at 5:30. Turn out the lights and close the door," Lamb said as he lay down and curled up under his blanket.

"Shouldn't we tell the President?" Alexander asked.

"What's the point? He won't remember it in the morning anyway," Lamb replied.

Alexander stood there like they had unfinished business. "Go away, Pres!" *Fucking academics,* Lamb thought. He changed gears and thought, *I should call Suliman. He might be able to use this information.*

CHAPTER 7

The fat Chechen colonel was sitting at his private table in the dining facility about to bite into his hot breakfast when his nephew, the captain, appeared in front of him to report. The colonel returned his utensils to the table. "What is it, Captain?" he asked.

"Colonel, the fighting has ended. The Ukrainian attack has been repulsed. We killed fifteen and recovered ten of the wounded they left on the battlefield. The prisoners are being interrogated as we speak. We incurred twenty-five dead and 42 wounded," he replied.

"Yes, yes, very well. What about the broker? Any news from him?" Sultanovich asked.

"Yes, sir. The broker wants every child we can obtain, and he promises the auction results will be better than the last. He also said he will pay a premium for the Catholic nun if she is delivered undamaged," he replied.

"How much more?" Sultanovich asked.

"Twice the usual amount for a female of her age," the captain replied.

"Excellent! Pass the word to the men. If any of them damage the nun, I will cut off one of their hands for stealing from me," the colonel said.

CHAPTER 8

Boss and his team had been sitting in the relative comfort of the Black Hawk's nylon seats for hours except for a twenty-minute period when they set up a security perimeter while the helicopter refueled in a temporary FARP on a bomb-damaged general aviation airport. Now they were rapidly approaching Lviv. Jon was asleep in the back row with his helmeted head resting in the corner between the aft bulkhead and the right-side crew door when Boss tapped his knee and transmitted over the team radio, "I called the brass back home and informed them of your situation. They took it all the way up to the DDO. He was sympathetic but refused to provide any support. He specifically forbade me from helping you, so sorry, but I can't help," he said.

Jon didn't bother moving his head but replied, "I understand, Boss. Thanks for the cache house. That will help a lot."

Boss shook his head at Jon and gave him the cut signal before he transmitted, "What was that? I think you broke up for a second."

"Oh, okay. Thanks anyway," Jon replied.

"Also, I just received intel that an air attack is imminent on Lviv. Heavy bombers and cruise missiles are inbound so don't be surprised if we drop you off in the middle of a maelstrom."

"A what?" Jon asked.

"An enormous clusterfuck," Boss clarified.

"Roger that, Boss, easy day. Are you hearing this, Angie? It's not too late to change your mind," Jon said.

"Fuck it, mate! Let's get this party started!" Angie feigned excitement.

***

Boss's intel was good. Twenty minutes later as the Black Hawk approached the outskirts of Lviv from the south everyone sitting on the right side of the helicopter could see a steady stream of cruise missiles coming toward the city low and fast from the east followed at high altitude by the bombers and their escorts. "Damn! It looks like the old black and white newsreel films of London being attacked by the German V2 rockets," Boss said. They were transfixed by the scene they were witnessing and by the knowledge the seemingly peaceful landscape they were approaching would soon be engulfed in flames and destruction. Innocent people were going to die, and they were helpless to prevent it.

Ukrainian air defense missiles, launched from sites ringing the city, raced toward the Russian missiles and bombers. Many of them were intercepted, their fiery debris tumbling from the sky well short of their intended targets, but many more were not. The Russian missiles slammed indiscriminately into civilian apartment buildings seemingly at random throughout the city. None could be even remotely considered valid military targets. The explosions caused massive fires and burning debris flew in all directions causing further death and destruction. Steel beams and concrete rubble rained down into the streets crushing vehicles and people.

Boss snapped out of his stupor. "Hey, that's a Patriot missile!" he transmitted on the team radio as he pointed out the window. The anti-aircraft missile was launched from the city's eastern edge and was flying directly toward a TU-95 Bear bomber at Mach 4.1. The missile exploded on the Bear's left wing causing it to roll upside down before spiraling toward the ground. The bomber didn't have an ejection system for the aircrew. Boss watched as the six-man crew began bailing out of the disintegrating bomber before it impacted the ground causing an even greater explosion. "There's one, two, three. I see three good chutes," Boss transmitted.

"Those boys are in for a rough day. The first rule of bomber flying is to not bailout over the target you just attacked," the Ghost 21 pilot said over the team radio frequency.

"Actually, I don't think they had time to release their load," the copilot replied.

"I don't think the kind people of Lviv will make that distinction," the pilot said.

Next time stay in Russia, Jon thought as he grew angrier by the second watching the ongoing destruction spread. He also didn't relish the idea of being dropped right in the middle of it.

"Okay, Jon, we're going to drop you off about three miles from your target, so we don't draw any unnecessary attention to the house. The area is built up so we're going to land on the flat roof of an abandoned building. Your target will be due north. Get ready, we'll be there in about three minutes," the pilot transmitted.

"Roger that, we'll be ready," Jon replied. He looked over at Angie and received a thumbs up.

"Landing checklist," the pilot called out on the ICS.

"Tail wheel switch locked. Parking brake on. Crew, passengers, and mission equipment check," the copilot replied as he held his thumb up in front of the instrument console where the pilot could see it.

"We'll see you guys when we get back," Jon transmitted to the team. The other guys responded with fist bumps and handed over their extra rifle magazines to make sure Jon and Angie had a full combat load when they hit the ground.

"If you get down there and you are absolutely out of options call me. I don't know what I'll be able to do but call me anyway. Otherwise, you boys be careful," Boss said.

The sun had been up for two hours when the Black Hawk came into a hover next to the flat roof of an old bombed-out two-story warehouse in a secluded wooded area on the outskirts of Lviv. The pilot slid his helicopter to the right and placed his right main mount tire on the corner of the roof as he maintained a steady hover. All the while, the Russian air attack continued around them. Jon's teammate, Charlie Three, slid the right door open and Jon and Angie, carrying their rifles and packs, stepped out of the helicopter onto the roof. They hunched over under the spinning rotor blades and hurried away to the stairs leading off the roof. Ghost 21 climbed away as Charlie Three closed the door. The crew chief waved goodbye from behind his minigun.

Jon and Angie shouldered their heavy packs before running down the stairs to the ground floor of the gutted building. All that remained of the original structure was part of the roof and the brick walls. Everything else had been scavenged long before the most recent Russian aggression. They headed north right away without looking at their GPS receivers. For now, they just wanted to create some distance between themselves and the drop-off point. The roads were empty in the immediate area. All of the sane people in town were taking cover below ground. They took turns bounding forward. One would run forward for three to five seconds while the other covered him. They continued the process for about ten minutes. Every step brought them closer to the chaos and destruction caused by the air attack. Cruise missiles continued to explode in front of them.

"I hope we don't get killed before we even start heading to Donetsk," Angie said as he ran by Jon.

"I hope the cache house is still in one piece when we get to it," Jon replied as he ran past Angie. They were entering a residential area of single-family homes. Many of the homes had been hit, one was razed to the foundation. Jon stopped at the end of a tall stone courtyard wall at the intersection of two streets. He peeked around the corner. He saw several damaged vehicles on the street, one was a van on its side burning. Beyond it, an old woman was on her knees in front of an old man lying in the street. She wailed uncontrollably. Jon waved Angie forward. Angie peeked around the corner. "She doesn't appear hurt, but the old man isn't moving. Let's see how fast we can get them into the church across the street," Jon said.

"Sounds good, mate," Angie replied.

Jon looked both ways before he ran around the corner. He took four strides before a missile exploded into a three-story brick house to his right. The shockwave knocked him off his feet and he flew twenty feet head-first into the roof of the overturned Ford Transit van. He crumpled to the pavement face first. Angie ran to him and rolled him over onto his side. Jon's nose was bleeding and he groaned as he sat up with his pack against the van. He opened his eyes wide and then blinked several times trying to get them to focus. "How bad am I hit?" he asked.

Angie ran his hands over Jon's body and replied, "Other than your bloody nose, I don't see any damage."

Jon slowly rolled over onto his knees and then used the van to steady himself as he stood up. He held his head high and wiped his nose on his sleeve. "Oh no, not my nose. That's my moneymaker. The ladies say it's my best feature. They'll be devastated," Jon said as he tried to smile.

"No worries, Jonny. Even now, broken, and bloodied, your nose is still your best feature," Angie said with a grin.

"Bullshit! My momma said I won a pretty baby contest just on my smile," Jon replied.

"I think you're a few stubbies short of a six-pack, mate. You may be worse off than I thought. You should sit back down," Angie said.

"Funny. Go check on the babushka. I'll be right behind you. First, I'll check these vehicles," Jon said.

***

Angie ran to the old couple. He dropped his pack and went to his knees to check on the unconscious man. "He has a bad wound to his calf. I'll put an Israeli bandage on it," he said in Ukrainian to the woman. He quickly applied the bandage, stopping the bleeding.

The woman watched him work, but seemed confused, "Are you Israeli?" she asked.

"No, Mother," Angie replied again in Ukrainian.

Jon quickly discovered there were no survivors in the vehicles and quickly walked over to Angie. He said, "They're all dead."

"What happened?" Angie asked the woman in Ukrainian as he began checking the old man for more injuries.

She took several deep breaths to steady herself as Angie worked. "My husband and I were walking to the market when the first missile hit that house." She pointed over her shoulder. "The explosion knocked us off our feet and a piece of jagged metal cut his leg. We tried to get to the church, but he collapsed, and I couldn't move him. Is he dead?" she asked, tears running down her dirty face.

"No, he lost some blood, but I think this bandage will stop the bleeding," he replied in Ukrainian. "Jon, can you carry him to the church while I help her?" Angie asked in English.

"Yeah, I got him," he replied. Jon was still operating at half speed. He went down to one knee and sat the old man up and then he and Angie hoisted him up onto Jon's shoulders in a fireman's carry. "Damn!" Jon grumbled. The added weight was almost more than his trembling legs could carry.

Angie patted Jon on the shoulder. "There you go, Jonny. Good lad. Easy day, right?" Angie said as he smiled. Between his pack and the old man, Jon was carrying over 250 pounds. He groaned as he slowly staggered off toward the church.

Angie quickly shrugged his pack onto his shoulders. "Mother, this will go much faster if I carry you," Angie said as he took her wrist in his hand and bent over to wrap his other arm around her leg. He stood up with her on his shoulders and turned to follow Jon.

"Wait! My purse! It has my money and identification!" she shouted.

"Yes, of course," Angie said as he bent over carefully to pick it up without dropping her before he hurried off behind Jon.

Jon struggled up the stone steps in front of the church, taking them one at a time and leading with his right foot. He was sucking air as he pushed the massive oak doors open. Angie followed close behind.

Angie called out for the padre in Ukrainian. A moment later he appeared. "Over here! We have been taking shelter in the basement! Come join us!" he beckoned them forward.

Angie asked, "Do you have a doctor here?" as he and Jon carried the couple toward the stairs. Another missile explosion nearby shook the building, causing dust and pieces of the plaster ceiling to fall on them.

The priest flinched, then looked up to see if the roof would collapse before he said, "Yes, downstairs! Please, hurry!"

Angie lowered the woman to her feet and led her to the stairway as Jon struggled down the stairs with the old man still on his shoulders. "Hurry, Mother," Angie said as he held her up.

Jon entered the basement right behind the priest who was already calling for the doctor. A man stood up from the group of fifty people sitting at the long tables and called for them to bring the old man to him. He cleared the table and two other men helped lower the old man from Jon's shoulders to the table. While everyone's attention was on the patient, Jon and Angie slipped away. They didn't want to answer any questions. They silently went back upstairs and stopped inside the front doors of the church. Jon sat down on a bench for a minute to catch his breath while he consulted the ATAK smartphone attached to his chest rig. ATAK stood for Android Tactical Assault Kit. The software was a mapping engine used for precision targeting, intelligence on surrounding land formations, navigation, and situational awareness. Jon was using it to navigate to the cache house. It also allowed Jon and Angie to keep track of each other if they got separated.

"While we're here I'm going to make a call," Jon said. He pulled out his satellite phone and dialed the number.

A throat cleared on the other end of the call. "Hello," Tom Adams said.

"Hey, Tom. It's Jon. Did I wake you?" Jon asked. Another missile exploded nearby shaking the building and causing an ungodly cracking sound.

"Yeah, but we were getting up in a half hour anyway. What the hell was that?" Tom asked after hearing the sound come across the phone.

"We're in the middle of a cruise missile attack in Lviv. How are you guys doing? Are you done with your vacation yet?" Jon asked.

"We're great, Jon. Ahhh no, Gwenn and I are still in Edinburgh researching Gwenn's family tree. After our Alaska trip got sidetracked, we decided to save up for a couple of years and treat ourselves to a special vacation. She's been looking forward to this trip for over a year. We're staying in a beautiful thousand-year-old bed and breakfast. Hold on a second, Jon... It's Jon. I don't know, he didn't say, yet. Gwenn wants to know why you are calling. Hold on, I'll put you on speaker," Tom said, "Go ahead."

"Hello, aaah, Gwenn, aaah, it's good to talk to you again. Sounds like, like you guys are having a great time," Jon said as he wiped the perspiration from his forehead. He could feel his neck getting stiff, which he knew would be followed quickly by a tension headache. It wasn't because he had been thrown head-first through the air by a cruise missile minutes ago. It was because he was talking to the one woman in the world who intimidated the hell out of him, Gwenn Adams. He held up the five fingers on his left hand and mouthed five aspirin to Angie. "Here's the thing. I need a pilot to..."

"Oh, lord. Here we go again," Gwenn said in exasperation. He could imagine her eyes rolling from 1,600 miles away. Angie handed him the aspirin.

Jon swallowed them without water. "Please, please, Gwenn, let me explain before you hang up. My goddaughter Kimmie is trapped behind the Russian line in Donetsk. I'm heading there now with a friend of mine, but it would be very helpful if I had a pilot with a helicopter to fly us out after I link up with her. I'm certain we're going to draw a lot of attention when we try to pull her out of there," Jon explained.

"What's she doing in a war zone?" Tom asked.

"Yeah! I know, right? That's what I asked her mom. Kimmie became a Catholic nun after her dad died in Iraq. She's only twenty-one years old and she's trying to do her part to make the world a better place. I know what you're thinking, young and dumb, right? So, anyway, she was assigned to a church in Austria, but a couple of weeks ago the church asked for volunteers to go to Ukraine to help with the humanitarian relief efforts. They sent her to St. Michael's Church in Donetsk. Last night Chechen soldiers came to the church, and she saw them beat her priest to death. She's scared out of her mind, and she can't get out on her own. I tried to get the company to help, but they refused," Jon explained.

"Jon, I have no clue where to get a helicopter in Europe. Besides, we'd need a team of pipe hitters to come in with me. We'll have to shoot our way in and out. We'll need at least a Huey," Tom said.

"Oh no! You are not going to Ukraine! You're a fifty-seven-year-old man with five grandchildren! You promised me you wouldn't go on any more of these crazy missions!" Gwenn laid down the law for Tom.

"Hon, if this was one of our kids, we'd be praying to God for someone to step up and help us get them out. We can't turn away. We have to try to help," Tom replied.

"This isn't for the government. You'll be a mercenary. If they catch you, you'll be executed," Gwenn said.

"Well, I think you have to get paid to be a mercenary," Tom quibbled. Gwenn gave him the wife look. "I probably won't be able to find a helicopter anyway. Jon, I'll make some calls and see what I can do."

"Thanks, Tom. Gwenn, I promise I'll make this up to you somehow," Jon said before he disconnected.

"Damn! That lady, Gwenn's a hard one!" Angie said.

"You don't know the half of it." Jon took three deep pulls from the drinking tube on his hydration system before rubbing his temples. "She hates hearing from me. Every time I talk to her, I bring bad news. Hopefully, Tom can help us out. He's a terrific pilot." He looked up to the ceiling before he said, "Do you hear that? The attack stopped. Let's head out," Jon said.

CHAPTER 9

0600Z (0900HR LOCAL)
CACHE HOUSE, LVIV, UKRAINE

The large stone house looked like the others in the quiet neighborhood, although this one was only mildly damaged in the air strikes. It backed up to wooded common ground and was built on a large lot surrounded by a ten-foot-high stone wall. Jon and Angie approached the rear of the property through the thick brush. There was a sturdy wooden door in the middle of the rear wall. Jon grabbed the handle and said, "The door is locked."

"Don't you have a key?" Angie asked.

"No, I don't, but even if I did there is no lock to put it in," Jon replied as he pointed at the door. Jon dropped his pack and put his back against the wall. He cupped his hands together and said, "Here, I'll help you climb the wall, then you can open it from the inside."

Angie dropped his pack and put his boots on Jon's shoulders before effortlessly pulling himself up and over the wall. "Aaah, we have a slight problem, mate," Angie said through the door.

"What is it?" Jon asked.

"There's a padlock through the handle," Angie replied.

"Combination or key lock?" Jon asked.

"Four-digit combination," Angie said.

"Try, zero, zero, zero, seven."

"Negative."

"Aaah, one, seven, seven, six."

"Nope."

"One, seven, eight, nine."

Seconds later Angie opened the door. Jon handed him his pack and stepped into the yard.

They began walking toward the garage doors which were on the back of the house. "What's so special about seventeen eighty-nine?" Angie asked.

Jon stopped and looked at Angie and then started walking again. "Even though you talk funny, sometimes I forget you're a foreigner. Seventeen eighty-nine was the year the Constitution went into effect," he explained as he arrived at the garage door.

"In case you haven't noticed where we are, you're a foreigner too," Angie said.

"Point taken," Jon replied. He looked around to see if anyone was watching them before he entered the code into the panel next to the door. The overhead door raised. He and Angie slipped inside and quickly closed the door. The windows were blacked out from the inside. He used his flashlight to find the light switch next to the interior door leading to the house and flipped it on. They quickly cleared the house and returned to the garage.

"Is this it?" Angie asked, clearly not impressed as he looked around the grungy garage.

"Were you expecting Q to greet us with a tricked-out Aston Martin that converts into a submarine and fighter jet?" Jon replied with his own question as he scanned the mostly empty garage.

"Well…yeah. You guys are the Arsenal of Democracy, right?" Angie asked.

Jon grabbed a rusty red coffee can off the workbench and turned it upside down. A pile of old screws fell from the can followed by two key fobs. Jon put one in his pocket and tossed the other to Angie. Only one vehicle was in the oversized garage, covered by a blue plastic tarp. They grabbed the tarp at the front bumper and pulled it to the rear. The tarp fell away to reveal a black Chevy Suburban. Jon opened the cargo hatch and whistled. "Christmas came early this year, Angie," Jon said with a smile on his face as he perused the contents of the cargo area, "Thank you, American Military Industrial Complex!"

"Now, this is more like it, mate," Angie said as he and Jon shared a fist bump. "You have restored my faith in Uncle Sam. We could overthrow a small country with this truck," Angie said.

"Run-flat tires, improved suspension, push bumper, over-sized gas tank, winch, ballistic glass, Kevlar armor, AM/FM stereo, Wi-Fi, Bluetooth, and a Rear Seat Entertainment System with a Disney Plus subscription so you can watch Bluey," Jon said while trying out his best Elwood Blues imitation.

"I'm really not a big Bluey fan," Angie replied.

"Bullshit! My nephew, Danny, loves Bluey. Bluey's the best thing to come out of Australia since Margot Robbie and Foster's beer," Jon shot back.

"We don't drink that shit; we export it to countries like yours where they don't know what good beer tastes like. I should check your head again, mate. You may have dain bramage," Angie joked, "I better drive."

***

Fifteen minutes later, Angie maneuvered them onto the M-09 highway, and they continued their journey to Donetsk. "Jon, there's no way we can stay alert all the way to Donetsk without sleep. Why don't you try to sleep for a couple of hours and then I'll wake you up to drive for a while?" Angie asked.

"Yeah, I guess you're right. Hey, I didn't thank you for coming along. I really appreciate it. I'd be screwed without anyone to help me," Jon said. The bleeding had stopped so he pulled the two small wads of bloody gauze from his nostrils and threw them out of his window. His nose hurt so much he didn't dare touch it. Earlier, Angie had offered to use his vast medical knowledge to mash it back into place, but Jon declined.

"No worries, mate. My calendar is clear. Besides, I still owe you from the time you saved my life in Sumatra," Angie said as he massaged his left shoulder. He would have lost his arm if it weren't for Jon. Several surgeries and a year of rehab were necessary to return him to duty.

"That was a shit show from the start. We were lucky to get out of there alive," Jon replied. He reclined his seat and closed his eyes.

"Did your people ever figure out why that classified AIM-174B missile fell off the Super Hornet into the jungle?" Angie asked.

"What missile?" Jon replied as he brought the bill of his cap down to cover his eyes.

It was quiet for a few minutes, but Angie could see Jon wasn't sleeping. His mind was in overdrive. Angie decided to help him unwind. "If you're not going to sleep, tell me more about Sister Joan," Angie said.

Jon put his seat back up and took off his cap. "Kimmie is the oldest of Clint and Carol's kids. She's always been a headstrong know-it-all daddy's girl. She's an overachiever and an idealist. Three-letter varsity athlete and National Honor Society in high school. She graduated with her bachelor's from Notre Dame in three years. She's maybe 5'4" and 120 lbs., but she storms through life like an NFL linebacker. She studies Grav Maga for fun. After her dad was killed, she turned her attention toward saving the world," Jon said.

CHAPTER 10

0630Z (0730HR LOCAL)
ROSSLYN GUEST HOUSE,
EDINBURGH, SCOTLAND

As Tom waited for Gwenn to finish her shower, he scrolled through his cell phone looking for a contact. "There he is," Tom said to himself and tapped the number. The call went to voicemail. He hung up and called again. *He'd better not be screening his calls,* Tom thought. The call went to voicemail again. This time Tom left a message, "Whitey, it's Chirp. I have a problem and I need your help. Call me back ASAP." His phone rang within a minute.

"Hey, Chirp, sorry for the delay. I've been getting a lot of scam calls since I started my new job," Whitey explained, "What's up?"

"Thanks for getting back to me so fast, Whitey. I figured I'd be waking you up. Are you already at work?" Chirp asked.

"Yeah, we're launching another rocket loaded with internet satellites this morning. The boss likes to be available just in case there are any issues. What are you up to?" Whitey asked.

"Gwenn and I are in Edinburgh on vacation," Tom said before being interrupted.

"Scotland?" Whitey asked.

"What? Yeah, Scotland." Tom replied, "Anyway, do you remember Commander Jon from the Alaska thing?"

"Yeah, I remember him. Why?" Whitey asked.

"He just called Gwenn and me from Ukraine. He said his goddaughter, is a nun now and this morning the Chechens came to her church behind the lines in Donetsk and beat her priest to death right in front of her. She's trapped and he's driving there to retrieve her. He asked me to find a helicopter and come and get them. Do you know where I can borrow a Huey for a few days? Also, I need you to send a plane to Homer, Alaska to pick up some people and bring them over here for the mission," Tom said.

Whitey leaned back in his plush leather chair. "Chirp, are you fucking with me? You gotta be joking, rescue a nun in a warzone," Whitey said as he laughed.

"I'm as serious as a heart attack," Chirp replied.

Whitey stopped laughing and sat up. He replied, "Fuck, Tom, that's a big favor." There was silence on the line. "Why doesn't he ask his friends at work to help him?" Whitey asked.

"He did and they can't. You're the Commandant of the Marine Corps. Can't you talk to one of your European counterparts?" Tom asked.

"I'm the retired Commandant, remember? There's a big difference. Getting a jet to fly a team to Europe is fucking expensive.

You know I don't have that kind of money. Do you?" Whitey asked.

"This trip to Scotland was my big splurge for the year and maybe next. I can check my sock drawer and under the sofa cushions," Tom replied.

"Okay, I'll talk to my new boss and see if he can help. I'll call you back," Whitey replied. General Bryan McKinley, callsign Whitey, had been in high demand upon retiring from the Marine Corps. There was a brief bidding war for his services before he had been hired by the richest man in the world, Alvin Monk. Monk owned many companies; the world's largest, most profitable electric car company, a space exploration company, and a satellite communications company, just to name a few. He was also very generous when it came to helping noble causes.

***

Tom started searching for another number.

"Who are you calling now?" Gwenn asked as she came out of the bathroom.

"Taco. He should have finished flight school last week. He was going to go back to Kodiak for a few weeks before reporting to the Coast Guard Aviation Training Center in Mobile," Tom replied. Lieutenant Junior Grade Ernesto "Taco" Ortega was a newly winged Coast Guard Aviator who had flown as copilot on a classified mission in Alaska with Tom. "Maybe he can round up some of the old team to help out. I think most of them are still up there around Cook Inlet." He found the number and hit send.

"Hello," Taco said after he cleared his throat.

"Hey, Taco, it's Tom Adams, congrats on getting your wings. Sorry to call so early, but I need your help," Tom said.

"Thank you, sir. I don't think it would have happened without your support. What's the problem?" he asked as he sat up on the side of his bed.

"Look, this is going to sound crazy so I'm just going to say it. Commander Jon's goddaughter is a Catholic nun and is trapped in Ukraine behind the Russian line. Her priest was beaten to death in front of her this morning by the Chechens. She can't get out, so Jon is going to sneak in to get her. He asked his bosses for help, and they said no. So, he asked me to find a helicopter and lift them out. I can't do it alone, so I'm asking you to round up the old team and come help me. I don't have any details, I don't have a Huey, and I don't know how I'll get you all to Europe. I have another friend working on that for me. I know I'm asking you to risk everything you've worked so hard for all of these years. I can't even promise we'll all come back from this. So, what do you say, Taco?" Tom asked.

There was silence on the other end of the line. It was true, Taco had worked hard to get where he was, and he wasn't exactly eager to throw it all away before he even reported to Mobile to learn to fly the Jayhawk. On the other hand, he wouldn't have been selected for flight school without Tom's recommendation. His mother was a devout Catholic, even more so than him. She had great affection for the sisters. She had often said when he was growing up that if she hadn't married his father, she would have become a nun. If it were his mother over there he'd go after her alone if he had to. He realized that was exactly how the commander felt about his goddaughter. This moment was a fork in the road in his life. Take the easy path or the risky one. He bowed his head and made a quick prayer for guidance.

Tom took his phone away from his ear and looked at the screen. He thought maybe the call had been disconnected. He was about to speak again when Taco said, "I'm in, sir. I'll start rounding everybody up. I'll call you when I have news." Just like that, the band was getting back together.

CHAPTER 11

Whitey looked around his massive, expensively appointed office like it could be his last time. He liked this office even more than the Commandant's office he occupied for three years. He got up from his large mahogany desk on the third floor and walked out to tell his secretary he was going to talk to the boss. He walked upstairs to the sixth floor and presented himself in front of Monk's secretary. He said, "Hi Monica, I have an emergency. Will you ask if Mr. Monk can see me for a few minutes?" She picked up the phone and seconds later he walked into Monk's stylish yet austere office.

"I'm a little busy right now, General. What can I do for you? Just the short version," Monk said with his desk phone handset in his hand. He was covering the microphone with the other.

"Sir, this is going to sound like a bad B-movie but I need to get a Huey helicopter for a friend of mine so he can fly it behind the Russian lines in Ukraine to pick up a covert agent friend of his who is there to rescue his goddaughter who is also a Catholic nun," Whitey explained.

Monk continued to maintain eye contact with Whitey while he said, "Aaah, I'm sorry, Mr. Secretary, I'll have to call you back. Something just came up… Yes, thank you," before he hung up. "Okay, General, maybe you should give me the long version." Whitey sat down in front of Monk's desk and told him everything he knew.

After five minutes, Monk asked, "Why is this so important to you, General?"

"Sir, I owe everything I have to Tom Adams. I wasn't a very good student at flight school. I barely squeaked by and when I got to my first fleet squadron, the Flying Tigers, it quickly became apparent that I wasn't going to last long. Tom was a deployment ahead of me, so he was already an aircraft commander and instructor pilot when I reported aboard. I embarrassed myself on a couple of flights with other instructors before Tom asked the C.O. if he could take over my training as a new copilot. His extra mentoring was just what I needed. So, without Tom, I would have lost my wings and never been in a position to become the Commandant of the Marine Corps. He saved my career and probably my life," Whitey explained.

Monk nodded his understanding and said, "General, do you have any idea where to get a Huey over there?"

"Sir, please, call me Whitey. There's a big private flying museum at the old RAF Berlin-Gatow Airport. I believe they have several flyable UH-1D Hueys that were retired from the German military," Whitey said.

"All right, call them and see if they'll sell one to us. Let me know what happens," Monk said.

"Sir, there's one more thing," Whitey said.

"Okay," Monk replied slowly, waiting for the other shoe to drop.

"I need a plane to fly a team of ten or eleven people over to Germany ASAP," Whitey said, worried he might be stretching his luck.

"Take one of the G700s," Monk replied.

Whitey smiled and said, "Thank you, sir." The Gulfstream G700 was one of two jets Monk had laid out $75,000,000 a piece for only two months earlier. They cruised at almost 600 knots and had a 7,500 nm range. Whitey rose and headed for the door.

"Good luck, General," Monk said as Whitey exited the office.

***

Ten minutes later, General Bryan "Whitey" McKinley, former Commandant of the United States Marine Corps, Devil Dog, and highly trained dealer of death and destruction, sat behind his desk staring at a piece of paper with a telephone number on it. He was trying to summon the courage to call the number. Finally, he wiped his sweaty palms on his trouser legs and picked up the phone. He dialed the number quickly before he lost his nerve.

"Ja," the man on the other end said.

"Hello, sir, my name is Bryan McKinley. Is Wolfgang Gerhardt there?" Whitey asked.

"Ah, yes, this is Wolfgang Gerhardt. How may I help you?" he replied in English.

"Sir, I believe you have several flyable UH-1D Hueys in your museum," Whitey said.

"Ah, yes! We have four!" Gerhardt responded excitedly. "They were some of the last built by Dornier in 1981! We have thousands of hours invested in their restoration! They are how do you say, ah yes, pristine."

"Mr. Gerhardt, I work for Alvin Monk. He is very impressed with your work, and he would like to buy one of your Hueys for one of his projects. He is willing to pay $3,000,000," Whitey said. There was silence on the other end of the line. "Mr. Gerhardt, are you still there?"

"Yes, ah, excuse me, but as I said the aircraft are pristine. We just finished them and will be flying them together in many airshows through October. They will generate much interest and many donations for the museum. I can't possibly sell one. I am sorry," Gerhardt explained.

"Sir, I understand your attachment to your aircraft, I was the same way when I commanded the Flying Tigers of HMH-361 in the United States Marine Corps, but..." Whitey said before being interrupted.

"Excuse me, Mr. McKinley, are you General McKinley, the Commandant of the United States Marine Corps?" Gerhardt asked.

"Well, I was. I retired about six months ago and came to work for Mr. Monk. Sir, he really wants one of the Hueys. What if he adds a $2,000,000 donation to the $3,000,000 price tag?" Whitey asked. There was silence on the other end of the line again. "Mr. Gerhardt?"

"General McKinley, would you be flying this Huey for the project?" Gerhardt asked.

"Well, the details haven't been ironed out, but yes, it's safe to say I will be one of the pilots," Whitey replied.

"Then we have a deal with one condition. After you complete Mr. Monk's project you must come to the museum and give our visitors a presentation on the part our Huey played in the project," Gerhardt countered.

Whitey wiped the perspiration from his brow and said, "I'd be happy to do that, Mr. Gerhardt. Thank you. Mr. Monk's bank will contact you shortly to arrange the wire transfer. I am operating under a strict timeline. My team and I should be there at Gatow around 0200hr local time. Can you have the aircraft ready for us by then?"

"Yes, this is not a problem, General. We will see you in the morning," Gerhardt replied.

CHAPTER 12

07002 (1000HR LOCAL)
HIGHWAY M-30 WEST OF
KHMELNYTSKYY, UKRAINE

Jon was the fourth man in a tight stack of seven standing in the
dark along a pockmarked, cinder block wall outside the back door
of a battle-damaged two-story house on the outskirts of Mosul.
Tonight, he and his teammates were wearing black Iraqi Army Special Forces uniforms. He yawned quietly as his stomach growled.
He had been awake and on the move for over thirty-six hours. The
only thing he had eaten was an unheated MRE spaghetti entrée ten
hours earlier. All he could think about was food and sleep. Despite
the early hour, the temperature hovered just over 100°F. Sweat
flowed steadily from under his helmet and into his eyes before
dripping off his nose into his beard. Under his body armor, his
pale pink skin was steaming. He grabbed his plate carrier below his
neck and pulled it out and back like a bellows several times to force

some fresh air under it for a little temporary relief. He was standing nut to butt behind his swim buddy, Clint.

He and his team were hunting Quds Force terrorists sent from Iran to plant improvised explosive devices, or IEDs, on the area roadways. These explosively formed penetrator-type IEDs were effective against mine-resistant vehicles and tanks. Their bombs resulted in the maiming and deaths of over 150 civilians and soldiers in the preceding month. Jon wiped the sweat from his eyes with his Nomex-gloved hand and sucked a mouthful of warm water from the drinking tube attached to his CamelBak hydration pack. He reflexively recoiled and closed his eyes as a powerful stench assaulted his senses. He had been subjected to another one of Clint's silent but deadly gastronomic attacks. In response, Jon pulled his collapsible baton from his plate carrier and slid it up between Clint's inner thighs and pressed it against his perineum. Through his night vision goggles, Jon saw Clint spring to his tippy toes and clench his cheeks.

Clint swatted the baton away and quietly said, "Asshole!"

Jon chuckled under his breath. The team leader began counting down from five seconds with his left hand. When he got to zero, they would breach the door and kill or capture the tangos—more likely kill, but a couple of prisoners for the interrogators would be preferable.

As the leader signaled three, the eight-inch-thick wall in front of Jon exploded, sending concrete shrapnel and an explosively formed penetrator flying from a fifteen-inch-diameter hole. Clint's head vaporized, spraying Jon's face and night vision goggles with hot blood, tissue, and bone. Some went in his mouth, causing him to gag. He froze for what seemed like an eternity. His mind screamed at his body to move, but nothing happened.

The operator behind Jon yanked him back out of the way and yelled, "Frag out!" as he threw two grenades through the hole.

They exploded and the breacher blew the door. The stack flooded through the smoky opening. Jon spit the coppery-tasting lump of brain matter onto the sand and wiped his face. His goggles were covered with the goo, and he flipped them up out of the way. He stepped over Clint and followed the team inside. They quickly swept the house, killing tangos. Tonight, there would be no prisoners. As the Team searched the house and gathered intel, Jon ran back outside to check on Clint. Maybe he hadn't seen what he thought he had. Jon pointed his flashlight at his friend then immediately turned away, retching uncontrollably until nothing remained. *No, Clint! Not Again! God, why?*

***

The first three hours of the journey on the M-30 highway were uneventful. Jon had slept through almost all of it. Angie was getting tired and would have to wake him up soon. Then he noticed the brake lights activate on the vehicles ahead of him. He came over a rise in the highway and at the crest saw traffic backed up for a half mile. Traffic was slowly moving forward. "Jonny, wake up," Angie said as he shook Jon's left shoulder. Jon's left hand was twitching.

"Not Again! God, why?" Jon blurted out as he woke. He raised his seat back and looked around before saying, "What's up?" Sweat poured from his forehead and dripped into his beard. His undershirt was soaked. He saw a line of brake lights in front of them leading to the flashing red and blue lights of police cars, "Where are we?" he said before mopping his face with his sleeve.

"We're about an hour west of Khmelnytskyy on the M-30 near a little town called Bokyivka. It looks like the National Police have a checkpoint set up. What do you think?" Angie asked.

"Well, one way or another we have to go through the checkpoint. We have our bogus papers. Maybe they'll just take a quick look and send us through," Jon replied, "I'll break out some food. See if you can sweet talk them and offer them some."

"You're sweating like a pig, mate. What should I say if they ask about you?" Angie asked.

Jon shrugged, "I don't know, tell them I had some bad sushi."

"Right, that'll work," Angie replied.

After a half hour of slowly inching forward, they arrived where the police officers were standing. Their white Toyota Prius police cars were parked on the shoulders of the highway with their red and blue light bars activated. There were four officers on the highway, one in each lane to talk to the driver and another officer to cover him. If they wanted to take a closer look at a vehicle, they made them turn off to the right on a two-lane gravel road to be searched by six other officers. The young constable stepped up to Angie's open window and saw the major's insignia on his Ukraine Army uniform and saluted him, "Hello, sir. May I see your papers, please?"

"Of course," Angie said in perfect Ukrainian as he handed over his and Jon's Ukrainian Army identification cards and orders. The orders indicated they had traveled to Poland from the President's office in Kyiv to visit the Polish Army and now they were returning to report to the President. If asked, he would tell the constable they were negotiating the delivery of more weapons from NATO. "Are you looking for someone in particular?" Angie asked. Jon sat next to him playing a disinterested officer while eating a cold spaghetti entrée from a brown plastic pouch.

"We have reports of sabotage in the area, more of Pichugin's little green men," he replied as he stared at Jon's spaghetti. The little green men were small Russian Spetsnaz units and private military contractors or PMCs. Pichugin was the president for life of the Russian Federation.

Angie feigned concern for the policeman and asked, "How long have you been out here?"

"Since last night, sir," the constable replied.

"Have you eaten?" Angie asked.

"No, sir," the constable replied again.

Angie looked around the area surrounding the Suburban. "Where is your lieutenant?" Angie asked.

"I haven't seen him today, sir?" the constable answered.

Angie nodded knowingly and said, "I'm sure he had his dinner last night and breakfast this morning. He is probably taking a nap with his feet up on his desk." Jon reached into the back seat and brought forward a cardboard case of commercial rations similar to MREs and handed it to Angie. "Here, share this with your comrades. Your lieutenant should be demoted back to constable," Angie said indignantly as he handed the case to the constable.

"Thank you, sir, and thank you, Major," the constable said as he stepped back with the box in his left hand and saluted with his right."

They returned the salute and Angie drove away as he raised his window. He said, "Do you believe that mate? These guys are busting their asses and their boss doesn't even arrange chow for them."

"Yeah, some things never change. I'm sure two thousand years ago there were Roman milites who were ignored and abused by their optio. Once we get clear, find a place to pull over and I'll swap seats with you," Jon replied. Milites were common Roman foot soldiers and optios were their junior officers.

An hour passed in silence before Angie asked, "Hey, mate, back there when I woke you up, you were having some sort of episode. We all have our demons. Do you want to talk about yours?"

As he drove, Jon looked out of his window watching the scenery go by for a few minutes, "You remember Clint, right? He died a couple of years ago in Mosul."

"Yeah, I knew Clint. He was a good man. I was sorry I couldn't come to pay my respects," Angie replied.

"I was standing behind him in the stack when he was killed. What no one outside the team knows is that his head was destroyed by an EFP. His blood and tissue sprayed all over my face. I guess someone in management decided it was too gory for the family to know about. I've seen teammates die or be horribly wounded but Clint and I were close. We went through BUDS together. I introduced him to his wife. It should have been me who died. I don't have a wife or children. They're Catholic and have a whole house full of beautiful kids," Jon said, still looking out of the window.

"Jonny, you're not responsible for Clint's death. We all take the same chances when we're out here," Angie tried to console him.

"You don't understand, I was supposed to be the third man in the stack. Clint and I were always pranking each other. Earlier in the day, I had blacked out his Oakleys with a black grease pencil. So, he was looking to get even with me. That night Clint jumped in line in front of me so he could release one of his nasty eye-watering farts on me. If I hadn't been fucking with him earlier in the day he'd still be alive," Jon said as he turned to look at Angie. Guilt was written across his face.

"That's bollicks, mate. No one appointed you guardian of all things great and small. I don't think they issue a cape to go with your Trident. When we get home, you need to talk to someone. It doesn't matter who, doctor, priest, even your bloody barber," Angie said.

"Yeah, okay. I will when you do," Jon replied as he wiped his eyes.

"Jonny, I have my shrink on speed dial. Although I must admit, she's quite a looker," Angie said, "If you don't want to talk to anyone else, you can always talk to me. I already know you're daft."

CHAPTER 13

A 2023 black GMC Yukon Denali pulled up on the ramp next to the Monk Industries white and blue Gulfstream G700. Whitey hopped out of the right rear passenger seat with his backpack over his shoulder and hustled up the jet's steps. He learned early on in his military career to always keep his go bag nearby. He was greeted by the flight attendants and two stern-looking security men packing sidearms. "Good morning, General McKinley, I just need your signature here and you'll be on your way," the first man holding out a clipboard said.

"What am I signing for?" Whitey asked.

"That, sir," he replied, pointing at a large black Pelican case sitting on the sofa.

"What's in the case?" Whitey asked.

"Two million dollars, sir," the man said.

"And what's the money for?" Whitey asked.

The security man looked at the paper on his clipboard and said, "Contingencies."

Whitey smiled and signed the paper before handing the clipboard back. "Thank you, sir. Enjoy your flight," the man said before he and his partner left the plane. Whitey was more and more impressed with Monk every day.

He stuck his head into the cockpit and said, "Are you guys ready to fly?"

The captain in the left seat said, "Yes, sir, we just need our destination in Alaska." He was a recently retired Air Force Special Operations Command pilot. The co-pilot had been a Navy Hornet driver.

"Damn! I don't remember. I'll make a call and find out. Just head for Anchorage for now," Whitey replied.

CHAPTER 14

National Security Advisor, Preston Alexander burst into Harold Lamb's office and flipped on the lights. "Harold, wake up!" Alexander shouted.

"Dammit, Pres!" Lamb yelled back from under his Harvard blanket, his head still covered, "What time is it?"

"4:15 AM. After the agency refused to help him, Commander Smith started calling his friends for support. He called Tom Adams, who then called General Brian McKinley," Alexander said.

"So, what? McKinley's retired. He can't order up any help in Ukraine," Lamb replied as he sat up squinting against the bright overhead lights.

"McKinley works for Alvin Monk, now. He just took off out of Austin in one of Monk's G700s heading for Anchorage.

He's going there to pick up a team of shooters to go with him to Ukraine. They intend to fly into Donetsk and rescue the commander and the nun. If we don't do something, they're going to fuck up Wynken's trip. What should we do?" Alexander said.

"We have to keep this quiet. Let me think for a minute," Lamb replied. Seconds later, he said, "Call the acting Administrator of the FAA and tell him to have inspectors waiting in Anchorage to ground Monk's jet and flight crew. That should stop them," Lamb said as he laid back down and pulled his blanket over his head, "Turn off the lights and close my door."

"Shouldn't we start planning for contingencies?" Alexander asked, mopping sweat from his forehead.

"Get out, Pres!" Lamb shouted. Alexander hurriedly closed the door and scurried back down the hall.

CHAPTER 15

0940Z (1240HR LOCAL)
HIGHWAY M-30 EAST OF HAISYN

Two and a half hours later, Jon was driving down the M-30 two-lane highway at a steady 60 mph when he had to slow to a stop for another checkpoint. This one must have just been set up because there were only ten vehicles in front of him. "Angie, wake up," Jon said as he nudged his left shoulder.

Angie sat up immediately. "What's happening, Jonny?" he asked.

"There's another police TCP ahead," Jon replied. TCP meant a traffic control point. "It looks like the national police again. Two cars and six officers."

Angie retrieved his binoculars from the back seat and scanned the area. "The police Prius on the right shoulder has its driver's side windows shot out and I see bullet holes in the doors," he said, "The cop on the left side of the first car in the line just yanked the driver out and smacked him across the face with a collapsible baton. He's down. The cop's going through his pockets. He has his wallet. He took the money out and tossed the wallet on the guy's back. He's yelling at him. He kicked him in the thigh. The guy's getting up and shaking his head. He's back in his vehicle and driving away. The other cop is laughing. His uniform is stained and too large for him, it's not his uniform."

"Are they green men or locals?" Jon asked.

"They're too unprofessional to be green men. What do you want to do?" Angie asked.

"I guess we'll do our good deed for the day. When we're fourth in line we'll initiate. You take out the three cops around the police car on the right shoulder. I'll take the other three on the left. If they look like they're going lethal on any of these people we'll start early," Jon replied.

"Okay, mate, sounds like a plan," Angie said. He reached into the backseat, pulled his plate carrier forward, and put it on. It was covered with 40mm grenades for the M-203 grenade launcher attached to his HK416 rifle. He loaded an M433 HEDP round into the launcher. HEDP meant high-explosive dual-purpose. It was effective against people and penetrated light armor.

Jon reached back, grabbed his plate carrier, and strapped it on. Next, he retrieved his short-barreled M249 Para (SAW). It had a collapsible stock, a 200-round cloth-covered box magazine, and an ACOG optic. Jon and Angie waited patiently while the people in front of them were systematically abused and robbed. They were sixth in line when Officer Baggy Pants grabbed a preteen girl by her hair with his left hand as he held his rifle with his right. He pulled her through the open right rear window and let her drop to the pavement. He kept his grip on her hair and used it to pull her to her feet. He let his rifle hang by its sling as he began slapping the girl in the face.

"Oh, hell no! Change of plans! Kill that motherfucker first and then the guys around the car!" Jon shouted.

"Roger, that!" Angie yelled back as he flipped his selector lever to fire.

Jon slammed the Suburban into Park and quickly leaped out onto the pavement. He saw the cop standing at the left driver's side door laughing as his partner beat the helpless girl. Jon fired a burst of ten rounds from his SAW into the laughing policeman's torso as he steadily advanced forward.

Officer Baggy Pants turned to see his comrade's chest and back erupt in a cloud of pink mist as he went down. Angie had closed the distance to fifty feet on his target and made the easy shot, putting an M855 ball round from his HK416 into the man's left temple. The right side of his skull erupted from under his scalp bringing half of his brain matter with it.

Next, Jon slewed his muzzle left and targeted the cop who had been leaning against the hood of the police Prius parked on the left side of the highway seventy-five feet away. The man ran behind the car and was headed for the trees when Jon sent a burst into his back dropping him instantly.

Angie adjusted his aim to the three cops in and around the other Prius. He fired the M433 HEDP round from his M-203. It traveled slowly enough for him to see it spiraling toward the car. The round exploded into a gray cloud full of shrapnel upon contacting the car door sending cops flying head over heels. The man inside the car was on fire. He fought frantically trying to open his door as the two men outside the car were struggling to their knees. Angie loaded another round and fired at the closest man who exploded on impact. His human shrapnel killed his partner.

Jon ran around the front of the car to make sure Officer Baggy Pants wasn't breathing. He leaned over and yelled, "What kind of pussy hits a little girl!" to the brainless corpse. Angie appeared at his side and Jon said, "Tell these people we were never here. I'll get the Suburban."

***

Angie helped the girl to her feet and put her back in her car. He leaned over to talk to her parents. "These men were not policemen. They murdered the real policemen and stole their uniforms and cars. Tell your friends and families to be very careful and stay off the highway except when it is absolutely necessary," he said in Ukrainian.

The girl's father said, "Thank you for stopping these criminals, Major. Where is your unit?"

"We are part of a classified unit hunting the green men, but if anyone asks, we were never here," Angie said before walking around the car and climbing into the Suburban. Jon stomped on the accelerator, and they sped away.

***

"I wish you would've left that asshole alive long enough for me to kill him! I hate bullies, a bunch of fucking cowards picking on little girls and the old and weak!" Jon was on a rant. He was rocking back and forth behind the steering wheel as he raced down the highway. He turned to look at Angie. Angie was staring at him. "What?" he asked.

"I think I just witnessed you battling your inner kryptonite, mate," Angie replied. "Normally, when you operate, you're cold as ice, but I've never seen you this amped up."

Jon took a deep breath and let it out. "Yeah, I have a few, power outages, being stuck in traffic, and tolerating bullshit, but bullies abusing the weak piss me off the most."

CHAPTER 16

M29 was sitting in the chow hall finishing a plate of Lamb, Pork, and Beef Pelmeni when M22 rushed through the door. He waved to M22 and said, "Come comrade, the Pelmeni is excellent today. This is my second serving."

M22 hurried over and sat down. He leaned across the table before saying, "I was just in the communications trailer. Two men in a black Suburban dressed as Ukrainian Army officers stopped at a traffic control checkpoint manned by some of our Separatist Militiamen on Highway M-30 east of Haisyn. The Americans killed all six of them in a matter of seconds. They are traveling toward us now. We must get on the road and intercept them. I can kill my brother's murderers before I contact my family tonight."

"This makes no sense. Why would an American Spetsnaz team fly away with Nikolaev and then return hours later in a Suburban? We have no idea who these men are and there must be hundreds of Suburbans in Ukraine. They were very popular before the war," M29 said.

"Not like this one. It had a large push bumper and off-road tires like the two the Americans blew up at the farmhouse," M22 replied. "I am leaving. You may stay here and stuff yourself if you wish," M22 said as he stood up and walked away.

M29 dropped his helmet on his head and shouted, "I'm coming! Slow down!" as he picked up his rifle and Styrofoam clamshell full of Pelmeni.

CHAPTER 17

Alaska State Troopers Eric Fuller and Mike Harmon were having another good day albeit with a very early start. They had been detailed to the Alaska Fugitive Task Force run by the US Marshal's Service and they were working for a man who had become a good friend over the last year or so. Supervisory US Deputy Marshal Kevin Bass had arranged a transfer from Chicago to Anchorage after surviving an attack by Russian Spetsnaz operators at a cabin on the shore of Eek Lake, Alaska. He had been one of a three deputy personal security detail assigned to protect a defector from the former Soviet Union. His friends Mark and Ronnie were murdered, and he was shot in the face and left for dead under a foot of snow. Eric and Mike were two of the men who had come to his rescue that freezing night. Now he literally owed them his life. This early morning, they were waiting in the woods about fifty feet off the road with three other lawmen drinking hot coffee. They were standing in a circle comparing their Alaskan sneakers. That's what everyone in Alaska called their knee-high rubber boots. This time of year, after everything thawed the ground became a swampy, smelly mess. When they finished their coffee, they would walk another two hundred feet through the bush to surround the cabin where Cooter "CJ" Wilson was hiding.

"So why is this guy called Cooter?" Mike asked.

"That's his first name," Kevin replied, "Maybe his parents were *Dukes of Hazzard* fans."

"Can you imagine being eight years old and everyone in school calling you Cooter all day? What did he do, anyway?" Eric asked.

Kevin pulled some papers out of his back pocket. He turned on the small blue LED light hanging from his neck on 550 Paracord and read from the papers, "Our boy, Cooter, got mad over the mailman not closing his mailbox tight enough to keep his mail from getting wet so he shot out the windshields of 107 US Postal Service vehicles with a high-powered BB gun. In court, he said he would've shot more, but his arms got tired from pumping up his rifle. The judge gave him two weeks to get his affairs in order before reporting to serve his sentence. That was four weeks ago."

***

Ten minutes later, they had the cabin surrounded. Kevin and three men were arrayed on the front porch. Mike and Eric were covering the back door. Kevin pounded on the front door three times and yelled, "Marshal's Service, arrest warrant!" then stepped back so another deputy could deploy a forty-pound battering ram. The wooden door jamb exploded as the door flew open. A high-pitched scream came from deep within the cabin, then a 300-pound man wearing powder blue man panties and Alaskan sneakers erupted from the backdoor followed by flashlight beams jiggling up and down as the lawmen scrambled to follow him outside.

Mike jumped in front of the desperado and yelled, "Guess who, motherfaa!" before Cooter ran right over him without breaking stride heading for the thick brush. Eric stood over Mike and took aim at the big man with the beanbag shotgun. He fired a round that struck Cooter in the right buttock but had little effect. He quickly chambered another round and fired. That one hit him right between the shoulder blades. Cooter danced the funky chicken for several steps, then fell face-first into the muck. The other lawmen quickly emerged from the backdoor of the cabin and made sure to laugh at Mike as they ran by.

"Are you okay, Devil Dog?" Eric said as he looked down at Mike.

Mike moaned softly, then croaked, "Next time, I get the bean bag gun."

Eric leaned over and offered his hand. Mike took it and Eric helped him get on his feet. They slowly walked over to where Cooter was being cuffed.

Kevin stood behind the young bucks yelling, "Stop resisting!" as they tried to get Cooter's hands close enough to handcuff him. They couldn't get his wrists close enough for one set of cuffs to close behind his back. "Use two sets," Kevin told the trio. By the time they stood Cooter up, he was covered front and back in the disgusting, smelly mud that came from thousands of years of rotting Alaskan flora and fauna.

"Congratulations! You guys caught him, so you get to transport him," Kevin said to Mike and Eric.

"Aw, come on, Kevin. We'll never get that stink out of the cloth upholstery," Mike complained.

Kevin and the others laughed. Kevin said, "Well, he's sure as fuck not getting in my Escalade." The Marshals had confiscated a Black 2021 Cadillac Escalade with tan leather interior. Chief Deputy Cameron thought it was gaudy, so he gave it to Kevin."

***

Two hours later, Mike and Eric had booked Cooter into the holdover. They were in the brightly lit parking lot of the Marshal's Service office cleaning the back seat of their SUV when Kevin walked out of the building. He was eating a chocolate-covered ice cream bar. "I like your spunk boys, but you need to learn to work smarter, not harder," he said, then sniffed the air. He shook his head and said, "You might need some professional help." He took another big bite.

Eric's cell phone rang. He wiped his left hand on his shirt and pulled his phone out of his back pocket. He pressed the button with his relatively clean pinkie finger and said, "Yeah?"

"Eric, this is Taco," he said.

Eric interrupted and said, "Hey, man it's good to hear you. Hang on, I'll put you on speaker for Mike. Okay, go ahead."

"Hi, Mike, what I was going to tell you guys is, well, you're not going to believe this shit, but Tom called me and said Jon is in Ukraine trying to rescue his goddaughter."

"Why the fuck is she in Ukraine?" Mike asked.

"She's a Catholic nun doing humanitarian work at a church. She got stuck behind the Russian lines and Jon needs a helicopter to lift them out. This mission is totally off the books. He's asking us to help him. I told Tom I'd round up the team. He's still working out the logistics of equipping us and getting us over there, but what do you guys think?" Taco asked.

Eric sniffed the car and said, "I'm in." He turned to Mike and said, "Maybe the car will smell better when I get back."

"Well, if you go, I have to go to protect your sorry ass," Mike said.

"What about Alice? Are you sure she'll let you go?" Eric teased.

"Alice ain't the boss of me. I think I'll just keep this mission on the down low. If she finds out, she'll want to go too. I'll tell her we're going up to the North Slope for a few days to track down a fugitive. Besides, I don't think I like the idea of her being in a combat zone anyway," Mike replied. Alice had been living with him since the mission to Eek Lake. They were even thinking about getting married.

"That's a big mistake, man! She's fucking psychic! She'll know you're lying?" Eric replied.

Mike waved him off and said, "She's my woman. You let me worry about Alice. She'll do what I say." Mike turned his attention to Taco on the phone. "Who will crew the helicopter?" Mike asked.

"I already talked to Chris Savage and Ed Hicks. Chris is coming, but Ed just had his ACL fixed," Taco replied.

"I'm going, too," Kevin replied.

"Who was that?" Taco asked.

"Remember the deputy we saved at Eek Lake, Kevin Bass? He works up here with us in Anchorage now. What's the deal, Kevin?" Eric asked.

"I should have died that night with Mark and Ronnie, but you guys saved me, and don't get me wrong, I thank God for you guys every day, but I need to find a way to pay this forward. I need to earn this new life that's been given to me, so I'm going with you. Saving a nun sounds like a good start," Kevin said.

CHAPTER 18

Over two hours had passed since Jon and Angie killed the fake cops east of Haisyn and they had traveled 120 miles. Now the sun was behind them as Jon drove sixty mph down the lonely highway swerving into the left lane occasionally to go around burned-out vehicles. Angie was trying to be a good copilot by scanning both sides of the highway for enemy positions. Jon was finally calming down from his earlier rampage when Angie quickly sat up erect and pointed as he yelled, "Tank in the trees at 11 o'clock! It's a kilometer away hull down on the edge of the farmer's field!"

Jon swerved left as he saw a blinding flash from the tank firing in the distance. The tank round screamed passed them on the right, exploding in the distance behind them. "Hang on!" Jon yelled as the SUV went airborne momentarily when it left the pavement on the other side of the highway. Neither of them was wearing a seatbelt. It careened down the grassy embankment and through a barbed wire fence. "Shit!" Jon yelled as he tried to stay behind the wheel as they bounced along on the uneven terrain.

"Stop the bloody car!" Angie screamed as he braced himself, his left hand on the headliner and his right grasping the handhold attached to the right A-pillar.

Jon bounced up and down so violently as they crossed the tall grass-covered washboard that his head kept slapping the headliner and he couldn't get his feet down to depress the brake pedal. The SUV charged through a row of thick brush before diving down a second embankment and splashing to an abrupt halt in a creek. A wave of brown water washed over the windshield. When everything settled the water was level with the bottom of the fenders. No words were necessary. They hopped out and sloshed their way to the cargo area to retrieve their FGM-148 Javelin anti-tank system. The Javelin was a fire-and-forget missile. Jon quickly uncased the launcher and attached the command launch unit to the tube. Angie loaded the missile before they scrambled up the far creek bank. Jon selected the top attack or curve ball mode, took aim, and fired the weapon. The Javelin missile was kicked out of the tube before the rocket motor fired. The missile climbed to an altitude of 500 feet as it raced 900 meters across the open field and dove into the tree line where it punched through the top of the T-90 main battle tank's turret and exploded inside killing the crew instantly. The turret flew off the tank flipping it through the air as if it were a giant coin before landing upside down in the field seventy feet away.

Deafening cheers erupted around them. They looked left and right and saw fighting positions on both sides of them near the crest of the tree-lined embankment. They were in the center of a Ukrainian infantry platoon.

A haggard-looking lieutenant stood below them in three inches of water. "Thank you for your assistance, gentlemen. We destroyed five of their six tanks several hours ago, but we ran out of Javelins. You just destroy their last tank. Now, we can go over there and burn the rats out of their holes. Would you like to join us?" he asked.

Angie carefully baby-stepped down the embankment toward the water, not wanting to slide down the muddy slope on his ass. He replied in Ukrainian, "As much as I would enjoy killing more Russians, I have to keep the major safe. The President would have my head if anything happened to him."

The lieutenant looked at Jon and then back to Angie. "Why is he more important than any other officer?" the lieutenant asked.

Angie looked left and right. He leaned in and said softly, "He is not Ukrainian. He is an American advisor. If he gets killed the Americans may stop supplying us with arms," Angie leaned back and said normally, "We have to get back on the road."

Jon took several steps down the slippery bank toward the creek with the launcher before losing his traction and sliding the rest of the way to the water like a world-class surfer. Upon arriving at the cargo area, he shouted, "Dammit! We have a flat!" Jon stared at the right rear tire. It was hanging off the rim. "Son of a bitch!" He kicked the tire. "We don't have time for this shit! This truck better have a jack!" he said as he put the launcher back in the case. He frantically moved the gear around enough to get to the jack. "This is gonna suck," Jon said mostly to himself before he went down to his knees in the water. He worked like a one-man NASCAR pit crew. He quickly loosened the lugs, set the jack up, and started ratcheting the Suburban's tire up off the creek bed. He looked around for Angie and saw him standing on the bank next to the lieutenant watching.

"You're doing great, Jonny. No reason for us both to get filthy," Angie said with a grin.

Jon yanked the bad tire off and threw it toward the bank. He retrieved the spare from under the SUV and quickly mounted it. He put the jack back inside and then bent over in the water to wash himself off. He looked to Angie and the lieutenant and said, "Easy day." Then he pulled three Javelin rounds from the stack of gear in the Suburban, gave them to the lieutenant, and said to him, "Kill some more Russians. Let's go," he said to Angie as he turned and sloshed his way back to the SUV and jumped in behind the steering wheel.

"Good luck, Lieutenant," Angie said before following Jon. He got in and closed his door.

Jon started the engine and set the transmission to 4WD low. He slowly depressed the gas pedal, but the SUV didn't move. He looked in his side mirror and saw a rooster tail of water flying off the spinning tire. He switched to reverse and tried again, but they didn't move. "Fuck! We're stuck!" Jon stated the obvious.

"Try rocking back and forth," Angie offered.

Jon looked at Angie as he began rocking back and forth in the driver's seat.

"Rock the truck back and forth, genius!" Angie yelled.

Jon alternated between drive and reverse several times, but they didn't move an inch. "Dammit! Hey, see if the lieutenant will get some of his men to help push us out," he said.

Angie stepped out into the calf-high water and walked over to the lieutenant. He said, "Would you mind if we borrowed some of your boys for a few minutes."

The lieutenant turned and yelled to his platoon sergeant, "Sergeant, bring the third squad over to lend a hand." The sergeant relayed the order and the seven surviving members of third squad walked down the embankment and into the creek behind the SUV.

Jon watched Angie as he leaned into the left rear corner. When the others were in position, Angie yelled in Ukrainian, "Okay, go!" Jon depressed the pedal slowly and watched as the rooster tail drenched Angie before the SUV lurched forward about a foot and stopped in another underwater pothole. Angie slipped off the fender and landed face-first in the creek.

Jon laughed, "You're doing great, Angie. Three or four more pushes like that and we'll be out." He saw Angie get up and glare back at him through the mirror. He was covered from head to toe in the slimy mud. He wiped his face with his hands and flung the mud back into the creek. Jon laughed again.

Angie and the men formed up on the SUV again and Angie yelled in Ukrainian, "Go!"

Jon gave it some gas and the SUV's tires spun in the mud drenching Angie and the men again, but the SUV didn't budge. "Hey, Major, try connecting the winch cable to that tree at the top of the creek bed and I'll see if it can help pull us out," Jon said. Angie bent over in the creek and rinsed his face and uniform off as best he could and then sloshed to the front of the SUV. He pulled the steel cable out between the slats in the grill guard, trudged up the slippery embankment to the large tree, and looped it around the trunk twice before hooking it on the cable and giving Jon the signal to take up the slack. Jon pressed the button on the winch controller and slowly added some gas. The SUV started slowly turning slightly to the left and toward the tree. Every couple of seconds it crept a foot closer to the edge of the creek. A minute later Jon stopped the winch with the SUV perched on top of the embankment above the creek. Angie unwrapped the cable from the tree and Jon retracted the cable with the controller.

Angie opened his door but rather than get in he looked at Jon and smiled. He said, "Jon, I think you have a dark side hiding behind that aw-shucks façade."

Jon smiled back and said, "I really wasn't trying to hide it."

"Before we hit the road why don't we change into civilian clothes? We don't want to be wearing these Ukrainian uniforms when we run into more Russians."

"I guess you're right. We'll have to keep both sets of ID handy," Jon said. They had Russian Federation SVR credentials from their original mission. They stripped down in the tall grassy field and cleaned up with wet wipes before putting on clean clothes.

The lieutenant emerged from the creek and walked over to them making sure he stayed on top of the tire tracks. "Gentlemen, I forgot to tell you to be careful crossing the field. There are Russian mines scattered randomly all over it," he said in Ukrainian.

"What was that?" Jon asked.

"The lieutenant said the Russians planted mines in this field," Angie said as he looked around where they were standing, "I'll ask what type." "Lieutenant, are they anti-personnel or tank mines?"

"Both. They plant anti-personnel mines around the TM-46 anti-tank mines to slow down our mine-clearing teams. The TM-46 mines are a mix of pressure and tilt-rod fuzes. The Toe Poppers are PFM-1 Butterfly mines. We haven't the time or equipment to make this field safe. Good luck," he said as he walked back to the creek again using the tire tracks.

"Anti-personnel mines are scattered around the tank mines to inhibit the mine-clearing teams," Angie translated for Jon.

"Shit! All I know about mines is I don't like them, except when I plant them. We don't have time to screw around. Do you want to walk back to the highway by following our tire tracks? After you're clear, I'll follow you in the truck. Otherwise, we can both go in the truck. There are probably a lot more toe poppers out there than tank mines. I think we're better off inside the truck," Jon said.

"I agree, but I'll drive," Angie replied as he gingerly moved to the driver's door. After they were both belted in Angie said," I'll take it slow until we get close to the embankment and then I'll speed up to help us get up the incline." Angie left the Suburban in 4WD low and began moving slowly across the farmer's furrows at a 30° angle being careful to stay in their original tracks. Their heads rocked left and right in time with the rows. As they neared the embankment Angie sped up. Halfway up to the pavement, the rear tires lost their grip causing several large rocks to be flung back onto the field. A toe popper exploded throwing a rock high into the air that landed on a TM-46 with a faulty pressure fuze. The mine exploded sending a geyser of dirt and rocks in a hundred-foot radius, cracking the Suburban's rear window, and pummeling the roof with gravel.

Angie pulled onto the empty highway and accelerated away from the mushroom cloud. As he headed for the bridge over the creek, he saw the lieutenant run up over the edge of the embankment. He was probably checking to see if the Suburban had been blown to a billion pieces. Angie honked and waved before they drove out of sight.

"Fuck! I've never been that close to a tank mine going off! I'm shaking!" Jon exclaimed. "How about you?"

"I was in one of your MRAPs in Afghanistan that drove over an IED. We flew up in the air about ten feet but landed on our wheels. My fillings almost came out. My ears rang for a week," Angie replied.

CHAPTER 19

M29 drove the Defender down Highway M-30 while M22 talked on his satellite phone. M22 disconnected the call and said, "Good news, comrade. They are very close. Men in a black Suburban destroyed a T-90 with a Javelin less than an hour ago outside of Velyka Vyska. They are heading this way."

"Is there any way to connect them to the farmhouse?' M29 asked.

"Just the black Suburban, but I do not believe in coincidences. I have not seen a black Suburban since the war started and now there are three in one day. If we catch them we can determine whether or not Officer Fyodor Nikolaev is a traitor or a captive. If he is captive and still in Ukraine we can take him back. Then I can kill the American Spetsnaz," M22 replied, "Pull off of the highway on the gravel road on the left. We will meet with our local militia commander, Leonid Vladislav. I was told he likes to be called Colonel. Before the war, he sold used cars. Over there, stop next to the technical," M22 said. In this case, the technical was a five-year-old blue Toyota Tundra pickup truck with a Dushka heavy machine gun mounted in its bed.

M22 and M29 walked across the road, helmets on and rifles held at low ready. The colonel was sitting on his truck's tailgate. Four of his men sat on the edge of both sides of the truck bed watching them approach. They looked more like refugees than soldiers. "Colonel Vladislav, I am pleased to finally meet you," M22 said as he held his right hand out for the colonel.

The scruffy colonel shook his hand as he looked him over suspiciously. "And who might you be?" he asked.

"Forgive me, Colonel. We are SVR Zaslon. Our names must remain secret. You may call me M22. He is M29. We are here on a mission vital to our country's national security. I was told you are a loyal Russian soldier. The motherland requires your help today," M22 said.

"We already have several national security missions planned for today. I suppose I may be able to fit yours in for the right reasons," the colonel said as his men laughed, "How many reasons do you have with you today?"

M22 turned to look at M29 briefly. M29 had seen that look many times and understood immediately. "Oh, I see. My apologies, Colonel. I was misinformed about your commitment. Today all I can promise you is pain if you do not help us," M22 explained. The colonel and his men began laughing again. The laughing stopped when M22 punched the colonel in his left temple and yanked him off the tailgate by his feet. The colonel's men moved to defend him but M29 stopped them with one shot fired into the air. M22 stood over the colonel with his pistol pointed at his face. "Colonel, I'm sorry we won't be working together," M22 said before pulling the trigger. "He looked up to the shocked men standing in the truck bed and asked, "Who is second in command?" Three men looked to the oldest man among them. "I am pleased to meet you, Colonel. Congratulations on your promotion. Please step down here."

CHAPTER 20

"I'm home," Alice York called out as she entered Mike Harmon's house. She had been living with him since they were temporarily forced back into active duty with the military over two years earlier to stop a team of Russian Spetsnaz that were tasked with extracting a Russian double agent from Alaska. Now she was making a decent living writing and self-publishing Amish Romance novels.

"I'm back here babe!" Mike said from their bedroom. He was sitting on their bed stuffing his clothes and hygiene kit into his backpack.

She leaned against the door frame with her arms crossed and watched for a minute. She said, "Why are you packing?"

"Eric and I are going up to the North Slope to find a fugitive," Mike lied, "We'll probably be gone for a few days. I'm sorry but it can't be helped. He's one dangerous hombre."

"Oh, Okay. That's too bad. While you're gone, I'll be flying to Europe to rescue Jon Smith's goddaughter, Kimmie. I guess you're gonna miss it," Alice said with an all-knowing smile.

Mike's chin dropped to his chest, and he murmured, "Fuckin' psychics."

She walked over to Mike and punched him in the arm.

"Ow! Dammit, that hurts!" Mike whined as he rubbed his arm.

"I don't need to be a psychic to figure out your sorry ass," she said, "You are the world's worst liar. You were really going to leave me behind, weren't you? You were going to leave me here to clean the house and bake cookies while you flew to Ukraine to save the world. Your last words to me might have been a lie."

"So how did you find out?" he asked, refusing to feel guilty.

"How do you think? Taco called me first. He needs a world-class sniper more than knuckle-dragging door kickers," Alice replied.

"Baby, it's too dangerous over there for you to go. How am I supposed to operate if I have to protect you the whole time?" Mike asked.

"You should know by now, I don't need any man's protection," she replied, "Besides, I'm the sniper. I'll be protecting all of you. My bag's already in the car. Hurry up or I'll leave you here and you can bake the cookies."

CHAPTER 21

M22 sat behind the steering wheel of a white Ford F-250 technical with M29 sitting at his side. Steel plates were welded onto all four sides. Their newly recruited ally, the freshly promoted separatist militia commander stood in the truck bed with two of his men, one manning the Dushka heavy machine gun. They were parked on the gravel road facing the highway a hundred feet away. Another team of five militiamen was manning the blue Tundra technical. It sat idling next to the Ford.

"The Suburban could be here any minute. My technical will fire first. It must not escape," M22 yelled to the men.

M29 rolled his eyes. "That's what you said half an hour ago. We have no idea if they are still coming this way or if they had anything to do with your brother's murder. So far all you have accomplished is killing two of our own people in cold blood with nothing to show for it. You are blinded by your rage to avenge your brother, comrade," M29 complained softly so no one else would hear him. He was coming to the end of his patience with his partner. It didn't matter that M22 was the senior officer. If his erratic behavior continued, he would have to report him.

"If you do not trust me to make sound decisions, you are free to return to Dnipro alone and report my activities," M22 replied calmly. He was growing tired of M29's negative attitude, "I will find these men and kill them before the night is over with or without you."

M29 turned to M22 and was about to respond when he saw a black Chevy Suburban approaching on the highway. He pointed as he shouted, "There it is! Shoot, shoot!" They heard a loud click come from the truck bed and then the sound of a gunner cycling a round into the Dushka's chamber. "Imbecile!" M29 shouted before a steady stream of rounds flew over their heads as the gunner fired. The blue Tundra raced forward toward the highway.

"Fucking militia!" M22 shouted as his back tires threw up a gray cloud of gravel. He quickly closed with the Tundra as it turned onto the highway.

***

An hour after swimming in the creek, Jon and Angie had covered over sixty miles and had just passed through Subottsi. Angie drove while Jon played navigator, looking for threats with the binoculars.

"Find a place to stop. I need to take a shit," Jon said as he squirmed in his seat.

"Why didn't you go back at the creek?" Angie asked. No sympathy.

"I didn't need to go back at the creek," Jon replied.

"No worries, mate. Climb in the back seat and go in a bag," Angie replied. It wasn't uncommon for special operations soldiers to crap in a Ziplock bag, but it was usually while on a patrol in the bush deep behind the lines when they were trying to keep their presence hidden from the enemy. The truly nasty part was carrying their bag of shit around with them in their pack for days at a time.

Jon looked at him. "Have you ever tried to shit in a moving vehicle? I have. It never goes as planned. The vehicle's bumping down the road, the bag's not wide enough or it's not big enough, and you don't just have to crap, you have to piss too. Plus, it's hard to see what you're doing," Jon complained.

Angie shrugged and said, "Give it a try, mate. What's the worst that can happen?"

"A big shitty, pissy mess, that's what!" Jon complained. He was getting annoyed, and his urge was growing exponentially. He could feel jumpers standing in the door, but Angie kept driving. "You're really not going to stop, are you?" Jon asked.

"I don't think we have the time, mate. We should Charlie Mike," Angie replied.

"Asshole. This is payback for the creek, isn't it," Jon said. It really wasn't a question.

"Whatever are you talking about?" Angie asked with a straight face.

"Yeah right! Okay, fuck it!" Jon said loudly. He took off his seat belt and climbed into the back seat. He rummaged around in the cargo area throwing random items in the air like an angry badger digging for his lunch. Jon couldn't see him, but he knew Angie was laughing. He found his pack and opened it. He pulled out a complete change of clothes in a two-gallon zip-lock bag and half a roll of toilet paper. The heavy-duty bag kept his clothes dry even when his pack was underwater. He removed the clothes from the bag and stuffed them back in the pack. He unbuckled his belt and dropped trou. He wasn't wearing underwear. After cleaning up earlier with wet wipes, he decided to let things air out. He strategized for a few seconds and then bent over at the waist holding the bag between his legs with one hand in front and one hand behind. Just as he was about to do his business a string of green tracers zipped across the road about ten feet behind the Suburban. "Incoming!" Jon yelled as he hunched over. The gun sounded like an old Dushka heavy machine gun. Instantly Jon felt the SUV lurch forward as Angie stomped on the gas. "Open the sunroof!" Jon yelled. Immediately, the glass began retracting. Jon rose up through the opening and planted his SAW's bipod firmly into the steel roof as he looked for a target, his trousers still around his ankles. He saw a blue pickup truck with the Dushka mounted in the bed turn onto the highway and race toward them. Angie's quick reaction gave them a growing 300-yard advantage. "They're coming after us!" Jon yelled down through the sunroof.

"I see'em!" Angie yelled back. He was pushing through 90 mph and still climbing as they raced along the undulating highway. More green tracers flew past the driver's side of the Suburban.

Jon responded with a string of red tracers and was rewarded by the driver's side headlight exploding. He fired another, longer burst that spidered the windshield in front of the driver. Jon watched the blue truck skid 90° to the right before it flipped upside down flinging several men out of the truck bed onto the pavement. It continued tumbling three more times before stopping upside down on the highway. A second technical, a white Ford F-250, swerved around the flaming wreck. Jon saw the truck bob up and down as it rumbled over the injured men. He fired a string into the vehicle, but the red tracers bounced harmlessly off in all directions. Jon dropped down through the sunroof and yelled, "It's up-armored! Give me your rifle!" He grabbed the HK416 with the attached M203 grenade launcher from Angie and stood up in the sunroof again.

Angie tapped him on the leg with an M406 round. "High explosive!" he yelled.

Jon pushed the round into the tube and slammed it shut. He yelled, "Stop!"

Angie realized immediately what Jon was doing and slammed on the brakes. After stopping, he took advantage of the brief pause in the action to snap a selfie of his smiling face with Jon's bare ass in the background. The photo would be lovely on the wall back in the team room in Virginia or perhaps as this year's team Christmas card.

Jon watched as the truck grew larger. Their green tracers danced wildly around the Suburban as the technical rose and fell with the curvy, undulating highway. Jon resisted the urge to squeeze the trigger. More tracers snapped through the air and spidered the right corner of the rear window before zipping by Jon on his left. He let the truck close to 150 meters before launching the grenade. It flew along a shallow arc back down the highway before it exploded into the steel plate bolted to the truck's grill. Jon saw the burning truck roll to a stop on the edge of the road. The men in the truck bed jumped onto the pavement. They were staggering around like they were confused. Jon yelled, "HE again!" Angie tapped him on the leg again and Jon loaded the round. He lobbed the grenade at the injured men. It exploded on top of the truck roof with devastating effects. "Let's go," Jon said as he came back down through the sunroof and pulled up his trousers, "I still need to take a shit."

***

"Shoot, damn you, shoot!" M22 yelled into his radio at the blue technical in front of him. His eyes went wide as he saw the Tundra slide sideways and tumble. The three militiamen in the bed were launched high into the air before falling to the pavement only to have the Tundra swat them further down the road. M22 swerved around the Tundra and unable to stop, ran over the three men writhing on the pavement. He didn't look back as he accelerated toward the Suburban. He saw the man standing in the sunroof and screamed at his gunner, "Shoot! Shoot, him!" Then the Suburban stopped in the road.

"They are stopping!" M29 shouted.

"Good, we have them!" M22 shouted back. Then the doubts came in rapid succession. *Why are they stopping? Is the truck disabled? Is it a trap?* he wondered to himself.

"RPG!" M29 screamed, as the high explosive grenade arced toward the truck.

M22 stomped on the brakes and slammed the transmission into Park as the grenade exploded into the truck's up-armored grill, destroying the engine. Within seconds another grenade exploded into the truck's up-armored roof. Everything went black for M22. Moments later, as his vision cleared he saw the Suburban driving away into the distance. His ears and nose were bleeding, but worst of all, he had a splitting headache. He turned and saw M29 moaning with his head hanging out of his open window. "Wake up, talk to me!" he shouted over the ringing in his ears. M29 slowly turned to look at him. His partner's nose and ears were also bleeding. M22 shouldered his door open and fell out onto the pavement. He staggered to his feet and emptied his pistol's magazine in the SUV's direction as he yelled, "Sooka sin! Unbju!" which meant 'son of a bitch, I'll kill you' in Russian.

M29 limped around the front of the truck and asked, "Did you hit anything?" before he dropped to one knee and grabbed the push bumper to steady himself.

CHAPTER 22

1400Z (1700HR LOCAL)
HIGHWAY M-30 KRYNYCHKY, UKRAINE

An hour later, as before Jon sat in the front passenger seat with the binoculars scanning for threats. He included frequent scans to the rear to make sure their six was clear. They were alone on this stretch of the divided four-lane highway. Jon was back to the cool, unflappable operator Angie was used to seeing, mostly, because after their last engagement, Angie found a secluded copse of trees to hide in while Jon disappeared behind the bushes to conduct his personal business. Now they were about a mile west of the exit for the city of Krynychky. Jon could see movement through his binoculars on top of the overpass. "Pull over. I see an armored vehicle and soldiers on the overpass."

"Cowboys or Indians?" Angie asked as he slowed to a stop on the shoulder behind a burned-out Mercedes E350.

"I can't tell from here. Take a look," Jon said as he handed the binoculars to Angie. "I think they have a BTR."

"Yeah, it's a BTR, but I still can't tell whose side they're on. Can you tell which model the BTR is?" Angie asked.

"Hell, I don't know. They all look alike to me. Let's break out the X2D and take a look," Jon said. The X2D was a folding quadcopter drone small enough to be carried in a rucksack. It had a 4K high-definition video camera and a 16x digital zoom FLIR camera. It could be launched in under seventy-five seconds. Angie pulled off the shoulder into the trees. They went to the rear of the SUV and raised the muddy hatch. Jon grabbed the X2D's case and opened it. He handed the controller to Angie so he could power it up while Jon unfolded the drone's four rotor arms. He walked over to the edge of the tree line and sat the drone on the ground. "Do you know how to fly this thing?" Jon asked.

"Yeah, more, or less. I did it once before," Angie replied. He turned to face the drone with the controller held in front of himself with both handles. He activated the camera and launched the X2D straight up to 200 feet above ground level. Then he steered it along the highway toward the overpass. At 200 feet he knew the soldiers couldn't hear the rotors beating the air.

Jon watched the drone lift off and followed it along its ascent until it leveled off and headed away. They both watched the small color screen as the images on the overpass grew larger. "Well, that's definitely a Russian BTR, nice of them to paint giant Zs on the sides and top. I count seven men on the overpass: one in the BTR turret, three manning the Dushka machine gun, and three riflemen on foot. There could be more inside the BTR. Underneath the overpass, I see two men manning the checkpoint," Jon said.

"Agreed. What do you want to do? We can drive up and show them our SVR creds," Angie offered.

"No, if they ask me any questions, we're screwed. Not to mention, the militia guys with the technical and the infantry with the tank we destroyed may have sent off a message saying our Suburban was hostile. Let's do what George Washington did to the Hessians at Trenton on Christmas. Let's blast the shit out of them before they even know we're here. We'll use the Switchblades, two 600s for the BTR and Dushka, and two of the 300s for the riflemen on the overpass and the two men manning the checkpoint underneath," Jon replied. He was referring to Switchblade Kamikaze drones. The Switchblade 600 weighed about fifty pounds and employed the same anti-armor warhead in the FGM-148 Javelin Anti-tank Guided Missile or ATGM. It was launched from what looked like a mortar tube. After the Switchblade exited the tube the wings and control surfaces would spring open, and it would fly away toward its target. It had a 40 km range and 40 minutes of endurance with a 70-mph cruise speed.

The Switchblade 300 was smaller and less lethal but still deadly. Its warhead was similar to a 40mm grenade. Angie left the X2D loitering above the target while he and Jon broke out the Switchblades. Ten minutes later four missiles were arrayed in their launchers two by two ready to fly. "I'll drive, you fly," Jon said as he closed the rear hatch and headed for the driver's door.

Angie climbed into the passenger seat next to Jon and sat the controller in his lap. He launched the missiles along their programmed route and said, "All right, mate. Let's go."

Jon slowly pulled out of the trees and accelerated toward the overpass. He didn't want to appear aggressive. He split his attention between the road and the missiles. He planned to arrive just after all of the debris from the explosions fell to the ground. Then hopefully he could just blow through the checkpoint. Angie set up the targeting priority as BTR, Dushka, rifleman on the overpass, and finally riflemen at the checkpoint.

A half mile from the targets, Angie said, "Fifteen seconds."

Jon began slowing down to give the drone attack time to do its damage.

"Five, four, three, two, one, impact," Angie said matter-of-factly.

Jon looked up in time to see the missile fly through the open turret hatch of the BTR and detonate inside. A brilliant explosion flashed before his eyes blasting fire out of the turret and the rear troop doors. A soldier engulfed in flames stumbled out and fell writhing to the pavement. Jon stopped the suburban abruptly so he could watch the action. The BTR continued to burn from the inside. Orange flames surrounded by black smoke rose above the rear troop hatches. The other Switchblade 600 exploded to the BTR's left inside the Dushka's sandbagged position. Two flaming human-sized objects flew into the air before landing outside the sandbagged emplacement. The riflemen on the overpass spun in circles looking for a safe place to run to but found none. Before they could disperse the first Switchblade 300 landed at their feet causing devastating wounds. They rolled around on the pavement screaming in agony. The two men manning the checkpoint on the highway were still underneath the overpass. They looked up but couldn't see the effect the missiles were having. They could hear the explosions and see the debris falling in front of them. Then they heard the screams, the agony of their burning and dismembered comrades. Since all the destruction occurred above them, they felt relatively safe for the moment. They took cover under their truck and waited. It only took a second for the final Switchblade to smash into their truck spraying them with shrapnel and burning fluids. They were only lightly injured and were able to crawl out from under the truck and put out the small fires on their backs.

Jon seized the opportunity to surprise them and raced forward. He stopped the Suburban about thirty meters from the checkpoint. He and Angie quickly advanced on foot toward their enemy. They were within about fifteen meters when the Russian soldiers saw them and began firing their rifles. A 7.62x39 round hit Jon in the center of his chest. The force of the impact rocked him back on his heels and he dropped to one knee gasping for air. He thrust his SAW out in front of himself and dropped to the pavement smacking his open mouth on the top of the receiver. He moaned in pain and saw stars swimming in front of his eyes. He shook off the pain and spit blood off to his side. He had the fore-thought to extend the bipod before the action started. He began firing bursts toward the Russians. One hid behind the flat rear tire. Jon kept firing until the steel-belted tire disintegrated to the point that his rounds hit the Russian.

At the start of the action, Angie dropped to the pavement and began firing at the second Russian who also took cover behind the other end of the truck. Angie fired an HEDP grenade round into the concrete pylon behind the truck. It exploded on the pylon spraying shrapnel all over the Russian's back. He yelped in pain and turned to run down the road. Angie fired a burst into his back, and he dropped lifeless onto the pavement.

"Angie! Check me for leaks!" Jon shouted from the asphalt, "I took a round in my plate!"

Angie ran to Jon and took a knee over him. Concern etched across his face, Angie said, "There's blood in your mouth, Jonny Boy."

"It's Okay. I smacked my mouth on the SAW. Check under my plate for holes," Jon replied.

Angie ripped the Velcro loose and put his hand on Jon's chest. It was wet with sweat but no blood. He said, "No blood or holes. I don't feel any broken ribs. Are you able to get up?" Angie held out his hand.

Jon took his hand and said, "Yeah, thanks, man. This is gonna hurt like a bitch for a while. Let's get out of here. You drive." Jon walked slowly back to the SUV as he rubbed his chest under his plate carrier. Angie grabbed the controller from the truck and brought the X2D down to land next to the truck. He shut it down and threw it in the cargo area. They cautiously drove under the overpass, weaving between the sandbags, truck, and bodies, then accelerated down the highway. "I think we can assume we are in Indian country from here on," Jon said.

Angie silently nodded his agreement. "We should be there in two and a half to three hours. Have you given any thought to what you're going to do if she refuses to leave?" Angie asked.

Jon continued to scan the road and its surroundings. "If I have to, I'll hog tie her ass and stuff her in a box. I've known that little girl since she was born. She's always been as headstrong as she is fearless. She has a bad habit of fighting above her weight. She thinks she's Saint Jude," Jon said. St. Jude was the patron saint of lost causes.

CHAPTER 23

M22 slowed the Land Rover Defender to a stop just before going under the overpass. He and M29 got out and approached the TCP cautiously.

"Both soldiers are dead. They were burned and shot," M29 said.

"Let's go on top," M22 said before he began making his way up the steep incline on all fours to the top of the overpass. M22 walked by the dead soldiers on his way to the BTR. It was white hot. The tires were still burning. He peeked inside through the open troop hatches. "The interior is totally burned out, but the outer shell is intact," he said. He didn't dare touch the scorching hot hatch.

"All of the soldiers are dead. Their bodies are riddled with shrapnel wounds. The Dushka and BTR did not get off any shots before they were disabled. They must have been totally surprised," M29 said. He looked to the sky. "How did they do this without air support?" he asked.

M22 shook his head and replied, "The Americans have more toys than 007."

CHAPTER 24

Jon was driving now. He couldn't get comfortable in his seat. Leaning back made his chest hurt from the AK round that hit his plate, so he had to sit erect. His swollen lip and the cut inside his mouth stung constantly and made drinking difficult, but worst of all, he had some extremely inflamed irritation in his groin that was growing by the minute. He scratched at the offending itch through the fabric of his trousers.

"Would you like some privacy, mate?" Angie asked with a smile.

"Either I have crotch rot, or I picked up some hitchhikers in the creek," Jon replied.

"Didn't you change your skivvies?" Angie asked.

"I decided to go commando to let things dry out," Jon explained. "How about you? Is anything irritated?" Jon asked.

"No, fresh as a daisy," Angie lied. Whenever Jon wasn't watching, Angie scratched to his heart's content.

"You're a medic. How about you break out your kit and rub some ointment on my afflicted area?" Jon asked wryly.

Angie laughed and replied, "You're on your own, mate. Why don't you follow Matthew's advice?"

"What's that, some kind of Bible remedy?" Jon asked.

"You could say that. Matthew said if thy right hand offend thee, cut it off. The same could apply to Willy," Angie said.

"Fuck that! Willy's my second-best feature, maybe my best now that I broke my nose!" Jon replied.

Angie laughed and shook his head. "I wish I had your sense of self-worth, mate."

***

Ten minutes passed and they were still peacefully driving down the lonely highway. Jon was getting nervous. "Two more hours, Angie and we'll be there. I wish the sun would go down. I feel naked driving down the highway like this not knowing if the troops we see are Ukrainian or Russian. I hope nobody back at that last TCP had time to get off a description of our vehicle," Jon said.

"The Ukrainians won't shoot at us until they're sure we're not friendly. The Russians on the other hand will shoot at anything not positively identified as an ally," Angie replied.

As Angie stopped speaking a green and brown camouflaged jet roared by Jon's side of the truck fifty feet above the ground at

200 knots. Jon flinched as he jerked the wheel to the right reflexively causing the truck to move to the shoulder. He could see the pilot looking at him as he flew by. The jet accelerated as it made a sharp climbing left turn to head back where it came from.

"Fuck! That's a Frogfoot! They fly in twos! His wingman is probably lining up on us right now! We have to find cover!" Jon yelled as he stomped on the gas pedal. The SU-25 Frogfoot was a Russian ground attack jet, but the Ukrainians flew them too. Its ground attack mission was similar to that of the American A-10.

Angie pointed ahead to the right and said, "Pull off up there by the metal building where the tree line parallels the highway."

Seconds later, Jon slammed on the brakes and turned right behind the building just before a salvo of S-8 air-to-ground rockets screamed by and exploded into the highway where the Suburban would have been. The dash 2 Frogfoot flew by seconds later at about 500 feet before climbing away to the left. It carried two B-8M1 rocket pods under each wing. Each pod could carry twenty rockets.

Jon made a quick left turn into the trees. He weaved the truck between the trees to get further into the thin strip of the wooded area between the highway and railroad tracks. Jon and Angie hopped out of the Suburban in time to see the second Frogfoot fly away back down the highway. The jets established a wagon wheel orbit 180° apart so one jet was always in a position to attack if the truck broke cover.

"They must really want us bad to be coming down low like that, but I don't think they can see us under the tree canopy," Angie said.

"Somebody must have told them about the tank and TCPs. We can't wait for them to run out of gas. They might be keeping us pinned down until they can get troops over here or call in artillery. Let's break out a Stinger," Jon said. They went to the back of the Suburban.

"Where are they?" Angie asked as he rummaged around the cargo area.

"Under the Javelin," Jon replied.

They pulled out a long green box.

"Have you ever used this thing?" Jon asked as they unlatched the lid.

"Just the simulator," Angie replied.

"Okay, I'll take this one," Jon said. He removed the FIM-92 Stinger shoulder-launched infrared ground-to-air missile from the case, lifted it onto his right shoulder, and attached the BCU. "Okay, the BCU is attached," he said before unfolding the antenna. The BCU was the Battery/Cooling Unit. He removed the end cap from the tube. Then he locked the sight assembly into place. Angie inserted the IFF cable into the gripstock for Jon. They hustled over to the edge of the tree line next to the highway. Jon grasped the uncaging switch with his left hand. The lead Frogfoot flew overhead low and slow at 200 feet and 150 knots with his landing gear and flaps down. The pilot punched off flares on top of the Suburban before raising its gear and flaps and quickly accelerating away in another predictable climbing left turn.

"He marked our position for his wingman! Do you see him?" Jon yelled as he looked through the peep sight and put the lead jet in the center of the range ring.

Angie yelled back, "Negative!" before he ran out into the center of the empty highway to get a better view of the sky. He pointed back down the highway and yelled, "Two just started his turn back toward us. Jon, get away from the flares!"

Jon stepped onto the pavement. He stood his ground and challenged the lead aircraft with the IFF. The IFF responded with a long series of beeps indicating the jet was an unknown or unfriendly target. Now Jon knew it wasn't Ukrainian.

Angie ran to the other side of the highway and slid down into the ditch. He yelled, "Hey, dickhead, get your bloody arse over here before Dash 2 comes back!"

Jon continued to track the jet as he activated the BCU with his right thumb. He waited the required three to five seconds for the weapon to warm up. Three seconds this time. He could hear the gyro spinning up.

"For fuck's sake, mate! He's on his attack run! Get over here, you stupid wanker!" Angie yelled.

Next, Jon heard the tone indicating the IR seeker had acquired the jet. He pressed the uncaging switch for the seeker head before he superelevated the launcher and fired the missile. The launch motor kicked the missile out of the tube about thirty feet before the main rocket motor fired.

The Stinger streaked away accelerating to more than twice the speed of sound as it homed in on the jet. "Fuck you, Ivan!" Jon yelled, transfixed by the missile's flight.

The Frogfoot's sensors recognized the incoming Stinger and alerted the pilot. He deployed chaff and flares as he frantically initiated a series of gyrating maneuvers across the cloudless sky as he tried to shake the missile. Jon continued to watch the action as he detached the single-use BCU and dropped it before it could damage the launcher. It was too hot to hold. The Stinger continued to close on the Frogfoot. Without pity, Jon imagined the terror the pilot must be experiencing. *Next time stay in fucking Russia!* He thought.

The Frogfoot pulled up and right popping off more flares in a final attempt to evade the missile, but the Stinger had a closure rate of over 1,000 knots and superior turning ability. It exploded in the jet's right engine exhaust sending it tumbling out of control toward the ground. Within seconds the ejection seat rocketed away from the burning inverted Frogfoot heading straight down toward the ground. The seat automatically turned 180° and climbed 100 feet in the air before the pilot separated from the seat and his parachute opened. He had barely enough time to swing once under its canopy before he hit the nicely plowed field next to the fiery remains of his jet.

"The wingman broke off his attack run and turned back to the right. He must have seen the missile hit his leader," Angie said as he walked back across the highway, "I think he is going to act as on-scene commander until their SAR assets arrive."

"Yeah, I'd like to stay here and stuff a Stinger up his ass, too, but he's probably calling in arty on us right now. We better haul ass," Jon said as they ran back to the Suburban, dodging between the fires started by the flares. Angie ran for the driver's side as Jon tossed the empty Stinger into the cargo area and jumped in the passenger side. "They could wipe out a whole fucking grid square just to make sure they got us after we smoked one of their Frogfoots. Hopefully, they don't have the time or resources to chase us," Jon replied.

"Hang on, mate," Angie said as he quickly backed the Suburban between the trees and brush to get back to the gravel road next to the steel building. He turned back onto the highway and accelerated away from the area. Seconds later the world behind them erupted sending sheet metal and flaming trees into the air for as far as the eye could see. Balls of orange flame surrounded by black smoke billowed above the tree line. "Crikey!" Angie yelled as he hunched down behind the steering wheel. He already had the gas pedal on the floor. All he could do was hope the explosions didn't follow them.

"Open the sunroof. I want to see if number two is coming after us," Jon said as he climbed into the backseat with his SAW. He stuck his head out and scanned the sky above the highway behind them. He ducked back down into the truck and said, "So far, so good," as he grabbed the Stinger tube from the cargo area. He reached down under the Javelin case and brought up another missile and BCU. He poked his head up again through the sunroof like a meerkat looking for eagles. He sat back down in the rear seat and pushed the missile out in front of him to slide it into the rear of the launcher.

Angie hit a bump in the pavement and the end of the missile smacked him in the side of the head. He winced in pain as he swerved into the oncoming lane. "For fuck's sake, Jon!" Angie complained as he rubbed his right ear.

Jon chuckled and said, "Hey, now you can say you were hit by a Stinger missile and lived." He attached the BCU and stood up through the sunroof opening again. He still didn't see any aircraft pursuing them.

"Shoot him, Jonny, shoot!" Angie yelled.

Jon frantically looked for the enemy who was going to kill them. "Where is it?" he yelled.

"Ten o'clock coming around to twelve!" Angie yelled back.

Jon had assumed the attack would come from behind them. He was going to be really embarrassed if they got killed because of his stupid assumption. He turned around and went through the sequence again to get the missile ready to launch. He skipped the IFF step this time.

"Twelve o'clock, two miles, Jon!" Angie yelled.

Jon could tell Angie was scared; he had never heard his voice that high. "Okay, I see him," he replied. He aimed the Stinger at the incoming Frogfoot and waited an eternity for the three seconds necessary for the seeker to cool and the gyro to spin up.

"Shoot dammit!" Angie screamed.

"I can't shoot, yet!" Jon yelled back.

"Fuck!" Angie yelled as he saw a salvo of S-8 rockets heading right at him from under the wings of the Frogfoot. The Stinger flew over his head and raced toward the jet flying between the rockets. The rockets landed short and exploded on the highway. Angie drove through the shower of debris as he watched the missile close on the jet. The pilot pulled his Frogfoot into a hard left turn and dove toward the ground as he deployed his flares. The Stinger turned with him and closed at an incredible rate. The missile exploded harmlessly among the flares above the Frogfoot as its left wing clipped a tree and it cartwheeled into the ground.

Jon tossed the used BCU into the ditch before he sat down next to Angie. "Is the little girl all right?" he asked.

"What girl?" Angie asked.

"The little girl that was in here screaming for her mommy?" Jon said before laughing.

"Fuck you, I almost shit myself," Angie said before laughing with Jon, "So now you have two subs and two fighters."

"What subs?" Jon asked.

"Yeah, okay, whatever, mate. You know, If Ivan ever finds out who you are they're going to put out wanted posters. Maybe we can get you the Ukrainian Medal of Honor or some shit," Angie said.

CHAPTER 25

Taco entered the terminal building and walked over to the group. "I guess it's kind of late to ask if everyone has a valid passport?" He asked. Taco stood in front of the other team members who were seated on a long wooden bench facing the floor-to-ceiling windows overlooking the ramp and runway. Tactical packs in varying shades of green, tan, and black littered the floor at their feet. Eric Fuller, Mike Harmon, Alice York, and Kevin Bass all raised passports over their heads.

"Hey, where are Chris and Ed?" Mike asked.

"Chris is on his way from Kodiak. He said not to leave without him. Ed is recovering from knee surgery. He blew out his ACL," Taco replied.

"Slacker! Some guys will do anything to get out of deploying," Mike joked.

"Good thing he can't hear you. He'd beat your ass with his crutches," Taco joked back.

Mike smirked and said, "He'd have to catch me first."

"Taco, have you heard anything more from Colonel Adams?" Eric asked.

"Just briefly, he said to get here ASAP and a plane was on the way to pick us up. It should be here any time now. He also said we were going to stop in Edinburgh to pick him up and then fly to Berlin to get the Huey," Taco replied.

"We missed breakfast. Are you guys hungry? We could run over to Khan's Kitchen and bring back Mongolian for everybody," Mike said.

"No!" Taco shouted, remembering the food poisoning that had incapacitated the pilots on the Eek Lake mission. Taco turned around to look out to the runway. He could hear the scream of jet engines outside ripping the air apart but couldn't see the plane. Then it appeared low and fast descending from right to left with its wheels and flaps down. It touched down on Runway 4. It stopped midway down the asphalt pavement, then it turned left 180° to taxi back down the runway to the ramp in front of the terminal. "Damn! Check it out! That's a Gulfstream G700," Taco said as he admired the sleek white business jet taxing toward the terminal. "They go for about 75 million a pop! Tiger must be coming up here to go fly fishing on the Kenai, again." He watched as the lineman directed the jet to its parking spot and chocked its tires. The door behind the cockpit opened from the top and folded out to become the stairs.

A pale but fit middle-aged man with short blonde hair wearing a green polo and khakis hurried down the stairs and rushed into the terminal. He stopped inside the door and looked right, then left. He quickly walked over to Taco, held out his hand, and said, "You must be Taco. I'm Whitey. Chirp sent me to get you." He turned to look at the group on the bench, "Is everyone here?"

"All but one, sir. He should be here any second," Taco replied.

Whitey checked his watch. "We can't wait. We need to get in the air before the Feds figure out what we're up to," Whitey said as he turned for the door, "Follow me." He marched off across the floor and out the door.

Mike hustled up next to Whitey with his eyes bugged out at whom he was seeing. "Sir, you're General Bryan McKinley, former Commandant of the Marine Corps!" he said excitedly. He was star-struck.

"Yes, I am and you're Staff Sergeant Mike Harmon. I've been following your career since you enlisted nine years ago," Whitey responded as he continued double timing it toward the jet.

"Really, sir!" Mike was shocked and flattered, he had no idea.

Whitey chuckled and said, "No, not really. Come on let's go before someone stops us."

The group busted out laughing as they followed Whitey across the ramp.

Eric stepped up next to Mike. "Really, sir!" He mocked Mike as he punched him in the shoulder, laughing even louder. "You're my hero, sir!" Eric stepped closer to study Mike's face and said, "You have a little bit of drool hanging off your bottom lip."

Mike tried to kick Eric on his backside, but Eric sidestepped the size 11 extra wide.

"Children, behave!" Alice said, then turned to the group. "I can't take them anywhere."

"Sir, don't we need to refuel?" Taco asked.

"No, we took off with a full bag. We're good for 7,500 nautical miles. We have plenty to continue to Edinburgh to pick up Chirp, and just call me Whitey," he replied. Whitey stopped at the bottom of the steps when he heard the familiar roar of a turbine-powered helicopter approaching. He looked to the right past the tail and saw an orange and white Coast Guard MH-60T Jayhawk approaching the ramp at high speed. The pilot flared the helicopter at 100 feet, standing it on its tail to rapidly decelerate, then nosed over to solidly plant the helicopter on the ramp with a rolling landing. The pilot braked to a stop fifty feet behind the G700. "Damn, we may be too late. I think we're busted." A man and woman in civilian clothes jumped out of the Jayhawk and ran for the jet.

"No, sir, it's cool. That's our missing man and Jon's fiancée," Taco said as Chris Savage ran up to the group.

"Great. Let's go," Whitey replied.

They followed Whitey up the stairs and were immediately impressed by the luxurious interior. Nineteen overstuffed tan leather seats that could be converted to ten beds were scattered along the walls of the 56-foot-long interior. There was an abundance of insanely expensive wood trim made of Bubinga hardwood from Africa. The cabin still had that new airplane smell.

"Find a seat and make yourselves comfortable. It'll take about six and a half hours to get to Edinburgh to pick up Chirp. If you're hungry, just wave at one of the attendants and they'll hook you up," Whitey said before taking a seat.

Mike's arm shot up in the air immediately for an attendant. "I think I'll go for the surf and turf," he said to his teammates and girlfriend, Alice.

"May I help you, sir?" the male attendant asked.

"The general said you have food for us. Do you have steak and lobster?" Mike asked.

"No, sir, I'm afraid not. This trip was on such short notice we didn't have time to get lobster, but I can whip up a mean Philly cheese steak sandwich in about fifteen minutes. How does that sound?" The young man replied.

"That sounds great, man. Thank you," Mike replied.

"Would anyone else like one?" the attendant asked. Seven hands shot up including Whitey's.

Whitey raised the intercom handset sitting next to his seat to his head and said, "Let's roll." The seatbelt light came on instantly and they began moving out of their parking spot. The female attendant walked the aisle to make certain everyone was buckled in before returning to the front and buckling her own seatbelt. The plane quickly taxied out onto the departure end of Runway 4 and stopped. The pilot kept the brake pedals depressed, then advanced the throttles for the two Rolls-Royce Pearl 700 turbofan engines, each putting out 18,250 pounds of thrust. They would push the jet up to 51,000 feet at 595 knots. When the engines stabilized at full power, the pilot released the brakes, and the jet lunged forward like a sprinter from the starting block. It raced down the centerline and leaped into the air with 500 feet of runway to spare.

***

Alice leaned forward, motioning toward Chris. "Kevin, have you met Chris, well of course you have, but you may not remember the first time. He was the EMT that helped you that night," she said.

"Yes, we met. I tracked him down, too. We got together a few months ago. The only guys I haven't met are the soldiers. Strasburg and Pope are deployed with their guard unit and Rogers was enjoying his honeymoon in Bermuda when I went to New York," Kevin who was sitting across from Alice replied and then asked, "Excuse me, Whitey, I know this mission popped up without notice but has anyone coordinated when and where we are going to get our weapons and equipment? I believe the Germans are pretty strict when it comes to automatic weapons being trafficked within their borders."

"Jon has a contact in the Moldovan SIS that will equip us with everything we need for the right price," Whitey replied, "We'll land outside of their capitol, Chisinau, to top off our fuel and load our equipment and ammo."

"What's the SIS?" Kevin asked.

"It's their Security and Intelligence Service," Whitey explained.

"Hey, everybody, this is Lieutenant Sarah Tuttle. She's Jon's fiancée," Taco said.

Sarah nervously waved at the team and said, "Hi, everyone."

Alice got up and sat down next to Sarah. "Hi, Sarah. Do you remember me? We never actually talked the other time we worked together. I'm Alice York. That insensitive caveman over there is my fiancée, Mike. How are you holding up?"

"I guess I'm still in shock. I know what Jon does for a living but when he deploys, he doesn't even hint at where he's going or what he'll be doing. He calls me every few days to check in, but I had no idea he was in Ukraine. I wouldn't have known about Kimmie needing help if I wasn't in the hangar with Chris when Taco called him. There's no way I'm staying behind if Jon's in trouble."

CHAPTER 26

Harold Lamb sat alone in his office wearing yesterday's clothes. He was leaning back with his feet on his desk. Despite spending an uncomfortable, near-sleepless night on his office couch, he had powered through his morning meetings fueled by donuts and caffeine. After eating a White House Cafeteria lunch consisting of roast turkey slices, mashed potatoes, and gravy he succumbed to the tryptophan coursing through his veins. The half-empty Styrofoam clamshell container resting precariously on his chest rose and fell in rhythm with his loud snores, like a dinghy bobbing in the ocean.

Preston Alexander burst through the office door, shouting at the top of his lungs, "Harold, wake up! We have another problem!"

BOB ASHER

Startled, Lamb fell backward out of his chair landing with his feet up in the air, the remaining half of his cold lunch sliding across his $300 shirt toward the rug. "God dammit, Pres! You almost gave me a stroke!" Lamb rolled over to his knees and braced his hands against the desk to help him stand up. Once erect, he looked down at the brown mess covering his shirt. "You owe me a shirt, Pres," he said as he bent over to grab the container and dropped it in his trash can. "What is it this time?" he asked as he unbuttoned his shirt. He took it off and dropped it in the can on top of his lunch. He bent over and pulled a shirt box from his lower right desk drawer. This one was only $275.

"The FAA inspectors at Anchorage Airport didn't stop General McKinley's jet as we planned," Pres said. The dark ring of sweat around his neck had spread from under his bowtie down to the second button on his shirt.

"Why not? How'd you screw that up?" Lamb asked, already assuming the incompetent National Security Advisor was to blame.

"I didn't screw up, Harold. McKinley's jet was about twenty minutes from Anchorage when the pilots canceled their IFR flight plan and continued VFR to Homer. By the time the inspectors figured out the plane wasn't landing at Anchorage, it was already halfway across Alaska heading for Edinburgh," Alexander explained.

"Christ, Pres, I gave you one damn job!" Harold added exasperation to his exhaustion.

"This isn't my fault. Can we call the President, now?" Alexander asked.

"Haven't you learned yet, we don't take stuff like this to the President? If we did, we'd be in World War III by now," Lamb replied. *This idiot, Alexander, is going to screw up my master plan to ascend to the Oval Office within the next ten years,* Lamb thought. "Okay, Pres, listen very carefully. Call Mayorkissass over at DHS. Have him call the Brits and say we suspect McKinley's plane is carrying contraband," Lamb said.

"What kind of contraband?" Alexander asked.

"Fuck, I don't know, drugs, guns, blood diamonds! You have a PhD from Princeton for God's sake! Figure it out!" Lamb replied.

"Harold, we should brief POTUS. This thing is getting out of hand," Alexander said defiantly.

"Pres, what did the President tell the entire staff right after he took office?" Lamb asked, trying to make a point.

"He said you were his right hand and when you spoke, you were speaking for him," Alexander replied.

"Keep going," Lamb pushed.

"He said to run everything by you, and you would decide when to get the President involved," Alexander said.

"That's right. Now get out of my office and call DHS," Lamb replied. "Next time I see you, you need to tell me this problem is over." Lamb was already wargaming in his head about how he was going to hang the blame around Alexander's neck if things went south.

CHAPTER 27

Zaslon officers M22 and M29 stopped on Highway M-30 parallel to the crash site of the first Frogfoot. They walked 100 meters out into the field. A green Russian Army Linza combat ambulance was parked between the Frogfoot wreckage and the injured pilot. A squad of infantry was deployed around the crash site to secure the classified equipment and sensitive items in the smoking Frogfoot debris. Two medics were putting a splint on the pilot's broken leg. His jagged white femur protruded from his left thigh. He writhed about, groaning in intense pain. Fortunately for him, the femoral artery was not severed.

M22 and M29 walked up to the group. "Lieutenant, we need to talk to you for a moment before the medics take you to the field hospital," M22 said.

"Please, stop the pain! I can't stand it!" the pilot begged them.

"You heard the lieutenant. Give him something for the pain," M29 ordered the medics.

"Sir, we have no painkillers to give him. We haven't had any for three days. Supplies are not making it to our outpost," the sergeant complained.

M29 handed morphine from his own IFAK to the medic. "Give this to him," he said. The medic injected the painkiller and within minutes the pilot had calmed down enough to talk. "Lieutenant, please tell us what happened to your aircraft?" M29 asked.

"During our pre-mission briefing the intel officer told us to look out for a black Suburban that had attacked several TCPs. We were returning from our mission when we saw a black Suburban on the highway. I dropped down low and slow to check it out. I tried to call them on the radio, but they didn't respond. Instead, after I flew by they drove off the road and tried to hide in the trees. I came around slowly again, so I could see where they were hiding and dropped flares to mark their position. As I climbed out and turned left to get back into position to attack them my wingman, Spider, told me the Stinger was coming at me and I heard the aural warning for the missile. I tried to evade it but got hit. As I ejected my leg broke on my way out of the cockpit. How is Spider?" the lieutenant asked. He looked around, instantly concerned for his friend, and asked, "Where is he?"

The sergeant replied solemnly, "I am sorry, sir. He was also shot down. He didn't make it out of the aircraft."

The Zaslon officers turned immediately and hurried across the uneven furrows in the farmer's field to get back to their Defender 110. "It appears your suspicions may have been correct," M29 said.

"We must find them before they switch vehicles. I'm surprised they haven't done so already," M22 replied.

"Perhaps they don't have time to stop. If they are in a hurry, they will make more mistakes," M29 posited.

They climbed into the Defender and M22 drove away quickly trying to make up time. However, he had to come to a crawl a mile later when they entered the artillery's impact zone. M22 slowly navigated around the random craters in the pavement. Large chunks of rock and asphalt were scattered everywhere. The small forests on both sides of the highway had been denuded and burned in the maelstrom. The burning tree trunks that remained standing had been snapped in half. The low sun disappearing behind the terrain gave the smoldering landscape a demonic feel.

"My God! This must be what Hell looks like. It even smells like Hell," M29 said.

"Why do you think soldiers call artillery the King of Battle?" M22 asked rhetorically.

CHAPTER 28

Jon lay prone fifty meters from the back door of St. Michael's Church behind a 300-year-old waist-high stone wall. The sun was just going down. He had surveyed the area for the last ten minutes. It was as dead as the church's cemetery. He keyed his team radio, "I found a fresh grave back here on the edge of the cemetery. The cross reads Father Del Toro. It looked like it was written with a magic marker. Otherwise, nothing's going on back here. How about your side?"

"All quiet on this front. There's a gap in the shrubs lining the driveway and deep ruts in the lawn. It looks like the Chechens did it just to be assholes. What do you want to do?" Angie asked from behind a row of low shrubs lining the circular driveway.

"Make your way around to the back door and we'll make entry from there," Jon replied. He received two clicks in response from Angie. Five minutes later they met up at the massive old oak door. Jon tried the door, but it was locked. "Do you want to give it a try?" Jon asked.

Angie smiled and went down to one knee and began working on the lock with his pick gun. He had the door unlocked in less than thirty seconds.

"What took so long?" Jon asked rhetorically as he smiled under his goggles. Jon entered first and they methodically cleared the nave and offices in the darkness on the first floor. They were unoccupied. Jon was getting nervous. He feared he might be too late.

"Let's check downstairs," Angie said. They silently made their way down the wide stone staircase.

Jon saw a cot in front of a closed door. Someone was sleeping on it. As Jon crept closer, he could tell the person was wearing a traditional nun's habit. He smiled when he saw Kimmie's angelic face quietly snoring. She had an old hockey stick leaning up against the wall next to her. He moved it out of reach. He raised his goggles out of the way. "Kimmie, it's Uncle Jon," he said. She didn't move. He wiggled her left foot. She stirred a little but continued to snore. "Kimmie, it's Uncle Jon." He said a little louder. He lightly kicked the cot. "Kimmie, I'm here," he said as he shined his blue lensed light on his face. Kimmie opened her eyes, gasped in fear, and swung her right fist at the goblin. Jon leaned back easily dodging the jab. It wasn't the first time a woman tried to punch him. "Kimmie, it's Jon," he said with a smile.

Her eyes focused on his blue face as she sat up. "Uncle Jon!" she said excitedly and wrapped her arms tight around his head. He wrapped his arms around her waist and stood up straight bringing her with him. "I was so scared. I didn't know what to do. I've been praying constantly," she said as her eyes teared up, "How did you know I needed help?"

"Your mom called me. She's worried sick about you, so my friend, Angus, and I came to get you out of here," Jon replied, "Tomorrow a Huey helicopter will come here to fly us out."

"Uncle Jon, I can't leave…" She said before Jon cut her off.

"There's no debate Kimmie. You're leaving with us tomorrow. Your sense of duty to the Church is noble but it's too dangerous for you to stay here any longer," Jon said impatiently. He didn't mention all of the people Angie and he had to kill to get to her.

"You don't understand, Uncle Jon," she replied, pushing the cot away from the door and opening it. She took Jon's hand and showed him into the large dimly lit room. She motioned with her arm for him to look.

Jon scanned the large room full of cots through his NVGs. It took a few seconds for the gravity of the problem to sink in. "Oh, my God," Jon said softly. Angie looked over Jon's shoulder and scratched his head under the side of his helmet. Jon slowly walked between the cots looking at all of the peaceful little faces. He returned to Kimmie and Angie. "How many are there?" he asked in a whisper.

"Ninety-two, ranging in age from three months to fourteen years. They're either orphans or the children of Ukrainian soldiers fighting on the line. The Chechen colonel wanted to take them away, but Father Del Toro wouldn't allow it, so they beat him to death. I prayed for God's help and the Chechens were called away to fight the Ukrainians before they could take the children. They're coming back soon. Their Colonel called the children his retirement plan. I know he will sell them to the sex traffickers. I can't let that happen. I'm all they have," she replied between sobs before bury-ing her head in Jon's chest.

Jon hugged her up, kissed the top of her head, then rested his chin there. "And you were going to stand here in front of the door and fight them off with a hockey stick," Jon said in awe of her courage, "You are definitely your father's daughter."

Jon looked up in time to see Angie wiping his eyes as he turned away.

Jon guided Kimmie back to the cot and he sat down beside her. "So, what else can you tell us?"

Kimmie wiped her face on her blanket and said, "We're almost out of food. I don't have enough to feed all of them breakfast in the morning. I have five babies, and I used the last of the formula when I put them to bed. We had enough for a week, but Yurochka stole most of it."

"Who's Yurochka?" Jon asked.

"Yurochka Yecoshenko is the church gardener and handy-man. He lives in the small house behind the cemetery. He stole almost everything from the pantry while Father Del Toro and I were taking care of the kids. The father was about to get the food back from Yurochka when the Chechens arrived," Kimmie replied.

Jon nodded his head and said, "Ok, I'll get the food back from Yurochka in a minute. Tell me about the Chechens."

"There were maybe twenty of them in five big trucks. I think they were like the kind Dad called a deuce and a half. They had a big fat colonel named Sultanovich. He said they were Special Forces, but he didn't look special, just fat," Kimmie replied.

Jon stood up and motioned for Angie to follow him over to the stairs. "Brother, I really appreciate you helping me get this far and finding Kimmie. I will never be able to repay you for what you've done for me and my family, but I know you didn't sign up to babysit a hundred rugrats. If you want to head back on your own now, I won't hold it against you," he said.

Angie smiled as he put his hand on Jon's shoulder and said, "Thanks mate, but I'd never forgive myself if I left the little ones to be taken by white slavers. I'll make my stand right here with you. I can't think of a better cause to die for."

Jon nodded as he choked back the lump in his throat and said, "All right then. What's our next step?"

"Well, we still have enough toys in the truck that with a little time we can set up a fine kill zone for them to drive into, but all of the noise will bring an overwhelming response down on us. I think we should find a temporary safe house big enough for all of us. For now, I'll go out to the road and keep watch," Angie replied and then headed up the stairs.

Jon sat down on the stone stairs and dialed his sat phone hoping to get a signal.

"Hello," Tom Adams replied.

"Tom, it's Jon. Where are you?" Jon asked.

"I'm at the airport in Edinburgh waiting for the team to get here from Homer. As soon as they pick me up, we'll fly to Berlin to get the Huey."

"Yeah, well I have another problem, Tom. We got to the church a little while ago and found Kimmie," Jon said.

"Well, that's great. What's the problem?" Tom asked.

"It turns out Kimmie has been taking care of 92 orphans I didn't know about and the Chechens that killed her priest were here to kidnap the kids to sell them into the sex trade. They got called away at the last minute to reinforce their FOB during an attack before they could snatch the kids," Jon explained.

"Oh my God!" Tom replied, "Jon, we'll need a whole fucking company of Hueys to get those kids out of there."

"We're going to look for a safe house to stash them in until we can figure out how to get them out of here, but first we have to find some food and baby formula before they wake up for breakfast," Jon said.

"All right, man. I'll call Whitey and see if he can pull another rabbit out of his hat. Talk to you later," Tom said before hanging up.

Jon walked back to Kimmie.

"Is Angie leaving?" Kimmie asked, already worrying about what was coming tomorrow.

"What? No, Angie's not leaving. He's going out to the road to protect us while we're down here," Jon explained.

"Why do you call him Angie," Kimmie asked.

"Well, long before I met him someone called him Angie instead of Angus and he made the mistake of letting people know he didn't like it so after that everybody started calling him Angie just to tease him. It's a military thing. Do you think your dad liked being called Mongo? Never let anyone know something bothers you. He's been called Angie so long it doesn't bother him anymore," Jon replied. "Angie, SITREP?" Jon asked over his team radio.

"I'm out front near the road looking for bloody Chechens," he replied.

"What's your plan on contact?" Jon asked.

"I'm going to shoot until every fucking one of them is dead," Angie replied.

Jon smiled. "Roger that. Kimmie says the church gardener named Yurochka stole a bunch of their food. He lives in a house near the cemetery. I'm going to go get the food back," Jon said.

"You want company, mate?" Angie asked.

"No, I'll handle that asshole. I'll check back with you in about fifteen minutes," Jon replied. He received two clicks in response. Jon turned to Kimmie and said, "I'll be back in a few with the food," before he lowered his goggles and walked off into the darkness.

"Please, be careful, Uncle Jon," Kimmie replied, "Yurochka is mean. He's been in prison."

Five minutes later, Jon was standing outside the back door of the gardener's house. He tried the knob and found it unlocked. He slowly pushed the door open. *No need to rush to my death,* he thought. He stepped inside the dark room and froze. He scanned the room through his GPNVGs. It was the kitchen area of a large room. He heard a squeal to his right and swung his rifle in that direction. He saw a large cat emerge from behind a sofa with a rat in his mouth. Jon stepped past him and checked the only other room in the house, the bedroom. There was a half-packed suitcase on the bed but no gardener. He returned to the other room and looked down at the cat as it eagerly ate its dinner. "Where's the other rat?" he asked before beginning his search for the stolen food.

***

"The food and Yurochka are gone," Jon told Kimmie after he returned to the church basement, "Do you know where the Father was buying the food?" He sat down on the cot next to Kimmie.

She nodded, "Father Del Toro prowled around until he found a black-market source. He said it was a bar about five miles from here called Casablanca."

"What did he trade for the food?" Jon asked.

"Anything the church had of value, relics, statuettes, even the church bus," Kimmie replied.

"How big's the bus?" Jon asked.

"It's small, maybe seats for twenty people. It's so old it barely runs," Kimmie replied.

"Okay, give me a list. Angie and I will get the food and be back in an hour or so," Jon said.

"No! Jon, please, don't leave me here alone with the children!" Kimmie pleaded with her head buried in his chest.

"Hey, hey, look at me. Come on, look," Jon said softly as he held her head in his hands and raised her face so she could look into his eyes," he smiled at her and said, "I didn't come all this way to look around for a few minutes and then leave without you. And now that Angie and I know you've been taking care of all of these kids, we're not leaving without them either, Okay? So, please, make a list and we'll go get the formula and food they need."

CHAPTER 29

"You gotta be shittin' me!" Whitey yelled into his sat phone, waking everyone on the plane, "My boss just paid $5,000,000 for a fucking Huey and now you say we need a Shitter! God dammit!" A Shitter was what old Marines, like Whitey, called the massive CH-53D Sea Stallion heavy lift helicopters the USMC used to fly before it was replaced by the even larger more capable CH-53E Super Stallion. Whitey sat listening for a minute, vigorously shaking his head before his demeanor changed instantly. "Well, shit, Chirp! Why didn't you say that in the first place? I'll call the boss and figure something out. That girl's got huevos the size of watermelons," he said before hanging up.

"What's the problem, General?" Kevin Bass asked. Everyone else was wide awake now and listening.

"Smith and his buddy got to the church safely to pick up the nun and then found out she's taking care of 92 orphans, babies all the way up to fourteen-year-old kids. Turns out the Chechens killed the priest because they were going to snatch the kids and sell them off to the highest bidder in Chechnya. Luckily, they were called back to their FOB to fight off an attack before they could take the kids. It would take nine or ten Hueys to lift all of us out of there and that's not going to happen, so, we need a helicopter a lot bigger than a Huey. Tom wants a CH-53 like we flew in the Corps," Whitey explained.

"I thought the 53s only carried thirty passengers. That was the limit when I rode in them," Kevin said.

"That was an arbitrary limit put on the aircraft by the Navy and Marine Corps in response to political pressure after a few bad accidents. Just like the 130-knot speed limit and the 45° angle of bank turn limit. Back in the day we ignored those limits and flew the Shitter the way Mr. Sikorsky intended, 170-knot cruise, sometimes up to 200 knots, 60-70° bank turns. When Saigon fell in 1975, the Marines loaded over ninety Vietnamese people in a Shitter and flew them out to the ship," Whitey explained, "So, one Shitter can fly all of the kids and us out, no problem, just as long as we don't shut down after we get there."

"Why's that a problem?" Mike asked.

"Because the 53 requires about thirty-man hours of maintenance for every hour it flies. We used to fly five-hour training missions. Our maintenance team was always working all night to get them ready for the next day. Chances are if we shut down somewhere in the field, something will break on startup. That's why it's called a Shitter," Whitey said, "Once you get it started, you fly it all day and keep hot refueling it until you're done. Excuse me,

I have to call Mr. Monk and tell him about the new information." Whitey turned in his seat and picked up the sat phone. Moments later he was talking to Alvin Monk. "Sir, this is Brian McKinley. I have an update to pass to you."

"Thanks, for calling, Whitey. What do you have?" Monk asked.

"Sir, Smith linked up with the nun at the church in Donetsk and found out she wasn't alone. He discovered that since the priest was murdered, she has been the sole caregiver for 92 Ukrainian orphans. The Chechen special forces commander made it clear during his first visit when he killed her priest that he intended to come back after repelling the Ukrainian attack on his FOB and seize the children in order to then sell them into sex slavery. He called them his retirement plan. So, the bottom line is a Huey won't work for this mission. You've been more than generous, sir, and I hate to ask but we need a large heavy-lift helicopter like the CH-53 Sea Stallion to get all of those kids out," Whitey said.

"Do you know about my childhood, Brian?" Monk asked.

"No, sir, not really," Whitey replied.

"I was born in Scotland and my parents died when I was three years old. I grew up in a Catholic orphanage in Edinburgh. I can't remember my parents, but I remember every one of the nuns who raised and taught me. You can have whatever you need to get those children out of there, Brian. There is no limit. Are you sure one CH-53 will be enough?" Monk asked.

"Thank you, sir. We know one will be big enough to carry all of the kids because 53s lifted more than ninety Vietnamese at a time when Saigon fell. It would be better if we had two or three helicopters, but we don't have time to find the people to crew the other helicopters," Whitey replied.

"Where can you get a 53 over there?" Monk asked.

"The same museum we got the Huey from has two German-built CH-53Gs that they just refurbished. The article I read a couple of days ago said they had been painted green and were ready to add their former German markings," Whitey replied.

"Okay, here's the plan. I'll put my best people on getting you access to that helicopter. Proceed to Berlin as if it's already a done deal. We'll call you if we run into any problems, talk to you later," Monk said.

CHAPTER 30

"Looks like we found where the gardener sold the kid's food," Angie said to Jon in English. They were standing in the stockroom of the Casablanca Bar surrounded by shelves overflowing with food, including baby formula just like that stolen from the church. "Did a man named Yurochka Yecoshenko sell this food to you earlier today?" Angie asked the bartender in Ukrainian.

"I do not know this man," the bartender replied.

Jon handed the man a list of food. "That's funny, you have the same food in your storeroom that was stolen from the orphans at St. Michael's Church," Jon said in English.

The bartender clearly understood but all he did was shrug his shoulders.

Angie said in Ukrainian, "So, how much for everything on the list?"

After studying the list for a good minute and a half, the bartender replied with a smile, "€5,000."

Angie shook his head in disgust and said, "Don't be ridiculous, that's five times what it's worth. I'll give you €1,300 and we can leave each other as friends."

The bartender shook his head and was about to speak when he heard someone at the bar call out for the bartender in Russian. He looked out to the bar through a peephole. "They look like SVR. What do you want me to do?" he asked Angie.

Jon put his hand on the bartender's chest and gently pushed him aside. He looked through the peephole and said, "Yeah, they're SVR."

Angie pulled his Glock 21SF from his holster and said, "Go talk to them, but know if they even look at the storeroom door, I'll kill you first."

The bartender smiled as he nodded, but he wasn't impressed. He grabbed a case of Obolon off the shelf and elbowed the door open. He sat the beer down behind the bar and asked, "What will it be, gentlemen?"

"Two Jewel of Russia," the tall agent with the acne-scarred face said as he looked past the bartender at the bottles on the shelf.

The bartender smiled and said, "Ah, yes, excellent choice." He pulled the expensive Jewel of Russia bottle down from the shelf and poured two shot glasses of cheap Russian Standard vodka from the bottle for them. He had been refilling that bottle with the cheap stuff for months. He could buy five bottles of Russian Standard for the price of one bottle of top-shelf Jewel of

Russia. He smiled as he set a jar of pickles on the bar between the two Russians.

"We are looking for a black Chevrolet Suburban. Have you seen any in the neighborhood?" the short rotund agent asked.

"No, sorry. What did they do?" the bartender asked.

"This does not concern you," Agent Scarface said and then motioned for another round.

The bartender shrugged and poured two more shots before he began wiping down the bar.

Scarface turned and saw two Chechen special forces soldiers, a sergeant, and a corporal, sitting at a table near the rear of the otherwise empty room. They sat with their backs to the wall sharing a half-empty bottle of Russian Standard. Their first bottle lay empty on its side. The SVR agents finished their shots and walked over to the soldiers. "Sergeant, have either of you seen a black Chevrolet Suburban in the area recently?"

The sergeant stared at the agent with contempt through his glassy eyes for several seconds before he replied loudly, "No, we have not seen anything. Now go away."

Scarface was immediately offended. "Sergeant where is your officer?" he asked.

"He is with your mother," the sergeant said before he and his corporal shared a laugh.

"Show me your military identification. You will be punished for your insolent behavior," Scarface said.

"Go to the dick! Real soldiers are drinking here. Go back to your cubicle and read your spreadsheets. Maybe this goat will crawl under your desk," the sergeant replied referring to the overweight agent. He and his corporal laughed again.

The sergeant's dismissive attitude infuriated Scarface. "I thought Muslims were prohibited from drinking alcohol. You are drunk, Sergeant. You are a disgrace to your uniform," Scarface said angrily. He wasn't accustomed to being disrespected by lowly enlisted men, especially Chechens. He pulled his notebook from his breast pocket to put the soldiers on report.

"And I thought all Russian men were impotent, but somehow your retarded bastards keep sprouting like weeds," the sergeant replied as he laughed with his partner.

The corporal said, "That is because Russian women whore themselves out to Chechen soldiers."

They laughed again as Scarface lunged for the sergeant. The sergeant fell backward in his chair with Scarface on top of him. Scarface pummeled the sergeant's face with punches opening cuts on the bridge of his nose and his right eyebrow.

"Laugh quickly, you Chechen dog, before all of your blood pours out on this filthy floor," Scarface said confidently.

As the sergeant absorbed the blows, he quickly jammed his left thumb up to the second knuckle into Scarface's right eye socket popping the eye out to dangle on his cheek. Scarface screamed in pain as he stood up to get away from the offending thumb. He grabbed his eye with his right hand and tried to push it back into the socket in an attempt to turn off the excruciating pain. Scarface grabbed the cheap Chinese four-inch folder he had clipped to his left trouser pocket and flipped it open. He bent over to stab the sergeant but was rebuffed by a boot to his left knee that buckled his leg and sent him crashing onto his back.

The sergeant sat up and spat blood on the floor. The sight of Scarface rolling back and forth holding his eye in one hand and his knee in the other, made him laugh through his own considerable pain. He staggered to his feet and bent over to pick up Scarface's cheap knife. "Even your knives are inferior," he said as he snapped the blade free from the handle with his hands and tossed the pieces aside. He drew his KAMPO bayonet from its sheath as he stood over his adversary. "I think I will castrate this pig before I gut him," the sergeant said coldly.

Agent Round Man was content to watch the fight in the beginning while Scarface was winning, but now the tide had turned, and he wasn't about to lose his own manhood for failure to act. He drew his GSh-18 pistol and swung it around to engage the sergeant. Three loud pops erupted causing his ears to ring. He turned to look at the corporal who was still sitting in his chair with a shot of vodka in his left hand and his smoking SR-1 Vektor pistol in his right. The corporal laughed again and turned his attention back to his vodka and the sergeant. Round Man fell to his knees and studied the three bloody holes in his jacket. He brought his pistol up and emptied it into the corporal before he himself fell over to bleed to death.

The sudden violence off to his side briefly startled the sergeant, but seeing the corporal had dutifully dispatched the threat, he returned his attention to Scarface. "Where was I? Oh yes, your testicles," the sergeant said as he unsteadily stepped between Scarface's legs. That's when the sergeant noticed Scarface's bloody right hand now held a GSh-18 pistol. Scarface began firing as the sergeant dropped on him and plunged the blade into his abdomen repeatedly.

After the shooting stopped, the bartender peeked out from behind the bar. The only motion he saw was gun smoke swirling under the low-hanging light fixture. He waved for Angie and Jon to come out. They burst out of the storeroom, guns up. Jon went straight for the front door and Angie went to the table. Jon lowered the GPNVGs on his helmet and looked outside through the window in the door. Seeing no movement, he cracked the door open to listen. After a minute, he opened the door and stepped out into the darkness. He walked around the building looking for any new vehicles and checking to see if they were occupied. Finding no one, he went back to the entrance.

"Friendly coming in," Jon said before walking into the bar. The bartender and Angie were standing over the dead men.

"Well, these are four shitheads we won't have to kill on our way home," Angie said.

"Too bad the rest of them aren't as accommodating," Jon replied, "Let's get loaded up and out of here before anyone else stumbles in for a drink."

"Wait! What am I supposed to do with these idiots?" the bartender asked as he motioned to the tiny warzone in the corner of his bar.

Angie pushed €1,300 into the bartender's chest and said, "Here is your money for the food. This mess is not our doing. It would have happened whether we were here or not. Maybe it's time to relocate your business to a safer part of the country."

CHAPTER 31

1900Z (2200 LOCAL)
ST. MICHAEL'S CATHOLIC CHURCH,
DONETSK, UKRAINE

Sister Joan was elated when Jon arrived and then devastated when
he insisted on going out to find food for the children. She decided
to lock the children in the nursery and go upstairs to stand guard
until Jon returned. She stopped by the father's office to get an
aluminum softball bat he kept behind the office door. She locked
the heavy oak front doors to the church and walked down to the
end of the long gravel driveway to hide in the darkness. She sat
down with her back against a tree. Despite her fear, exhaustion
overtook her, and she fell asleep. She woke up in what seemed like
seconds later when she heard trucks approaching in the distance.
She stood up behind the tall bushes next to the three-foot-high
stone wall next to the road. *Uncle Jon, please, come back,* she thought.
As the first truck turned off the road and onto the driveway, she

threw a baseball-sized rock that spidered the windshield. The truck stopped abruptly.

***

"There she is. Sergeant, take two men and bring her to me. Remember, do not hurt her. She is worth a fortune," Colonel Sultanovich ordered. The men hopped down from the back of the truck and ran into the darkness. "Continue to the church," Sultanovich said to his driver. The trucks drove away leaving the soldiers in darkness. The men moved off into the bushes, resisting the urge to use their flashlights.

***

Sister Joan ran about a hundred feet and stopped behind a tree. *Help me, Lord. Please, give me strength,* she prayed silently. She was on the verge of crying. The soldiers following her were cautiously advancing. She heard one of them say something to the others and then heard them move away from each other. She stood behind a large oak tree and cocked the softball bat over her shoulder. One of the soldiers passed within three feet of the tree and Sister Joan swung for the fences. She was rewarded with a sickening ping as the bat fractured the soldier's skull. He went down in a heap and didn't move. The sergeant and the other soldier heard the bat's blow in the distance but didn't recognize the sound for what it was. Sister Joan dropped the bat and felt around the man's body until she found his rifle. It felt like the AK-47 rifles that her father had taught her to shoot. She slung the rifle over her shoulder and patted the man's equipment for more ammo. She stopped after she came across two hand grenades and an extra magazine. She put them in her pockets and quickly moved about fifty feet to another tree. She stopped to listen. The other two soldiers were getting closer. She heard one whisper to the other. She pulled the pin and tossed a grenade about fifty feet and ducked behind another large oak. She closed her eyes and covered her ears. Three seconds later the grenade exploded. She heard a scream and then silence except for the ringing in her ears. She headed back toward the church.

***

The trucks stopped in front of the church and the colonel, and his men dismounted. They heard the grenade explode 500 feet back toward the road. "Idiots! I told them not to hurt the nun! Corporal, take two men and help them find her," Sultanovich barked. The soldiers turned and hurried into the darkness.

***

Sister Joan was about halfway to the church when she heard voices approaching her. It sounded like the men were angry. They were complaining to each other about something, probably her. She hid behind another tree and pulled the last grenade from her pocket. She pulled the pin and tossed it toward the sounds. Seconds later it exploded, and she ran away from the men so she could arc around them to get back to the church.

***

Colonel Sultanovich and his men were stymied by the locked church doors. They had not brought any breaching equipment. The second grenade exploded in the distance. Sultanovich turned to his nephew, the captain, and said, "I swear if those morons damage the nun, I will kill them myself. Sergeant connect a tow chain to the doors and pull them off with the truck." They watched expectantly as the men attached the chain to the door but before the truck could move the trucks and men were riddled with automatic fire from an AK-74 rifle. The men dropped to the ground and scrambled for cover. Sultanovich was face down behind the front tire of his truck trying to get smaller.

"Colonel, may we return fire?" his nephew asked as he cowered behind the rear tires.

"Yes, you imbecile! Return fire and find the gunman," Sultanovich bellowed.

***

Sister Joan fired the rifle until it ran dry. She moved twenty feet to the left, reloaded, and dumped the second magazine into the trucks and men hiding behind them. She dropped the rifle and ran laterally to get to the side of the church out of sight of the men in front. She felt along the stone wall of the church until she found the downspout. She shimmied up the pipe to a second-floor window that she had left unlatched. She climbed inside and hurried down the stairs to the basement. A thunderous crack came from upstairs as the massive oak doors were ripped from their hinges. She was immediately terrified when she heard Chechen voices shouting upstairs. She began crying as she ran back to the kids' room. She kicked her cot away from the door and grabbed her hockey stick. Seconds later she saw beams of light coming down the stairs.

"Lord Jesus Christ, Son of the living God, please send Jon back to save us from these evil men. Lord Jesus Christ, Son of the living God, please send Jon back to save us from these evil men," she quickly prayed aloud as she cried. Ten Chechen soldiers led by Colonel Sultanovich approached her confidently. Then the church gardener, Yurochka Yecoshenko, appeared at his side. She screamed, "Yecoshenko, you will burn in hell for what you've done!" She lunged forward to spear him in the chest but missed. He jumped back and managed a weak laugh. The other soldiers inched forward. "Stay back!" she yelled as she swung the hockey stick in a wide arc in front of the men causing her black habit to swirl around her body like a martial arts expert from a Jackie Chan film. The soldiers jumped back and laughed at the sight, but some admired her will to keep fighting despite the overwhelming odds.

Sultanovich chuckled and said in English, "Sister, please, there is no need to fear us. We are here to save you and the children."

"That's what you told Father Del Toro before you murdered him!" she yelled. She heard children behind the door wailing. "Stay back!" she said as she lunged forward again with the stick bloodying the colonel's knuckles.

Sultanovich quickly jumped back to avoid another swing of the stick. He looked to his men and said, "Very well. Take her and the children to the trucks, but do not damage them." The men rushed forward and the first was promptly dropped to the floor by a high stick to the head swung fast enough to break the shaft in half. Bobby Plager would have been proud. The second man reflexively punched Sister Joan in the temple so hard he knocked her unconscious.

Sultanovich stepped forward and punched the soldier in the back of the head, knocking him to the floor. "Idiot! I said do not damage them. If her price is lowered, I will take your left hand," he said menacingly. Sultanovich turned the doorknob only to find the door locked. He stepped back and said, "Kick it in." A sergeant came forward and shattered the thin door with one kick. The colonel stepped into the room and was hit on the side of the head with a mop handle wielded by a thirteen-year-old girl named Katya. Her grandfather was a Ukrainian Army officer and she had heard him tell her parents stories about how evil the Chechen soldiers were. Her younger brothers were behind her, and she refused to let them be taken without a fight. The colonel cried out in pain as he collapsed in a heap. Two soldiers picked him up off the floor. The colonel stood swaying and shook his head. Two of his men held the girl by her arms. Sultanovich grabbed her by her hair. "Load the children on the trucks. I will be along shortly," he said to the captain in Russian. "Come along my dear. Let's find somewhere to get comfortable." He pulled her deeper into the nursery as she struggled against him. She kicked him in the shin, and he responded by slapping her across the side of her head. Stars danced before her eyes. He threw her onto a cot and undid his trousers as his men carried and otherwise herded the children out of the room. She could hear her younger brothers screaming her name as they were dragged away. The fat old man dropped on top of her. He groped up and down her body as he smothered her face with wet, disgusting kisses.

She bit his cheek as hard as she could just above his beard and pounded his chest with her tiny fists as she shouted, "Pig!" He groaned like a wounded walrus as he rolled off of her onto the floor. She jumped to her feet to run but he grabbed her ankle and pulled her to him. "You fucking whore!" he bellowed before he unsheathed his blade.

CHAPTER 32

2000Z (2300 LOCAL)
ST. MICHAEL'S CATHOLIC CHURCH,
DONETSK, UKRAINE

"I'm glad we found the baby formula. Babies crying is another one of my Kryptonites. Hearing babies cry is like a knife going through my heart," Jon said as he rode shotgun on the way back to the church. He was rubbing his sore chest under his front plate. They were running with the headlights off as they used their GPNVGs. "We need to find a hiding place within walking distance of the church to stash everyone until the helicopter gets here."

Jon could see Angie's helmeted head shaking back and forth before he said, "I don't know, Jonny Boy. Where are they going to find a heavy lift helicopter in the middle of the night and get it here today? If we had government support, it might be doable. We should start thinking about stealing a semitrailer big enough to carry the sprogs."

"I trust these people with my life, Angie. We've been places and done shit together. They'll find a helicopter and get here on time," Jon said.

"They're the ones who helped you take the subs," Angie said.

"What subs?" Jon asked.

"Relax, mate. I know you can't talk about it," Angie replied as he turned onto the gravel driveway in front of the church.

"Stop the car," Jon said with concern in his voice. Angie stopped immediately. Jon said, "We have a problem. There's a light on inside the church. I told Kimmie to keep the lights out." They dismounted and bounded from cover to cover until they reached the entrance to the church. They saw the doors were broken on the driveway. "Dammit!" Jon exclaimed softly. *Please, lord let Kimmie and the kids be okay,* Jon prayed silently. They crept inside and made their way downstairs to the nursery. The lights were on, and they saw a lone figure lying on a cot at the far end of the room. Kimmie and the other children were gone. Jon felt queasy as he dropped to his knees before he said, "Oh my God. We're too late. They took them. I swear to God, I thought we had more time." Jon turned his attention to the body on the cot. He rolled the girl over and she moaned. She looked to be around twelve or so. She groaned in pain as she held her abdomen. Her pajama bottoms were around her ankles. Jon opened her shirt and saw three large stab wounds next to her belly button. She had lost a lot of blood. Jon pulled a dressing from his kit and held it to her wounds to slow the bleeding.

Angie appeared at Jon's side. He held up a broken hockey stick. "Kimmie put up a fight before they took her."

The girl opened her eyes and looked at Jon and Angie with terror. She begged in Ukrainian, "Please, don't hurt me anymore."

"Rest easy child. Sister Joan sent us to help you. This man is the sister's godfather. We won't let anyone hurt you ever again," Angie replied in Ukrainian. He looked over to Jon, who shook his head to signal the severity of her injuries. Angie dug into his IFAK and retrieved his ketamine. "This will take your pain away," he said as he gave her the injection. Within seconds she began showing relief. "What is your name?" Angie asked.

"Katya," she said quietly. The drug was already making her drowsy.

"Katya is a beautiful name. Who did this to you, Katya?" he asked.

"The old fat man with the long beard. The soldiers called him Colonel. He tried to kiss me, so I bit him on the cheek. He was so angry; he stabbed me and then raped me. I heard Sister Joan curse the gardener. She told him he would burn in hell," she said. "I want to go home. Will you take me home?" she asked. She was pale now and her breathing labored.

"Yes, Katya, you will be back with your family very soon," Angie said as he tried to smile for her but all he could do was weep. Jon held the dressing to her stomach with one hand and wiped his eyes with the other. The minutes passed slowly as Angie talked soothingly to the girl. Jon brushed her hair away from her face with his free hand. In the civilized world, they would've scooped her up and raced to the nearest trauma center, but there was nothing civilized about the Russian-controlled sectors of Ukraine. All of the hospitals had been destroyed early in the war. So, they sat vigil with this innocent child and prayed for her silently, each in his own way. Whenever she moaned, Angie gave her more of his precious ketamine. Eventually, she rattled her last breath and Angie and Jon cried for her again.

Jon pulled the blanket over her head and cleared his throat before he spoke, "Angie, we don't have time to bury her. Let's take her to the cemetery and put her in one of the family crypts."

**

Thirty minutes later, Jon and Angie were sitting in the Suburban trying to decide on their next move when Jon's sat phone buzzed. "Hello," he answered.

"Jon, it's Gwenn. I'm up and running at Monk's Edinburgh facility. I see you parked in front of the church. How can I help?" she asked.

"Thank God you are watching. Gwenn, I fucked up big time. We got here ahead of the Chechens, but I left Kimmie, and the kids unprotected while we went looking for baby formula. The Chechens came back and took all of them while we were gone except for one little girl the Chechen colonel raped and stabbed. She died in our arms just a few minutes ago. Please, tell me you can track where they took them," Jon said.

"Oh, dear. Jon, I'm sorry for what happened to the girl, but you must know you wouldn't have stopped anything. There are only two of you. You might have killed a few of them but the result would have been the same. They would have killed you and Angus and then taken Kimmie and the children. Give me a few minutes and I'll find them. Then you can tail them until Tom and the team arrive," Gwenn said.

"Thank you, Gwenn. We're standing by," Jon replied before Gwenn disconnected. "Okay, we're back in the fight. She'll find them. I don't know how she does it, but she will."

"She's right, you know? We didn't have the time or a location to move the kids to before the Chechens got here and even if we had been here, we would have had to hide and watch what they did. If we engaged them, they would have run right over us and more of the kids could have been hurt or killed. Our best option is to tag along behind them until the chopper arrives. Then we'll have to arrange a hasty ambush somewhere along their route," Angie said.

Jon nodded his agreement and said, "Keep an eye on the truck. I'm going up in the bell tower to take a look around." He hopped out and started walking across the front lawn toward the church entrance. Minutes later, his sat phone buzzed. "Hello," he said.

"Jon, it's Gwenn. A Chechen Special Forces colonel named Marvan Sultanovich took the children. It's not the first time he's done this. Since the war started in March 2022, he's averaging about one roundup a month. He gathers a hundred or so children, sometimes including young women, and takes them back to his hometown, Grozny. There he sells them to the highest bidder. Tonight, we have EO coverage of Donetsk. Sultanovich brought two large tour buses to the church for the kids and two military trucks for his soldiers. After a short shootout, he took them back to his FOB adjacent to the airport. If he follows his previous pattern, he'll convoy them to Grozny tomorrow morning under the guise of relocating them for humanitarian reasons and then they'll never be seen again."

Jon raised the wooden hatch at the top of the bell tower and climbed onto the platform next to the bell. "Thank you, Gwenn. Please, let me know if you see any movement over there tonight. I'll talk to you later." He looked east into the distance about five miles away through his PGNVGs. It was deathly quiet around the church except for the faint hum of the aircraft he saw flying around the airport in the traffic pattern preparing to land. He wished he was cutting through the perimeter fence right now and slipping inside the FOB, but he knew he had to wait for the team to arrive with the helicopter before he could make his move. *Hang on, Kimmie, we're coming,* he thought. He hoped the children were being fed. He had an SUV overloaded with food, but he couldn't get it to them. He scanned the area for 360° looking for any suspicious activity. Then he looked down and noticed a dim light was on in the gardener's house. A figure passed in front of the window. "Angie, I see movement in the gardener's house. I'm going to check it out," Jon transmitted over his team radio.

"Do you want backup, mate?" Angie asked.

"No, I want to do this myself," Jon replied, deadly calm. He was in beast mode now.

"Understood," Angie transmitted.

In two minutes, Jon was listening outside the cottage's kitchen door. There was an old Toyota Corolla parked feet away. He heard the gardener quickly moving back and forth across the large open room. He decided to disregard his training and do things the old-fashioned way, he kicked the door open and rushed inside. The burly gardener screamed like a little girl and fell backward over an overnight bag on the floor. He recovered quickly and sprang to his feet. He lowered his head and charged Jon like a bull. Jon sidestepped and pushed him headfirst into the wall, but the man was able to grab Jon's rifle sling and pull him along. The gardener crumpled to the floor again, followed immediately by Jon who slapped the back of his helmet against the wall as he landed on his ass next to Yecoshenko. Jon shook off the stars. *Thank you for fighting back*, Jon thought as he drove his right elbow into the back of Yecoshenko's head eliciting a satisfying groan. Jon pushed off of him to get to his feet.

"Good evening, Yurochka Yecoshenko. Sister Joan said to say hi!" Jon said as he stood over the man. Jon pushed his rifle behind his back before he grabbed Yecoshenko by the front of his shirt pulling him up to his feet. Yecoshenko weakly grabbed at Jon's forearms, but he was still dizzy from his fall. He said something in Ukrainian that Jon didn't understand.

Once they were eye to eye Jon threw a quick left jab into his face. Yecoshenko's nose exploded with a sickening crack as his head snapped back. His eyes rolled up in his head as his knees buckled and he collapsed to the ground again. Jon grabbed one of the old wooden chairs from the kitchen and placed it next to the gardener. Yecoshenko's hand grabbed the poker next to the fireplace and swung it at Jon striking his thigh. Jon caught the poker in his gloved hand before Yecoshenko could swing it again. He acted like it didn't hurt but he had to take the weight off of it to ease the pain. He angrily wrenched it away from Yecoshenko and flung it across the room. Yecoshenko whimpered something unintelligible again.

"I didn't understand that Yurochka. Try it again in English." Jon picked him up again and dropped him in the chair." Yecoshenko didn't respond so Jon slapped him upside the head. "Again, in English!" Jon yelled in his face.

"Who, who are you? Why are you here? I will report you to Colonel Sultanovich," Yecoshenko complained in highly accented English. That was exactly the wrong thing to say.

Jon gave him another jab to the face; this one targeting his right eye opened a wide cut across his eyebrow. Yecoshenko's head flew back again, and the front legs of his chair came off the floor. Jon grabbed his shirt to keep him from falling over. Jon didn't care if his head smacked the floor, but he didn't want him to blackout before he got some answers. Jon shook his hand to ward off the pain in his knuckles. *Good thing I'm wearing gloves,* he thought. Jon looked past Yecoshenko's shoulder at an open suitcase on the bed. Five stacks of Euros sat on top. "Why did Sultanovich take the children and where is he taking them?"

Yecoshenko winced in pain and shook his head, trying to clear it. "He is evacuating them from the warzone to Grozny for their safety," he replied.

Jon's hand was still sore, so he pulled his collapsible baton from his plate carrier and flicked it open. Yecoshenko's eyes sprang wide open at the sound. Jon brought down a crushing blow on Yecoshenko's right knee shattering his kneecap. Yecoshenko tried to scream but the intense pain took his breath away. He fell out of the chair yelping like an injured dog. He rocked back and forth holding his knee with his hands. The nasty gash exposed white bone and gushed a steady ribbon of blood down his pant leg. "We both know that's not true, Yurochka," Jon said before slapping the side of his head, this time rupturing his left eardrum. Blood issued forth and ran down his neck before being absorbed by his dark sweater. Jon sat him back in the chair.

"The sooner you tell me what I want to know, the sooner the pain will stop. You don't want to walk out of here a cripple, do you? Well, you won't actually walk out of here with your leg fucked up that way, but you get my meaning, right?" Jon asked, not expecting an answer. "This will be the last time I ask, Yurochka, why did Sultanovich take the children?"

Yecoshenko nodded his head rapidly. He said "Okay, yes! Yes! Sultanovich will take the children to Grozny to sell them to the sex traders or anyone else who pays the highest price."

"Why did you tell Sultanovich about the children? Before you speak, know that I will take your other knee if you waste my time," Jon said as he lightly tapped Yurochka's left kneecap with the baton.

"I needed money to escape this shithole," Yecoshenko said as his voice broke. He knew how bad he sounded, so devoid of humanity.

"And how much did you sell your soul for?" Jon asked.

"What do you mean?" Yecoshenko asked.

"It's simple, you condemned 92 children and a young nun to a long-drawn-out horrible death. How much were you paid?"

"€50,000!" Yecoshenko said as he sobbed. He knew he was condemned.

Jon stepped around him and grabbed the stack of Euros from the suitcase. There were five €10,000 stacks. Each held one hundred €100 bills. Jon held them in front of Yecoshenko's face for a moment while he continued to cry for himself. Jon set the money on the table. "So, you sold innocent babies and children for a little over €500 each." Jon stopped talking to let that sink in for a minute. "Yurochka, you're gonna leave this earth tonight. Do you want a moment to talk to your god?" Jon circled behind Yecoshenko. He drew his Glock and silently threaded his suppressor onto the barrel. He wasn't a heartless man and he believed in redemption, but he also knew he could not leave Yecoshenko alive. He had no respect for any human life other than his own.

"I have no god. There is no god," Yecoshenko sobbed, "My life has been one of pain and death and bad choices. Do what you will with me."

Jon stepped back and fired a 230-grain jacketed hollow point round into the back of Yecoshenko's skull. He didn't want any of the blood or brain matter to blow back on him. The body slowly began listing to the right before building up momentum and flopping head-first onto the floor. Jon stuffed the Euros into his cargo pockets. He would give the money to Kimmie after they were out of harm's way. It would pay to feed and house the children temporarily until something permanent could be worked out. "Angie, the gardener is dead. I'm coming back to the truck," Jon transmitted.

"Roger that, mate," Angie replied unconcerned. Big boy rules were in effect.

Jon turned off the lights in the house and lowered his four-banger goggles. He cautiously opened the back door and looked out past the Toyota. All he heard were insects and frogs. He stepped into the doorway and sensed more than saw something swinging from his right toward his head. He quickly leaned back like he was in a limbo contest. His head moved back inside the doorway, and he took a glancing blow to the side of his helmet just before an aluminum softball bat bounced off the door jam. Stars momentarily swarmed in front of the green image of a man in the doorway provided by his goggles. He instantly considered shooting his new opponent but rejected the idea. He wanted to know who this man was and what he knew. He stepped back further into the kitchen and flicked open his baton again. The man in the doorway hesitated a second. He couldn't see Jon in the dark room, but he began swinging the bat wildly back and forth, destroying Yurochka's glassware and toaster. Jon waited for an opening then lunged forward swinging his baton laterally at knee height. The man yelped in pain as he crumpled to the floor falling on top of Yecoshenko's warm body. The man began fighting with Yecoshenko, smacking his head with short strokes from the bat, and screaming something in Chechen Jon couldn't understand. Jon snatched the bat from his hand. He looked at the baton, then hefted the bat. The bat had merit, but he decided to stick with his baton and set the bat on the kitchen counter.

The man was choking the dead Yecoshenko to death with both hands when Jon flipped the kitchen lights on. The man screamed when he saw Yecoshenko's dead eyes staring back at him. He quickly rolled off the body, soaking his camouflage uniform in a pool of Yecoshenko's blood.

Jon saw the man was a Chechen Spetsnaz soldier. "Relax Ivan, I think you got him," Jon mocked him in English. The soldier had an ugly oozing wound to the side of his head and his left eye was swollen shut. "Jesus! Have you always been this ugly?" Jon asked. He looked like a member of the Borg with his enhancements removed. His rifle was missing. Jon went behind him and lifted him off the floor onto Yecoshenko's chair. He began to zip-tie the soldier's arms to the chair, but the man resisted. Jon smacked him on the uninjured side of his head. The soldier winced and stopped resisting. Jon zip-tied the other arm and called Angie, "Hey, Angie, just as I was leaving the house a Chechen soldier tried to ambush me. Watch your six, there may be more of them creeping around."

"Will do, mate. I'll have a walkabout," Angie replied.

"How many of your buddies are sneaking around outside?" Jon asked. The man remained silent. Jon stepped into the bedroom and picked up a dirty sock and a roll of packing tape. Jon stepped in front of Ivan and poked the side of the man's wounded head with his finger.

"Ubl'udak!" the man cursed Jon. Jon jammed the sock into his mouth and wrapped the tape around his head four times. Now he was hopping mad, shaking his head, and stomping his feet. Jon pinched his nostrils closed for a few seconds, long enough for the man to realize he couldn't breathe. He stopped fussing.

"Did you just call me a son of a bitch? I don't know much Russian, but I've heard that one," Jon said before shaking his head with a frown, "Do you kiss your babushka with that mouth? Sit tight, I'll be right back." Jon flipped off the lights and walked around outside the house for a few minutes to see if anyone else was around. Satisfied they were alone; he went back inside. He flipped on the lights and searched the soldier. Jon grabbed the end of the tape and slowly unwrapped it, pulling ample amounts of facial hair from his beard with every pass. The man closed his eyes and winced in time with every orbit. Jon removed the sock and Ivan stuck his tongue out, trying to clean it off with his teeth. "Do you want some water?" Jon asked. Ivan nodded. Jon found an unbroken glass in the cupboard and filled it with water. Jon leaned down in front of Ivan and said, "If you spit on me I'm going to punch you right here as hard as I can." Jon was pointing to his remaining good eye. Ivan shook his head and Jon helped him drink the water.

Jon sat down across from him. "Okay, where were we? Oh yeah, do you speak English?" Jon asked. The man mumbled something unintelligible. Jon pressed his baton against the man's injured knee. "Hey, bud, you need to start talking or I'm about to go all Al Capone on your ass," Jon said as he pointed at the softball bat. The man looked at Jon through his good eye, then looked at the bat, then back to Jon again. "Really, you've never heard of Al Capone or the Untouchables? Don't you guys get Netflix?"

"Chicago, bang, bang!" the soldier said with a smirk.

"Good, so you do speak English," Jon said.

"I speak fuck you, American puzzy," the man said before laughing.

Jon tapped the man's knee again and over-enunciated, "It's pussy, not puzzy, but that's close enough. What happened to your head?" Jon asked as he pointed at the man's head injury with his baton.

"Fuck you, Joe!" the man yelled.

"Is that all you have? Fuck you? How about suck my cock or kiss my ass?" Jon asked.

"Fuck you," the man repeated.

"Look, man, I'm tired. Today I've been blown up by a cruise missile, busted my nose and lip, shot in the chest by an AK, this motherfucker smacked my head against the wall," Jon pointed at Yecoshenko, "and my junk is burning like it's covered in fire ants. So, start fucking talking!" Jon yelled as he scratched the boys. Ivan smirked. Jon gave him a firm rap on his oozing head injury with his baton. The man grimaced but did not speak. Jon pointed to Yecoshenko and said, "He didn't want to talk either, so I had no further use for him." The soldier looked down at the gardener's body but remained silent. Jon gave him another rap. "Come on man, I don't have all night." Rap, rap. "I'm about to get one of Yurochka's dirty spoons out of the sink and pluck that good eye out." Rap, rap.

The soldier winced and moved his head away from the baton. He took several rapid deep breaths through his nose. His head was so red it looked like it would explode. He was so angry his chair was vibrating off the floor. Jon smiled at him and gave him three more raps; harder than before but still he did not speak. "Okay you win," Jon said before reaching into the sink and retrieving a spoon with dried food stuck to it. Jon stood over Ivan and put him in a headlock with his left arm, then brought the spoon forward toward his eye.

Ivan closed his good eye and started talking rapidly, "Colonel order not hurt nun, but she run around in dark, be pain in ass. Colonel order us to catch nun but he tie hands. Fucking bitch nun hit me with bat. Steal my rifle and grenades. Wound seven soldiers. Colonel blame me. I know he pay gardener €50,000 for children. I think I take money from gardener, go to Aruba."

Jon smiled at hearing how much chaos Kimmie had caused the Chechens. *Clint, you must be proud as shit of Kimmie for fucking these Chechens up so badly. I know I am,* Jon thought. "€50,000 doesn't seem like enough to escape to Aruba and start a new life," Jon said.

"I have money. This my ten mission," the soldier said.

Jon's demeanor changed with that news, "You've sent ten groups of kids back to Chechnya! That's over 900 kids!"

The soldier nodded, "Yes, business good."

Jon's face went red. "No! Business very bad!" Jon shouted before he shot the soldier twice in the chest and once in the forehead with his suppressed Glock. The soldier slumped forward in his chair. Jon kicked him and the chair over backward. "Angie, status," Jon transmitted.

"All quiet out front. It looks like the Chechens expended a lot of ammo in front of the church. There's spent brass all over the driveway. It wasn't here before we went to get the food," Angie replied.

"Yeah, the soldier said Kimmie was being a real pain in the ass before they caught her. She wounded about a third of them. I'm done back here. I'm coming to you," Jon transmitted.

CHAPTER 33

The G700 followed the yellow taxiway lines to the ramp where a lineman with lighted wands waited to guide them. After the wheels were chocked, the engines spooled down.

"The business center normally closes at 2200 hours, but Mr. Monk arranged for them to stay open for us. Everyone, please, stay on the plane. We need to leave as soon as Tom gets aboard," Whitey said.

The captain came out of the cockpit and approached Whitey. He said, "Sir, we have a problem. Someone reported we're carrying contraband, so the local police are ordering us to stay on the plane until the Border Force officers come out to search us and the plane."

Whitey bent over to look out his window and saw a marked police car idling in front of the business center. "Son of a bitch! Did they say how long it will be before they can get out here?"

"No, sir, but they're coming over from the main terminal, so it shouldn't take too long," the captain replied.

The rest of the team was listening. "This sounds like someone in the Administration is trying to slow us down," Kevin Bass said. Eric and Mike nodded in agreement.

"Or it could be someone from the business center who got pissed because they had to work late and decided to inconvenience us rich folks in the fancy jet," Alice countered.

"We'll probably find out one way or the other after they get here," Whitey replied. He turned to the captain and asked, "Did they say anything about Tom Adams?"

"Just that he can't come out to the plane until he is searched," the captain replied.

"OK, thanks," Whitey said. He pulled out his cell phone and dialed Tom before sitting back down in his seat. "Hey, Chirp, do you know why we're being delayed? Is anyone pissed about working late?"

"No, everybody in the FBO has been extremely polite. I guess with Monk's facility here in town they want to maintain good relations with him," Tom replied.

"Well, somebody is fucking with us. I've flown all over the world in Monk's planes since I started working for him and we've never been searched or delayed in any way," Whitey said.

"Well, after President Pichugin threatened a nuclear response if the United States interfered in Ukraine, the Administration got really skittish about angering him. Jon asked his bosses for help, so they know he was operating in Russian-controlled southern Ukraine. It makes sense that when they said no, he would reach out to his friends for help. They might try to stop us all the way up to the point we cross the border into Ukraine. After that, I think they'll leave us alone," Tom said.

"Then I'm surprised they didn't stop us before we left Homer," Whitey said.

"You probably tripped them up by leaving from Homer instead of Anchorage. They might not have had time to adjust," Tom replied.

"I'm going to give Monk a call and see if he can send some legal support out here to speed things up. Talk to you later, Tom," Whitey said. He dialed the number. "Hey, sir, it's Whitey again, I have another problem."

"What is it, Whitey?" Monk asked.

"Sir, we're being delayed at Edinburgh. They are going to search us and the plane for contraband," Whitey explained.

"What for? We never get searched," Monk replied.

"I think the White House is trying to keep us from accomplishing our mission. They're afraid of what Pichugin might do if we're discovered," Whitey replied.

"Do you think the president would aid and abet children being sex trafficked?" Monk asked.

"He might not even know about it. They could just tell him about the nun and leave the kids out of their brief," Whitey explained, "They just have to buy enough time for the Chechens to get them out of Ukraine for our mission to fail. I don't think they would actually tell the Russians about the mission," Whitey said.

"What do you need from me?" Monk asked.

"Sir, right now, I need legal support. Two or three Scottish lawyers out here at the plane ASAP might help a lot. Otherwise, we're just a bunch of foreigners up to no good," Whitey said.

"Okay, they're on their way," Monk replied.

"Sir, just to save time, can you have your lawyers also meet us when we land in Berlin?" Whitey asked.

"You bet. Good luck," Monk replied.

***

Thirty minutes later Taco saw some movement and said, "Whitey, someone just came out of the FBO and is talking to the cops in the car."

Everyone in the plane stuck their faces to a window to watch the action. After a minute the man dressed in jeans and a V-neck sweater to ward off the cool humid air turned and began walking toward the plane. Seconds later he entered the cabin. Whitey was standing ready to meet him.

"Are you General McKinley?" he asked.

"Yes, I am," Whitey replied.

The man held out his hand and said, "I'm James McFadden, lead council for Monk Industries Scotland. Mr. Monk asked me to help expedite your release."

"You sure don't dress like a lawyer," Mike said.

McFadden turned to face Mike. "I can't speak for the states, but this is what we solicitors in Scotland wear when we're dragged out of bed to rescue what you Mericans call brigands, ne'er-do-wells, and scallywags," McFadden said with a smile. He scanned the interior of the plane, then turned back to Whitey. "Before the Border Force officers get here, are you carrying anything controversial?"

"Just that," Whitey replied as he pointed to a large black Pelican case at the back of the cabin.

"What's in the case?" McFadden asked.

"Cash," Whitey replied.

"How much?" McFadden asked.

"$2,000,000," Whitey said.

"I see, and where are you heading tonight?" McFadden asked.

"Berlin and we have a tight deadline. Beyond that, it's confidential work for Mr. Monk. He's funding this venture," Whitey said.

"Whitey, a van just pulled up in front of the FBO," Taco said.

McFadden saw the Border Force's officers marching away from the van and said as he went outside, "All right, time to go to work. Excuse me." He came back in five minutes and said, "All right then, this is the plan, General. Have everyone except the flight crew line up outside the plane with their luggage and the officers will search you out there and then they will search the plane. We should be able to get you in the air within the hour."

Whitey turned to the team and said, "You heard the man, grab your shit and line up outside."

The group stood en masse. Mike shouldered his pack and said to Eric, "I hope you didn't pack your Austin Powers Swedish Made Penis Enlarger."

Eric pushed him in the back and replied, "You never returned it after the last time you borrowed it."

Kevin laughed and said, "You two are like an old married couple. No, I take that back. It would be an insult to old married couples."

Four Border Force officers were lined up outside in their dark blue uniforms ready to begin the inspection with McFadden standing next to their leader. The officer at the end of the line addressed the group, "Good morning, everyone, I'm Inspector Douglas McDougall. Please, line up in front of my team and we will start the inspection."

Everyone did as instructed with Whitey first in line. "Good morning, Inspector McDougall," Whitey said as he sat his pack down on the tarmac and handed over his passport.

McDougall read the name in the passport, "Brian McKinley. Would you be General McKinley of the American Marines?"

"Formerly, yes. I'm retired," Whitey explained.

"Are you traveling for business or pleasure, General?" the inspector asked.

"Business, I work for Monk Industries now," Whitey replied.

"Mr. McFadden said you have $2,000,000 on board. Is this correct?" McDougall asked.

"Yes, sir," Whitey replied.

"May I ask for what purpose?" McDougall asked.

Whitey smiled and replied, "Travel expenses."

"I see. And your companions are a United States Deputy Marshal, two Alaska State Troopers, two Coast Guard Officers, and a novelist specializing in Amish romance novels. Why are they traveling with you?" McDougall asked.

"They're providing security for the money," Whitey replied.

The inspector chuckled. "Really. An Amish romance novelist is providing security," he said.

"To be fair she was an Air Force Security Forces sergeant before the writing bug bit her," Whitey replied.

Inspector McDougall turned to address Alice and asked, "Ms. York, what titles have you published?"

"Most recently, *Getting Hitched, Amish You More, and Yodel for Your Supper*," Alice replied.

The inspector did a quick Amazon search on his phone and found her books. "I see," McDougall said as he handed Whitey's passport back to him. He took a knee and searched Whitey's pack quickly before zipping it back up.

"May I ask a question?" Whitey asked.

"Of course, sir," McDougall replied.

"The only reason we stopped here tonight was to pick up Tom Adams and then we were going to take off immediately. We're on a very important confidential mission, and we have very little time to accomplish it. I've flown all over the world for Monk Industries and we've never been stopped like this. Do you know why we were delayed tonight?" Whitey asked.

"Sorry, sir. They didn't say, but the request did come from your government," McDougall replied. He turned to his Border Force officers and saw they had completed their inspections. "All right gentlemen, have at it." The three officers boarded the plane.

CHAPTER 34

After landing in the darkness at Berlin Brandenburg Airport, the team quickly cleared customs, despite the US government's best efforts to delay them, thanks to a squad of Monk Industries lawyers. The team quickly boarded a German Army surplus UH-1D Huey helicopter from the flying museum flown by a couple of crusty old, retired German Army pilots sporting huge gray mustaches that would have made Kaiser Wilhelm II proud. They flew directly to the former RAF Gatow airfield and landed on the brightly lit ramp in front of the main hangar. Whitey and Tom exited the Huey and saw a pudgy bespectacled man in his fifties with a salt-and-pepper mustache and beard approaching them from the hangar. The giant hangar doors were open, and a tug was pulling a massive CH-53G out of the hangar by its nose landing gear.

"Tom and I are going to talk to the museum director. The rest of you go with Chris and get that Shitter ready to fly," Whitey said to the team before he and Tom turned to head for the man. "Herr Gerhardt I presume, I'm Brian McKinley and this is Tom Adams," Whitey said as he held out his hand.

Wolfgang Gerhardt shook his hand and said, "Yes, General. It is good to meet you and you also Mr. Adams. Please, call me Wolfgang."

"Will do, please, call me Whitey," he said, "I see the Sea Stallion behind you being pulled out of the hangar. It looks incredible, like it's fresh out of the Sikorsky factory. I assume Mr. Monk made a deal with you for us to use it for a few days?"

"Oh no! He tried but as I told him this is quite impossible. The helicopter is going to the paint shop. This morning it will be repainted in German Army livery just as it was before being retired from active service. We have big plans for the, what do you call them? Shitters. We will raise a lot of money and awareness for the museum with a pair of CH-53s. Imagine them flying over an airshow low and fast with one carrying a 105mm howitzer on a line below it and the other carrying a trailer full of simulated artillery rounds," Gerhardt replied, "They release the howitzer and trailer on the grass between the runways and then land nearby. A squad of soldiers runs out of the helicopters and quickly fires off several salvos. Then they load everything back up and fly away within a few minutes. It will be spectacular."

Tom and Whitey shared a knowing look. They had done just as Gerhardt described many times in exercises and airshows while they were young Marine aviators. Those were the good ole days when they were still new to military flying and every new experience was a thrill. Tom turned to Whitey, "We must have the 53," he said.

"Yeah, I know. Do you think we should read Wolfgang into what we're doing?" Whitey asked.

"I guess we don't have a choice. Wolfgang, can we talk somewhere in private?" Tom asked.

"Yes, of course. Follow me," he replied. They walked back into the hangar and then into his office. "Please, have a seat," he said as he motioned to the chairs in front of his desk as he sat down behind it. It was decorated with military airplane and helicopter models. "So, what wild promotion does Mr. Monk have planned for my Sea Stallion? Let me guess, he will paint it white like an ice cream truck and fly it over the World Cup to drop thousands of his cell phones on the crowd," Gerhardt said before chuckling at his own joke.

Tom and Whitey didn't laugh. Tom leaned forward with his hands clasped, elbows resting on his knees. "Wolfgang, a friend of mine is in Russian-occupied Donetsk tonight trying to rescue a twenty-one-year-old Catholic nun. Her name is Sister Joan. She is also his goddaughter. Before she called home for help, she saw her priest beaten to death by a group of Chechen soldiers. They were at her church to seize the 92 orphans she and her priest were caring for to take them to Grozny to sell as sex slaves. We're going to stop them and take the kids back, but we can't do it without your helicopter," Tom explained.

Whitey piled on, "Wolfgang you said you would sell us the Huey if I would agree to come back afterward and give a presentation on what we did. How about if I do the same thing after we get back with the orphans? Imagine the good press you'll get after people see your helicopter was used to rescue 92 beautiful little children. We could even make a documentary. How does that sound?"

"It sounds like a fantasy, General. What you propose is ridiculous. You intend to fly one helicopter across Ukraine and take almost one hundred children away from the Chechen Army by force. You are talking about a suicide mission. You will be shot down within an hour of crossing the border," Gerhardt replied.

"We are willing to take that risk, Wolfgang. We can't turn our backs on these innocent boys and girls," Whitey said.

"Well, gentlemen, I can't stop you from your fool's errand, but I can keep the helicopter here with me. You may take the Huey with you as we agreed, but that is all. Later, you will thank me for saving your lives," Gerhardt said.

Tom was stunned. "I can't believe you have such a callous disregard for so many lives," Tom said.

Gerhardt chuckled, "Please, Mr. Adams, thousands of children die every day all over the world under horrible circumstances. These children are, how do you say, a drop in a bucket? I will shed no more tears for them than any other."

Tom lunged forward and grabbed Gerhardt by his shirt. He dragged him across the desk as he squealed like the pathetic coward he truly was. Tiny aircraft from two world wars crashed into the floor. Tom dumped Gerhardt on the carpet and dropped on top of him. He yelled, "You heartless bastard!" as he drew his fist back already anticipating the satisfying crunch Gerhardt's nose would make when it shattered.

Whitey grabbed the back of Tom's jacket and pulled him off causing them both to roll back onto the floor. He wrapped his arms and legs around Tom immobilizing him. "Knock it off! We can't have you breaking your hand right now. After we get back, I'll hold your coat while you kick his ass," Whitey said. Gerhardt rolled over and scrambled behind his desk on all fours.

"Let go of me, Whitey! Let me teach this motherfucker a lesson!" Tom yelled.

"Look, if we have to, we'll round up the museum staff, hogtie them, and lock them in the janitor's closet before we steal the damn thing," Whitey whispered in Tom's ear.

There was a knock in the open doorway behind them. "Excuse me, for interrupting, gentlemen. I'm looking for Herr Wolfgang Gerhardt," the man wearing a conservative charcoal gray suit said in heavily accented English.

"He's the fucking cockroach hiding under the desk," Tom said as he stood up, "Who are you?"

"I am Sebastian Gunter. I represent Mr. Monk in all legal matters in Deutschland," he said. Turning his attention to Gerhardt, he said in German, "Herr Gerhardt, please, come out from under the desk. You are embarrassing yourself." Gerhardt stood up with an umbrella in his hand to defend himself but took a step back to make certain he was out of Tom's reach. His gaze flitted back and forth between Tom and Gunter. Gunter stepped forward between Tom and Whitey to hand Gerhardt an envelope. "This document serves to notify you that Monk Industries now owns 73% of this museum. Mr. Monk is willing to buy your 3% share from you right now and you will be escorted off of the airfield or you may keep your current title and 3% for the time being as long as you cooperate immediately with these gentlemen. What is your decision, Herr Gerhardt?" Gunter asked.

Gerhardt scanned the document and replied, "I would like to stay with the museum! Just keep that madman away from me!" He relied upon the museum for his livelihood.

"Very well, I am certain as long as you comply with the general's wishes you will have no more trouble," Gunter said. He turned to Whitey and asked, "General, what support do you require of Herr Gerhardt?" Gunter asked.

Whitey turned to Gerhardt and said, "I want that 53 you just rolled out of the hangar topped off with fuel. I want the chaff and flare dispensers mounted and loaded. I want the GAU-21 machine gun mounts installed in the windows and on the ramp. I want 150 sets of foam earplugs. I want five flight helmets for my aircrew. Tom, do you think we should load up the internal fuel tanks?"

"No, we don't need them to get to our first stop and we would have to remove them before we flew into Ukraine," Tom replied. Seven 170-gallon internal fuel tanks could be loaded inside the cabin to give the helicopter an extra 1,190 gallons of fuel but it could take a couple of hours to remove them at Chisinau.

Whitey turned back to Gerhardt and said, "Give the aircraft logbook to Tom so, he and Mr. Savage can confirm that the helicopter is ready to fly. I want to launch in two hours."

Gerhardt pulled the logbook off the shelf behind his desk and handed it to Tom who hurried out of the office to join Chris at the helicopter. Gerhardt sat down behind his desk and called his number two to pass on Whitey's requirements.

"One more thing, Wolfgang. Hey, look at me!" Whitey shouted as he drew the Ka-Bar knife from the brown leather sheath on his belt. "Do you know what this is?" he asked as he pointed to the groove running along the upper half of the seven-inch blade. Gerhardt shook his head. "This is the blood groove. It makes it easier to pull the blade out of a body so you can make faster reattacks. If you tell anyone about our intentions to fly into Ukraine, they will never find enough of your body to bury," Whitey said. Whitey sheathed his knife and walked out of the office to talk to Gunter. "What happened to just buying the 53 from the museum?" Whitey asked.

"I tried to negotiate the sale of the helicopter with Gerhardt last night, but he was quite unmovable, so Mr. Monk made a personal plea of his own that he also rejected. Mr. Monk does not like being told no. He directed me to find a way to make the deal happen. I did some research and determined Gerhardt is just the frontman for a small group of investors who own the bulk of the museum. They are aviation enthusiasts, but they are also shrewd businessmen who enjoy making a profit. They weren't interested in selling the helicopter but then Mr. Monk offered to buy the entire museum. His generous offer and the possibility of working on future projects with Monk Industries was too good to refuse," Gunter explained.

***

Tom hurried across the brightly lit ramp to the helicopter where Chris and Taco were giving it a thorough preflight inspection. They had every access panel open. They knew that Tom and Whitey being Naval Aviators would also conduct their own preflight inspection before they agreed to fly the helicopter. "Chris, I have the logbook. How does it look?" Tom asked as he handed him the logbook.

"It's beautiful, sir. I've never seen a helicopter this clean. Everything looks brand new. There are no hydraulic leaks at all. I don't have to tell you, the only time a Shitter isn't leaking hydraulic fluid is when it's empty. They even have all of the soundproofing insulation installed in the cabin. Do you want us to strip it out? It'll save us about 300 pounds," Chris asked.

"No, let's keep it. The little kids might pull their earplugs out during the flight. The soundproofing may help save some of their hearing. Also, find a pig for us to take on the flight and five cans of hydraulic fluid," Tom replied. A pig was a manual pump used for transferring hydraulic fluid from the can directly into the 3,000 psi hydraulic systems from inside the helicopter. The 1980 mission to rescue the American hostages in Iran, Operation Eagle Claw, failed and good men died because one of the MH-53 helicopters had a hydraulic leak and nobody thought ahead to bring a pig. "Excuse me, I need to call Jon," Tom said. He walked away from the helicopter and dialed Jon's number.

CHAPTER 35

0030Z (0330 LOCAL)
ST. MICHAEL'S CATHOLIC CHURCH,
DONETSK, UKRAINE

The sat phone vibrated and Jon saw Tom's name on the screen. "Hey, Tom, what do you have?" Jon asked.

"We got the 53, Jon. Monk bought the whole fucking museum to get it. I couldn't believe it, but he did. We owe him big time. We plan to launch around 0230 Zulu. So far, we have lawyers and money, but we need guns for the 53 and the team. Did you find what we need?" Tom asked.

"Yeah, I have a guy in Chisinau. I already called to alert him, so he's expecting you. He owes me a favor, but it won't be cheap. How much do I have to spend?" Jon asked.

"Monk gave us $2,000,000 but please, get the best deal you can. I'd hate to blow through all of this money and then have to go back and ask for more. Who is your guy? Can we trust him?" Tom asked.

"He's a major in Moldovan military intelligence and yes you can trust him. Send me your list and I'll get what you need," Jon replied.

"Sounds good. So, what's your situation down there?" Tom asked.

Jon cleared his throat. His voice broke as he said, "It's, ahhh, it's not good. While we were out looking for baby formula, the Chechens came to the church and took Kimmie and the kids away to the FOB at the airport. That fuckin' colonel raped and murdered a little girl in the church. It's my fault, Tom. I should have stopped it. I swear to God, I thought I had more time," Jon replied, as he began to tear up. He hadn't cried in years before tonight. He didn't even cry the night Clint died.

"I'm sorry, Jon. I know it sucks, but you have to put it behind you and focus on the kids you can help," Tom replied.

"I know you're right, but this is so fuckin' frustrating. I need to be doing something. There's no telling what's happening to Kimmie and those kids right now," Jon said before the floodgates opened. He couldn't stop crying. "Clint made me her godfather because he believed I would protect her. I failed him and Kimmie. I feel so useless right now. I desperately need to kill some more of these motherfuckers," Jon said as he sniffled and wiped his nose on his sleeve.

"Hang on, Jon, we're coming. Don't engage anyone until we get there. I'll send you my list," Tom said before disconnecting.

Jon wiped tears from his eyes and put the phone away. Angie remained quiet and let him have his moment. "If you tell anyone I was sitting here balling like a little bitch, I'll fuckin' kill ya'," he said.

"Relax, mate, we're all human and if this particular untimely disaster just happened to occur during your time of the month, who am I to judge," Angie said with a shit-eating grin.

Jon, wiped his eyes again as he laughed, "Fuck you, asshole."

Angie reached into the center console and offered Jon what looked like a hundred-year-old paper napkin. "Would you like a tissue, sweetheart?"

Jon punched him in the arm as Angie laughed, "Kiss my ass, shithead… And thanks again for coming. I'd be dead without you."

"No worries, mate. If I ever have a goddaughter who becomes a nun and calls me to rescue her and a metric fuck ton of orphans from a hellish warzone, expect my call," Angie said with a straight face.

"You bet, brother. I'm serious. You have my word, Angie. I'm your man, whatever it is," Jon replied as he held his fist up between them. Angie nodded and gave him a bump.

CHAPTER 36

The team assembled in the museum's conference room. Whitey stood at the head of the large oval table with Tom sitting off to his right side. "Everyone, please, take a seat so we can brief you. This won't take long because we don't know very much." The small talk stopped and those who weren't sitting did so. "A force of approximately twenty Chechen Spetsnaz soldiers led by Colonel Sultanovich murdered the priest at St. Michael's Church in Donetsk. They have since taken Jon's goddaughter, Kimmie, known as Sister Joan, and ninety-one orphans ranging in age from a few months to around fourteen to their airport FOB. According to their pattern, they'll convoy them to Grozny tomorrow. We anticipate the convoy will consist of an SUV for the colonel, two Ural 4320 6x6 trucks for the twenty or so soldiers, and two tour buses for the children. Thanks to Mr. Monk's constellation of satellites Gwenn was able to quickly locate them at the airport FOB and will alert us when they move. Jon and Angus will follow them in their Suburban until we can catch up to the convoy. Then to abbreviate the kill chain, we will find, fix, and kill the enemy by hasty ambush somewhere along the highway. We must strike with sudden, overwhelming force.

"Now there's one important difference to this mission that you should take a moment to consider very seriously. You have all been told since the beginning of your military training that we don't leave anyone behind. We will risk a hundred warfighters to rescue one. I have firmly believed that throughout my time in uniform.

"This mission is different. The children have to come first. Taking them back and getting them safely away from the warzone is paramount. We'll follow the pirate code. We are all expendable. If you're wounded and fall behind, you'll be left behind. We can't risk delaying on the ground for even a minute. That 53 is a giant bullet magnet and one round in the right or wrong place can bring it down. As soon as we get the children on board you need to haul ass for the ramp. If you aren't okay with the idea that the kids come first, you shouldn't get in the helicopter tonight," Whitey stopped talking and looked around the room. No one spoke. Some nodded their ascent and others gave thumbs up. Mike looked like he wanted to say something but remained silent. "Go ahead, Mike. Do you have a problem?" Whitey asked.

"No, sir, not me. I'm a Marine. I've always known I was expendable, but these Air Farce people might need to bring a time-out card just in case things get scary," Mike said with a smile as he looked at Alice and Eric.

"The way I remember it, the last time you were in combat you screamed like a baby when you got a little boo-boo on your leg," Alice replied.

"A boo-boo! I got fucking shot!" Mike shouted, "I have a Purple Heart to prove it."

"Yeah, you got shot so bad, Eric had to put a Hello Kitty band-aid on it," Alice said.

Mike went to reply, but Eric put his hand on Mike's forearm and said, "Dude, you better quit while you're behind."

Whitey continued, "Once we have the kids on board we'll buster for Kyiv. We'll have to remain flexible depending on how much opposition we encounter. If we're cut off, we'll turn south and head for Turkey if we have enough fuel. No matter what way we go when we get done we can plan on spending some time in someone's jail.

"Chirp will take the right seat. I'll take the left. Taco will man the left gun and Chris will be the crew chief and man the right gun. Kevin since you were a heavy weapons platoon sergeant, I'd like you to take the tail gun," Whitey said.

"Aye, aye, sir," Kevin replied.

"Eric, Mike, and Alice will be the ground element on the ambush. Sarah, I don't know your background in the Coast Guard. Where would we best use you?" Whitey asked.

"Sir, I'm an intelligence officer now but during my enlisted days, I led boarding parties and was qualified in every weapon we had on the cutter including the .50 cals," Sarah replied.

"Okay, Sarah, you'll join the ground element. Mike, you were infantry. Were you a squad leader?" Whitey asked.

"Yes, sir," he replied.

"You'll lead the ground element," Whitey said.

"Aye, aye, sir," Mike replied.

"We can assume at some point along the route to Grozny we'll catch up with Jon and the convoy. Then, we'll move ahead of the convoy to set up the ambush. We'll rely on surprise and violence of action. Once we engage, we must keep shooting until all of the enemy soldiers are dead. We can't allow them to delay us. We must get the kids off the buses and on the helicopter as fast as possible. Door gunners, if you see a QRF responding we are relying on you to stop them before they get close enough to engage us. We are going to max out on fuel. That's 13,256 pounds of Jet-A1. That will give us a range of 860 nautical miles and a time aloft of just over five hours at 170 knots. We'll refuel in Chisinau when we pick up our weapons and personal military gear. After refueling, we'll have another 860 nautical miles of range. When we takeoff from there we'll be well above the 53's max takeoff weight of 42,000 pounds so we'll perform a rolling takeoff," Whitey said.

"Excuse me sir, but doesn't the 53 have roll-on internal auxiliary fuel tanks to extend its range? Can't we use a couple of them?" Taco asked.

"Yes, it can carry up to seven 170-gallon roll-on internal tanks, but we don't need them to reach Chisinau and once we get to Donetsk, we can't use the internal tanks while firing the guns because of the high risk of the fuel fumes causing a fire or explosion inside the cabin. In our experience, every time we used the tanks the fumes leaked out. And we need the room inside the cabin for the kids. It'll be a tight fit with all of us and ninety children. Besides, we have more than enough fuel to fly to Donetsk and then fly to Ukrainian-controlled territory.

"Okay, that concludes the brief. Tom and I are going to remain here to pray for a successful mission. You're all welcome to join us if you wish," Whitey said. No one left the room.

***

Just past four in the morning Tom and Whitey sat in the cockpit of the CH-53G. It was like coming home again. The auxiliary powerplant or APP was running to power the cockpit lights and intercom system. The APP was a small jet engine used to power all of the systems necessary to get the main engines started. The APP allowed the helicopter to be started out in the field where no outside power was available. It also created an ear-splitting whine that was unbearable without wearing hearing protection. In the old days, the crews in CH-53s were told to use foam earplugs under their helmet's sound suppression earphones to save their hearing. But then it made the radios too difficult to hear so they would have to turn up the volume on the radios and negate the protection of their foam earplugs. So, they either took out the earplugs or turned up the radio. Either way damaged their hearing. Fortunately, today they had helmets with noise-canceling technology built in so Tom and Whitey could talk over the ICS without yelling. Tom had completed a very detailed pre-flight inspection of the helicopter with Chris and Taco. Both were highly trained and experienced helicopter airframe and powerplant mechanics and crew chiefs. Chris had experience working on and crewing 53s during several Marine Corps deployments. They found the helicopter was in superb condition thanks to the German restoration team.

Since Tom had more recent flying experience and more flight time in the 53, he would act as the aircraft commander. Whitey would be the H2P or copilot. "Ok, Chris and Taco are you up?" Tom asked over the intercom system or ICS.

Chris, the crew chief, stood outside the helicopter in front of Tom's chin bubble where they could see each other. He was connected to the ICS through a forty-foot extension cord called a long cord. Chris keyed the push-to-talk button clipped to the top of his flight jacket and said, "Roger, I have you loud and clear, Chirp."

Taco stood on the left side of the helicopter in front of Whitey's chin bubble. He raised his right thumb, then keyed his own microphone with his right hand before saying, "Loud and clear, sir."

Chirp keyed his ICS and said, "Ok, here's the brief. If anyone asks our callsign is Whitey five three and we are on a humanitarian mission sponsored by Monk Industries. As Whitey said, we have enough fuel for about 860 nautical miles and five hours of flight time. That will get us to Chisinau International Airport in Moldova. Moldova's airspace is already closed to commercial air traffic due to its proximity to combat operations in Ukraine, so we will land on Runway 08 and take the first taxiway to the westernmost ramp to arm up and hot refuel. Since the airport is closed there should be very little activity. Jon's intel contact, Cujo, will inform the local officials that we are part of a Moldovan intelligence operation and to stay clear of us. Then after we refuel, we'll have another five hours of flight time. If we don't get the kids somewhere safe within those five hours we're screwed. I don't see a scenario where we sneak into a Russian-controlled airfield to refuel and then get out safely.

"Once we start the engines, we aren't shutting them down until the mission's over. We'll fly VFR and stay under the radar as much as possible. If we have an inflight emergency depending on the severity, we might not follow the NATOPS procedures to the letter. If it's a land as soon as practical emergency, we will probably continue on the mission. If it's a land as soon as possible emergency, we'll decide what to do when it happens. If it's a land immediately emergency, we'll probably have to land except if we're over water. I don't care if the main transmission starts seizing up, we are not going in the water with a helicopter full of kids. We'll land on the nearest ship if we have to.

"Before we cross the border into Ukraine, we'll drop down to between fifty and 100 feet AGL to mitigate the shoulder-launched SAM threat. If we do get shot down and are on fire, keep your heads down and meet in front of the helicopter well beyond the rotor arc. We'll make constant altitude and heading changes to mitigate ground fire. Does anyone have any questions?" Chirp asked. No one did. "Chris, did you get us a pig and hydraulic fluid?"

Chris keyed his PTT and said, "Yes, sir. It's inside."

"Good. Okay, let's get this beast started. Prestart checklist, Whitey," Chirp said. Whitey and Chirp proceeded to go through the NATOPS checklist using the challenge and response method they had used throughout their careers. Twenty minutes later the rotor blades were turning at 100%, the anti-collision light and the red and green navigation lights were on. Chris led the team into the helicopter using the ramp under the tail pylon. Chirp taxied out to what was left of Runway 26R and stopped. Before he could start his roll, a glaring spotlight appeared above the 53 and began orbiting overhead. "What is it? Can you see?" Chirp asked over the ICS.

"It looks like an Aérospatiale Puma. It says Bundespolizei on the side," Chris replied.

"Shit! That's the Federal Police!" Whitey said.

Kevin stood up and looked over Chris's shoulder. He said, "Those troops in black with their feet hanging out of the helicopter are GSG 9." Grenzschutzgruppe or GSG 9 was Germany's premiere counterterrorism police force.

The Bundespolizei pilot made an aggressive no-hover landing thirty meters to the right of the 53 and elite operators poured from the cabin and raced toward the 53.

"Hurry, Chirp! They're coming fast!" Chris said.

"Roger that, I'm rolling," Chirp said as he released the brake pedals on top of the anti-torque pedals, pushed the cyclic forward, and raised the collective to accelerate down the shortened runway.

"Helicopter Delta Alpha Mike Five Three, this is the German Federal Police. You are ordered to stop immediately and present your passengers for inspection," the highly accented German voice said in English over the emergency frequency, 121.5 MHz.

Mike and Eric sat on the ramp waving at the policemen chasing them on the runway as they fell further and further behind. "Auf Wiedersehen!" Mike yelled as Eric laughed. They couldn't resist poking the bear. The policemen turned and ran back to their Puma.

Chirp continued to accelerate and lifted off, climbing to 500 feet AGL in the dark night sky as he turned to the southeast. He intended to maintain that general heading across Germany, Poland, and western Ukraine before entering Moldova.

"Chirp the Puma just lifted off, it's following us," Taco transmitted from the left gunner's window.

"Fuck'em! That Puma tops out around 150 knots. We can cruise at 175 and bump up to 200 if we need to. In twenty minutes, we'll be in Poland," Chirp replied over the ICS. Lightning flashed in the distance in front of the helicopter and jumped laterally from cloud to cloud. Chirp looked at Whitey, surprise in his eyes. "What the fuck was that? You didn't say anything about thunderstorms!" Chirp shouted at Whitey.

Whitey was surprised too, "I thought you checked the weather!" he replied.

"You're the fucking copilot! I pre-flighted the helicopter! All the planning shit was yours!" Chirp corrected him.

"I did the weight and balance and the fuel calculations! You had my tablet! I thought you were checking the weather!" Whitey defended himself. Lightning cracked brighter and closer.

"Well, you better get on that tablet right fuckin' now and check the weather ASAP or this mission may end in a smokin' hole right here in Germany!" Chirp said as he slowed down to 130 knots. Thunderstorms came with heavy rain, lightning, hail, and microbursts. Chirp knew better than to fuck around with that shit, especially at night.

"Chirp, the Puma is catching up and he's bringing a friend," Kevin transmitted from the open ramp.

"Helicopter Delta Alpha Mike Five Three, this is the German Federal Police. You are flying into danger. Turn right heading one eight zero and follow me to the Bundespolizei Dresden Heliport," the pilot transmitted again on the guard frequency, 121.5 MHz.

A heavy downpour enveloped the 53 and Chirp immediately lost all visual references to the world outside his cockpit and began scanning his cockpit instruments to maintain the helicopter in controlled flight. "I'm coming up," he called out. He began climbing. As a young lieutenant, he had been taught, when you inadvertently fly into IMC or Instrument Metrological Conditions you start climbing immediately and turn 180° to fly back out of the clouds. If he did that tonight he would be condemning almost a hundred kids to misery and death. Instead of turning he made a silent prayer and kept climbing straight ahead. Lightning flashed again bigger and louder than before. Turbulence shook the helicopter. "I can't see shit outside, Whitey! Turn on the wipers! What's the MSA for this area?" Chirp asked.

Whitey was head down looking up the local weather on his tablet. He looked up to the overhead panel and turned the windshield wiper switch to high. Then he paged over to the en route chart on his tablet and replied, "1,500 feet." He moved to the weather radar page and said, "Turn left to 090°. We should exit the storm in about five miles."

Chirp turned left and continued to climb in the turbulence for two minutes and felt a little relief when he saw the altimeter needle pass 5,000 feet. Then the 53 shook violently as the turbulence became severe. Chirp yelled into the ICS, "Make sure everybody is belted into their seats!" He immediately felt himself get light in his seat. The helicopter was falling. He pulled the collective up to his armpit as he looked down at the Vertical Velocity Indicator and saw the helicopter was dropping at 4,000 feet per minute. The engines were screaming at their maximum capability, unable to arrest the descent. "Microburst!" Chirp shouted over the ICS. The sudden downdraft could swat the 53 into the ground. Jumbo jets had succumbed to the powerful winds many times. Most jets carried weather radar so they could fly around them. He pressed the button on the eight-day clock to start the timer. He figured he had a little over a minute to get out of the downdraft before they burned in. "Drop the gear," Chirp called out to Whitey. He wanted the gear down just in case he came out of the downdraft in time to make a roll-on landing.

Whitey checked to make sure they were flying below the landing gear activation speed of 140 knots and lowered the gear knob. He watched the landing gear panel until the lights turned green. He said, "Three down and locked. Nr's down to 97%. I'll try to bring it back up with the Engine Trim," Whitey shouted back. Nr was the speed of the rotor blades. If it dropped much below 95%, they could lose the lift provided by the rotor system and fall out of the sky. The Engine Speed Trim Switches were on both collectives and controlled by the right thumb. Whitey pushed the switches forward until the Nr came back up. "Nr's a 100% again," Whitey said.

"We're still dropping at 4,000 feet a minute," Chirp said before he checked the clock. "We have about twenty seconds before we hit. Chris, Taco tell everyone to brace for impact. Whitey, turn the landing light on." Bright white light reflected off the clouds and back through the heavy rain into the cockpit as the wipers swept back and forth. Chirp looked to the right out of his window and saw an ever so small dark break in the clouds. "I'm coming right. Count off, Whitey," Chirp said.

"Clear right," Chris replied as he stood and looked out of the window in the crew door.

"Chris, get back in your seat and strap in," Chirp said.

"Fifteen, fourteen, thirteen, twelve, eleven," Whitey called out as the turbulence lessened. Chirp still held the collective up at full extension. "Ten, nine, eight, seven." The clouds cleared but the heavy rain continued as the helicopter continued down. "Six, five, four."

"Hang on!" Chirp yelled as he jerked the cyclic to the right to dodge an obstruction.

Whitey instinctively pulled his feet up off the floor and yelled. "Was that a church steeple?"

The windshield cleared and the rain stopped just as the helicopter leveled off. Chirp found himself flying down a wide boulevard just above the buildings on each side. He lowered the collective back to where it should be in normal flight. He looked up and saw a clear predawn sky. "Coming up to 500 AGL. Whitey, suck the gear and turn off the landing light and wipers," Chirp asked, "Is everyone all right in back?"

"They're all in one piece. Mike hurled but he caught it all in a bag," Taco replied.

***

The Puma pilot was a good Christian man and a firm believer in a life after this one. He hoped to join his maker in the hereafter someday, but he preferred that it not be this day. When he saw the Sea Stallion disappear into the thunderstorm, he shook his head in disbelief and turned north to fly around it.

"My God, that pilot must be insane! We'll find the helicopter burning in a farmer's pasture," his copilot exclaimed.

"No, not insane. That one, he has balls the size of Texas. We will not find him," the pilot replied.

CHAPTER 37

M22 and M29 stormed into the bar through the front door like they owned the place. Their commanding officer in Dnipro had called to tell them two SVR officers had been killed in a bar fight with two Chechen soldiers. They were ordered to investigate and report back. A Ukrainian man sat at a table near the bar surrounded by four Russian soldiers who stood over him making threats. It was clear he had been beaten. They could see four bodies on the floor at the far end of the room.

"Who is this man, Sergeant?" M22 asked.

"Sir, he is the owner of the bar. He told us," the sergeant said before M22 stopped him.

"Thank you, Sergeant but I want to hear the story from him," M22 said. He turned his attention to the barkeeper and said, "Why are four men lying dead in the corner?"

"I already told them what happened before they started beating me! There was no reason to hurt me. I am cooperating!" the barkeeper complained.

M22 slapped the man on the side of the head hard enough to let him know he was serious and said, "Stop whining and tell me before I introduce you to real pain."

"The bar was empty when the Chechen sergeant and corporal came in. Over several hours they drank three bottles of vodka. The two SVR officers came in and ordered a couple of drinks and asked me if I had seen a black Chevrolet Suburban. I told them I had not. After they finished their drinks they walked over to ask the soldiers if they had seen the Suburban. The sergeant was disrespectful. He told them no and to go away. The tall SVR man was insulted and argued with the sergeant. The argument quickly became physical and soon they were all shooting each other," the barkeeper said.

"Sergeant, did you search him?" M22 asked.

"Yes, sir. He had this in his pocket," the sergeant said as he held out a wad of cash totaling €1,300.

M22 turned to M29 and said, "Go have a look around." M29 checked behind the bar and then disappeared into the storeroom. M22 addressed the barkeeper again, "You are leaving out part of the story. Do not waste any more of my time. You should have Ukrainian hryvnia or rubles, not euros. Who gave you €1,300?"

M29 came out of the storeroom and said, "It looks like a secondhand store back there. He runs a black market."

M22 drew back his gloved hand and punched the barkeeper in the left eye. A soldier caught the barkeeper before he could fall out of his chair. "No more lies!" M22 shouted before drawing his pistol and pressing it into the man's forehead between his eyes.

"Who gave you the euros?" The soldier standing behind the bar-keeper took two steps to the side.

"Two men came in after the Chechens. They asked about food for the children at St. Michael's Church. I took them to the storeroom. While we were negotiating the SVR officers came in. They hid in the storeroom until after the SVR men and Chechens killed each other. They gave me the money, took the food, and left," the barkeeper confessed.

"Be very careful how you answer my last question. Were they driving a black Suburban?" M22 asked.

The barkeeper closed his eyes tightly before shaking his head. Seconds passed and he was still alive. He opened his eyes just in time to see the fist that broke his nose.

M22 and M29 left immediately. M22 drove out of the lot as M29 turned on his tablet to check the map.

***

Jon and Angie were lying behind a couple of trees in the dark near the Suburban. If it was attacked, they didn't want to be inside. It was parked on the lawn between the road and the church. They were well-hidden but could see if anyone pulled off the road onto the driveway. Angie was getting some sleep while Jon stood watch. The sat phone vibrated and Jon answered quietly, "Hello, Gwenn."

"Jon two men just parked on the far side of the cemetery and are cautiously walking toward you between the tombstones. They're armed," Gwenn said.

"Thanks, Gwenn, stay on the line. Send updates when needed," Jon replied. He crawled over to Angie and woke him.

"What's up, mate?" Angie asked quietly.

"Gwenn says we have two armed men creeping up on us from the far side of the cemetery. Let's see if we can get to the stone wall on this side of the cemetery before they do." The old stone wall was waist-high and ringed the cemetery. Jon traded his SAW for his suppressed HK-416 he had in the Suburban. "Try to take them out with suppressed weapons. If we go loud the neighbors might rat on us." They ran off as fast as they could using their GPNVGs to show the way. As they rounded the church they scanned the area, then moved forward at a crouch.

"They're about a hundred yards out moving from headstone to headstone," Gwenn said from over 1,500 miles away in the Monk facility in Edinburgh.

"Roger, we see them. Watch our six," Jon said.

"Always," came the response.

"You think these guys have goggles?" Jon whispered to Angie.

"We have to assume so," he replied.

"Make sure your IR laser's off until you need it," Jon said as he checked his own. He didn't want to get killed because he gave away their location too soon. "Wait until they get within 25 yards before you shoot. You take the one on the left. Don't pop up in the same place twice. They probably have body armor so go for the head or pelvis."

"Understood," Angie replied before he raised his head high enough to see over the wall. He ducked back down. "It's no good. They're moving one at a time. One covers while the other one moves." Angie moved down the wall about five feet.

"Okay, we'll take the first one together, then you pin the other one down while I flank him," Jon replied before flipping his laser on and taking a peek. "Now, Angie." They popped up and stitched M29 with 5.56mm rounds. He dropped immediately between the tombstones. His partner, M22, returned fire. He missed but got Jon and Angie to duck behind the wall. He ran over and grabbed M29 by his drag handle and pulled him behind the nearest granite headstone.

***

M22 rolled M29 over on his stomach behind the headstone and handed M29 his rifle. He moaned in pain. Most of the rounds hit his armor but two caught him below his belt. He was bleeding profusely. "You must keep fighting comrade. Return fire to the front. They will try to flank us. I will intercept him. After I kill them, I will get you to the hospital," he said before he fired a string of tracers around the left side of the headstone toward the wall where Angie had been and then rushed laterally toward the side wall. He could hear M29 firing behind him toward their enemy's original position. M22 dove head-first over the short stone wall to get away from Angie's tracers. As his head cleared the wall he came face to face with Jon as he rose to fire his rifle. Their helmets collided and they collapsed into a tumbling ball of knees, fists, and elbows.

***

"Keep their heads down and I'll circle around," Jon said to Angie before crawling away on all fours. Angie popped up with his rifle and fired four or five rounds before ducking and moving to a new spot then repeating the process. He burned through his thirty-round magazine in less than a minute, causing the granite headstone to crack at the bottom and fall over crushing M29. The constant firing gave Jon enough time to move around and attack from the side. Jon came up over the wall with his rifle and was immediately bowled over by M22 diving over to his side. *Fuckin' soccer ninja!* he thought as he fell backward onto the ground trading punches with the Russian. They were so close neither was able to bring his rifle to bear so they grappled trying to gain an advantage.

"Who are you assholes?" Jon asked through clenched teeth. *This wiry bastard is strong,* he thought.

M22 ignored the question and said in English, "You fight like you have Russian blood in your veins."

"No, but I have plenty of it on my boots," Jon said before mustering enough strength to finally pull his suppressor under M22's chin. The Russian's face exploded spraying Jon's face with blood and tissue. A small gray geyser erupted from the top of his helmet. Jon froze. Suddenly he was back in Mosul standing behind Clint watching his head disappear.

"Jon, are you good?" Angie asked over the radio. "Hey, Jon."

Jon snapped out of it. "Yeah, I'm good," he replied, Gwenn, can you tell if these guys called for help before they died?"

"Negative, but one of them has a sat phone," she replied.

"Yeah, I found it, thanks," Jon said. As he searched his Russian he dropped what he found in a small pile next to the body.

Seconds later, Angie approached cautiously. "Friendly coming in," he said softly.

"You're clear," Jon acknowledged him. Angie took a knee next to Jon. Jon pointed at M22 and said, "Ole number 22 there had this sat phone in his pocket." He handed the phone to Angie.

The phone was unlocked. Angie scrolled through the messages written in Russian Cyrillic script. "These men are SVR Zaslon. Apparently, his brother was one of the SVR officers we killed when we picked up Fyodor. They have been looking for our Suburban since we took out the green men at the TCP," Angie said.

"How did they know we were here?" Jon asked.

"They were ordered to investigate the barfight. The bartender told them we bought food for the church, and we had a black Suburban," Angie replied.

"Gwenn saved our asses, again," Jon said to Angie. "Gwenn, where did these guys park their vehicle?" Jon asked over his sat phone.

"It's parked half a block from the far side of the cemetery. It looks like an SUV," she replied.

Jon picked up the Land Rover key fob from the pile of M22's belongings piled up on the grass. "Angie go get the Suburban. I'll get their Land Rover. We'll swap vehicles with them and sink these guys in the pond with the Suburban," Jon said.

Angie smiled and said, "You're starting to sound like a Mafia hitman," before he ran off into the darkness.

Five minutes later, they met up near the bodies. They transferred their weapons and gear to the Land Rover Defender 110. Then they carried the bodies over to the cargo area of the Suburban.

"How come all of these Zaslon guys smell like cheap tobacco, but they're built like soccer-playing ninjas?" Jon asked.

"Fuck if I know, mate. Just be happy they don't smell like old sushi and aren't built like sumo wrestlers," Angie replied.

They drove around the cemetery to the pond behind the gardener's house with the headlights out. Jon stopped the Suburban about twenty feet from the slope leading down to the water. He left the truck in neutral and jumped in the Defender next to Angie. Angie slowly maneuvered the Defender up behind the Suburban until the push bumper contacted the Suburban's rear bumper.

"Okay, good job, Angie. Now just ease it into the water," Jon said.

Angie began pushing the Suburban toward the bank and said, "No worries, mate."

"Easy, easy, Angie, not too fast," Jon said nervously.

"I got it, Jonny, I got it," Angie said. The Suburban rolled over the edge of the bank and nosed down for the water picking up speed and momentum.

"Okay, that's far enough. Stop! Stop, Angie!" Jon shouted as the front of the Suburban entered the water with the Defender still on its bumper.

"I can't stop, the bloody Suburban's pulling us in!" Angie shouted as all four of the Defender's wheels spun in reverse.

"Fuck, get ready to bail!" Jon yelled as he cracked his door open.

As the Defender's front wheels submerged, the slope under the Suburban changed and the bumpers came loose from one another. The Defender stopped and the Suburban quickly floated out into the pond. Angie slowly backed the Defender up the bank and onto level ground.

"Easy peasy, right, Jonny boy," Angie said, his greenish grin glowing under his goggles.

"Wait! Why isn't it sinking? It's just sitting there like a fucking lighthouse alerting everyone that passes by!" Jon was flummoxed. "I can't believe we have the only water-tight SUV Chevy ever built."

"You should have left a window open a little bit," Angie offered.

"The water's not even up to the fucking windows," Jon replied.

"Swim out there and poke a few holes in it," Angie recommended, knowing Jon was the only SEAL he ever met who didn't like the water.

"Dammit!" Jon said before giving up. He stripped all of his gear off except his pistol and walked down to the water. He was up to his chest wading out to the SUV when large bubbles began roiling up from underneath it on all four sides. The Suburban slowly disappeared under the surface. "Son of a bitch!" Jon said as he slapped the water before turning back for dry land.

***

"Did Jon just wade out into the water?" Gwenn asked over the sat phone.

"Yes, ma'am, and by his body language, I'd say he's madder than a wet hen right now," Angie replied with a laugh. "He's almost back. Radio silence."

"Well done, mate! Your mere presence was enough to force the vehicle to withdraw," Angie teased.

"Funny. I'm fucking soaked. Pop the rear hatch. I'm going to change into my last set of clean clothes," Jon said. He stripped down and gave extra attention to his inflamed areas with the tub of wet wipes.

CHAPTER 38

0230Z (0530 LOCAL)
FORWARD OPERATING BASE,
DONETSK AIRPORT, DONETSK, UKRAINE

The young captain knocked on the door to Sultanovich's room and said in Chechen, "Colonel, it's time to get up." There was no response. He knocked again, harder this time. "Colonel, it is time to wake up." Something hit the door from the inside with a loud thump. It was usually a boot.

"Come in!" Colonel Sultanovich yelled back in Chechen. He had a splitting headache from his vodka-induced hangover. Sultanovich enjoyed gathering his officers together in the evening after dinner to gamble, drink, and regale them with apocryphal stories of his extraordinary prowess as a warrior. The captain entered and flipped on the bright overhead lights as Sultanovich sat up on the edge of his bunk wearing his typical wife-beater shirt and stained boxers. He closed his eyes tight in an attempt to ward off the pain.

"I think you enjoy watching my discomfort," he said as he held out his hands palms up. The captain placed a cup of coffee in one and four aspirin in the other. Sultanovich pried one eye open for a millisecond to check what he was handed. He knew there were soldiers in his battalion who preferred him dead. "You know if your mother were not my cousin, I would have you shot for the pain you cause me every morning," Sultanovich said.

"Yes, sir, you tell me every morning," the captain replied.

"Report," the colonel said.

"Sir, the merchandise is all accounted for, and I doubled the guard last night as you ordered to keep the Russians from taking or damaging any of it. They are being fed as we speak. I contacted the broker. He assured me that his storage facility is ready to receive the merchandise and he has the amount you agreed upon in Euros ready for your arrival," the captain reported.

"Excellent. I want the merchandise to be clean and well-fed when I deliver them. I don't want the broker to have any complaints. He is always looking for reasons to lower the price. What was the total amount again?" Sultanovich asked as he stood and scratched his ass.

"€65,000,000, sir," the captain replied.

Sultanovich nodded his approval as he smoothed his long coarse beard with his left hand. "Excellent. Which wholesaler won the auction this time; sex, adoptions, or body snatchers?" Sultanovich asked. He really didn't care. It was all about the money. The infidels had a voracious appetite for his products. They were no better than dogs or pigs. His products weren't Muslim, so his conscience was clear.

"The body snatchers won this auction, sir," the captain replied.

"Very good, removing another ninety-two infidels from the world is a good start to the day," he replied, "I'm going to shower. I want my breakfast delivered to my quarters in fifteen minutes."

***

An hour later, Colonel Sultanovich stepped out of the latrine tent shaking his hands back and forth trying to dry them. Apparently, the Supply Officer couldn't requisition any paper towels. *The man had probably diverted enough rubles by now to build a mansion on the best beach in Sochi,* Sultanovich thought. He was certain the man had some sort of side hustle going on. All of the senior officers did. The cool moist morning air felt good on his face. He walked over to the small convoy of five vehicles. The captain was standing next to the first tour bus with a clipboard in his hand. He saluted as the colonel approached. Sultanovich returned the salute and said, "Report, Captain."

"Colonel, as you ordered the merchandise has been cleaned and fed. The security detail has also finished chow and is standing by," The captain said as he pointed to the thirty soldiers standing in formation next to the first green Ural 4320 6x6 truck. "Sir, I've been informed that there was an incident about three hours ago."

"What sort of incident?" Sultanovich asked. He did not like the word, incident. It could be something benign or something signaling a pending disaster.

"A junior sergeant on the guard detail was caught trying to rape one of the 12-year-old boys," the captain said.

"Was there any damage?" Sultanovich asked. He was so angry, he was shaking.

"The boy resisted and received a black eye," the captain replied as if he were talking about a dented bumper on a car dealership's Volkswagen.

"Where is this thief?" Sultanovich said as he spun around hoping to see him.

"He is in the sick call tent. He resisted arrest and required medical attention," the captain said.

"Come with me. I will show you how to deal with this sort of issue in the future," Sultanovich said as they walked to the tent. He threw open the door and zeroed in on the soldier sitting on an examination table with a bandage on his head. Two armed soldiers stood at the end of the table guarding him. Sultanovich walked past the wounded soldiers in the cots on both sides of the aisle and bent forward invading the soldier's personal space. "Do you deny attempting to rape the boy?" he bellowed demanding an answer. The soldier looked down and shook his head. "Do you deny striking him in the face when he tried to stop you?" spittle flew from his mouth. The soldier flinched as the spray landed on his face. Again, he looked at the floor and shook his head. He didn't dare look at the colonel or speak.

"Very well. You are obviously guilty of damaging my property. However, I am a merciful man. I will allow you to choose your punishment. I will put a hood on your head to protect your identity then lock it and your hands into the stocks. You will be stripped bare from the waist down to allow your fellow soldiers access to you until sunset today or I will have the captain shoot you in the head and leave your body in the forest for the animals. Which do you prefer?"

The man sobbed openly. He wanted to beg for another option but the thought of either of the first two punishments was so unpalatable he couldn't bring himself to speak. A third option would certainly be worse than the first two.

Sultanovich slapped him on the side of his head, rupturing his eardrum. The pain was overwhelming. "Speak man, I have other duties to attend to!" the colonel yelled in his good ear.

The soldier took three deep breaths and mumbled, "I'll take the stocks, sir."

Sultanovich shook his head in disgust and said, "Pity, a good Chechen soldier would have asked for the bullet. Guards take him to the stocks. Captain, after sunset, have him transferred out of my battalion. Walk with me and continue your report." They exited the tent and walked back to the convoy.

"Sir, the route to the storage facility in Grozny is 1,036 km. With refueling stops, it will take approximately sixteen hours. The route is the same as the last two trips," the captain read from the clipboard.

"Very well. Mount up," Sultanovich yelled to his men. The soldiers ran to their trucks and climbed aboard. The convoy rumbled to life. Sultanovich, his driver, and two-man security detail walked to his Mercedes AMG G 63 SUV. He had liberated it from a wealthy Ukrainian dentist after the doctor had failed to save one of his rotting molars. The dentist wouldn't need a vehicle ever again. Sultanovich didn't much care for the Emerald Green Metallic paint. He would have preferred the Obsidian Black Metallic himself. Before this Special Military Operation in Ukraine, he would have never been able to raise enough goats to buy even a used G-Wagen. After the war, he would buy a new G-Wagen in all of his favorite colors. They rolled out of the main gate of the FOB and were soon speeding away from Donetsk on Highway H-21. Sultanovich reclined his seat and said to his driver, "Wake me if anything interesting happens." He lowered the brim of his cap to cover his eyes. In moments he was snoring.

***

"Angie, get in the fast lane and slowly cruise up alongside the convoy. I want to try to pass Kimmie a message," Jon said as they followed the last Ural truck from a safe distance as they traveled east on the H-21. Jon pulled the cardboard top off a case of commercial MREs and wrote his message with a black marker.

Angie accelerated in the fast lane and slowly passed the last truck and continued ahead to the tour bus. "I don't see her. Do you?" Angie asked as he sped up slightly.

"No, go to the next bus," Jon said as he held the cardboard sign face down in his lap.

Angie sped up again.

"There she is. The fourth row behind the driver," Jon said unsuccessfully trying to hide his excitement. He flipped the sign over in his lap and angled it to give Kimmie a good view. He looked up and saw Kimmie had her head down and her eyes closed. She was praying. "Come on, Kimmie, look over here for a second. God, make her look," Jon said. On cue, she looked outside and saw Jon in the SUV. He was smiling at her with a Tootsie Pop in his mouth. He showed her the sign. "I know you're praying. God sent us to help you. Hang on! Our friends are coming!"

***

She nodded her head with tears in her eyes. She had been praying constantly since before Father Del Toro was murdered except for the few hours last night when she passed out from exhaustion. She had hope again as she watched the SUV continue past the bus and G-Wagen before accelerating out of sight.

***

Jon dialed Whitey's sat phone. "Whitey, this is Jon. The convoy with the kids left the FOB about twenty minutes ago. They're heading east on Highway H-21. How far out are you guys?"

"Assuming everything goes as planned in Chisinau, we should get to Donetsk around 0900Z. I guess that's noon your time. How fast is the convoy moving away from us?" Whitey said.

"It's pretty congested right now, maybe fifty miles per hour. It should pick up to around sixty as we get out into the countryside. We'll see if we can find a way to slow them down. I'd rather not let them get across the border into Russia," Jon replied.

"How about the weather? We almost got knocked out of the air by a German thunderstorm a little while ago," Whitey said.

"It's clear skies here in every direction," Jon replied.

CHAPTER 39

Jon had his head down looking at the moving map on his ATAK-equipped Samsung smartphone. He was looking for a good spot to cause a traffic jam on Highway H-21. They were five miles east of Chystiakove in a rural area covered in farmland when Jon said, "Angie, take the next right turn. Okay, now drive down to the end of this gravel road and take another right onto the dirt road. See the copse of trees on the left? Pull us up into the trees. This should give you a clear 250-meter shot to the highway."

Angie parked under the trees, and they went to the cargo hatch. "Do you want me to use the Barrett or the AR-10?" Angie asked.

"Use the AR-10. It has a suppressor. The Barrett is too loud and would kick up a big dust cloud. The convoy security would zero in on us in a heartbeat," Jon replied.

"Where's my target?" he asked.

"Remember the Russian Army convoy we passed with the BMPs loaded on trailers? See if you can cause one of them to jackknife. I want you to take out the right front tire on the truck. If it doesn't lose control right away, go for the right rear trailer tires," Jon said.

Angie pulled out a black Pelican case and retrieved the rifle with a Nightforce scope. He could hit moving targets out to 800 yards. He loaded a twenty-round magazine with armor-piercing ammo and chambered a round. He went prone behind a tree five meters back from the edge of the copse facing the highway so no one would see his muzzle flash and extended the bipod.

Jon glassed the highway with his binoculars. "I see the convoy. It's about two miles out. There's a gun truck at the front of the convoy. They have soldiers scanning the countryside with binoculars. If they see us, disregard the attack and haul ass back to the Land Rover. We'll run away bravely," Jon said.

A minute later, Angie said, "Okay, I see them." They were moving at a brisk 95 kilometers per hour. Angie waited for them to close the distance and then squeezed the trigger. The round flew through the side wall of the right front tire, disintegrating it immediately. The truck swerved right but stayed on the pavement. Angie had already moved his crosshairs to the rear tire and released another round. The tire ripped to shreds and the bare wheel dug into the pavement causing the truck to be pulled further right until the left front tire left the pavement before it flipped onto its left side and slid into the ditch. The trailer also tilted left, lifting the right wheel off the pavement, causing the trailer to swing across the opposing lanes of traffic before it rolled over on its side, dumping the BMPs upside down in the far ditch. The first BMP smoked for a few seconds before the ammunition it was carrying inside lit off causing a loud explosion and a bright orange and black fireball. The flaming BMP flew fifteen feet into the air before falling back to earth. Angie and Jon felt a satisfying shockwave. Immediately the gun truck stopped and two Dushka heavy machine guns began raking all of the wooded areas on the right side of the highway in an effort to suppress the enemy attack. The massive 12.7x108mm rounds snapped large limbs and small trees in half, raining the foliage down on Jon and Angie.

"Good shooting, Angie. Time to GTFO," Jon said as he hunched over and ran back to the Land Rover.

Angie ran close behind. He quickly closed the rifle back up in its case and ran to the driver's door. "Where to, Kemosabe?" he asked.

"Uh, back the way we came and then down the highway," Jon replied. After they were safely out of the area Jon looked at Angie quizzically and asked, "Where did you learn Kemosabe?"

"YouTube," Angie replied.

"Well, if I'm Kemosabe you know that makes you Tonto," Jon said.

"Oh, no. I don't think so," Angie said.

"Yep, you're Tonto. My faithful companion!" Jon said as he laughed.

"Fuck you. One lame callsign's enough, mate. If I'm Tonto, I'll turn this fuckin' bus around right now," Angie replied.

"Okay, okay. You're not Tonto!" Jon said as he continued to laugh. "Let's find a place to pull over somewhere to wait for the kids. I'll call Gwenn." He dialed the number.

"Hello, Jon," Gwenn replied from Edinburgh.

"Hi, Gwenn. Are you still tracking the convoy," Jon asked.

"Yes, they just came to a stop about a half mile behind the mayhem you caused with the BMPs. With all of the military convoys stacking up, the line will be a couple of miles long in a few minutes," Gwenn said.

CHAPTER 40

0600Z (0200 LOCAL)
OFFICE OF THE WHITE HOUSE
CHIEF OF STAFF

Following his usual pattern, National Security Advisor Preston Alexander grabbed the doorknob to barge into Chief of Staff Howard Lamb's office, but the door was locked. "Harold, let me in! We have a problem!" Alexander said urgently as he pounded on the door.

"Go away, Pres!" Lamb shouted from behind the door. This was the third night in a row he had to sleep in his office. He was tempted to move into the Lincoln bedroom if this kept up.

"We need to talk! Let me in!" Alexander continued banging. He heard the door unlock. He rushed into the dark room in time to see Lamb drop back onto the sofa. Alexander flipped on the overhead lights.

"Dammit, Pres!" Lamb yelled as he pulled his Harvard blanket over his head. "What now?"

"The Monk crew evaded capture all the way through Poland, Ukraine, and Romania. Now they're about thirty minutes from Chisinau. It looks like they'll land at Chisinau International. CDR Smith worked with a Moldovan intel officer during his Navy days, a guy named Maximilian Cojocari. He has a side hustle selling guns and equipment to friendly causes. The Monk crew will probably go to him to be supplied before heading into Ukraine," Alexander explained.

"I'm tired of this bullshit. I have a country to run," Lamb said as he sat up on the couch. He rubbed his eyes, then took a deep breath and exhaled. He walked over to his desk and sat down before retrieving a card from his middle drawer. He dialed the number on his secure telephone.

"Hello," a man answered.

"Hey, Matt, this is Harold Lamb. How are you liking your new assignment in Moldova? It must be better than the last shithole they exiled you to," Lamb said. Harold knew Matt from his years working for the State Department.

"Good morning, Harold. Yes, it's a step up. It's not a shithole, but I can smell it from here. Considering it's 2:00 AM in DC, you must be calling for something important," the Agency chief of station replied.

"I'll get right to it. In about twenty-five minutes a civilian CH-53 helicopter will land at Chisinau International. The people on the chopper will buy a load of illegal weapons and equipment from a Moldovan intelligence officer named, hold on. Pres, what's the guy's name? Yeah, Maximilian Cojocari. He supplements his Army salary as a gun runner on the black market. After they get the guns, they'll fly them into Russian-controlled Ukraine. We need you to send someone to the airport to stop the helicopter from taking off," Lamb explained.

"I see. Do you want lethal or less than?" Matt asked.

"Geez, Matt, less than lethal. We don't want to kill anybody. Well…you know, maybe, only if it's absolutely necessary," Lamb quibbled.

"Did you clear it with the ambassador?" Matt asked.

"Matt, the ambassador doesn't need to hear about this. This comes straight from POTUS. Do this for the old man and you'll be back in Virginia in no time," Lamb said.

"Understood. I may have a man in position to help us. I'll get back to you afterward," he said before disconnecting the call.

***

The station chief pulled a pay-as-you-go burner phone from a Faraday bag in the bottom drawer of his desk. He opened the Signal app and sent a secure message:

I have a job for you. A civilian helicopter will land at the transient ramp at Chisinau Intl in about twenty minutes to conduct an arms deal. You need to stop the helicopter from leaving the airport. Lethal force is authorized only if absolutely necessary. $250,000 upon completion.

The reply came immediately:

What makes you think I'm in a position to stop it?

The chief:

You arrived in Chisinau three days ago on a private contract which you completed yesterday. Now you are in the airport terminal waiting for the Moldovan government to lift the temporary no-fly order.

The contractor:

What about my shoot-on-sight order?

The chief:

It's still in effect. Maybe I can help you with that when I get back to Langley.

The contractor:

If you try to fuck me, you'll never see me coming before I slit your throat.

The chief:

No tricks, scouts honor.

The contractor:

You were never a fucking boy scout.

CHAPTER 41

Chirp keyed his ICS and said, "Landing checklist." After their near-death experience in Germany, the team had flown four hours straight through Poland, Ukraine, Romania, and Moldova without incident. The airspace in Moldova had been closed by the government to all traffic except the military due to the Russian aggression occurring in nearby Ukraine. Jon contacted his friend, Major Maximilian "Cujo" Cojocari, and asked for his help. Cojocari had arranged a Moldovan Army callsign for them and a military transponder code, but they were directed to maintain radio silence and land on the westernmost edge of the ramp at Chisinau International Airport near a fuel truck and several green army trucks. The transponder code would keep the air defense artillery from launching an attack on them.

"Speed control levers 100%, landing gear down and locked, parking brake off, seat belts fastened, crew set in back, anti-ice off," Whitey replied as he held his thumb up in front of the instrument console where Chirp could see it.

Chirp slowed to 40 knots and performed a roll-on landing at the approach end of runway 08. He made an immediate left turn onto the taxiway leading to the ramp. "Everyone stay belted in. If anything looks wrong, I'll pull pitch and take off straight ahead," Chirp said.

"Chirp, the ramp is empty except for the four men standing behind the cargo truck," Taco replied.

Chirp came to a stop sixty feet from the men facing the trucks. "Set the parking brake, Whitey," he called out. Whitey did as requested. "I wonder why one of the trucks has a Ma Deuce mounted in the bed. I hope they're not expecting trouble." Chirp said. "Taco wave the refueling guy in to start the hot refuel."

"Roger that," Taco replied as he left the cargo compartment.

"Okay, I'll stay on the controls. Go make your deal," Chirp said. Whitey unstrapped and climbed out of the cockpit between the seats and out of the crew door on the right. Chris followed close behind.

"Good morning, General. You can call me Cujo," Major Cojocari said as he saluted and then proffered his hand.

"Good to meet you, Cujo. Call me Whitey. I'm afraid we don't have time for pleasantries. Do you have the equipment we requested?" Whitey asked as he shook the little man's hand.

"Yes, sir, but your reputation precedes you. I would be too embarrassed to call you anything but General. My good friend, Jon, told me what you need and why you are here. You are on a noble quest. We have everything you need in the trucks. Come with me," Cujo replied. He led them over to the truck and gave orders in Romanian to his men. Two of them climbed into the back of the truck and open the cases for Whitey to see. They showed him three Browning M-2 .50 caliber machine guns in like new condition and thirty 100-round boxes of armor-piercing and incendiary-tracer. Every fifth round was a tracer.

"Please, take a look, Chris," Whitey said.

"Aye, aye, sir," Chris climbed into the truck with the men. He quickly examined the guns that he had years of experience operating while flying with HMLA-369. "They're good, sir. Clean, lubed, and ready to go," he said.

"What about the personal gear?" Whitey asked Cujo.

"Show them," Cujo told his men. They opened the other crates for Chris's inspection.

Chris rummaged around for a few minutes and said, "M-4s with ten thirty-round mags, Glock 17s with four 17-round mags, M-9 bayonets, MICH helmets, AN/PRC-154A Rifleman team radios, IFAKs, plates and plate carriers, M-Pact tactical gloves, and clear lensed Oakley military eye protection. Everything is copacetic, sir."

***

The contractor, dressed in the unconscious refueling truck driver's military coveralls, was dragging the hose toward the helicopter when Taco intercepted him. "Hey, man, let me take the hose. I'll hook everything up and signal you went to start pumping," he yelled over the roar of the engines and rotor blades turning at 100%. The man nodded like he understood. Taco connected the grounding wire to a pad eye in the ramp, then connected the hose nozzle to the pressure refueling port. Taco signaled the refueler and he flipped on the pump.

The contractor looked past the nose of the helicopter and saw Whitey walking toward the Moldovan Major. He recognized him immediately as retired General Brian McKinley, USMC. *Son of a bitch! There's no way he's a fucking gunrunner! Matt set me up!* he thought. He walked around to the other side of the truck to call his old boss. It rang ten times before it was answered.

"Authenticate," Matt said.

"You set me up, motherfucker! You have ten seconds to come clean or the next time you hear from me you won't hear from me because you'll be fucking dead!" the contractor shouted over the roaring helicopter thirty yards away. He paced back and forth behind the truck as he scanned the area around him. He didn't want to stand in one place for more than a second.

"I don't know what you mean! What happened?" the chief asked. He was clearly shaken.

"Former Commandant of the Marine Corps, General Brian "fucking" McKinley flew in on the helicopter! Hell, he's one of the pilots! I'm pretty sure he's not running guns!" the contractor yelled.

"You weren't set up, I was! Get out of there! Once you're clear let me know. I'll make this up to you somehow!" the chief replied before he hung up.

The contractor put the phone back in his pocket and walked back around the truck to the pump controls.

***

"Cujo, how in the hell did you get a hold of those Rifleman radios? They're not available for foreign sale," Whitey asked.

"The same place I bought the rest of this equipment. I got it from the Taliban in an online auction. After America left Afghanistan all sorts of goodies became available through trusted online brokers. If you give me two weeks' notice and $3,000,000, I can get you a slightly used Black Hawk helicopter."

"Okay, Cujo, how much for all of this gear and a full bag of gas?" Whitey asked.

"As I said, Jon told me about your mission. I have no desire to profit off the misery of helpless children and nuns, but I am not a rich man and I have to pay for the equipment and my men's time. I need $250,000 to cover my expenses. Can you cover that?" Cujo asked.

"Yes, we can. Chris, please get the money," Whitey said.

"Oh, General, I also have some gifts for the children," Cujo said as he turned to his men in the truck and pointed at several cardboard boxes. The men slid the boxes to the edge of the truck bed and opened them. "The smaller boxes have candy and teddy bears. The larger boxes have 100 children's skateboarding helmets," Cujo said. "I am not a perfect man, General, but I cannot tolerate anyone who would abuse a child. I hope you treat these savages harshly when you find them."

"I can guarantee that much," Whitey replied as he shook Cujo's hand.

Five minutes later, the pressure refueling was almost completed when four military trucks drove around the side of the nearest hangar and accelerated toward the helicopter. The weapons and personal equipment were being brought on board the helicopter.

Chirp and Whitey were sitting in the cockpit monitoring the gauges. "That doesn't look good," Chirp said to Whitey. He keyed the ICS and said to everyone in the back, "Get ready. Four trucks are hauling ass our way. We may have to shoot our way out of here."

Cujo was standing in front of the helicopter next to his truck watching the refueling when he noticed Whitey waving at him from the cockpit and pointing behind him. He turned and saw the trucks approaching. He took several steps toward the trucks and waited with his arms crossed. The trucks formed a semi-circle on the right side of the helicopter and forty soldiers poured out of them. They formed a line in front of the trucks with their rifles at low ready and awaited further orders. Their officer, a tall, thin lieutenant, stepped forward, stopped in front of Cujo, looked down, and saluted. Cujo returned the salute and began a very animated discussion with the young officer. The lieutenant pointed past Cujo's head at the helicopter and said something that Cujo clearly did not appreciate. He stepped forward and began dressing down the young officer in front of his men. Some of them were laughing.

Alice climbed the step to the cockpit and sat on the fold-down seat between the pilots. She looked out through the windshield and said, "What's going on out there?"

"Looks like Cujo's chewing some ass," Whitey stated the obvious.

"I hope he has enough juice to get rid of these guys," Chirp replied.

Alice said, "I'll try to translate. The kid is saying he apologizes for interrupting the major's business but someone in the terminal reported suspicious activity on the ramp. Cujo says you're fucking up my classified operation just by being here. I should jam my boot so far up your ass you taste the polish. The lieutenant's smiling. He says will you forgive me if I agree to take your snaggle-toothed hag of a cousin on a date. Cujo smiles and says she's not a hag, but she could use a trip to the dentist. The soldiers are all laughing again. Now round up your men and redeploy them at the perimeter fence to keep others away from my operation. The kid says yes sir. Cujo says to tell your mother I'll be home in time for dinner." They watched as the lieutenant saluted and gestured for his men to get back in the trucks. Cujo lightly kicked the kid's backside as he walked away.

Cujo turned toward the helicopter with a smile on his face. He climbed the stairs to the crew door and stuck his head in the cockpit next to Alice's. "It is no problem. He is my son. I told him to go to the perimeter fence gate and keep others away from us. The refueling is complete. Good hunting and Godspeed," Cujo said as he offered his hand again to Whitey and Chirp. Then he looked Alice up and down. She was a head taller than him. He shook his head, and said, "Magnificent!" before leaving the helicopter.

The contractor shut down the pump and walked over to Taco to get the hose. As he reached for it his left foot was swatted out from under him. He fell to the concrete on his side. He tried to get up, but intense pain shot up his leg. He looked down to see blood flowing from his mangled boot. Another bullet skipped across the pavement next to him. No one heard the shots, but they saw the contractor go down and the second bullet chip the concrete.

"Sniper! A sniper shot the refueler! Let's get out of here!" Taco shouted into the ICS as he ran for the door.

Cujo and his men took cover behind the cargo trucks. Unfortunately, no one was manning the fifty cal. in the gun truck. The contractor hopped and crawled until he got to cover behind the bed of the gun truck. Another round thumped into the side of the truck bed.

***

"Get in! Hurry, Taco!" Chirp yelled as he looked up to confirm the power control levers were set to the Fly position. He skipped the pre-takeoff and takeoff checklists.

Whitey keyed his ICS, "Are crew and passengers secured?"

"Waiting for Chris, sir," Taco replied.

Whitey continued, "Pull chocks, Chris, and get in!"

Chris grabbed the rope connecting the two wooden chocks around the right main mount and pulled them loose, before tossing them inside the cabin and hustling up the steps attached to the inside of the lower half of the crew door. He pulled the crew door up and locked it in position before swiveling his machine gun mount into position above the door and pinning it in place with the large barrel sticking outside. "Chocks removed and the crew door is secure. All set in back, sir."

"Roger that. We're maxed out on fuel again, so I'll be making a rolling takeoff to the east. Coming right," Chirp said quickly as he pulled pitch on the collective and pushed the cyclic forward a couple of inches to get the helicopter moving forward. After it rolled a few feet he pushed the right anti-torque pedal forward and tilted the pedal with his toes to activate the right brake to begin the right turn on the ramp.

"Chris leaned out of his window with his hands on the M2 machine gun's butterfly trigger while looking for a target and said, "Clear right," over the ICS.

"Tail cleared left," Taco called.

"Roger," Chirp said as he straightened out and began to accelerate forward.

Whitey moved his right hand up to hold the speed control levers fully forward. He would keep it there until after the helicopter had safely climbed away from the ramp. Chirp smoothly pulled up on the collective to accelerate across the empty ramp. Whitey began calling out their airspeed, "10, 15, 20, 25, 30." At 30 knots Chirp lifted the front wheels off the concrete. When the rear wheels were ten feet off the ground he rotated the nose down 5° and climbed away as he accelerated in a max performance takeoff. After reaching 100 feet AGL he leveled off and called out, "Landing gear up." He would continue accelerating until reaching 170 knots.

Whitey grabbed the circular knob and raised it. He watched the landing gear status lights until they turned green before activating his floor ICS switch with his boot, "Three up and locked." He pointed at the lights on the center console and gave Chirp a thumbs-up.

"Cujo's men are blasting the shit out of someone in the control tower with their Ma Deuce. A guy just crawled out of the backdoor and jumped off the walkway! Jesus, that's gotta be at least sixty feet!" Kevin shouted over the ICS from his gun position on the ramp.

"We'll be crossing the border into Russian-controlled Ukraine in about fifteen minutes. I'll drop us down a little to stay between fifty to 100 feet AGL to keep us under the MANPAD threat. I'll also be making small heading changes every fifteen to thirty seconds to avoid groundfire. When we get close to the border, we'll test-fire the guns. Be careful not to destroy some poor farmer's property," Chirp said, "Whitey, keep giving me fuel checks every thirty minutes."

"Roger that," he replied.

CHAPTER 42

After the Chechen convoy found a way around the BMP ambush, they continued unabated to the Russian border near the small town, of Kh Chernikov. Jon and Angie followed them from a distance. They watched as the Russian border guards waved the convoy through without any inspections. A few minutes later Angie drove up to the Guard's booth and presented his and Jon's bogus SVR-RF credentials.

The young man looked down at the ID cards and badges then nodded his approval. "What is wrong with him?" the guard asked.

Angie looked at Jon then back to the guard. Jon was snoring as his head rested in the gap between the headrest and passenger window. Angie chuckled and said in Russian, "Too much vodka last night. He can't hold his liquor."

The guard laughed. "We have been told to look for a Black Suburban SUV. One was seen in the area of a SU-25 that was shot down and in Donetsk where two SVR officers and two Chechen soldiers were found dead in a bar," said the guard in Russian.

Angie nodded and said, "We heard about the barfight, but I thought they were keeping it a secret for now. It will look bad when the news reports the SVR and Chechens are killing each other. I heard one of the SVR men had his eye gouged out. It was just dangling out there on his cheek. Those Chechen dogs are disgusting."

The guard shook his head like he was trying to shake the image loose from his brain. "Yes, they are. One of their convoys just went through."

"Oh, what were they stealing this time?" Angie asked.

"Their colonel said they were transferring orphans from the warzone to be adopted by good Russian families," the guard said.

"Do you believe him?" Angie asked.

"No, sir. I think they will be sold to someone, but certainly not to good families," he replied.

"Why don't you stop them?" Angie asked already knowing the answer.

"We have orders to leave them alone. As long as they support President Pichugin's war they may do as they please. Our world is upside down now. Good is bad, bad is good," the guard replied as he handed back the credentials.

"Maybe we can do something about that," Angie said before driving away.

CHAPTER 43

09002 (1200 LOCAL)
AMBUSH SITE BETWEEN
KH KRINITSA AND FASTOVETSKAYA, RUSSIA

"Is this a causeway or a bridge?" Jon asked as he divided his attention between the digital image on his ATAK smartphone attached to his chest plate and the world around him.

"There may be drainage pipes under the water but it's definitely not a bridge. It doesn't matter, the soldiers who try to run will still wind up in the water, face down," Angie replied. 200 yards later he turned off the pavement and down the shallow incline leading to the tree line on the southwest side of the highway. Traffic was sparse here. Most of the military traffic at the border had continued east toward Volgograd or north toward Moscow. He backed into the trees so he could see the convoy when it drove across the causeway.

"I guess there's only one thing to decide before the helicopter and convoy get here," Jon said as he held up the black nun's habit they had brought along from the church.

"Don't look at me, mate! This is your party!" Angie said, serious as a heart attack.

"Angie, we need the element of surprise to keep any of the kids from getting hurt. I have a beard, you don't. I'm 6'3', you're what? 5'7"?" Jon asked.

"5'9", thank you, very much," Angie replied.

Jon's tone was dubious as he said, "Yeah, okay, 5'9". Either way, if I'm standing in the middle of the road wearing this, they're going to see a tall dude with a white beard wearing combat boots. This thing will fit you even while you're wearing your plate carrier. You can even hide your grenade launcher under it. This is no different from us wearing burkas in Afghanistan."

Angie thought for a moment. He remembered several times burkas allowed him and his team to slip right through checkpoints unnoticed on their way to targets. "Fucking logic! Give it to me!" Angie snapped, before snatching the habit out of Jon's hand. "If I see so much as a smirk out of you, you can forget this charade."

Jon fought mightily to keep from laughing again and managed a nod before looking away out his window.

"What was that?" Angie asked as he pushed on the back of Jon's left shoulder. "Did you say something, mate?" Angie asked before pushing Jon's shoulder again while looking at the back of his head.

Jon kept looking out of his window and shook his head.

"No? I didn't think so," Angie said. Now he was smiling.

"I better call Whitey and give him the plan," Jon said as he dialed his sat phone.

"Go for Whitey," he said.

"Hey, Whitey. We found an ambush site just south of the causeway on the A270 Highway between Kh Krinitsa and Fastovetskaya. Gwenn is tracking us. She'll send you the coordinates. It's a secluded stretch of road. No houses for miles. There's a strip of trees about 200 feet wide lining both sides of the highway. We need you to land the helicopter behind the trees in a farmer's field. We'll put out a VS17 signal panel to mark the spot. We need Alice to be in the middle of the line to be in a position to take out both bus drivers. We have a scoped AR-10 rifle for her. Angie and I will take out the lead SUV and the troop truck behind it. I need the rest of your ground element to take care of the last troop truck. The gunners on the helicopter should handle any squirters. After we send the all-clear the helicopter should land in front of our Land Rover with the ramp facing us so we can just run aboard and take off. How far out are you?"

"Standby, I'm receiving your coordinates now," Whitey said as he entered them into the GPS. "Looks like fifteen minutes. Gwenn texted the Chechens will be there in twenty minutes, so we only have a five-minute window to get ready. Get your shit wired. We'll fly overhead to check the LZ and then land on the marker panel. See ya soon," he said before disconnecting.

"Okay, the helicopter is fifteen minutes out. That's five minutes before the convoy. Get dressed and I'll go stage the AR-10 for Alice and stake out the VS17," Jon said. While Jon was unpacking the rifle, he watched Angie pull the habit on over his plate carrier and then put the veil on his head. He looked like he would have rather taken a beating than wear the outfit. Jon threw him a bone. "Thanks for doing this, Angie. I swear none of the guys will ever hear about this from me." Jon jogged off into the trees with the rifle and VS17. He staked out the panel on the edge of the plowed field next to the tree line. He laid the rifle and four twenty-round magazines down on the panel and ran back to the Land Rover. Angie was sitting behind the steering wheel hating life.

"Are you okay, man?" Jon asked.

"I will be when they get here so I can blow shit up," Angie replied as he donned his Ray-Ban Wayfarer sunglasses.

Jon looked down to check his watch as a massive shadow raced across the ground and an ear-splitting roar came from above. He looked up in time to see the CH-53 race overhead at an un-heard-of speed for a helicopter before it banked into a sharp 45° angle of bank turn and decelerated much like he had seen them do at Navy and Marine Corps airfields except they were normally at 700' to 1,000' AGL. This time Chirp was down on the deck barely clearing the treetops with his rotor blades. The helicopter disappeared behind the trees, and they saw a brown dust cloud rise above the trees. "I'll go put the ground element in position. Be ready for the convoy."

"Oh, believe me, mate, I'm ready," Angie replied as he dropped the transmission into drive while he held the brake pedal down.

Jon ran off to meet the team. He found them advancing halfway through the trees. He was about to greet them when he saw his fiancée, Sarah Tuttle. He did a double take and shouted, "Sarah, what are you doing here!"

"Excuse me! I guess I was supposed to sit at home knitting you a sweater while you're over here taking on the Chechen Special Forces by yourself. You're welcome, asshole!" she replied.

"Baby, I'm glad you want to help me but how am I supposed to operate if I'm worrying about protecting you?" he asked, digging his hole deeper.

Mike turned to Alice and said, "See."

"Shut up, dumbass," Alice replied.

Sarah replied to Jon, "Well you better figure it out fast, Captain Caveman because that convoy will be here in about three minutes."

"Well…well…fuck!" was all Jon could think of saying before he went back to business. "Everyone, follow me," he said before running through the brush to the highway. He stopped short of the edge of the trees. He pointed to the right down the highway. "Angie and the Land Rover are about two hundred feet that way in the trees. When the convoy gets close, he's going to pull out and block the road. When Angie starts shooting, you start shooting. The last vehicle in the convoy is a truck with about ten soldiers. Mike, Eric, and uh, Sarah, you'll need to neutralize that threat."

"To be clear, what does neutralize mean?" Eric asked.

"I mean you kill every human being in that truck as fast as possible before they can hurt any of the kids or us. Don't hesitate for a second. These assholes sealed their fate when they signed on to kill priests and steal children. Understood?"

"Roger that," Eric replied.

"Then move to the buses and help get the kids to the helicopter. Okay, Alice let's go," Jon said. He and Alice ran another one hundred feet closer to the Land Rover. "We're relying on you to take out both bus drivers."

"No problem. I really don't need a scope for this," she replied.

"Okay, good hunting," Jon said before rushing back to Angie. Alice went down the embankment to take cover in the trees.

Jon had just returned to Angie's driver's door when his sat phone rang, "Hello, Gwenn."

"Get ready, Jon. The convoy is about two miles away," Gwenn said.

"Are any other vehicles between us and the convoy?" Jon asked.

"No and the road's clear for about two miles behind it," she said before hanging up.

"Okay, Angie get out there," Jon said as he ran about fifty feet back down the road and hid behind a tree.

Angie drove out of the trees and up onto the highway blocking both lanes of the southeast bound lanes of the highway. He climbed out of the truck and stood waiting. The convoy came into view as it drove across the causeway. Despite the habit, he felt naked standing in the middle of the highway with five vehicles and over twenty soldiers barreling down on him. As the G-Wagen approached, Angie took several steps forward and held up his left hand.

CHAPTER 44

The colonel woke up as the G-Wagen slowed to a stop. Sultanovich sat up in his seat and raised the bill of his cap. "What is that stupid cow doing in the road?" he asked. Then his eyes went wide as he saw the nun produce a rifle with a grenade launcher from the folds of her habit and point it at him. "Drive!" he yelled in terror as the first grenade left the tube. The HEDP round crashed through the windshield and detonated inside the driver blowing out the windows. Shrapnel sprayed the left side of Sultanovich's head and body as a fireball engulfed the cabin. He opened his door and fell out onto the pavement with his long gray beard burning bright red and orange. He screamed in agony as he frantically tried to put out the flames with his hands.

***

As soon as Jon saw Angie raise the grenade launcher, he brought his SAW to his shoulder and raked the troop truck with continuous eight-round bursts of tracer and armor-piercing ammunition. The red tracers made killing easy as they allowed Jon to quickly zero in on his prey from less than one hundred feet away. He burned through his first two-hundred-round box in seconds as soldiers spilled out of the truck bed and scattered as they tried to get away from the deadly red hose. Some, though grievously wounded, re-turned fire haphazardly toward the trees without any clear targets. Jon swapped the empty box magazine for a fresh one and rushed up the embankment toward the highway. He saw a soldier running away, headed for the river. Jon shot him in the back then turned his attention to those trying to crawl under the truck to hide. He methodically finished each one with headshots. Two soldiers on the far side of the truck got up and ran for the river but Angie saw them and expertly launched a grenade out 100 meters that killed them instantly. Finding no more soldiers, Jon turned his attention to Sultanovich. He was trying to crawl away into the brush with his remaining good right arm and leg. Jon let his SAW dangle by its sling as he bent down to roll Sultanovich over. "Hey, asshole! Can you hear me? Katya sent me! I promised her you would never hurt another beautiful little girl!" Sultanovich drew his pistol with surprising speed with his right hand but failed to get off a shot before Jon grabbed it and threw it away. *Thanks, for attempting to fight back,* he thought. That was all of the time he had to waste on this human excrement. Jon went to one knee, pulled his knife from its sheath, and drove it down at an angle into Sultanovich's neck before wrenching it back and forth to open up the wound channel. Hot blood gushed out around his blade soaking his gloved hand. Sultanovich lost consciousness in a few seconds. Jon saw his cell phone sticking out of the top of his breast pocket. He grabbed it and stuffed it in his cargo pocket.

***

Alice was standing behind a tree when Angie initiated the ambush. She decided to engage the second bus driver first hoping it would keep the first bus driver from trying to escape. The driver was sitting behind the steering wheel constantly scanning the area he could see from his seat. Alice moved to another tree to improve the angle of her shot to avoid accidentally hurting one of the children with a through-and-through shot. She took aim and shot the driver center mass. She hoped he would look like he was sleeping when the children walked by him. As soon as his chin hit his chest the bus started slowly rolling forward. She heard the children screaming over the gunshots and explosions. The bus rolled twenty feet into the first bus and stopped.

Alice ran back to her original tree and saw the first bus driver was out of his seat, hiding behind two teenage girls. He opened the door and pushed them forward to the bottom step and stepped down behind them. He was hunched over trying to keep his head behind theirs. His head darted back and forth as if he was looking for an escape route. Alice couldn't get a clear shot. The driver produced a pistol and held it to one of the girls' heads. She wondered what her Great-Great-Grandpa would do and then it came to her. She yelled, "Gobble, gobble, gobble," at the top of her lungs. The driver got a confused look on his face and popped his head up above the girls to see where the sound came from. Alice smiled as she sent a 168 grain 7.62x51mm FMJ round crashing through the bridge of his nose stopping all of his motor functions as though his internal switch had been flipped off. He crumpled in a heap on the steps.

The two girls ran screaming toward the trees. Alice stepped out in the open and yelled to the girls in English, "Girls, come to me!" as the sound of automatic weapons and grenades reverberated around her. They saw the tall red-headed Viking princess and ran to her screaming. "Do you speak English?" she asked. They both nodded as they continued to cry. "Do you see that helicopter?" Alice pointed to the sky. They nodded again. "That's my helicopter. Sister Joan asked my friends and me to come to get you. When the helicopter lands in front of that big SUV, I need you to help me get the other children inside it so we can fly away from here to safety. Do you understand?" they nodded again. "Good, come with me." She led them back to the bus. Alice slung her rifle and grabbed the driver by his boots. As she dragged him down the stairs, the back of his head made a satisfying crunching sound as it hit each step. Alice dragged him to the shoulder of the road and then rolled him down the embankment and out of sight.

Sister Joan arrived at her side and said, "Where is Uncle Jon?"

Alice pointed past the troop truck to the G-Wagen just in time for Sister Joan to see Jon thrust his knife viciously into the colonel's neck. The sight shocked and pleased her at the same time. She might have to mention it during her next confession.

"Sister, I need your help. The helicopter will land behind Jon's SUV in a minute. When it does you must have all of the children in the first bus hurry to the rear ramp and go as far inside the helicopter as they can, so we'll have room for the kids in the second bus. Do you understand?" Kimmie nodded. "Okay keep your kids in the bus until the helicopter lands. Do you know how to use this?" Alice asked as she offered her Glock pistol to her. Sister Joan smiled as she took the pistol, performed a press check, and ran back to her bus. For the first time since Father Del Toro was murdered, she felt good about her chances to save the children.

***

Mike's ground element was hiding in the trees just to the rear of the trailing troop truck. They were lying prone behind trees about five meters apart. When Angie initiated the ambush, Mike yelled, "Pour it on!" as Sarah, Eric, and he began firing at the truck simultaneously. The cargo area was covered by green canvas so all they could do was spray the cover and hope for the best. Soldiers began spilling out of the back of the bed. Instead of the expected ten soldiers, this truck carried around twenty. Five of the soldiers followed their training and rushed toward the ambushers to get out of the kill zone. Five more ran to the other side of the road and took cover behind the embankment. The remaining ten lay dead or dying in the truck bed or on the pavement. "Guess who, Motherfucker!" Mike shouted at the five Chechen soldiers as they charged down the embankment at them. They were mowed down easily by the three defenders.

Mike got on his team radio to call Jon for support, "Jon this is Mike, the last truck has at least twenty soldiers. Half of them are still fighting. Some took cover on the other side of the highway. We need help before they start maneuvering on us."

Jon's electronic voice responded immediately, "Understood. Hang on. We're going to envelop them."

Something rolled down the embankment and exploded causing Mike to flinch. "What was that?" Mike yelled with his ears ringing.

"Grenade!" Sarah yelled back as she loaded a fresh magazine.

"Mike, I'm going to move up to the top of the embankment," Eric called over the team radio from the far end of the line.

"Roger that. We'll cover you until you're in position and then we'll move up next to you," Mike replied.

Eric stood up and ran to a tree at the edge of the tree line. He looked both ways, then ran up the embankment and dropped to the ground. He waved Mike and Sarah forward and moments later they joined him.

Mike called Jon on his radio, "Jon we moved up to the top of the embankment, but we haven't seen any activity."

Jon responded, "Mike, Angie and I moved across the highway and into the tree line. I want you guys to lay down a steady rate of fire across the road to keep their heads down and we'll hit them from the side."

"You mean right now?" Mike asked.

Jon looked at Angie and Angie shook his head. "Yeah, Mike, right now, please," Jon replied.

Before Mike could give the order to fire, another grenade skipped across the pavement and down the slope behind him. He yelled, "Grenade!" as it exploded and then, "Fuck, I'm hit!" after it kicked him in the ass. "Return fire!" he yelled as he started shooting across the road. Eric and Sarah immediately joined him.

***

Angie and Jon stepped out of the tree line and began lobbing M203 grenades and spraying the remaining five Chechens with machine gun fire. It was almost over before it started. It wasn't a fair fight. Angie and Jon were the champions of not fighting fair. If they found themselves in a fair fight it meant they had fucked up somehow. Jon keyed his radio, "Okay, Mike. You're clear. Beat feet for the Land Rover. I'm calling in the helicopter."

"Uh, yeah, I may have a minor problem," Mike replied.

"What? What's the problem?" Jon asked as he turned and started jogging toward Mike's position. Angie joined him.

"One of the Chechen grenades bit me in the ass," Mike replied.

Jon yelled to Angie, "Here, take the sat phone and go help get the kids ready and tell Whitey to land the helicopter. I'll go get Mike!"

"Don't be late, mate!" Angie replied as he took the phone and turned for the buses, his black habit flapping in the wind.

Jon quickly ran to Mike. He was lying on his stomach with Eric bandaging his hip and ass cheek. "Mike, can you walk?"

"No but I can hop on one leg," he replied.

"Eric, stop what you're doing. The helicopter is inbound. You and Sarah go help the kids get on the helicopter. I'll take care of Mike. Help me get him up," Jon said as he bent over to get Mike up on his one good leg. Eric helped stand Mike up. "Okay, I got him. Get Sarah and the kids to the helicopter. Don't wait for us," Jon said. Jon put Mike's arm over his shoulder and started step dragging him back to the helicopter.

"I'm not leaving you. We'll go together," Sarah replied.

"Baby, I love you, but you have to cooperate with me or you're going to fuck everything up. I do this shit for a living. Now, please, get out of here," Jon begged.

Eric started pulling her toward the helicopter. After a few seconds, she accepted what was happening and ran back to the helicopter with Eric.

A few steps down the road, Mike said, "Jon, something's wrong with my other leg. It feels like my hamstring is pulled."

Jon stopped and looked at Mike's leg. "You're bleeding from another shrapnel wound," Jon said as he took Mike's arm by the wrist and raised him onto his shoulders in a fireman's carry. Jon strained under the 240-pound load and stepped off at a double-time march. "Fuck! What have you been eating, lard? All of you, Marines, are grenade magnets. You probably jumped on this one on purpose." Jon saw one of the supposed-to-be dead Chechens on the ground under the last truck trying to bring his rifle to bear on him, but he was lying on top of it. Jon struggled to get his SAW sling loose so he could shoot the man.

"I'll get him," Mike said as he fired three rounds from his pistol into the soldier, finishing him.

Sister Joan led the way from her bus with a baby in her left hand and Glock in the other. The older kids were carrying the rest of the babies and shepherding the younger children behind her. She fought against every instinct in her body to panic and continued walking calmly at a child's pace to the helicopter that had just flown over her and landed beyond the Land Rover. Alice and her kids were lined up and following the first group. Sister Joan glanced movement to her left and saw a wounded Chechen soldier under the first truck roll over onto his stomach. His bloody face grimaced as he slowly scraped his rifle across the pavement in an arc trying to bring it to bear on the infidel nun. Sister Joan spun around and stuck her Glock under the truck bed. She pumped five rapid shots into the man's head and shoulders. The baby wailed into her ear, frightened by the gunfire. She kissed the infant in an attempt to calm her. "Come children, the bad man can't hurt you," she said in broken Ukrainian. She kept the Glock at low ready as she scanned for more targets. The three minutes it took to cover the 200 feet from the buses to the helicopter felt like an eternity. Finally, Sister Joan stepped onto the ramp and walked to the front of the cabin where she and her helpers began strapping the kids into the canvas troop seats, two and sometimes three kids to a seatbelt.

Back at the ramp, a five-year-old girl excitedly yelled, "Tato! Tato!" and wrapped her arms around Kevin's neck as he sat behind the M2 machine gun. He patted the girl on the back to calm her, but she continued to cling to him. One of the older girls talked calmly to her and managed to untangle her from Kevin.

"What was she saying?" Kevin asked in English.

"She thought you were her papa," the girl replied before taking her forward.

Emotions Kevin had kept hidden for two years exploded to the surface. He began crying uncontrollably. Since the night in Alaska when his partners, Mark and Ronnie, were murdered by their own protectee, he had been living two lives. One for his friends and family where he was completely recovered from the vicious attack and the other only for himself where he knew the truth. He had recovered physically from being shot in the face within six months, the fresh scars hidden neatly under a fashionable beard. His missing teeth replaced with perfect implants. He had fended off the temptations of opioid painkillers and alcohol before they had a chance to take hold. By all rights, he should have been back to normal. The morass he found himself mired in was one of intense depression and confusion brought on by his inability to snap out of his funk. He had lost count of the nights spent lying in bed waiting for morning to come. Now suddenly, he felt it was all behind him, the result of a little girl's brief affection. He was ready to live again, maybe even find a wife and start a family.

***

Chaos spread like wildfire on the highway. Within a minute of the ambush initiating, civilian vehicles began arriving in the kill zone on both sides of the highway. They skidded to a stop and tried to back away from the area before a stray round caught up to them. The first few oncoming vehicles were treated to the bizarre sight of a Catholic nun standing in the middle of the highway launching 40mm grenades into a military convoy. A soldier with his face on fire tumbled out of a green SUV as everyone else burned inside. Some drivers had the where with all to turn around and drive down the shoulder past the other cars stuck in the traffic jam to get away. Several green military trucks were scattered among the others. Chirp flew the CH-53 parallel to the highway at 100 feet AGL and 60 knots while all three of his gunners engaged the military vehicles with their M2 heavy machine guns to keep them from advancing to help the Chechen convoy before he landed beyond the Land Rover. Sister Joan followed by Alice quickly led their children to the helicopter and rushed them up the ramp. The older kids were excited, and the little kids were scared. All of them were screaming but they all ran to the helicopter.

***

Jon waddled between the burning G-Wagen and Sultanovich's blood-soaked corpse. He wished he could stop and kill him all over again, only better this time. He was sucking air like he had just sprinted through a marathon. He still had another hundred feet to get to the ramp. Angie and Eric were waving for him to hurry up. Their concern was emphasized when Kevin fired a string of .50 cal. BMG rounds past Jon's left shoulder at a mob of angry locals that had traded their pitchforks for rifles recovered from dead soldiers. One head exploding into pink mist from a 619-grain bullet was sufficient to pacify the crowd for the moment. Angie and Eric ran out to help Jon carry Mike.

"I can carry him!" Jon complained loudly.

"Yes, of course, you can, mate but we don't have all bloody day," Angie replied as he and Eric took Mike from Jon's shoulders.

CHAPTER 45

Kevin sat behind his M2 heavy machine gun mounted to the ramp scanning for threats behind the trio carrying Mike. He worried they had already been on the ground too long. His quick burst of fire had a devastating effect on the handful of locals who had armed themselves, but the deterrence was fading fast. *Come on, come on! We don't have time to fuck around!* He thought as he watched Mike and his rescuers inch ever closer at what seemed a sloth's pace. "Hurry the fuck up, dammit!" he screamed at the top of his voice. Finally, they stepped onto the ramp and Kevin immediately keyed his ICS, "All aboard! Let's go!" The helicopter jumped from the pavement and accelerated away from the carnage. Kevin watched as two police cars raced toward him driving on the wrong side of the highway. They screeched to a stop parallel to the burning G-Wagen. "Hurry up!

The cops are here!" Kevin shouted into the ICS. Four policemen emerged from their cruisers with AK rifles and began firing at the helicopter. Kevin saw a spark fly from the tail skid under the tail boom. He didn't want to hurt a policeman, but he did target their cars with his M2 to deter them. He shredded their cars, sparks, and glass flying in all directions, followed by one satisfying gas tank explosion. The men dropped their rifles and scrambled like keystone cops trying to get away from the burning car.

***

Chirp had been watching the action through the rearview mirror above the instrument panel. As soon as the men stepped onto the ramp, he pulled pitch and the giant helicopter leaped from the pavement. He nosed the helicopter over to make a maximum performance takeoff and as soon as he was above the trees, he turned left to use them for cover and accelerated away to the northwest. "Whitey call Gwenn. See if she has a good route for us to get back to Ukraine without flying over a bunch of pissed-off Russians," Chirp said before asking, "Chris is everyone accounted for?"

"Yes, sir, 91 orphans, one nun, four from our ground element, five aircrew, and two hitchhikers. That's 103 souls total," Chris reported.

"Good. Make sure they strap the kids in as best they can. How's Mike doing?" Tom asked.

"He took grenade shrapnel in his ass cheek and hamstring. No major arteries were hit. Eric gave him some morphine, so he's chill right now," Chris replied.

"How are the kids doing?" Tom asked.

"Alice, Sarah, and Sister Joan have the helmets on all of the kids. Now they're working on the earplugs and teddy bears. They also gave them some of the gum and candy Cujo provided so they're happy for now. The older girls are feeding the babies," Chris replied.

***

Angie was still wearing the habit when he plopped down on the ramp next to Kevin and retrieved an Mk152 radio detonator from his chest rig. He pressed the button and smiled as the Land Rover exploded sending a gray and black smoke plume hundreds of feet into the air. It wouldn't do to leave anything useful behind for the Russians. Jon was sitting on the deck just inside the ramp across from Angie chugging his second bottle of water. He nodded his approval when Angie looked over at him. Next, Angie stripped off the habit and threw it at Jon. He caught it and then laughed as he stuffed it under the canvas troop seat next to him. It had served its purpose.

CHAPTER 46

Russian Federation President Vladimir Pichugin mumbled obscenities as he paced back and forth in front of the eighty-inch television mounted to the wall. "Bring General Gennady to me immediately!" he shouted to his bodyguards. He looked down to button the navy blue Brioni jacket of his €5000 suit and straightened his maroon Valentino tie. He was in his underground bunker office fifty meters below his massive fortress palace on the bluffs overlooking the Black Sea. The palace was a billion-dollar gift from his billionaire oligarch cronies.

Ten minutes later the Russian Federation Minister of Defense, General of the Army Sergei Gennady stood before Pichugin's desk clad in a white terrycloth robe and flip flops. Water dripped on Pichugin's ornate Persian rug. Gennady had been swimming laps in the indoor pool. "How may I help you, Mr. President?" he asked as he ran a towel through his short gray hair.

"Have you seen the news?" Pichugin baited him.

"No, sir, I was in the pool," Gennady stated the obvious. He had learned long ago to let the little man vent his frustrations on him rather than make excuses.

"While you were swimming, the Americans invaded our country," Pichugin said as he pressed play on the TV remote. A Russian news report played video of the ambush from several cellphones. It started with a video shot from a passenger car on the north side of the highway showing a Catholic nun wearing a flowing black habit standing in front of a black Land Rover block- ing the southbound lanes. The nun produced a grenade launcher from under her habit and began firing grenades into a Mercedes G-Wagen and military truck. Chaos ensued as a military convoy was destroyed and a platoon of Chechen Spetsnaz soldiers were killed by a small group of fighters. This was followed by a long string of children walking down the southbound lanes to board a CH-53 helicopter that had landed on the highway. Then two police cars arrived and were shredded by the tail gunner on the helicopter as it flew away. The video ended as the Land Rover exploded.

"Colonel Marvan Sultanovich and thirty Chechen soldiers are dead. Sultanovich was the Chechen President's cousin. He demands satisfaction. These videos have already spread around the world!" Pichugin yelled as he pointed at the TV. "The Americans are secretly using their F-22s and F-35s to shoot down our aircraft over Ukraine. An unending supply of NATO tanks and artillery are flowing in from Poland. We are running out of men, missiles, aircraft, tanks, and ammunition. I have to grovel to China and Iran for support. How can I deter NATO from helping Ukraine if you can't even defend our borders?" Pichugin vented.

"Mr. President, I advised against this special military operation from the beginning. I told you the readiness reports from our combatant commanders were grossly inflated. Fortunately, we still control from Luhansk down to Kherson. Negotiate peace with NATO and promise to go no further into Ukraine. The Ukrainians won't like it, but NATO will agree to let us keep what we have. They grow tired of war very quickly. The Ukrainians are toothless without NATO support," Gennady reasoned.

"No! I will reclaim what rightly belongs to Russia! Alert the tactical nuclear missile forces in Belarus! Tell them to be prepared to launch on the Mariinskyi Palace within fifteen minutes of my command!" Pichugin demanded. Mariinskyi Palace was the Ukrainian President's official residence.

"Mr. President I strongly advise against alerting the nuclear forces. NATO will detect the preparations and the Americans have already vowed to respond," Gennady replied.

"Do as I say old man, or I will remove you from your post! Now, get out!" Pichugin screamed.

"Yes, Mr. President, as you wish," Gennady bowed his head and stepped back before turning to leave the office.

"Wait! Find that American helicopter and shoot it down!" Pichugin spat.

"Mr. President, What of the children?" Gennady reminded him.

"They are of no concern!" he shouted.

"Yes, Mr. President," Gennady replied before he left the room. Pichugin was becoming more unstable every day. He would require close monitoring. The nation was coming to a crossroads. Today might be the day that Mother Russia's future was finally determined. Ten minutes later, Gennady was back in his room. He turned on his secure cellphone and made the call.

"Dah," Colonel General Arseni Sevastian said from his headquarters in the General Staff Building in Saint Petersburg. He was the commanding general of the Western Military District that included Moscow.

"Arseni, it's Sergei. The time has come. Are you still on-board?" Gennady asked.

Sevastian stood up from his desk and said with great enthusiasm, "Yes, of course, my brother!"

"Good, man. Today we will change the fate of our country. Have your men standing by. Soon this nightmare will be over. Goodbye, comrade," Gennady said. Gennady and Sevastian had been young lieutenants in Afghanistan. They were in a Mi-17 Hip helicopter that dropped them in a landing zone the Mujahideen had prepped. Mortars started impacting the zone as soon as the helicopter landed. Sevastian was there when shrapnel ripped into Gennady's thigh. His soldiers scattered when the attack started, but Sevastian ran to Gennady and applied a tourniquet that saved his life. He still carried some of the Muj steel in his leg.

CHAPTER 47

"We have a big problem, Chirp," Whitey said over the ICS, "Gwenn says we stirred up a hornet's nest. Two Mi-24P Hind helicopters launched out of Mariupol and are heading our way. They're crossing the Tahanroz'ka Gulf right now."

"Damn, they're blocking our path back to free Ukraine. Do we have enough fuel to get across the Black Sea to Turkey?" Chirp asked, already knowing the answer.

"No, we'll be about twenty minutes short. We'd have to ditch in the water," Whitey replied.

"Which means certain death for these kids. We don't have any life rafts," Tom said.

"How about we fly as far as we can and then land in the water? We might be close enough for a Turkish trawler to tow us in or at least take the kids," Whitey said.

"We'd still be 50 or 60 miles out from the coast when we went in the water. Did you check the drain plugs? I didn't crawl under the belly to check them before we left. We might sink before anyone came to help us. The water temperature this time of year is around 60°F. That's too cold to go swimming," Chirp said. "What about islands, are there any Turkish islands we can land on?"

"There are only a few and they are all out of range," Whitey replied.

"I guess we'll have to do some pilot shit. If we can get past the Hinds, they won't be able to catch up to us," Chirp said.

"What if they sent Frogfoots?" Whitey asked.

"Well, shit, Whitey, I don't know. Let's worry about the real Hinds before the imaginary jets," Chirp replied, "Here. Take the controls."

Whitey put the sat phone down on the center console. "Roger, I have the controls," he said as he wiggled the cyclic.

"You have the controls," Chirp replied, as he picked up the phone. "I'll ask Gwenn for heading guidance to get us back to free Ukraine. Keep us at 100 feet AGL and 170 knots. Make sure you make a slight heading change every fifteen seconds or so. We don't want to catch an RPG or SAM."

"Roger that," Whitey replied.

Chirp plugged the sat phone into his helmet and said with a smile, "So, ah, what are you wearing?" He wanted to make Gwenn laugh one more time before one of the Hinds killed them.

"Excuse me, sir? Oh, you must be Colonel Adams. Mrs. Adams went to the loo. Oh, here she is. It's Colonel Adams," the young female voice said from Edinburgh as she handed the phone over to Gwenn.

"What did you do?" Gwenn asked suspiciously.

"What do you mean? I didn't do anything," Chirp denied.

"Bullshit! Her face is as red as her hair. Back to work, the Hinds just crossed the beach, heading straight at you. ETA five minutes. Turn left 15°."

"Whitey, the Hinds are five minutes out. Come left 15°. Chris, Taco, and Kevin, you are still weapons-free. We're going to be maneuvering like a madman. We won't have time to call out everything in advance. Okay, Gwenn, from here out, I want to keep the line open between us. I'm going to get Alice to come up here and sit in the jump seat. I'll give her the phone." Chirp keyed his ICS, "Alice come up to the cockpit." Chirp lowered the jump seat for her, and she sat down. "Alice, I want you to monitor the sat phone with Gwenn and relay any info she gives you." He gave her the phone. "Jon, Angie, Eric, we're going to be in a shootout in a few minutes. I want you to help keep the fifties loaded. They'll burn through the 100-round belts in a matter of seconds." Angie and Eric moved forward carefully stepping over and around the children jammed together shoulder to shoulder in the canvas troop seats lining the cargo compartment.

"Gwenn says the Hinds altered course to intercept us. They're two minutes out," Alice reported.

"Okay, Whitey, remember, they have a dual-barreled 30mm autocannon on the right side of their fuselage next to their nose so don't engage them head-on. I think it's the same one the Frogfoot employs. I recommend we come up to 1,500 feet AGL to give us more options. The Hind has a slight edge in the climb, but we're more maneuverable. We need to stay above them and shoot down on them through their rotors. As long as we're looking down on them through their rotor blades they can't shoot us with their cannon," Chirp said. *Lord Jesus, please, save us,* Chirp prayed silently.

"Hind one o'clock, two miles," Chris said calmly over the ICS.

"Whitey, come left 20° and climb to 2,000 feet AGL." *Get'em, Chris, kill that motherfucker!* Chirp thought. He knew Chris was an excellent aerial gunfighter based on his experience as a Huey Viper gunner with HMLA-369. Whitey turned left 20°. He already had the collective pulled up as high as he could raise it, so he pulled the cyclic back to 10° nose up to zoom skyward. "Be looking out for dash two," Chirp said before a string of 30mm cannon rounds flew in front of the helicopter and came back toward the cockpit before traveling under the troop compartment missing the helicopter by less than ten feet.

***

Chris leaned out of his right gunner's window, pointed his gun down at two o'clock, and squeezed his butterfly triggers. The huge 619 grain .50 caliber BMG armor-piercing-incendiary and tracer rounds raced across the 500 meters separating the two helicopters, the first few missed off to the left, but Chris smoothly corrected and sent a burst through the top of the rotor disc and into the fuselage. Rounds ricocheted off the engine armor and back into the rotor blades. The Hind pilot reacted to the hits by pulling off and down to the right. "Kevin, Hind coming your way low and to your left!" Chris yelled into the ICS. He instantly heard Kevin's gun begin firing.

***

Kevin immediately pointed his gun down and left and a micro-second later he was rewarded by the sight of the smoking Hind crossing behind the 53 from left to right. He squeezed his triggers and yelled into the ether, "Fuck you!" He sprayed the Hind's tail rotor and main transmission area below the main rotor head. "That's for Mark and Ronnie you fuckin' assholes!" he yelled into the slipstream. He reluctantly stopped firing as his rounds began falling short of the Hind. At first, he was pissed because the Hind kept flying away but then seconds later it entered a sharp right turn and a large piece of rotor blade flew off. A second later the entire rotor head above the transmission snapped off causing the Hind to tumble tail over cockpit down into the ground where it exploded upside down throwing three dead soldiers from the troop compartment out into the plowed earth. Burning jet fuel sent orange flames and black smoke mushrooming up from the Russian farmer's field. Four S-5M air-to-ground rockets cooked off in their pod and screamed across the field before exploding into the tree line.

"Good shooting, Kevin! He just splashed that Hind!" Jon transmitted over the team radio before slapping him on the shoulder.

"Well, it was already smoking before I shot it. Chris hit it first. I just finished it off," Kevin explained.

"Well done, Kevin. Keep looking for dash two. He's out there somewhere," Chirp replied.

"Gwenn says dash two is coming up behind us at our eight o'clock and a mile," Alice said.

"Whitey, turn to two o'clock and bump it up to 185 knots. We'll leave him in our dust. Taco, Kevin, do you see him?" Chirp asked on the ICS.

"Dash-2 is still at 8 o'clock, one mile, and 200 feet AGL," Taco replied on the ICS.

"Gwenn says two SU-25 Frogfoots are approaching from the east, ETA 15 minutes," Alice reported.

"Damn, we can't go north. Whitey, I have the controls," Chirp said as he took the collective and cyclic in his hands.

"Roger, you have the controls," Whitey replied as he held his hands up in front of the instrument console between them.

"I have the controls," Chirp said completing the three-way change of controls, "We're going to have to engage the other Hind as we escape to the south. Taco and Kevin, get ready. I'm going to make a hard, climbing left turn to the south. Be ready to shoot down into the Hind as he climbs into us." Chirp was already at 185 knots when he rapidly entered a 60° angle of bank climbing left turn. "Get ready, he should be coming into range," Chirp said but no one fired. He rolled out of the turn heading south, "What's happening?" he asked.

"Chirp, the Hind turned right to keep his distance. Now he's turning back left to follow us," Taco replied.

"Damn, he's smarter than the first Hind pilot," Chirp said, "If he starts climbing, sing out. We can't let him get above us. If he does, we'll be having a knife fight in a phone booth. Alice, ask Gwenn if there are any US Navy warships in the Black Sea. Sometimes we have a destroyer or two out there."

"Chirp, the Hind's at 6 o'clock and a mile. He's climbing through about 500 feet," Kevin called out.

"Shit! We can climb higher than him, but we don't want to be fighting with him at 15,000 feet when the Frogfoots show up. We have to kill him now. Hang on!" Chirp yelled as he pulled the cyclic back into his abdomen. The 53's nose went up and up to an unnatural angle where the helicopter was standing on its tail. Chirp could hear the children screaming over the sound of the massive jet engines. It broke his heart to scare the kids, but he had to save them.

"Chirp! What, what are you doing? Get the nose down," Whitey yelled as he braced himself. He had never been that afraid before in a helicopter even when the first Hind was shooting at them. He expected the helicopter to depart controlled flight any second and tumble helplessly out of the sky until it crashed into a fiery ball of unrecognizable burning flesh and metal. Surprisingly, the helicopter's nose continued up around the arc until the helicopter was upside down. After the nose passed 5° nose down, Chirp rolled the helicopter to the right 210° to return the helicopter to level flight at 3,000 feet AGL and a coordinated 30° angle of bank turn to the right. He looked down through his side window and saw the Hind heading north and climbing from 1,000 feet below. "Chris, do you see the Hind at 2 o'clock low?" Chirp called out.

Chris responded with a long string of .50 cal. BMG aimed down at his three o'clock. "Kevin, he's coming through your 5 o'clock," Chris called over the ICS.

Kevin sprayed several bursts through the Hind's rotor system as it flew out of range. "I had a lot of hits on the Hind, but I don't see any damage. He's turning around to chase us," Kevin called out, "Jon, I need more .50 cal."

Jon grabbed another 100-round ammo can and attached the first link of the belt to the end of the belt already in the gun. He kicked the empty can off the ramp.

"What the fuck? Was that an Immelmann?" Whitey yelled into the ICS.

"Yeah, I guess so," Chirp replied.

"This helicopter is not approved for acrobatics," Whitey replied.

"It's not approved to fly at 185 knots or carry 103 people either but here we are," Chirp replied.

"Well, next time give me a heads up so I can clench my cheeks. I don't want to die with soiled skivvies," Whitey said with a grin.

Jon and Kevin watched as the Hind pointed its nose about 10° above the horizon and fired a salvo of S-5 rockets from its left pod.

"The Hind just fired a salvo of rockets at us!" Jon yelled into the ICS.

Chirp immediately pulled back on the cyclic to climb another 500 feet. "Where are the rockets!" he yelled into the radio.

"We're good! The rockets' burned out and they're falling away," Jon replied.

"Where's the Hind now?" Chirp asked.

"He's still about a mile behind us and 1,000 feet below," Kevin said.

"Coming left and down, get ready, Taco," Chirp said as he entered a 70° angle of bank turn that caused the helicopter to lose altitude rapidly.

CHAPTER 48

"Alice, any word from Gwenn?" Chirp asked.

Alice read from her notebook, "Yeah, she said the Turks gave the US Navy permission to bring an amphibious ready group through the Turkish straits last night into the Black Sea."

"What about that treaty the Turks have saying they won't allow any aircraft carriers to transit into the Black Sea?" Whitey asked.

Alice read from her notes again, "Ah, yeah, it's called the Montreux Convention of 1936. The Turks are pissed because the Russians shot down a Turkish civilian airliner yesterday over Odesa that was carrying Turkey's ambassador to Ukraine and some Turkish pop singer, I can't pronounce her name. The Russians claim it wasn't their missile."

"Does she know which ships are in that amphibious ready group?" Chirp asked.

Referring to her notes again, she said, "It has the Wasp-class amphibious assault ship, USS Kearsarge, LHD 3, the amphibious transport dock ship, USS Arlington, LPD 24, and the dock landing ship, USS Gunston Hall, LSD 44. There's also a destroyer escorting them. It's the guided-missile destroyer, USS Arleigh Burke DDG-51."

"Sweet, the ACE on the Kearsarge is a reinforced tiltrotor squadron with twelve MV-22B Osprey assault support tiltrotors, six F-35B Lightning II stealth strike-fighters, Four AH-1Z Viper attack helicopters, four UH-1Y Venom utility helicopters, and four CH-53E Super Stallion heavy-lift helicopters. The F-35s can handle any Russian fighters they send out after us. Alice, ask Gwenn for a vector," Whitey said.

"Whitey, can you call someone with enough juice to get us aboard the Kearsarge?" Chirp asked.

"I'll try. I gave Paul Bane command of the 22nd MEU before I retired. He should be deployed on the Kearsarge now. Alice let me have the phone," Whitey said before accepting the Sat phone. "Hey, Gwenn, I'm going to put you on hold while I call the Marine colonel on the Kearsarge to see if he can help us," Whitey said before finding the number in his tablet. The phone rang five times before it was answered, "Go for Wolf!" Bane barked into the phone.

"Wolf, it's Whitey, do you have a minute?" he asked.

"Hell, sir, I have all the time in the world for you. Everyone wants to talk to you. You're in the eye of a giant shitstorm. I'm sittin' here with the Commander of the Kearsarge ARG. We're waiting for orders about what to do with you. They're sayin' you attacked Russia and started WWIII with a Shitter you plucked out of a museum," Wolf said before laughing.

"Wolf, we flew this 53 into Russia chasing a Chechen Special Forces convoy carrying 91 Ukrainian orphans to be auctioned off in Grozny by human traffickers. They were going to use these kids for spare parts. Now, we're being pursued toward the Black Sea by a Hind and a couple of Frogfoots," Whitey explained.

"Yeah, we're watching them too, but they're not alone. You'll be within range of three of their frigates in a few minutes. You need to get back on the deck soon or they'll smoke your ass," Wolf warned.

"How about you guys come out here and escort us back to the Kearsarge? You can take us into custody as war criminals and rescue all of these poor kids from us," Whitey offered.

"Sir, there's nothing I'd like better, but you know I can't scratch my ass without orders. We'll be manned up and standing by just in case those orders come down, but seriously, sir, start wave hopping, ASAP, before you get lit up. Wolf out."

Whitey handed the phone back to Alice and said, "Chirp we need to get back on the deck before one of the Russian frigates gets a lock on us. Wolf said there are three of them out here. He also said they can't help us without orders."

"Catch 22. If we come down the Hind will get us and if we stay up here the frigates or jets will. We have to deal with this guy now. Where's the Hind?" Chirp asked.

"Still a mile behind us and 1,000 feet below," Kevin replied.

"Okay, we have to take this guy on now. I'm going to make a hard descending right turn. Chris, you should get the first crack at him. Remember, the engines are armored, and the rotor blades are titanium. Concentrate on the rotor head and tail rotor," Chirp said.

Chirp received two ICS clicks in response before he said, "Coming down and right."

"Clear down and right," Chris replied with his head and shoulders outside of his window as he leaned on his gun and strained to see the Hind that would soon be coming into view above the tail fin on the right external fuel tank. Seconds later he called, "Tally, on the Hind," before firing a long burst at the Hind through the front of its rotor disc to the rear and down the tail pylon to the tail rotor. The Russian pilot pulled up and right in an attempt to bring his autocannon into action, but the Shitter was more maneuverable in the turn and faster as it flew downhill. The Russian stomped on his right anti-torque pedal to bring his nose around quickly to the right and squeezed off a string of 30mm shells that flew past the Shitter's tail and exploded harmlessly.

Chris was hosing the right side of the Hind's rotor head again when he noticed the upper half of the passenger door was open and a machine gun was firing back at him.

"Pull up! The Hind has a machine gun in the troop compartment!" Chris yelled into the ICS.

Chirp stopped his descent and reduced his angle of bank to 20° to extend his range to the Hind. The Shitter's speed advantage allowed them to get behind the Russian to his 6 o'clock. The Russian stopped his turn and accelerated northeast at his max limit. "Chris, were we hit? Everyone, check the kids," Chirp called out.

"I don't see any damage to our helicopter," Chris replied.

"The kids are screaming again but no one is hurt," Sarah replied.

"Okay, good," Chirp replied. "I'm coming down to the deck." He nosed over 5° and lowered the collective slightly to maintain 185 knots. "Maybe we can break contact with him before the fast movers show up," he said as he dropped dangerously close to the ground. He was skimming the trees at only 50 feet AGL. He was so low that before turning, he had to climb a little to keep his rotor tips from impacting the ground. "Where's the Hind?" Chirp asked again.

"He hasn't noticed our turn yet. He's still hauling ass to the northeast," Kevin said.

"Gwenn says the Frogfoots are about ten minutes out," Alice said.

"I'm going to keep us over land as we head southwest toward the Black Sea. The terrain should help us hide," Chirp replied.

"Gwenn says a Ka-52 Alligator Assault Helicopter just lifted off out of Kerch and is heading east to intercept us," Alice said.

"Aw shit! That helicopter is more deadly than the Hind!" Chirp complained, "We can't get caught between them. Ask Gwenn for a vector for the Alligator. We'll have to take it on fast and then haul ass for the water." By water, Chirp was referring to the Black Sea. He was hoping to go feet wet and then beg the Navy for help on the guard frequency in the clear in front of God and everybody. Maybe the pressure from the public would force the White House to help.

CHAPTER 49

1010Z (1310 LOCAL)
SKY ABOVE KRASNODAR KRAI, RUSSIA

Jon was sitting on the cargo deck of the Shitter with his back to the wall at the end of the nylon troop seats. He was looking past Kevin's right shoulder trying to help spot hostile aircraft. He could hear Chirp and the others going back and forth on the ICS wishing he could help when he remembered what Boss said to him over Lviv before he stepped out of the Black Hawk onto the warehouse roof, 'If you get down there and you are absolutely out of options, call me. I don't know what I'll be able to do but call me anyway.'

Jon pulled his sat phone out of the pouch on his plate carrier and selected his number. He connected the phone to his helmet.

"Hey, Jon, is that you?" Boss asked.

"Yeah, Boss. I'm at that point in the mission where I don't know if I should shit or go blind, so I took your advice and called you. You probably heard we were successful in taking the kids away from the Chechens. We killed every one of those worthless motherfuckers. Now we have 91 orphans in our helicopter hauling ass for the Black Sea with the Russians only a few minutes behind us. We called the Kearsarge ARG for help and they said the White House is refusing to let them engage. Pretty soon we're either going to get shot down or ditch in the water. We all knew death was a definite possibility on this trip. That was a risk we agreed to take but these kids are completely innocent. The Chechens were going to sell them off for spare parts. We can't fail, Boss, it just can't be allowed to happen," Jon said. He didn't know what Boss could do to help from hundreds of miles away, but it felt a little better to talk to someone.

"Jon, I have one arrow left in my quiver. I read the names on the list of orphans you sent. Did you know three of them are the grandchildren of a Ukrainian general?" Boss asked.

"No, I didn't," Jon replied.

"I'm going to have a talk with him. He may be able to help. Just stay alive no matter what. I'll do what I can from here. You're not out of the fight yet. Boss out," he said before ending the call.

***

Boss looked out of the open troop door of his Agency MH-60 DAP Black Hawk helicopter as it flared for landing in a farmer's pasture outside of Mali Prokhody north of Kharkiv. Boss was traveling with his whole team minus Jon and Angie. He was sticking his neck out a mile on this hop. He didn't really have a legitimate excuse to be landing at the temporary field headquarters of the Ukrainian Army's Rocket Forces and Artillery. It had expanded so much in recent months due to the influx of arms from America and NATO that now it was commanded by a major general named Marko Shevchenko.

Boss and his team hopped out of the chopper. He stopped next to the pilot in command and said, "If the camp is attacked leave us here." The pilot nodded his agreement. The team quickly strode over to the closest Ukrainian officer. Boss showed him an identification card created for him by the Ukrainian government and said, "I have information for General Shevchenko about his grandchildren."

"You can come with me but your men will have to wait here," the young captain said in English as he motioned to the pickup truck behind him.

"Two, you guys stay with the chopper. If the area comes under attack, get in the chopper, and leave me here. We can link up later," Boss said before climbing into the truck.

"Roger, that Boss," Two replied.

Several minutes later, Boss was standing in front of the general's desk. "So, you are another one of the men who are not here. What do you know of my grandchildren?" Shevchenko asked.

"General, a good friend of mine went on a personal rescue mission to the St. Michael's Church in Donetsk to rescue his god-daughter who is a Catholic nun. When he got there, he found out the nun was trying to care for 92 Ukrainian orphans by herself. Her priest had been murdered by Chechen Special Forces the day before. He arranged through a wealthy benefactor to send a team in a CH-53 heavy lift helicopter to rescue the children but before the helicopter arrived the Chechens took them. They were convoying them to Grozny to be auctioned off to organ traffickers. My friend's team ambushed the convoy inside Russia and retrieved the children.

"They are trying to escape but the Russians have cut off their route to Ukraine. Now they are flying south to the Black Sea where they hope to land on a US Navy ship. My government is refusing to help them because the Russians have threatened to use nuclear weapons if we interfere with the war. I need your help convincing my government and Russia to allow the children to escape. They are being pursued by attack helicopters and jets," Boss explained.

"This is a very sad tale, and I would help if I could but even I have to operate within the bounds of my orders. How are my grandchildren related to this story?" the general asked.

"Sir, your son died in the defense of Mariupol. When your daughter-in-law learned of her husband's death, she took her children to her parent's home in Donetsk and then joined the militia in Mariupol where she was also killed in action. Two weeks ago, her parents were killed in a Russian missile attack while the children were in school. The fire department took the children to the church. Sister Joan has a list of all of the children under her care and photos of each child saved on her email account," Boss said as he handed the general a copy of the list and a piece of paper with photos of his twelve-year-old granddaughter and his eleven and eight-year-old grandsons.

Shevchenko read their names on the list and then studied their photos. He had not seen them since Christmas before the war started. They looked so much older now in the photos as if their youth had been stolen from them.

"Sir, would you like to speak to them?" Boss asked.

"What? Is this possible? Yes, of course, please," Shevchenko said as he sprang to his feet. He folded the papers quickly and put them in his breast pocket as Boss made the call.

"Jon, it's Boss. I'm standing here with Major General Marko Shevchenko, commanding general of Ukraine's Rocket Artillery. He would like to talk to his grandchildren. Please, ask Sister Joan to put the Shevchenko children on the phone."

***

Jon quickly but carefully stepped over and around the children packed into the helicopter's cabin. He told Sister Joan, who was on the line and what he wanted, before handing her the phone. Her face was filled with indecision for a moment and then she handed the phone to Viktor, the general's eleven-year-old grandson.

"Hello!" Viktor yelled into the sat phone over the sounds of the screaming children and the helicopter.

"Viktor, is that you? This is your Didus. Are you all right?" Shevchenko said, struggling not to lose control. Didus was Ukrainian for grandpa.

"Yes, Didus! It's Viktor! Are you coming for us? Russians are trying to kill us in this helicopter! Please, come and get us!" Viktor pleaded.

"Trust me, son, you will not be harmed! I will stop the attacks and come for you very soon. How is Marko? Is he afraid? Tell him to be strong. He is safe now. I will protect you," Shevchenko said, hardly able to control himself.

"Yes, Didus! I will tell him!" Viktor yelled.

"Good, let me speak to your sister, Katya," Shevchenko said.

"Didus! Katya is dead! The fat Chechen colonel killed her when he took us from the church! He did bad things to her, Didus!" Viktor exclaimed through his tears.

Shevchenko lowered his head and closed his eyes. The world began to spin as he felt his way behind his desk with his left hand while he held the phone in his right. He collapsed into his chair. His shoulders were shaking. "Viktor, I'm so sorry you had to witness that, but for now you must be brave for little Marko. Can you do that?" Shevchenko asked as he fought the rage welling inside himself.

Viktor sniffled and said, "Yes, sir."

"Good. I cannot bring your sister back to you, but I swear I will avenge her and your mommy and daddy. I love you, Viktor. Now please, let me speak to little Marko," he said.

"Hello, Didus! Please, take us home!" Marko cried into the phone.

"Hello, Marko. I promise I will come to bring you home very soon. Are the Americans treating you well?" Shevchenko asked.

"Yes, they gave us candy and teddy bears after they killed the Chechens. Sister Joan gives us hugs and kisses," Marko explained.

"Good, Marko. I need you to be strong for the sister and do what she says. She is bringing you back to me. Can you do that, Marko?"

"Yes, Didus," Little Marko said.

"Good, let me speak to the sister," Shevchenko said.

"Hello," she said.

"Sister Joan, I am Major General Shevchenko, the boys' grandfather. I understand you cared for all of these orphans alone and put yourself in danger to protect them. Viktor and Marko are all I have left. I will always be in your debt. I only hope that someday I can repay you. Please, let me speak to the leader of your rescue team," he said.

"Yes, sir," Jon said into the phone.

"I am Major General Shevchenko. Do you lead this rescue mission? What is your name?" he asked.

"Sir, you can call me Jon," he replied.

"You are obviously a military man. What is your rank?" the general asked.

"I was a commander, sir," Jon replied.

"Commander, thank you for saving our children. As I told Sister Joan, Viktor and Marko are all I have left. I am forever in your debt. Someday I hope I can repay you," he said.

"Sir, I understand how you feel. Sister Joan is my goddaughter. I would do anything to protect her, even invade Russia. You can help us right now by getting the Russians to stop attacking us and convince the US Navy to let us land on the USS Kearsarge. The Russians are minutes away from catching up to us. They already tried to shoot us down several times," Jon explained.

"Commander, did the Chechen animal rape my granddaughter before he killed her?" Shevchenko asked, trying to control his temper.

Jon swallowed hard and said, "Yes, sir, he did. She was still alive when my partner and I found her in the church, but she had been stabbed in the abdomen. We gave her morphine to take away her pain and we stayed with her until she passed. We cleaned her as best we could and interned her in a family crypt in the church cemetery. I hope you can take comfort in knowing that I caught that Chechen bastard at the ambush and killed him with my knife. He will never hurt another child," Jon replied.

"Thank you, for this, Commander. Keep fighting. I will get their attention for you," Shevchenko said before disconnecting. He handed the phone back to Boss.

"I'm very sorry, General. I had no idea your granddaughter had been killed," Boss said. His contrition was evident across his face.

"Thank you for giving me two wonderful reasons to keep fighting," Shevchenko said. He walked over to his wall map of the battlefield and studied it for a moment. He picked up his desk phone and said, "Take a message, Sergeant. Are you ready? It has come to my attention that 91 Ukrainian orphans including my grandchildren are in a civilian helicopter fleeing Russia toward the Black Sea at this very moment. They are being pursued by Russian attack aircraft. If any of the children are harmed, I will respond by removing the city of Belgorod, Russia from the map with my rocket artillery, signed Major General Marko Shevchenko. Did you get all of that? Read it back to me." The nervous radioman did so. "Good, send the message in the clear to my Russian counterpart." Shevchenko knew the Americans and his own government would also hear the message.

CHAPTER 50

"Harold, I have an update on the orphan rescue mission," the National Security Advisor, Preston Alexander said upon entering Harold Lamb's office and handing him a report, "Somehow the commanding general of the Ukrainian Rocket Forces and Artillery found out his grandkids are included in the 91 orphans that were rescued. He says he'll wipe out Belgorod, Russia if any of the kids are harmed. We've been telling the Navy not to help them but there are Russian attack jets and helicopters within about five minutes of intercepting them. They don't have a chance in Hell without our military. The Russians are refusing to back down. They are claiming the children were evacuated from an active warzone for their own safety. Of course, we know that's horseshit. They've been actively stealing kids and selling them to the highest bidders.

We need POTUS to authorize military intervention, ASAP, before the Ukrainians start WWIII."

"He doesn't want to be bothered with Ukraine. Give me the order. He gave me the authority to sign for him a couple of weeks ago when he went home for vacation," Harold Lamb, White House Chief of Staff said before signing the order.

CHAPTER 51

1020Z (1320 LOCAL)
SKY ABOVE KRASNODAR KRAI, RUSSIA

"Break left!" Taco yelled over the ICS as the Alligator flew in from 10 o'clock low and began firing its cannon from over a mile away. The cannon rounds were passing well below the helicopter. Taco returned fire from his Ma Deuce not really thinking he would score hits but instead hoping he would deter the Gator from coming closer. As he wished, the Gator turned right to increase the distance.

Chirp wrapped the helicopter up into a tight 60° bank left turn before Whitey said, "I have the controls!"

"You have the controls!" Chirp responded.

Whitey was looking over his left shoulder through his side window, watching the Alligator pilot maneuver his helicopter to stay out of Taco's reach. Whitey continued the turn and used his 1,000 feet altitude advantage to close on the Gator and put Taco in position to fire down into the Gator's rotor system from behind.

"Get him, Taco!" Whitey said. Taco fired down through the Alligator's rotor disc. The Alligator broke hard right and flew under the 53. "He's coming your way, Chris. Chirp, take the controls." Whitey called.

"I have the controls," Chirp replied.

The top half of Chris's body was leaning out of the helicopter. He had his fifty pointed straight down when the Alligator appeared trying to escape to 3 o'clock. Chris raked his rounds back and forth between the engines and rotor disc. Chirp turned right and paralleled the Gator from above so Chris could continue his attack. Seconds later, smoke erupted from the Gator's right engine quickly followed by flames. The Russian helicopter began a slow roll to the right before all six rotor blades from the coaxial rotor system flew away from the rotor mast. A fraction of a second later the upper canopy exploded outward sending shards in all directions followed immediately by a rocket-assisted tether that yanked the pilot out of the right seat horizontally to the ground and slammed him into a grain silo before his parachute could open. The helicopter continued its roll and crashed into a farmer's field upside down. "Splash one Gator!" Chris said over the ICS.

"Good shooting, boys!" Chirp replied.

"I've never seen an ejection from a helicopter. That looked really violent. I think I'd rather ride it in," Chris said.

"Okay, we'll be feet wet in a minute. I'm going to drop down to 200' AGL," Chirp called out as he turned to a south-southwest heading, "Watch out for the jets. They should be here any minute."

"No sign of the jets, but the Hind is back on our tail about a mile back and 500' AGL," Kevin called.

"Coming up," Chirp said as he pulled back on the cyclic to zoom climb to 1,000' AGL. He couldn't pull any more torque out of the collective. "We have to stay above him," Chirp said as the helicopter crossed the beach into the Black Sea.

Kevin elevated his barrel and lobbed a string of rounds back to the Hind. He couldn't tell if he was hitting it, but it did maneuver out of the way and began climbing. "The Hind is climbing after us," Kevin called out, "Jon, I only have one more box. Get two more from under the cargo seat."

"Roger, that," Jon replied. He turned and got on his knees and reached under the kids' legs to unstrap the ammo cans.

"Okay, we don't have time to fuck around with this guy. Hang on!" Chirp yelled as he pulled the cyclic back to its stop.

"Dammit, Chirp!" Whitey shouted. He expected the forty-year-old helicopter to disintegrate any second. "This isn't a fucking Hornet."

Chirp watched his attitude indicator to maintain wings level as the nose continued to come up to an abnormal level. The screams in the back became so loud Chirp could hear them inside his helmet but he kept watching the nose as it came up and up past 90°.

***

Kevin dug his boots into the deck as he looked behind the helicopter which was now straight down at the water. The Hind came into view a thousand feet below. He fired a long burst through the Hind's rotor disc. He watched as the tracer rounds ricocheted off the armored engine housings until his gun ran dry. He reached for his last ammo can, but it was out of reach. He stood up, grabbed the can, and loaded the belt into the gun. Centrifugal force kept his feet planted firmly on the deck for the moment. Kevin stepped back toward his seat, but his boot slipped on the empty brass causing him to fall to the ramp. He felt himself sliding toward the edge. He was confident his gunner's belt would keep him from falling to his death, but he didn't know if it was short enough to keep him inside the helicopter. "Help," he screamed as he glided along atop the loose brass as if it were a conveyor belt.

Jon turned around with the ammo cans in time to see Kevin sliding toward the abyss like a kayak approaching a waterfall. He dropped the cans and lunged for Kevin. Jon grabbed Kevin's gloved right hand just as he slid off the ramp. Kevin's weight pulled Jon toward the edge, but Jon's left boot caught on the leg of the M2 mount. Jon came to a stop with his head and arms hanging outside the helicopter looking down at the water. Jon couldn't press his push-to-talk button because his hands were holding Kevin's hand. "Kevin, call for help!" Jon yelled into the slipstream.

Kevin pressed his PTT button and yelled on the ICS, "Help! I fell off the ramp! Help us!" Unfortunately, the only thing the rest of the crew heard was the rush of air blasting the microphone.

"Hang on, Kevin. Try to pull yourself up my arms!" Jon yelled to Kevin. Kevin tried to grab Jon's sleeve with his free hand but there was nothing to hold on to. Under Jon's arm, Kevin could see his nylon gunner's belt strap was already cut nearly in half by the sharp metal edge of the ramp.

*****

In the cockpit, all Chirp could see out of the windshield was blue sky. He kept pulling back as he climbed to 1,700' AGL while maintaining a steady one G of gravity. After rotating past 180° the 53 was inverted. Taco and Chris's feet were still planted firmly on the deck by centrifugal force as they stood behind their guns. Chirp kept pulling until he was arcing down toward the water. He saw the Hind fly by below him still at 500 feet above the water. Within seconds the 53 was screaming past 500 feet heading down for the waves. Chirp had the collective held firmly against the stop, but the helicopter continued down. "Come on, pull out, pull out you fucking pig!" Chirp yelled. At the bottom of the loop, the helicopter was pulling over two and a half times the force of gravity as it clawed the air for lift. It dropped to fifty feet above the waves and slowed to 80 knots before it stopped descending and finally started accelerating over the water.

***

"Hang on, Kevin! I got you!" Jon yelled over the slipstream as the helicopter began to bottom out and the Gs began to build. Jon's boot lost its hold, and he screamed as he slid off the ramp to join Kevin dangling below the helicopter on his own gunner's belt strap. Despite the death grips they both held, Kevin's hand slipped out of his glove. After five feet his nylon strap arrested his fall. He looked up at Jon and grinned with relief. Then his strap broke and he screamed as he fell until he disappeared into the waves fifty feet below.

CHAPTER 52

1030Z (1330 LOCAL)
BLACK SEA SOUTH OF
NOVOROSSIYSK, RUSSIA

"Kevin!" Jon shouted as he spun around on his strap frantically searching for him as the 53 raced away after the Hind. *Not again!* he thought. He was tired of losing good people. He clenched his thin three-inch-wide nylon strap with both hands and began pulling himself back up to the ramp. He was within a couple of feet when the helicopter quickly turned right, and the centrifugal force pulled him back down to the bottom of the strap. "God dammit!" he yelled. He keyed his radio, "Angie! Help me! I fell off the ramp!" No one responded. "Fuck!!!"

***

Sister Joan was consoling some of the younger children when Chirp entered the loop. The helicopter was falling out of the sky when she looked toward the ramp and saw Jon disappear off the end. "No!" she screamed in horror. She began crying uncontrollably. Her father had been killed in combat in Mosul two years earlier and now the man who moved Heaven and Earth to arrange to save her and the children in less than a day was dead. The man she thought of as her favorite uncle, the man who had cheated death a hundred times had just fallen to his death. The shock to her system was so great, she was teetering on the edge of a mental shutdown. Now the children were trying to console her. She took deep breaths to keep herself from hyperventilating while she said a silent prayer for strength. After regaining control, she smiled at the children and nodded to them. She stood up, stumbled to the ramp, and sat down behind the machine gun. She pulled the charging handle back and let it fly forward just as her father had shown her years ago when he taught her to shoot the Ma Deuce during the SEAL Squadron's Family Day. She wanted revenge. She wiped her eyes on the sleeve of her habit and began searching for targets.

***

Chirp was climbing back through 500' headed for 1,000' to get above the Hind when he had an epiphany. He stopped his climb and came back down to 500'. "I think these guys have been told to stay down low to make it easier for the Russian frigates to target us with their missiles. We should probably stay low too if we can," Chirp said over the ICS.

"Chirp, Gwenn says the Frogfoots are here. One is two miles in front of us turning to hit us head-on at 1,000 feet and the other is a couple of miles behind us at 10,000 feet," Alice said.

"I have the Frogfoot at 10,000 in sight," Chris said as he stuck the upper half of his body out into the slipstream and twisted his torso around to look up through the rotor blades.

"Stay on him, Chris. Whitey, remember how we trained against the A-4s when we went down to Yuma?" Chirp asked.

"Yeah, we got our asses kicked," Whitey replied.

"Well, most of the time but Mac and I beat them a few times when they came at us head-on," Chirp replied as he watched the Frogfoot roll out of its turn to attack the 53 from 12 o'clock. "Hang on!" Chirp said as he quickly jinked the nose 15° to the left. He was already flying at 185 knots. The Frogfoot was also approaching at his max speed. Chirp figured it was something over 500 knots. He watched as the Frogfoot jinked 15° to match Chirp's turn. Chirp immediately jinked back 15° to the right. The Frogfoot again turned back to match Chirp. Now, Chirp pushed the nose over and descended from 500 to 100 feet at his max airspeed. They were now within gun range and the Frogfoot pilot pushed his nose over to put his gunsight on the huge lumbering helicopter. It was impossible to miss at this distance but before he could squeeze his trigger, he felt the sudden rush of negative Gs lift him off his ejection seat. His helmet smacked the canopy snapping him out of his target fixation as he realized all he could see out of his windshield was the helicopter and the angry surface of the Black Sea rising up at 500 knots to snatch him out of the sky. He immediately pulled out of the dive and banked right to circle around the helicopter. Chirp turned hard left to stay inside the Frogfoot's radius. Chirp kept his tight turn in and within seconds the Frogfoot appeared on

Chris's side of the helicopter's nose. He fired an exceptionally long string of rounds as Chirp easily maintained his position inside the arc of the Frogfoot's turn. The Su-25 pilot's jet was on fire before he tried to evade but by then the damage was done. The jet rolled to the right continuously as it dove at a 45° angle into the waves. There was no ejection.

"Splash one Frogfoot," Chris said calmly over the ICS.

"Well done, Chris! Great shootin'," Chirp replied.

CHAPTER 53

1035Z (1335 LOCAL)
BLACK SEA SOUTH OF KERCH, CRIMEA

Sister Joan could hear Chris firing his gun, but she couldn't see any of the action. She did catch the Hind trying to sneak in behind them. She was instantly angry and afraid. She lined up the Hind in her crosshairs and fired a long burst. The tracer rounds fell short, but the Hind turned away to stay out of range.

***

Chirp began climbing to prepare for the attack he knew would be coming from the other Frogfoot. "Listen up Taco and Chris, I think the next Frogfoot will dive in overhead and attack us through our rotor head just like our own Hornets do in training. I'll try to maneuver to give you guys a clear shot back at him," Chirp said.

"Chirp, there's a huge container ship at our 10 o'clock and one mile heading south. I think it's Russian," Taco said.

"Sweet," Chirp replied, as he turned immediately for the ship. Thirty seconds later he performed a quick stop maneuver behind a stack of containers six high. The 53 was maintaining position off the port side of the ship with its rotor tips about fifty feet away from the containers as the ship sailed forward at a steady fifteen knots. "If anyone comes out on the deck with a weapon, light them up," Chirp said.

"Roger that," Taco replied.

Chris pressed his PTT button twice in the affirmative.

"Whitey, get on Guard and ask the Kearsarge for help," Chirp said.

Whitey switched up 243.0 Megahertz on the UHF radio and transmitted, "Mayday! Mayday! Mayday! This is a Monk Industries helicopter calling the USS Kearsarge on Guard. We are a civilian helicopter carrying 103 souls including 91 orphans being attacked by Russian military helicopters and jets approximately fifty miles south of Kerch. We are low on fuel. We need immediate assistance, over." Whitey waited for a response, but none came. He repeated his call. "They're not going for it, Chirp," Whitey said. "You know how us Marines are. They'll curse the president and hate watching us go down, but they won't disobey their lawful orders."

Chirp nodded his understanding.

"Chirp the Frogfoot is orbiting the ship at two miles and 500 feet," Taco called out.

"The Hind is coming back straight at us on the deck from 6 o'clock," Chris said with the upper half of his body outside the helicopter looking back toward the tail.

Chirp air taxied the 53 forward to the ship's bow and then pedal turned it 90° so he could see the Hind. It was a half mile away and closing rapidly. "Get ready, Chris," Chirp said as he moved the helicopter in front of the bow and then climbed just above the top of the containers and bridge.

***

The Hind was approaching the stern when the 53 popped up above the ship. Chris fired down on the Russians with devastating accuracy. The armor-piercing incendiary rounds spidered the gunner's armored windshield rendering him virtually blind. The pilot sitting behind and above the gunner slowed abruptly and moved to cover behind the containers stacked on the ship's stern. Seconds later, the Hind popped up to fire its cannon at the Sea Stallion 800 feet away in front of the ship, but it was no longer there. Chirp had dropped down below the level of the containers and flown down the starboard side of the ship and stopped at the corner of the stern. Chris took great pleasure in seeing the giant target so close and utterly defenseless. He blasted the right side of the Hind from less than seventy feet away, unleashing a long string of death that started at the passenger compartment door where a machine gunner had surprised them earlier. Next was the right engine, then he moved up to the rotor head, and ended at the pilot's canopy. The pilot must have been hit because the Hind slowly slid forward until its rotor blades shattered upon impacting the steel containers sending shrapnel in all directions. The Hind dropped instantly into the ship's wake and promptly rolled upside down.

***

Chris was enjoying inflicting punishment on the Hind when he saw the splintered rotor blades flying toward him at incredible speed. He had no time to move or warn anyone before it all slammed into the right side of the 53. Chirp maneuvered away immediately but whatever damage occurred had already been done. Chris leaned out to survey the damage. The right landing gear was now extended, and the two tires were shredded. He looked up at the engine cowling and saw dark liquid coming from underneath it. He knew it had to be engine oil. "Chirp, we've been hit. The right-side landing gear is down, and the tires are destroyed. Also, there's oil leaking from the #2 engine," Chris said over the ICS.

"Yeah, my chin bubble is blown out and the avionics door is gone. Whitey, drop the gear handle and see if the other two come down," Chirp said.

Whitey reached down with his right hand and lowered the landing gear handle. "Chirp, the left and right main mounts indicate they are down and locked, but the nose gear is still red. Do you want me to cycle the gear?"

"No, with the right-side tires damaged, they might get stuck in the up position. Try the emergency extension handle," Chirp replied.

Whitey grabbed the handle next to the landing gear handle and turned it and then pulled. Nothing happened. "The nose gear panel light still indicated it's up."

"Fuck! How are the kids?" Chirp asked.

"None are wounded but most of them are scared to death," Taco replied.

"We need to make a run for it. Watch that #2 engine oil pressure for me," Chirp said as he turned south and accelerated past the ship. Soon the helicopter was at 150 knots and 500 feet.

"Chirp, the Frogfoot is climbing above us," Taco said.

"How high?" Chirp replied.

"Hard to say, ten or fifteen thousand feet," Taco replied.

"Sing out when he rolls in on us and I'll try to put you and Chris in position to shoot him," Chirp said.

"He just rolled inverted. He's coming down," Chris said.

"Everybody, hang on!" Chirp yelled over the ICS. He pulled the nose up 10° and pushed the cyclic to the left causing the helicopter to roll.

"Dammit, Chirp!" Whitey yelled. He grabbed the handhold above his helmet with his left hand and braced his left foot on the lower window frame as he watched the world spin around. Chirp rolled the massive helicopter three times in an incredible eighteen seconds with no loss of altitude. As the helicopter rolled left from 60° to 150° for a second time, Chris fired a sustained burst toward the Frogfoot still 8,000 feet above them before the pilot fired any rounds from his 30mm cannon. Upon seeing the .50 caliber tracers the pilot broke off his attack to think of a better option.

***

Jon was climbing up his strap for the third time when the helicopter entered the first roll. He was about to put his hand on the ramp when the centrifugal force pulled him away from the ramp again. He was terrified out there on the end of his nylon strap, but he was also fascinated by the view of the world spinning around him without the hindrance of being belted inside an aircraft. He had many HALO jumps in his logbook, but this was different. He felt like a yo-yo being spun in a circle by its string. After the third roll the helicopter stopped abruptly. He cursed several times before he began climbing again.

***

"I got some good hits on the Frogfoot before he broke off his run but he's still following us, 2 miles at 4 o'clock and about 300 feet," Chris said.

"Why did he drop down so low?" Whitey asked.

"Three surface-to-air missiles are inbound from the west in 20 seconds!" Alice relayed from Gwenn.

Whitey and Chirp both punched their clocks on the instrument panel to reset the second hands.

"Whitey, make sure the chaff and flare dispensers are armed! I'm going to head for that tanker at 2 o'clock!" Chirp yelled over the ICS as he flew dangerously close to the waves.

"I see the missile! Hurry, Chirp! Chaff and flares, now!" Chris yelled back.

Whitey fired off a continuous string of chaff and flares from the dispensers on both sides of the 53. The helicopter disappeared along the port side of the tanker as the first surface-to-air missile flew through the chaff and flares and exploded into the ship's fantail. The second and third missiles arrived seconds later, causing even greater explosions that turned the tanker into a colossal inferno.

Chirp stayed low flying along the port side of the tanker until he passed the bow and then he climbed to 300 feet and continued on course. "Where's that Frogfoot?" Chirp called out.

"He's coming fast at 6 o'clock!" shouted Taco.

Chirp began a series of quick turns left and right, climbing up and down. He stepped on the pedals alternately to push the tail pylon out of trim in an effort to confuse the Frogfoot pilot's aim. Sister Joan saw the jet closing in, and she depressed her triggers and fired continuously until he turned left which allowed Taco to engage him. The Frogfoot pulled off and began climbing.

"Chirp, the Frogfoot is climbing above us, again!" Taco called.

Chirp climbed to 500 feet to give himself more room to maneuver. "He's probably going to dive on us again. Get ready. I'll try to roll us over to give you guys a good shot. It takes about six seconds for a complete roll so if you want me to keep going say something. Whitey, try the Kearsarge again."

"Mayday! Mayday! Mayday! This is a Monk Industries helicopter calling the USS Kearsarge on Guard! We are a civilian helicopter carrying 103 souls including 91 orphans! We are under attack by a Russian Frogfoot approximately sixty miles south of Kerch! Our helicopter is badly damaged, and we are low on fuel! We need help now or we're all dead!" Whitey transmitted on Guard. He waited but there was no reply. "I can't believe they're going to stand by and let all of these innocent kids die," Whitey said over the ICS.

"Fuck that! We're not dead yet! Give me a clear shot and I'll deep-six that motherfucker!" Chris replied.

CHAPTER 54

Taco was leaning out of his window looking up through the spinning rotor blades. "He's rolling in inverted from 10,000 feet!" Taco called out.

"Hang on!" Chirp yelled as he snapped the cyclic over to the left to initiate a rapid roll.

A second later, Chris fired a quick string of API into the Frogfoot as it came into view. Another second later, the Frogfoot disappeared behind the right external fuel tank. After two more seconds, Taco saw the Frogfoot passing through 6,500 feet. He fired a short burst before an explosion erupted from the Frogfoot's left wing root. The jet snap rolled a full rotation to the left before the left wing separated from the fuselage. The jet spiraled into the water behind the 53 as Chirp stopped the roll after one revolution. There was no ejection. "Splash another Frogfoot," Chris called out.

"Shit hot, boys!" Chirp replied.

"I don't think that was us. That looked like a missile impact," Taco said.

"Whitey, this is Wolf on guard, turn to 190°. Mother is steaming to you at flank speed. Rendezvous in approximately 20 minutes," Colonel Paul Bane transmitted from the cockpit of his USMC F-35B Lightning II.

"Thanks for coming out, Wolf. We're shot up pretty bad. Can you come down and look us over?" Whitey asked.

"Roger that. I'll join off your starboard side. Tell your gunners to make their weapons safe," Wolf transmitted.

"You guys heard the man," Whitey called on the ICS.

Two minutes later, Wolf flew down and approached the helicopter from 5 o'clock. He was within a half mile when Sister Joan saw his evil black jet racing in to attack them. She screamed thinking he was another enemy fighter and lit him up with her fifty. Upon seeing the tracers Wolf broke right and up to get clear. He stayed above out of reach and sent a blistering call to Whitey, "Whitey, what the hell was that! Is your tail gunner a nun? She just fuckin' shot at me! Get your shit together! And do you know one of your people is hanging off the ramp on a pendant?"

***

Chirp and Whitey both leaned to the middle of the cockpit to look in the rearview mirror on top of the instrument console. They caught glimpses of Sister Joan's back as Angie and Eric blocked their view as they moved as fast as possible from the front of the cabin to the ramp all the while stepping over and around the children. "Sorry about that, Wolf. She wasn't supposed to be on the gun. I guess our gunner fell off the ramp. We're reeling him in now," Whitey replied.

"I'd never live it down if I got splashed by a nun. They'd probably give me a new fucked up callsign," Wolf said.

***

Angie and Eric hooked their gunner's belts to pad eyes on the bulkhead and carefully stepped to the edge just as Jon's gloved hands appeared on top of the ramp. They grabbed him by his wrists and dragged him up onto the ramp and sat him down next to the M2. "I could have got back inside by myself," Jon groused.

"Yes, of course, you could, mate. Why did you go out there in the first place, fancy a bit of fresh air?" Angie asked with a smile.

Sister Joan squealed with joy and wrapped herself around Jon, "I thought you were dead, Uncle Jon! I prayed so hard for God to save you!"

"I did a lot of praying too while I was on the end of the line," Jon said. He looked up at Angie and Eric and said, "Kevin slid off the ramp. I tried to pull him back in, but I ended up following him out. At the bottom of that loop when the Gs built up his strap broke and he fell. I tried to hold on to him, but the Gs were too much," Jon replied. He held up Kevin's glove for emphasis.

"Kevin fell!" Eric yelled and spun around to make sure Kevin wasn't actually still on board. "We have to go back for him!" He hurried back to the front of the cabin to tell Chirp and Whitey as Sarah passed him heading for Jon.

"Oh, my God! Are you all right?" Sarah asked as she went to her knees to hug Jon.

He hugged her back. "Yeah, just a little wrung out from being whipped around on the end of the strap. I'll take over the tail gun and you too can go back to taking care of the kids," Jon said. He was a little embarrassed by the attention especially since Kevin made the ultimate sacrifice a few minutes earlier. He knew they couldn't go back to look for him. The primary mission was still to get the kids to safety.

***

"Wolf, our man on the strap advised we did lose a man off the ramp when his gunner's belt snapped. He fell about ten minutes ago. Can you send someone to look for him?" Whitey asked.

"I'll let the ship know," Wolf said as he observed the right-side machine gun. It was pointing straight down, and the ammo belt had been removed. Chris leaned out of the window above his M2 and saluted the colonel. Wolf returned the salute. "I'm coming up on your right side now. Your right main mount looks like it's down and locked, but the tires are shredded. The external fuel tank and the sponson are peppered with small holes. The sponson is streaming fuel, it's a small leak but I can see it. The right engine cowling and the hump in front of the rotor head have small holes too. Something dark is leaking from the bottom of the hump." Wolf moved forward to check the nose gear. "The avionics door on your nose is missing. The nose landing gear door is missing, and the wheels are twisted in the wheel well. I'm going to cross under to your left side." Seconds later, he said, "There's a gash about six inches wide running all the way across the bottom of the cabin between the sponsons. The left side looks good. Are you sure nobody inside got hit?" Wolf pulled up level with Whitey's seat about thirty feet outside the rotor arc. They made eye contact.

"The only wounded man we have on board was hit on the ground during the rescue," Whitey replied.

Wolf shook his head and said, "That's fucking incredible. How do you want to handle your landing gear problem?"

Chirp and Whitey talked for a moment and then Whitey looked back at Wolf and transmitted, "We'll land on the main mounts and keep the nose up so the Marine helicopter maintenance crew can try to pry the nose gear down. Just in case that doesn't work, have them strap down a stack of mattresses and pallets about five feet high and we'll set the nose down on it."

"Are you serious, pallets and mattresses?" Wolf asked.

"Yeah, the Super Stallion mechanics and crewman will know what to do," Whitey assured him.

"We just got word the Russians aren't giving up. They have four Mig-29s and two Su-57s headed our way. My boys and I are going to ask them to turn around. Keep heading 190° and you'll be aboard the boat shortly," Wolf said as he broke away from the helicopter in a rapidly accelerating climbing left turn and disappeared from view. "Whitey, be advised, three more surface-to-air missiles were just launched from a Russian frigate west of you. Impact in 25 seconds," Wolf transmitted.

Whitey and Chirp punched their clocks again to countdown the 25 seconds. "We would appreciate it if you'd do something about that," Whitey replied.

"We're working on it," Wolf responded.

"Standing by on the chaff and flares. You guys sound off if you see anything," Whitey called out on the ICS.

"Coming back down to fifty feet," Chirp said.

"Chirp, the number two engine oil pressure is low!" Whitey said as he pointed at the caution panel before he reset the master caution light at the top of the instrument panel.

Chirp continued the descent to fifty feet and said, "Dammit! Leave the engine at 100%! We'll deal with it after the missiles! Let's find something to hide behind!"

***

The guided-missile destroyer USS Arleigh Burke (DDG-51) maintained its position three miles off the port side of the USS Kearsarge. The ship detected the surface-to-air missile launch from the Russian Frigate and seconds later fired three RIM-66 Standard MR missiles in response. The medium-range missiles arced away from the ship accelerating to Mach 3.5.

***

"Chirp, that fishing trawler is the only thing close enough," Whitey said as he pointed straight ahead.

Seconds later, Chirp performed a quick stop maneuver to come to a near hover behind the ship. "How much time left?" Chirp asked.

"Fifteen, fourteen, thirteen," Whitey counted down.

"I see the missiles, three o'clock high coming down! Chaff and flares now!" Chris called out from behind his gun as he began firing. Whitey began punching them off immediately. "Three more missiles coming from twelve o'clock high! Hey, they're going for the other missiles! One down, two down, three, splash all three Russian missiles. They must have come from the Burke!" Chris yelled overjoyed with their reprieve.

"Argh! Help! I'm blind!" Taco yelled in pain from behind the left machine gun. He dropped to the deck covering his eyes with his hands.

"What happened, Taco!" Eric asked as he tried to pull Taco's hands out of the way. As an Air Force Pararescueman, he was a highly trained medic.

"That fucking fishing boat lased me! I can't see shit!" Taco yelled in a panic. It was an open secret that Russia operated a fleet of over fifty surveillance ships disguised as ordinary fishing trawlers. Many of them had military-grade laser target designators. They had a habit of shadowing US Navy Carrier Groups.

***

"Chirp, give me a pedal turn facing the boat, fast! I'll take care of it!" Jon called from the ramp. Jon realized immediately that he had to get the pilot's eyes pointed in a safe direction before they too were lased. If both were hit by the high-powered military laser designator and blinded, they would all die soon after as they crashed into the water. Chirp did as was requested and Jon targeted the three laughing Russians standing behind the laser before they realized there was a tail gunner on the ramp. The .50 cal. BMG rounds riddled them sending bloody body parts flying in all directions. *You're not laughing now, assholes!* Jon thought. Next, he targeted the laser, making certain it could do no further damage. Then, Jon rained hell on the pilothouse, blowing out all of the windows and killing the captain who didn't have the good sense to take cover like the rest of the bridge crew. He watched without remorse as his rounds decimated the superstructure until no one was left standing. Then he went to work on the stern. The armor-piercing incendiary rounds quickly started a fire which caused the trawler's fuel tank to explode, sending an angry orange fireball and billowing black smoke hundreds of feet into the sky. "Target destroyed," was all Jon said before he loaded a fresh belt of ammo into his gun. Then he heard screaming behind him over the roar of the engines and rotor blades. He turned to see what the problem was.

All of the children were terrified again. Those who didn't have their heads buried in their laps were staring wide-eyed at him, horrified at the destruction he had unleashed on the defenseless fishermen on the boat. He realized instantly that they'd had a front-row seat to his carnage. For most of the flight, the kids just saw each other. They weren't on the ICS, so they had no way

311

of knowing the fisherman had used a high-powered laser target designator to blind one of the people who had traveled over 5,000 miles to save them from a terrible death. For all they knew, Jon was just as bad as the Chechens.

CHAPTER 55

Chirp climbed to 1,000 feet above the water as his eyes darted back and forth between the clear blue sky in front of him and the ever-increasing oil temperature and ever-decreasing oil pressure in the #2 engine. "I say we leave #2 at 100% until it fails. What do you guys think?" Chirp was asking mostly Whitey and Chris. Normally, if an engine failed it would be a land as soon as practical emergency, but over water, this was out of the question. CH-53s were designed to land in the water but the Marine Corps had learned painful lessons through decades of experience that it was usually a bad idea. If all of the drain plugs weren't in place the helicopter could take on so much water it could sink or at a minimum get so heavy it would not be able to take off again. Plus, a random wave might capsize the top-heavy helicopter. But the six-inch wide gash running across the bottom of the fuselage prevented any possibility of a water landing.

"I agree. Let's get every second we can out of it," Whitey said.

"If you get increased vibrations through the speed control levers or airframe, the engine is about to seize up. Shut the engine down ASAP," Chris advised.

"Whitey, this is Mother. Do you read on Guard?" the controller on board the USS Kearsarge transmitted on the Guard frequency.

"Whitey reads you five by five, Mother," He was using his Chuck Yeager test pilot voice. He wanted to portray the cool, calm Marine Aviator and former Commandant of the Marine Corps and not the scared sixty-year-old retiree who hadn't flown anything in over seven years.

"Whitey, we have you on course at ten miles. Recommend you slow to 120 knots to prepare for landing. I understand your right main mount tires are flat and you have a hung nose gear. We have a maintenance crew standing by to pry your nose gear loose. The pallets and mattresses are chained down on the tramline just forward of spots eight and nine. The deck is clear from the fantail to the island. Do you have any other mechanical problems?"

"Mother, Whitey, we also have an oil leak in our #2 engine. We anticipate it will fail before we get on deck, so we are planning on a single-engine landing," Whitey replied.

"Whitey, Mother, understood. Confirm your altitude, fuel, and souls on board," the controller said.

"Angels one, zero plus one five, and 103 souls on board, including 91 children," Whitey transmitted.

"Fire in #2 engine! Flames are coming from under the engine cover!" Chris shouted into the ICS. Chirp and Whitey both looked up at the fire t-handles next to the engine speed control levers. The #2 fire T-handle was illuminated.

"Whitey, confirm the #2 T-handle is illuminated," Chirp said.

"Confirmed," Whitey replied immediately. He knew not to touch it.

"Place your hand on the #2 T-handle," Chirp said.

Whitey placed his right hand on the T-handle.

"Confirmed. Pull the #2 T-handle aft," Chirp said.

Whitey did as ordered.

"Main Engine Fire Extinguisher switch to Main," Chirp said.

Whitey flipped the switch to main, dispersing fire retardant into the #2 engine compartment. "How does the fire look, Chris?" Whitey asked over the ICS.

"I still see a few small flames. Hit it again," Chris replied.

"Whitey, switch from Main to Reserve," Chirp said.

"Reserve activated," Whitey replied.

"The fire's out!" Chris shouted into the ICS seconds later.

"We need to lighten the load on our good engine. Toss all of the guns, ammo, and anything else we don't need overboard," Chirp ordered.

The gunners and their assistants helped get the M2 machine guns off their mounts and dropped them into the waves. Next, the mounts went overboard, then all of the ammo cans and tactical gear. The kids saw what was happening and understood immediately. Some started offering up their candy and teddy bears. Eric choked up for a moment as he looked up and down the length of the cabin at the terrified children. He realized they could all be dead in a few minutes. He smiled at them and signaled with his hands that they could keep them.

"Chirp, do you want to jettison the external fuel tanks?" Whitey asked.

"No! I know they're empty, but I've heard too many horror stories about one of them getting hung up and causing a death spiral. With the damage to our right sponson there's no telling if both tanks will come off normally," Chirp replied.

"Roger, I'll call the Kearsarge," Whitey said over the ICS. He switched over to the UHF radio and transmitted, "Mother, this is Whitey."

"Whitey, go ahead for Mother," the controller replied.

"We had a fire in the number two engine. The fire's out but now we'll be conducting a single-engine landing. We'll skip trying to pry the nose gear down and instead, we'll conduct a no-hover landing to the mattresses, over."

***

"Roger, do you have Mother insight at your 12 o'clock and seven miles?" the Air Boss asked.

"Affirmative, Mother," Whitey replied.

"The deck is clear, sir. You are cleared to land. Godspeed," the Air Boss replied trying to sound like this was just a normal day for the Kearsarge. Then he picked up his handset and broadcasted over the loudspeaker to his men and women manning the flight deck, "Crash and firefighting crews standby. Everyone, stay behind cover until the 53 lands and the rotor blades have stopped. I'll give the order to advance."

***

"Make sure the kids are strapped in tight. We're going to be making a steep approach to a no-hover landing so it might seem like a crash landing but it's not. Don't worry. I've done this a hundred times. I always walk away," Chirp said over the ICS. He turned to Whitey, who gave him a sarcastic and somewhat doubtful look. Chirp smiled and shrugged. Everything was relatively copacetic for about thirty seconds and then Whitey and Chirp saw the BLADE PRESS caution light illuminate on the caution panel. The rotor blades had a hollow spar that was pressurized with nitrogen to approximately 10 psi. The caution light indicated there could be a crack in one or more of the rotor blades. If even one rotor blade failed the resulting imbalance in the rotor system would cause the rest of the blades to rip themselves apart in a matter of seconds and the helicopter would tumble out of control into the sea.

Chirp pounded the top of the instrument panel. "Well fuck! What's left? Maybe a Tsunami will swamp the ship just as we land or a damn meteor will knock us out of the sky," Chirp said in exasperation.

"Do you think it's actually cracked?" Whitey asked.

"Oh, with all of the other shrapnel damage we have, I'm pretty sure it's cracked. I just hope it stays together for another four minutes," Chirp replied. "Get set in back. Whitey, give me the landing checklist."

"Speed Control Levers to Fly. Landing Gear Lever down. Parking Brake locked. Harnesses locked," Whitey responded.

"Two miles out, one minute to go," Chirp said before he tensed up on the cyclic and collective. "Dammit! The AFCS just failed," he said as he struggled to control the helicopter. The Automatic Flight Control System was similar to a car's power steering, except it was used in addition to the 3,000 psi hydraulic systems used to reduce the level of effort necessary to move the cyclic, collective, and anti-torque pedals. "Whitey, reset the AFCS dc circuit breaker," Chirp said.

Whitey found the circuit breaker on the panel. "It's reset," he replied.

"It's still tango uniform. The controls are super heavy. Get on the controls with me. I'll set my ICS to hot mic and call out the inputs I need from you. Everybody in back, get set, we're coming in for landing. Make sure everyone stays inside the helicopter until the rotors stop. Whitey, pull back on the cyclic, hold. Good, now lower the collective, stop. Add left pedal, hold. We need to slow down to 60 knots. 500 feet. Lower the collective and pull back on the cyclic, stop. Hold that. Slow to 30 knots. 250 feet. Pull back, hold. Raise the collective with me, hold," Chirp said. They came down to 110 feet on the radar altimeter at the fantail. As they crossed the fantail the rad alt dropped to 50 feet. "Add left pedal to straighten the nose, hold. 50 feet, 10 knots. Raise collective, hold. 20 feet, raise the collective. Touchdown," Chirp said as the helicopter made jarring contact with the steel deck and the rotor blade tips flexed dangerously low. "Forward on the cyclic. Engage the rotor brake and I'll shut down #1. Chris as soon as the rotors stop get the kids out of the helicopter," Chirp called over the ICS. Whitey engaged the rotor brake and the rotor head abruptly stopped, followed immediately by a thunderous crack. One of the six rotor blades snapped in two and a piece of the blade flew over Chirp's head as he sat in the cockpit shutting down their one remaining good engine. Whitey and Chirp looked outside in time to see the twenty-foot-long blade fragment skip across the deck for another 200 feet.

***

"Now! Move, move, move! Get those kids inside the island and down below!" The Air Boss shouted into the loudspeaker handset as he stood behind the glass in pri-fly or primary flight control. Over a hundred sailors and Marines spilled out of every hatch on the island. Their orders were simple, run to the helicopter, grab a child, and run back to the island as fast as possible. Then get them inside before the helicopter could burst into flames or explode. It was a frantic scene of organized chaos as sailors and Marines ran to the ramp and passenger door and then waited impatiently in line while children were handed over in ones and twos by their original rescuers. Jon and Angie were on the ramp handing children off while trying to get a good headcount. Chris and Eric were at the passenger door doing the same. Inside the cabin, Sister Joan, Sarah, and Alice were helping a few of the older girls tend to the infants. Within two minutes all of the children were safely and efficiently moved from the helicopter to the island.

Sarah and Sister Joan took Taco by his arms and led him out of the helicopter and over to the island. He was nearly catatonic with fear over the prospect of being blind for the rest of his life.

Eric, Chris, and Alice stood over Mike. Eric went to one knee to talk to him. Mike was sleeping sitting up in his cargo strap seat. Eric looked up at Chris and Alice and said, "They grow up so fast," emphasizing Mike's well-earned reputation as a big dumb kid. "Sometimes, I think he gets shot or blown up just so he can get high."

"What did you give him this time?" Chris asked.

"The kit the Moldovan major gave us was stocked with morphine," Eric replied.

"Oh, yeah, morphine is the best," Alice admitted.

Eric studied Alice for a moment wondering when she needed the drug then decided against asking. "Earth to Devil Dog! Are you in there? It's time to come out of orbit!" Eric said as he lightly shook Mike's shoulder. Mike's eyes opened for a second as he sat up straight, then they closed, and he slumped dead asleep again.

"Don't know about you guys but I don't feel like carrying his lazy ass to sickbay. Stay with him. I'll get some people in here with a stretcher," Chris said before exiting through the passenger door.

***

"Russian fighter aircraft approaching the U.S.S. Kearsarge, this is a United States military fighter aircraft, you are flying into danger. Russian aircraft have demonstrated hostile intent today and have been shot down. Turn away immediately or you will be destroyed," Wolf transmitted in the clear on the UHF Guard frequency.

"Yankee Air Pirates, I am Major Dimitri Georgy. You have violated airspace under Russian Federation control to help war criminals escape justice. Return them immediately or you will be destroyed," the Russian Air Force pilot replied.

"Major, we are in a superior position with better aircraft and weapons, but you don't know that because you can't see us. If you fly south of 44° North you will all be destroyed. I have four eager captains with me who are praying you all keep coming," Wolf called out.

"I am speaking to Colonel Paul Bane of the United States Marine Corps correct?" Georgy asked. His question was met with dead air. "Come now Colonel, or should I say Wolf? I have been listening to you on Guard while you talked with General McKinley. There is no point in remaining silent. This is what we have trained so long for, yes? Finally, we have worthy adversaries. We have come too far to turn around without testing each other. We may never get another chance to fight with your, what do you call her, Fat Amy? It will be my great honor to defeat you today," Major Georgy replied.

"Major, if you cross the 44th parallel, I guarantee it will be your last fight with any aircraft," Wolf replied.

"Fights on!" the major replied as his flight accelerated in afterburner across 44° North.

"Wolf switched frequencies to call his pilots. "Cowboy, Bluto, engage the Felons. Spanky, Barstow, engage the Fulcrums."

Seconds later, Cowboy transmitted, "Fox three," after his AIM-120D AMRAAM radar-guided air-to-air missile dropped away from his F-35B's internal ordinance bay and raced away at four times the speed of sound.

Bluto's Lightning coordinated with Cowboy's aircraft nearly instantaneously and he launched his AIM-120D missile seconds later at the second Felon, "Fox three," Bluto echoed Cowboy's call. Spanky and Barstow launched their missiles at the first two Fulcrums seconds after Bluto fired.

Cowboy's missile traveled forty nautical miles in less than a minute. Cowboy watched as the lead SU-57 Felon disappeared from his helmet-mounted display. "Splash one Felon," the young captain transmitted, calmly.

Bluto transmitted, "Splash dash two."

"Splash the lead Fulcrum," Spanky transmitted.

"Splash the second Fulcrum. It looks like the other two are hauling ass for home," Barstow transmitted.

Wolf shook his head in disgust. *Why would any military leader send his pilots on a suicide mission with no chance of success?* he thought. "Sierra Hotel gents. Cowboy and Bluto RTB to refuel and rearm. I'll remain on BARCAP with Spanky and Barstow," Wolf replied.

***

Chirp and Whitey sat in the cockpit trying to get their shit together. Their hands were shaking, partly as a side effect of the stress and fear from the flight but mostly from the physical effort expended flying the helicopter after the automatic flight control system failed.

"I think my arms and legs are going to be sore for weeks," Whitey said as he massaged his thighs.

"Did you see the elephant?" Chirp asked.

Whitey nodded and thought for a minute, "Yeah, I did. I hope I never see it again." Seeing the elephant for military men referred to the fear and anxiety soldiers faced preparing for war and then dealing with the aftermath of what they did and experienced in battle.

"C'mon, let's get out of here. I need to find a head," Chirp said as he climbed out of his seat and stepped down into the cargo area. He stretched his sore body. "I feel like I just went twelve rounds with a gorilla."

***

Angie and Jon stepped off the ramp onto the nonskid-covered steel flight deck. They were both dead tired and sore down to the bone. Jon put his arms over his head to stretch then bent over to place his palms on the deck. He straightened up and looked at Angie. He smiled and shook his head. He shouted, "I can't believe we just fucking did that!" He exchanged high-fives with Angie and then wrapped him up in a bear hug, raising his boots off the deck.

"If you kiss me, mate, I'll kill you," Angie warned before Jon let him go.

"This mission would have been perfect if we hadn't lost Katya and Kevin," Jon said suddenly melancholy.

"Jonny Boy, we're blessed to have survived at all. We're lucky most of these rugrats weren't killed along the way," Angie replied. "All of the rounds and rockets expended and none of the kids were hurt. It's a bloody miracle."

A monstrously built Master at Arms and four of his biggest petty officers approached Jon and Angie. "Excuse me, gentlemen, we have orders to search you for weapons," he said.

Jon looked the men over and asked, "What for, Senior Chief? Are you taking us into custody?"

"No, not yet sir. I don't think the captain has decided if you're heroes or criminals. Hands up and spread your legs," the Senior Chief Petty Officer ordered.

Angie and Jon complied.

"We're unarmed, mate. We dropped all of our guns in the drink. Besides, if we wanted weapons, we'd take yours," Angie said with a smile as the petty officers searched them. He jumped a little. "How is it you sailors always dilly-dally when you come to a man's crotch?"

"Oh, good, you're a tough guy, huh, like some little Tasmanian Devil," the Senior Chief replied. His boys chuckled.

"Angie, please! I've been blown up by a cruise missile, shot in my chest plate, and whipped around the helicopter on a string like a fucking yo-yo. I'd like to visit the shower, not the brig. Besides, they just saved us from certain death," Jon said before turning his attention back to the Master at Arms. "Senior Chief, before you start swinging your batons, I'd like to introduce us. I'm Commander Jon Smith retired, formerly of SEAL Team Three and Dev Gru. He's Warrant Officer Angus Hawkins retired from the Australian Special Air Service Regiment," Jon said.

The Senior Chief looked down and made eye contact with Angie and smiled. "Aussie SASR, huh? Pleased to meet you Mr. Hawkins. You guys did some crazy shit in Afghanistan."

Whitey and Chirp approached the group and Whitey asked, "Senior Chief is there a problem?"

The Master at Arms recognized the retired former Commandant of the Marine Corps and replied, "No problem, General, the captain ordered us to come out here and secure any weapons you may have brought on board with you. That includes searching the more nefarious members of your crew." He turned to look over at

Angie and Jon again. "I also have orders to take you and your team to see the captain. Follow me, please."

There was a tremendous roar from overhead. The group stopped and looked toward the fantail to find two Marine F-35B jets in tight formation flying over the ship at 400 knots. Cowboy in the lead performed a snap roll and then broke hard to the left to enter the landing pattern. It was called entering the break. The roll signified he had shot down a plane on his sortie or made a kill. Two seconds after Cowboy's roll and turn Bluto made a roll of his own before laying his jet over in a sharp left decelerating turn to follow his leader. They both dropped their flaps and landing gear before turning to approach the deck at a 45° angle to land on spots two and four.

"Did you see the rolls? Those Devil Dogs made some kills!" the senior chief shouted to be heard over the jet noise.

Just as the two jets shut down their engines, Jon heard the familiar roar of a Navy Knighthawk helicopter approaching the ship and turned to look off the port side. Over his twenty-year Navy career and four more with the agency, he had ridden in every H-60 model; Seahawk, Knighthawk, Black Hawk, Jayhawk, Pave Hawk, and the President's VH-60N White Hawks flown by the Marines of HMX-1. They were all different with unique missions, but they all sounded the same. This time it was a Navy MH-60S Knighthawk multi-mission helicopter. Jon watched as the helicopter approached the deck at a 45° angle to spot six forward of the port side elevator. It slowly crossed the edge of the deck with ten feet between its tailwheel and the nonskid deck. The pilot came to a hover over the landing spot and pedal turned 45° to the left to point the nose straight down the deck. He timed the rocking and rolling motion of the deck as the ship plowed through the ten-foot waves. Just as the deck reached the apex of its rise the pilot lowered the collective to firmly plant the helicopter on the deck. The crew chief hopped down from the open right cabin door and chocked the right main mount tires. Moments later four sailors wearing cranial flightdeck helmets and white flightdeck vests ran to the helicopter. They pulled a stretcher from the cabin as an aircrewman held an IV bag above it at shoulder height. In unison, they began walking to the island.

Recognition registered on Jon's face immediately. "Angie, that's Kevin!" he yelled as he sprinted toward him. Seconds later he arrived at Kevin's side with Angie right behind him. "Kevin, I thought you were fuckin' dead!"

Kevin locked eyes with Jon. "Me too, man. I almost froze my ass off. You know that trick they teach us at boot camp where you take your trousers off and blow air into them to make a flotation collar?" Kevin asked. Jon nodded. "That shit actually worked. I couldn't believe it."

Jon took a deep breath and said, "I'm sorry I dropped you, brother. I thought I could hold on." Tears were forming in his eyes.

Kevin saw Jon's pain. He held up an arm and said to his stretcher bearers, "Hey hold up a minute." Kevin looked up at Jon and said, "You need to get that shit out of your head right now, Jon. You didn't drop me, my strap broke. And we had to be pulling over 2 Gs at the bottom of that loop. Nobody can hold on to five hundred pounds with one hand. It's fuckin' impossible. We're good, man. Don't sweat it." He held his fist up and Jon bumped it. "Can you believe how Chirp flew that Shitter? I didn't know a 53 could loop like that. I almost lost my shit. Okay, boys. Let's go."

Angie stepped up next to Jon as they watched the stretcher disappear inside the island. "That lad is one lucky bastard. I was gobsmacked when I saw him on the stretcher," Angie said.

"This is the second time I've seen that cat cheat death. The first time he took a .308 round in the face. It almost blew his jaw off. Then the Russians left him for dead buried under a foot of snow. Eric and Chris did some amazing work keeping him alive. I think his heart stopped three or four times on the flight to the hospital," Jon said.

"Was that when you captured the submarines?" Angie asked hoping Jon would slip.

"What submarines?" Jon replied without missing a beat.

CHAPTER 56

"I told you to shoot down the American helicopter! Now it has escaped and landed safely on their ship!" Pichugin railed at General Gennady from relative safety behind his desk. Three of his most trusted bodyguards stood behind him. They were meeting in Pichugin's underground office again only this time Gennady was in his combat uniform. Gennady checked the floor beneath him for a plastic drop cloth as he stood in front of the desk.

"Mr. President, I sent every available aircraft after the helicopter, even two of our Sukhoi T-50s stealth fighters flown by our best pilots," Gennady tried to defend himself. The T50 was what NATO called the SU-57 Felon.

"And only two pilots returned with their tails between their legs! Your pilots are incompetent, and your aircraft are second-rate!

Every time our pilots engage with Western pilots we lose! Your commanders siphon off so much training and operating funds our military is left hollow! Fortunately, our missiles are exceptional! Today I will make history! I will finally defeat Ukraine and bring NATO to its knees!" Pichugin was beaming.

"Mr. President, please, reconsider what you are contemplating. There will be no coming back from this decision once you give the order. You are holding the future of Mother Russia in your hands," Gennady warned him.

"Exactly, General! I am determining the future of Mother Russia! We will regain our rightful place as a world-dominating superpower! Now, how do I give the order to launch the Iskander missile into the Mariinskyi Palace?" Pichugin asked.

"With your permission, Mr. President, I must bring in my communications team with the equipment. They are waiting in the outer office," Gennady said.

"Yes, be quick. No more stalling, General. I won't change my mind," Pichugin replied, anxious to fulfill his destiny.

Gennady opened the office door and motioned to his men, "Set up the equipment on the conference table. Five Russian soldiers in combat uniforms entered the office. Two carried large black plastic cases containing the equipment necessary to transmit the launch order to the missile battery in Belarus. The other three armed with submachine guns were there to safeguard the classified equipment. The two technicians quickly set up the equipment in the center of the table where Pichugin usually sat and then stood back along the wall. It looked like a clunky twenty-year-old portable computer stuffed in a hardened green plastic box.

Gennady walked around the table and stood next to the empty chair. "To be clear, Mr. President, you intend to authorize the launch of an Iskander missile armed with a tactical nuclear warhead from Belarus at the Ukrainian Presidential Palace," General Gennady stated.

"Yes, General Gennady, proceed," President Pichugin said.

Gennady pointed to the keyboard attached to the communications gear on the conference table and said, "Just enter your twenty-digit authorization code into the code box at the bottom of the screen and press enter."

Pichugin stood up from his desk and walked over to the conference table followed closely by his bodyguards. The paranoid Pichugin motioned for them to stop on the other side of the table so they couldn't see his code when he entered it. They stood in front of the three equipment guards to block their view of the equipment. Pichugin turned to the communications technicians and said, "You two, go to the other side of the table." They quickly did as instructed. Pichugin pulled his cell phone from his pocket and handed it to the leader of his security detail and said, "Get a video of me entering my code to order the attack. We will put it on the news after the strike." The bodyguard did as he was told. Pichugin sat down in front of the equipment and studied the monochrome screen. Pichugin reached into his jacket's inside breast pocket and produced a card with thirty twenty-digit codes on it. He placed it on the table in front of the keyboard. There were several input boxes at the bottom of the screen. "Which box does the code go in?" he asked.

"The middle box, Mr. President," Gennady said as he leaned over Pichugin's shoulder and pointed at the box.

Pichugin began entering the characters on the thirteenth line into the box. He was almost giddy with anticipation. Suddenly, Gennady pulled a piano wire garrote from his steel-reinforced leather watchband and wrapped it around Pichugin's neck pulling it tight with all of his might, cinching it so tight the wire cut through Pichugin's neck down to his spine in less than a second. Blood sprayed across the equipment and table. The bodyguards reacted before Gennady could cut Pichugin's throat but not before the three soldiers behind them gunned them down with their submachine guns.

Gennady stood there frozen next to the partially decapitated former President of the Russian Federation for several seconds. His bloody hands were shaking. He had expected to die during the attack.

"Mr. President!" the young captain from the communications team shouted, but Gennady was transfixed on the gory scene. "Mr. President! What are your orders!" he yelled again as he shook Gennady's shoulder.

Gennady turned to look at the captain and realized he was being addressed as Mr. President. "Sasha, post two guards outside the door. Then get your father on the phone. We have a republic to rebuild," Gennady said as he moved on wobbly legs to sit down next to the headless former head of state. Sasha was General Arseni Sevastian's son and Gennady's godson.

CHAPTER 57

Chirp and most of the rescue team were sitting around the large dining table in the USS Kearsarge's commanding officer's cabin when Whitey's sat phone rang. "Hello," he said. He listened for a moment and said, "Sure, but before I hand you off, I want to thank you for your help. I lost count of the number of times you saved us out there. Hey, Chirp, Gwenn wants you."

Chirp took the phone and said, "You bet she does," as he laughed with the others around the table. "So, what are you wearing, sweetheart?" he said into the phone.

"You scared the shit out of me! Are you out of your mind? I know helicopters aren't supposed to fly upside down like that! You could have killed yourself and everyone else!" Gwenn yelled loud enough that everyone around the table could hear it. He could hear her tears.

Chirp grimaced and got up from the table. Everyone's eyes followed him out of the room. "Hon, I didn't have a choice. We were scrambling for our lives. You saw it and I wouldn't have attempted those maneuvers if I wasn't sure I could do it," he explained as he picked at paint chips on the steel bulkhead. Truthfully, he thought his chances were at least 60%.

"That's it! You are done! Do you understand me? You are grounded! No more John Wayne bullshit, Grandpa!" He felt the heat burning his ear.

"C'mon, babe," he said but the line was already dead. He looked at the phone and said, "Love you." He turned and walked back into the room, giving Whitey back the phone as he passed him. He sat down, looked around the table with a straight face honed from over a decade of experience as a police officer, and said, "Gwenn asked me to tell you all what an outstanding job you did saving the kids." The room erupted with laughter. Chirp laughed with them. "And to say what a dumbass I was to fly the helicopter the way I did."

"Chirp, we'd all be whale shit by now if you hadn't flown like a madman out there, but I have to admit the loop and rolls scared me," Eric said.

"Aerobatics like that are prohibited in a 53 for good reasons, but in the training squadron, the HMT-302 instructors showed us a video of the test pilots looping and rolling a 53 back in the 60s so we always knew it was possible," Whitey said.

"Actually, I heard that helicopter was overstressed so bad it never flew again," Chirp added.

"I hope we can get the 53 back to the museum. Can you imagine the attention it will get if it's left just as it is with all of the battle damage," Whitey opined.

Captain Wallace Booker stepped through the hatch to his formal cabin. His executive officer, Captain Howell, stood and ordered, "Attention on deck." All assembled rose to their feet out of respect for the office, including Whitey.

"Please, be seated everyone," Booker said as he made a bee-line for the former Commandant of the Marine Corps. "General McKinley, it's an honor to have you aboard." He held his hand out to shake.

"The honor is mine, Captain Booker. Please, call me Whitey," he said as he shook the captain's hand before they sat down at Booker's large dining room table.

"Yes, sir, I'll try," Booker replied.

"Thank you, for saving our asses out there, Captain," Whitey said.

"I want to apologize for leaving you hanging in the wind out there for so long, but we had strict orders not to interfere. National Command Authority is scared to death by the Russian threats to use tactical nukes in Ukraine. I want you to know every sailor and Marine on this ship was chomping at the bit to come after you. They were borderline insubordinate," Booker explained.

"We understood, Captain. Everyone on this team is military," Whitey said.

"Thank you, sir. If you don't mind, could you make the introductions?" Booker asked.

Whitey motioned across the table, "We have our aircraft commander, Lieutenant Colonel Tom Adams, US Army Reserve retired."

"Colonel, I was watching the ISR feed while you put on your airshow. I didn't think a Sea Stallion could fly like that. The loop and rolls were incredible," the captain said.

"Desperate times call for desperate measures, sir, but I think Whitey did the rolls," Chirp responded as he smiled at Whitey.

Whitey coughed as he sipped his coffee, "Your ass, I did! Uh, Captain, this is our crew chief, Chief Petty Officer Chris Savage, US Coast Guard," Whitey said.

"Your gunnery was very impressive Chief. How many aircraft did you knock down?" the captain asked.

"I'm not really sure, sir. Taco and Kevin did a lot of damage too. They came at us so fast; we were just trying to stay alive. I think your pilot, Wolf, splashed the Frogfoot that was diving on us as Chirp rolled the helicopter," Chris replied.

"Captain, this is Commander Jon Smith, US Navy retired. He's the man responsible for bringing this rescue mission together," Whitey said.

"Your reputation precedes you, Commander. Quite impressive," the captain said as he patted a stack of manila folders on the table in front of him. Jon's was over two inches thick.

"Next, we have Lieutenant Sarah Tuttle, US Coast Guard. When she learned of the mission, we couldn't stop her from coming," Whitey said.

"It took great courage to risk everything on the spur of the moment, Lieutenant," the captain said.

Sarah smiled as she looked into Jon's eyes and squeezed his hand under the table. "It really wasn't a difficult choice at all, sir." Jon smiled back at her.

"Captain, this is Warrant Officer Angus Hawkins, Australian Special Air Service Regiment retired. He was in theater doing some work with Commander Smith when Sister Joan called for help. He volunteered immediately," Whitey explained.

"Welcome aboard, Mr. Hawkins. I remember reading about some of your exploits in Afghanistan. You and your team racked up a spectacular series of successful missions," the captain said.

Angie nodded once and said, "Thank you, sir."

"This is Technical Sergeant Eric Fuller, Alaska Air National Guard," Whitey said as he motioned further down the table.

Booker held up Fuller's folder and said, "Sergeant, you've done a lot in a relatively short career. Welcome aboard."

"Thank you, Captain," Eric replied.

"And finally, this is Alice York, formerly a staff sergeant in the Air Force," Whitey said.

The captain stared at her for a moment and finally asked, "Do you write a series of Amish romance novels?"

"Yes, sir, I do," she replied.

"I thought so. My wife loves your books, especially, that one called *Your Barn or Mine*," Booker said.

"The other three men on our team were wounded and are being treated in your sick bay. They are Deputy United States Marshal Kevin Bass formerly a staff sergeant in the USMC, Alaska State Trooper Mike Harmon also formerly a staff sergeant in the USMC, and Lieutenant Junior Grade Ernesto Ortega, US Coast Guard. Do you have any news on them, Captain?" Whitey asked.

"No, sir, nothing new. They were still being treated when I came back here," Booker replied. "You can go check on them as soon as we're done. Okay, here's your situation. You are all being detained until we get some federal law enforcement agents out here. We don't have an NCIS agent aboard at the moment, so the Master at Arms will keep an eye on you," Booker said.

"Sir, why are we being detained?" Sarah asked.

"Because right now the White House can't decide if you should be hailed as heroes or prosecuted as international war criminals. The Russians are screaming bloody murder. They are claiming you invaded their sovereign homeland, destroyed a military convoy, murdered thirty Chechen Special Forces soldiers, and kidnapped ninety-one orphans who were being relocated from a deadly war zone to safety inside Russia. They also said you attacked a container ship loaded with humanitarian relief supplies headed for Crimea and killed a bunch of fishermen when you sank their boat. So far they haven't complained about the tanker ship they set on fire. The Russians want to fly a helicopter out here right now and take you all back to Russia with them. The White House Chief of Staff recommended I put you in the brig but that seems harsh considering what you did," the captain explained.

Angie leaned over and whispered into Jon's ear, "Add a sunken Russian spy ship to the two captured subs. Very impressive."

"Not now, dude," Jon replied while keeping his eyes on the captain.

"Sir, that's ridiculous!" Sarah responded to Captain Booker.

The captain nodded and put his hand up to stop her. "Yes, of course, it is but if you are from the part of the world that already hates America it makes sense." He changed the subject. "I went to the mess deck to see the children and talk to Sister Joan. The kids are in amazing condition considering what they've been through. None were wounded and the only complaints are that they are a little air sick, and some are hard of hearing. I guess an hour or so in a CH-53 will do that. We're stuffing them with tacos, cheeseburgers, cake, and ice cream." He turned his attention to Jon. "Sister Joan said you're her godfather. She was amazed that you were able to come for her so fast," Booker said as he looked at Jon.

Jon nodded and said, "Her father, Clint, was a highly decorated Naval Special Warfare Operator. He died fighting in Iraq. She gets her tenacity from him. She doesn't have any back down in her. I couldn't let her die fighting alone in Ukraine."

"It's amazing what we're willing to do for our families. Major General Marko Shevchenko, commanding general of Ukraine's Rocket Artillery had two grandsons on your helicopter. He threatened to wipe Belgorod, Russia from the map if the kids were harmed. He launched a couple of HIMARS rockets over the city into a Russian Army supply depot to prove he had the range. He was nowhere near Donetsk. I wonder how he found out about the Chechens stealing the orphans?" Captain Booker asked. Jon remained silent.

"Captain, what's your opinion? What would you have done in our place? Just stand by and let those innocent children be sold off to be murdered for their organs," Chirp asked.

"I think what you did was truly noble and altruistic. I'm embarrassed to say, I don't know if I have that courage," Booker replied.

A lieutenant entered the room and whispered in the XO's ear. "Sir, there's a Fox News Alert concerning the rescue. We have a recording," the XO said as he motioned for the lieutenant to turn on the massive TV attached to the wall.

The talking head said, "We have a Fox News Alert. We received a tip that there has been a civilian-led rescue of a large number of Ukrainian orphans that were kidnapped by Chechen soldiers from St. Michael's Catholic Church in Donetsk, Ukraine. It is reported the Chechens murdered the priest, Father Domingo Del Toro. Colonel Marvan Sultanovich commanded the Chechens. The rescue team ambushed the Chechens inside Russia near the town of Fastovetskaya. The rescue team successfully retrieved the ninety-one orphans and flew them out of Russia in a CH-53 Sea Stallion helicopter owned by Monk Industries and landed aboard the USS Kearsarge in the Black Sea. The White House is refusing to comment at this time, but we are in possession of an audio recording purported to be a mayday call from the rescue helicopter to the Kearsarge claiming they are under attack by Russian jets and helicopters. Here is the call played in its entirety:

"Mayday! Mayday! Mayday! This is a Monk Industries helicopter calling the USS Kearsarge on Guard. We are a civilian helicopter carrying 103 souls including ninety-one orphans being attacked by Russian military helicopters and jets approximately fifty miles south of Kerch. We are low on fuel. We need immediate assistance, over."

The reporter continued, "We have also received confirmation from Alvin Monk. Mr. Monk has released the following video statement on his social networking website."

"A group of civilian volunteers led by Monk Industries Executive Vice President and former Commandant of the United States Marine Corps, General Brian McKinley have successfully rescued a Catholic nun and 91 Ukrainian orphans kidnapped from St. Michael's Catholic Church in Donetsk, Ukraine by Chechen Special Forces soldiers commanded by Colonel Marvan Sultanovich. Sultanovich had already auctioned off the orphans to the highest bidder in Grozny who intended to murder the children in order to harvest their organs to be sold on the black market. The Chechens were convoying them to Grozny when the rescue team confronted them and took the children back by force. The team loaded the children into a Monk Industries Sea Stallion helicopter and flew them out of Russia to the Black Sea being attacked all the way by Russian jets and helicopters. Even though the helicopter was severely damaged, General McKinley and his copilot were able to land on the Kearsarge. All of the children are unharmed and being cared for on the ship. Three members of the rescue team were wounded and are being treated. I don't have the words to express how thankful and proud I am of the actions of General McKinley and his team," Monk said.

"That's all we have for now. We will return to this story as more information becomes available," The reporter said before the recording ended.

The team gave a collective sigh of relief.

"There's no way the administration can sell us out now," Alice said as she high-fived Eric and Sarah.

Jon's sat phone started ringing with an incoming call from Major General Marko Shevchenko. "Hello." Jon listened for a moment and said, "Sir, I'm sitting in the captain's stateroom on the USS Kearsarge with the rest of the rescue team and Captain Booker. Can I put you on speaker?" Jon hit the speaker button and put the phone on the table. He said, "Ladies and Gentlemen, I have Major General Marko Shevchenko, commanding general of Ukraine's Rocket Artillery on the phone. He would like to speak to you. Go ahead, sir."

"Thank you, Commander, for this opportunity to address your team. I was able to speak to my grandsons a few minutes ago. They were eating pizza and ice cream in the ship's, what is it called, chow hall. They are still heartbroken over the murder of their sister but thanks to you, they will live on and remember her fondly. You have done an amazing thing. You saw children in desperate need, and you saved them at the risk of your own lives and freedom. You stopped a terrible crime in progress, a crime my country, your country, and NATO refused to acknowledge or act on. Human trafficking has been occurring since the very beginning of this ugly invasion. The Russians claim they are evacuating our children from the warzone for their own safety, but they are stealing them and selling them to the highest bidder. Thousands have gone missing, never to be seen again. Are General McKinley and the captain there?" Shevchenko asked.

"Yes, this is Brian McKinley and Captain Wallace Booker is sitting next to me," Whitey said.

"Captain Booker, thank you for allowing the helicopter to land on the Kearsarge. I am forever in your debt. General, thank you for your part in organizing and leading this rescue. I do not know what stake you have in this mission but without you, I fear my grandsons and the other children would have already disappeared by now. If I am ever in a position to help you in any way, please, contact me. I will reach out to you shortly to arrange the transfer of my grandsons. If you will excuse me I need to cancel the pending attack on downtown Belgorod," Shevchenko said before he disconnected.

"Do you think he was serious about destroying Belgorod?" Captain Booker asked the group.

The team shook their heads. "Like you said, it's amazing what you'll do for your family," Whitey said.

CHAPTER 58

123OZ (1530 LOCAL)
BLACK SEA, USS KEARSARGE
LHD 3, SICKBAY

Jon stopped at the foot of Taco's bed. His eyes were bandaged with gauze. Jon tried to sound upbeat, "Hey, amigo. It's Jon. How are you doing?"

Taco brightened instantly and sat up, "Hey, sir, I'm okay. How are the kids?"

Jon swallowed the lump in his throat, "They're aaah, doing fine thanks to you, Taco. They were fed a little while ago. Now they're playing games and watching Disney movies. Have the docs told you anything about your eyes?"

"They ran a bunch of tests, but they haven't come back to see me yet," Taco explained.

"Look, man, I'm sorry I got you into this mess. I needed to get Kimmie out of danger, but I shouldn't have brought you guys into it. It was almost guaranteed that someone would get hurt or killed. It's a miracle we all made it out alive. Bottom line, I shouldn't have made my problem, your problem," Jon said.

"Sir, I'll admit, I freaked out when that laser hit me, and everything went dark. I sat there in the helicopter feeling sorry for myself, while everyone around me was fighting for our lives. I was just waiting for death to come, and I made my peace with God. Now, I've been sitting here thinking and it occurred to me that even if I had known I would be permanently blinded, I still would have come on the mission. That's just the way I was raised. It's a big part of why I joined the Coast Guard. I like saving people. If someone's in danger I come running," Taco said. He seemed at peace.

"You're a good man, Taco. You humble me. Compared to you, I'm just another self-absorbed arrogant asshole," Jon choked up again. "So, what can I do for you?" Jon asked.

Taco held his left hand out, "Will you pray with me?"

Jon teared up, "Absolutely," Jon said as he took his hand.

"Lord, Jesus Christ, please, forgive us for all of the lives we took while retrieving the children. Let the children find peace and happiness outside the war zone. In Jesus' name, we pray, Amen," Taco said.

And Jesus, please, let Taco recover his vision. If anyone should be held to account let it be me, Jon prayed silently. "Amen. You know, Taco, it wouldn't hurt to ask for something just for yourself once in a while," Jon said.

"No worries, the Lord will decide what is best for me. We speak every day," Taco replied.

Someone knocked on the wall outside the curtain. "Excuse me, gentlemen. I'm Doctor Welby. Lieutenant, I have your test results."

"I'll give you some privacy, Taco," Jon said as he stepped back to leave.

"It's okay, sir, stick around. Go ahead doc," Taco said as he steeled himself for the worst.

"We have good news. The bottom line is, we expect your vision to come back in a few days. Whatever burned your retinas wasn't strong enough to permanently blind you. If it was a military laser targeting system it must have malfunctioned or been really dirty. You're a lucky man, lieutenant. I'll be back to check on you in a while," he said and walked away.

"That's great news, Taco! You'll be back flying before you know it!" Jon said. He was excited for Taco.

"I was ready to be told I would spend the rest of my life in darkness and now I have a second chance. It's a little overwhelming. Thank you, for praying with me, Jon," Taco said.

"You're welcome, brother. If you don't mind, I'm going to tell the team. If you're up for it, I'll come back and take you to meet Kimmie and the kids," Jon said.

"Thanks, Jon," I'd like that," Taco replied.

***

Jon walked over to Mike's bed, four curtains down the row. "How's our favorite bullet magnet?" Jon asked as he stood at the end of

Mike's bed in sick bay. Mike was lying on his side with a seven-inch zipper running from his left ass cheek down to the top of his thigh. A drain tube ran from the bottom of the incision down the side of his bed to a bag. Alice sat in a chair next to him.

"Hey, man, I'm great. How you doin'?" Mike replied, slurring his words before he nodded off. He was high as a kite.

"Every time the corpsman walks by he whines like a little girl, so they pump him back up to keep him quiet," Alice said. She had a yellow legal pad in her lap. She had written on half of the pad.

"Hey, have you heard, Taco's blindness is temporary. He should recover in a few days," Jon said.

"That's great news," Alice said.

"What are you working on?" Jon asked.

"A new story called *Black Hawk Down on the Farm*," Alice replied.

"What's it about?" Jon asked.

"A Catholic nun in Mexico is helping take care of a bunch of orphans when the drug cartel sicarios show up and kill her priest and kidnap her and the children. Her godfather rounds up a team to shoot their way in and rescue them," Alice said.

"Ha! That's ludicrous, no one would ever believe such a crazy story," Jon replied, sarcasm intended, "What's the Amish Romance angle?"

"There's an Amish community in Chihuahua. A sixteen-year-old Amish couple will hide the nun and the orphans in a barn. A big battle will ensue between the godfather's team and the Sicarios. Eventually, the Mexican Marines will show up, crashing one of their Black Hawks near the barn," Alice replied.

CHAPTER 59

The Russian ambassador, Kazimir Vasili's driver pulled up to the White House's guard shack. The uniformed Secret Service agent checked them in and let them pass. Minutes later the ambassador was escorted into the Oval Office by four Secret Service Special Agents from the president's personal security detail. Vasili had called ahead and asked for an emergency meeting with POTUS. He approached the president who was standing behind the Resolute Desk. They leaned across it to shake hands. "Thank you, for meeting with me on such short notice, Mr. President."

"Mr. Ambassador, please, have a seat," POTUS motioned to the chair in front of his desk. The Vice President, White House Chief of Staff, National Security Advisor, Secretary of State, and Secretary of Defense sat on the sofas behind the ambassador. Two

Secret Service Agents flanked POTUS, and the other two flanked the ambassador.

POTUS motioned for his PSD leader to step forward. The agent leaned down near the president's right shoulder. "Are there any cards for this meeting?" he whispered in the agent's ear. The agent walked over to Harold Lamb and quietly relayed the question to him. Lamb quickly made eye contact with POTUS and shook his head no.

POTUS smiled and asked, "What can I do for you, Mr. Ambassador?"

"Mr. President an extraordinary event has occurred in my homeland today. After you ordered your Navy to help the Monk helicopter escape Russia, my president tried to order a tactical nuclear missile attack on Kyiv as he warned he would do on many occasions if you interfered in Ukraine," the ambassador said.

"Hold on, man! Are you saying I ordered my Navy to interfere?" POTUS said before seeing his chief of staff nodding the affirmative beyond the ambassador's shoulder. "Oh yeah, right. Go on. What was that? Something about a nuke?"

"Yes, as I said, President Pichugin tried to launch a tactical nuclear missile strike against the Ukrainian Presidential Palace in Kyiv, but he was stopped by the Minister of Defense, General Gennady. The general is now the interim president of the Russian Federation. He wishes to negotiate a cease-fire for the special military operation in Ukraine so a peaceful resolution to the ongoing conflict may be found. General Gennady will be contacting you shortly on the secure video-conferencing system we share. I am here to vouch for the veracity of his claim to be our president," the ambassador explained.

The chief of staff, Harold Lamb, opened the door leading to the President's study and pulled the cart carrying the teleconferencing system back into the Oval Office. POTUS didn't like having the system in his office eavesdropping on him. The system alerted indicating an incoming call. "Are you ready, Mr. President?" Lamb asked before he activated the system.

"Go ahead," he replied. Lamb turned it on.

"Mr. President, thank you for agreeing to meet with me. You may not remember but we met when you were Vice President in 2012 during the G8 summit at Camp David. I am the former Russian Federation minister of defense, General of the Army Sergei Gennady. I have been elevated to my current position as the interim president of the Russian Federation due to the illegal actions of my predecessor, Vladimir Pichugin," Gennady said. His English was excellent with only the slightest accent.

"General, how did you prevent President Pichugin from launching his attack on Kyiv?" POTUS asked.

Gennady motioned for his cameraman to pan to his left. The camera came to rest on the still-warm decapitated corpse of the former president sitting in the chair next to Gennady in the Sochi Palace's bunker conference room. Pichugin's near-severed head was resting on his right shoulder. POTUS recoiled at the sight, "Jesus Christ, man! What did you do to him?" he exclaimed.

"I apologize for the theatrics, Mr. President, but I had to act decisively before this maniac could start World War III. My deputies in Moscow have already arrested or eliminated most of Mr. Pichugin's acolytes. Sadly, many of them chose to throw themselves off of the balconies of their penthouse suites rather than surrender for prosecution. Our new administration is eager to start an era of cooperation and trade with you and our neighbors in

Europe that will be beneficial to all. We are weary of war and have no interest in forcing our neighbors to return to old alliances." There was silence for a moment, then, Gennady said with a smile, "Perhaps one day we can join NATO."

National Security Advisor Preston Alexander was feverishly scribbling on a sheet of paper with a black marker. He handed it to Lamb who read it quickly and held it up for POTUS to see. POTUS read the paper out loud, "Ask him when Russia will stop offensive operations so we can urge Ukraine to reciprocate."

Ambassador Vasili looked back over his shoulder in time to see Lamb hide the paper on the sofa next to his leg. Ever the professional diplomat, he refrained from laughing.

"Excuse me, Mr. President. What did you say?" Gennady pretended to be confused.

Ambassador Vasili leaned in and said to POTUS, "If I may Mr. President." And then addressed President Gennady, "The president asked when will Russia stop offensive operations so they can urge Ukraine to reciprocate."

"I will contact my field commanders as soon as we finish this call," President Gennady replied, "I suggest our staffs begin coordinating immediately so we can stop the useless death and destruction occurring in Ukraine and along the Russian border."

POTUS looked over to Lamb who was emphatically nodding his head. POTUS said, "Yes, Mr. President, that sounds like a splendid idea. I hope to meet with you soon once we work out the details."

"Thank you, Mr. President. I will be in touch. If you need me for anything, ask Ambassador Vasili to contact me. Goodbye, for now," Gennady said before ending the call.

POTUS turned back to Vasili and asked, "Mr. Ambassador, how will the people of the Russian Federation react to the country's government being overthrown by a military coup d'état?"

"Frankly, Mr. President, the vast majority of the people will be thrilled for the time being. It was common knowledge among the people that President Pichugin was corrupt. If the army had swept into Ukraine and won the war within a few weeks, as planned, the people would have celebrated but after seeing the war drag on for over two years and the staggering death toll on both sides, and the massive destruction of population centers in Ukraine, the Russian people just want it to end. My country has become a pariah in the Western world and the sanctions are making life uncomfortable for the average Russian. Mothers hated giving up their sons for Pichugin's meat grinder. If the generals end the war in Ukraine and stop the corruption rampant in our government and commercial sectors, the people will embrace them with open arms whether they are allowed to vote or not," the ambassador said candidly. He stood up and said, "Now with your permission may I begin negotiations with your Secretary of State?"

CHAPTER 60

Thirty minutes earlier Harold Lamb had enjoyed an excellent medium rare sixteen-ounce ribeye steak and baked potato prepared by his chef/housekeeper. After being served in the dining room he sent her home early. He ate alone in his six-bedroom colonial farmhouse situated on a ten-acre lot adjacent to the golf course. There was plenty of room for the stable and horses his wife and children were so fond of riding. It was deathly quiet with no kids in the house. Now he stood in front of the floor-to-ceiling window in his home office. He was sipping on a crystal tumbler of extremely expensive twenty-three-year-old Pappy Van Winkle's Family Reserve bourbon as he watched the sun slowly drop below the horizon on the far side of the golf course. His $500 Cuban Cohiba cigar smoldered on his desk unattended. He was pleased with himself. It had been a week since General Gennady and his cohorts decapitated the Russian Federation's civilian leadership and seized control of the government. They were moving at light speed to withdraw their soldiers from all Ukrainian territories except for Crimea. They insisted on keeping their Black Sea naval base in Sevastopol but were also desperate to resume normal relations with the West. So far Lamb had dodged any responsibility for his repeated attempts to stop the Monk rescue team from saving the children.

"Is that a Cohiba?" Jon asked from the doorway behind Lamb. His ever-present Glock 30SF remained holstered under his favorite barn coat.

Lamb shrieked and dropped the heavy tumbler on his left foot sending a jolt of pain up his leg. "Fuck!" he yelled as he hopped around on his good foot to face the voice. "I know who you are! You're Commander Smith! How did you get into my house? Where are my marshals?" he said. Two Deputy United States Marshals protected him at all times when he wasn't on the White House grounds. He looked past Jon's shoulder expecting them to rush in to rescue him.

"They're resting peacefully in the trunk of their car," Jon answered. He would never actually harm any American law enforcement officer. He had too much respect for the thankless job they did. He had been sworn in as a Special Deputy U.S. Marshal several years earlier when he helped federal law enforcement with a few domestic cases. He still had the badge and credentials at home in his safe just in case he was called upon again. "Have a seat over here on the sofa so we can talk," Jon said as he pointed to the plush brown leather couch. His hands were still empty. He hoped Lamb would try something physical so he could beat him to death.

Lamb sidestepped to the sofa, never taking his eyes off of Jon. He noticed Smith was wearing black nitrile gloves. "My wife and children will be home any minute," Lamb warned.

Jon walked past him to the wall next to the window and pressed the button to close the curtains. "Ahhh, no they won't. They're on another one of those Caribbean cruises they love so much," Jon called his bluff. "So, how long have you been working with human traffickers? Is that how you can afford this property and your country club dues? I know the government doesn't pay this well," Jon said as he looked around at the large home office and expensive furniture.

"I have no idea what you are talking about," Lamb replied nervously.

Jon pulled a cell phone from his pocket and held it up for Lamb to see. "I borrowed this phone from Colonel Sultanovich after I killed him."

"I had never heard of him until you ambushed him and rescued the children," Lamb said.

"Well, he knew the human trafficker, Suliman Kulayev, in Chechnya, and Kulayev knows you. I can't read Russian, but my terp says there are texts on this phone where Kulayev tells Sultanovich that he keeps a man on retainer in the White House, he referred to him as Harry. Harry alerts him whenever we or our allies are considering taking actions that run counter to his business activities. Actions like sending civilian helicopters to rescue a nun and 92 orphans before they can be delivered to him in Grozny. After we gave that info to the investigators they had no trouble linking you to Kulayev. You've been in pretty much constant contact with him since you were a foreign service officer at our embassy in Kazakhstan fifteen years ago. Everyone called you Harry back then, didn't they? I'm guessing he was still working for the GRU when he recruited you and then he continued to pay you after he retired," Jon said. "How much intel did you sell to the Russians before you started selling kids?"

"I still don't know what you're talking about!" Lamb shouted. He stood up and yelled, "Now, get the fuck out of my house!"

Jon stepped forward and slapped him across the face with his open hand. "Sit your ass down and don't move until I tell you to," Jon said calmly. Lamb quickly complied as he rubbed his sore cheek. "Does that shit ever work? You just bow up on people, yell a little bit, and they do what you say?" Lamb didn't respond. "Where was I? Oh yeah, the money. You're not very good at hiding your blood money. Why does a civil servant need eight LLCs that receive over $70,000 every month while his companies don't issue any invoices or provide any goods or services? The forensic accountants have already identified your shell companies and seized your offshore accounts in Switzerland, Liechtenstein, the Channel Islands, the Cayman Islands, and Curacao. They also found the $250,000 transfer you sent to the Chisinau Chief of Station from your Curacao account. That was to pay for the contract hitter he sent to the airport to stop our helicopter from getting into Ukraine. He ratted you out immediately in order to avoid prison and keep his pension."

Sweat was beading on Lamb's forehead and above his lip. "I'm the White House Chief of Staff for Christ's sake! You can't fucking touch me! I'm the president's right hand!" he shouted. He was in a panic.

"You were his right hand. Now some dude named Alexander has your job. He's moving into your office as we speak. You're fair game now. PNG. POTUS cut you loose," Jon said. "So, how does this end for you? Do you want to have a heart attack on the shitter or accidentally strangle yourself during autoerotic asphyxiation?"

"You can't do that! I deserve due process. I have rights! You can't just execute me!" Lamb complained.

"Are you fucking serious? You sold out your country for over a decade to our mortal enemies and then you aided and abetted selling thousands of children to the highest bidder to be molested by pedophiles or murdered for their vital organs so your family could ride horses and go on cruises. Fuck your due process. We're playing by big boy rules," Jon replied before slapping Lamb on the side of his head. "Get up." Jon reached for Lamb's shirt as Lamb pulled a small pistol from between the sofa cushions and began firing it at him. Jon leaped onto Lamb and wrestled with him over control of the weapon. Lamb fired three more times into Jon's chest before Jon took the pistol from him. Jon saw the slide was locked back indicating the magazine was empty. He tossed the gun aside before they rolled off of the sofa onto the Persian rug with Jon on top. *I can't believe this motherfucker shot me. Fuck him. Forget the pain. Keep fighting until he's dead,* he thought. Jon sat up and rolled Lamb over face down on the rug and laid down on Lamb's back. He placed him in a rear naked chokehold. Lamb tried to peel Jon's arms away from his neck, but Jon's hold remained tight like an anaconda. Within nine seconds the lack of blood flowing to Lamb's brain rendered him unconscious. Jon maintained the hold as he counted off two minutes in his head. He released the hold and rolled off of Lamb onto his back to catch his breath. The pain in his chest made it hard to breathe. He ripped open his shirt and inspected his Level IIIA+ soft body armor. Seven .380 ACP hollow point bullets had mushroomed into the first several layers of Kevlar, but none penetrated. He released the elastic band holding the armor against his chest and ran his hand under his t-shirt. There was no blood. "Thank you, Lord," Jon said as he looked toward the ceiling. He rolled over onto all fours and slowly stood up. He stepped into the office's private bathroom and held his armor and his t-shirt up to look at his chest in the mirror. It was still covered with the purple and green contusions he had suffered during the rescue mission a week before. Now the fresh red welts spreading around his sternum would blossom into new angry bruises. "Dammit!" he shouted.

Jon opened the medicine cabinet and borrowed four aspirin tablets from Lamb. He secured his armor and tucked his shirt in. He returned to Lamb and dragged him to the bathroom. Jon leaned him up against the open door. He removed the necktie that was hanging loose around Lamb's neck. He tied two slip knots in the tie and put one loop around Lamb's neck. The other went around the doorknob. Jon pulled them snug and then pushed on Lamb's shoulder until the body slid sideways far enough to tighten the noose. Jon returned to the office and collected the pistol and spent brass before leaving.

***

Angie heard pounding coming from the trunk behind him. The senior deputy was furious, "Open the fucking trunk, motherfucker! We're Deputy United States Marshals you fucking bastards!"

"What took so long, mate?" Angie asked as Jon approached in the darkness. He had been sitting behind the steering wheel of the deputies' car babysitting. The pounding and muffled threats from the trunk continued.

"Come on. Let's go. I'll tell you on the way. Bring their key fob with you," Jon said. They walked off into the brush as they headed for the Potomac River. "Okay, let's stop. Hit the trunk release so the deputies can get out."

"Are you sure? They're going to be pissed," Angie said as he aimed the key fob at the car from fifty yards away.

The car's lights came on and the trunk lid sprang open. Seconds later a deputy wiggled over the edge of the trunk with his hands zip tied behind his back. Gravity took over and he fell to the asphalt face-first with a thud. "Motherfucker!" he shouted. He rolled onto his back in time to see his partner falling out of the trunk and landing on top of him. "Fuck! Get off of me dammit!"

"Where are their weapons?" Jon asked.

"They're locked inside the car field stripped. I may have accidentally dropped a few of the smaller parts into the sewer," Angie replied.

"Cool. Give them back their key fob," Jon said.

"Sure thing," Angie said before he reared back and threw the fob as far as he could toward the car. It fell about thirty yards short into the tall weeds. They made their way back toward their boat. "So, how did it go with Mr. Lamb?" Angie asked.

"He's a sneaky bastard. I was discussing his options with him when that traitorous shithead pulled this 380 from between the sofa cushions and emptied it into my chest," Jon said as he held out the little black pistol. "I'll drop this in the river on the way home. He ruined my favorite shirt. My chest is about every color of the spectrum. I feel like I got stampeded by a crash of rhinos. Thank God for Kevlar."

"A what of rhinos?" Angie asked.

"A crash, it's like a herd," Jon replied.

"Why didn't you just say a herd?" Angie asked.

"Ask your king. It's his language," Jon answered.

"Did the wanker opt for the heart attack or asphyxiation?" Angie asked.

"After what he did, he didn't deserve the heart attack," Jon replied.

CHAPTER 61

Jon and Angie were lying next to each other in the brush fifty feet from the fifteen-foot-high compound wall. They surveyed the area with their quad-tubed GPNVGs. They had been observing the activities in and around the palace for three days.

"Crikey! What's that disgusting smell, mate? You smell like shit," Angie said softly.

"I laid down in a fresh pile of dog shit a couple of hours ago," Jon replied. "Is it that bad?"

"Nooo, I hardly noticed," Angie said before moving away a couple of feet. "Do you want to go over the plan one more time?" Angie asked.

"No changes, you take the rover coming around the wall from the left and I'll take the one coming from the right. We'll meet back here and go over the wall together. Let's go," Jon replied. They crawled away in different directions. Minutes later Jon's guard walked around the corner of the compound wall smoking a cigarette with his rifle slung over his left shoulder. He smelled worse than Jon and seemed larger than Jon remembered. As the man passed by oblivious to his surroundings, Jon stepped from behind a tall bush and quietly threw his gloved left hand over the man's mouth crushing the burning cigarette into his face. Before he could react to the pain, Jon drove his Ka-Bar knife into the man's right kidney. His groan was muffled by Jon's vice grip on his mouth. The guard grabbed Jon's left arm and flipped him over his shoulder. That briefly puzzled Jon until his back hit the ground. This had never happened to Jon before. The guard's move surprised him. *Maybe I missed the kidney,* he thought. Jon held on to the man's head as he landed on top of Jon. Jon withdrew the blood-drenched blade and thrust it into the sentry's jugular vein and wrenched it back and forth. Blood gushed from the gaping wound onto Jon's goggles and face. He turned his head away to keep from choking. Within seconds, the guard went limp, and Jon pushed him off onto the ground. He grabbed the man's collar and dragged him behind a bush. He went back to the original meeting place and hid in the darkness for a couple of minutes until Angie returned. "What took so long?" Jon asked.

"My guard stopped about fifty feet short of me and took a shit. Are you sure you laid down in dog shit, earlier?" Angie asked.

"No, I'm not!" Jon replied and sniffed the front of his plate carrier. "I don't know which would be worse!" Jon said.

"Jesus! What happened to you? Are you wounded?" Angie asked after seeing Jon covered in blood.

"No. After I stabbed that shithead in the kidney, he flipped me over his shoulder," Jon replied.

"I've never seen that before. You must've missed the kidney," Angie said.

"I didn't miss it. He was just a big motherfucker, and it took a minute to kill him," Jon explained. He took a knee and used his drinking tube to clean off his face and goggles. Next, he shrugged off his backpack and pulled out a rubber-coated grappling hook attached to a small coil of climbing rope. He and Angie crept up to the wall and Jon swung the hook over the top as Angie covered their backs. Jon quickly climbed the rope and sat on top straddling the wall while Angie came up.

"Have you seen the dogs?" Angie asked. They had counted three guard dogs on the property the day before. The dogs were Belgian Malinois' and Jon and Angie had agreed they were military-trained war dogs because they didn't bark.

Jon gave one short toot on his dog whistle and the dogs appeared in seconds below them. They were softly growling like they hoped the men would fall. Jon reached into his pack again and retrieved a large zip-locked bag full of raw sirloin steaks laced with a tranquilizer. "I hope they haven't been trained not to accept food from strangers. I really don't want to shoot them," Jon said. He had a Ruger MK IV suppressed .22LR caliber pistol in his pack for that possibility. He dropped the steaks to the dogs one at a time to make sure they all got some. They ate the meat quickly and looked up to Jon for more. They weren't growling anymore. Within a minute they were on their sides. Within two minutes they were out cold.

Angie turned the hook around and dropped the rope to the manicured lawn inside the compound wall. He slid down the rope and stood between the snoozing maneaters while Jon put his pack back on and followed him down. They quickly moved fifty feet to the palace wall. Angie turned and leaned against the wall with his intertwined gloved hands held down below his belt. Jon put his left boot in Angie's hands and Angie stiffened so Jon could climb up his compact torso. Jon's right boot stepped on Angie's left shoulder and Angie helped Jon raise his left boot up to Angie's right shoulder. Angie sniffed Jon's boots and recoiled. "Are you sure you didn't step in that dog shit?" he whispered.

"No, I don't think so," Jon replied. He put his hands on top of the balcony floor, but he smiled as he whispered, "I'm still about eight inches short."

"Oh, for fuck's sake...Go ahead," Angie whispered back, dreading what was about to happen. He tried to flex his neck muscles before Jon's right boot landed on top of his helmet. He felt Jon's full weight for a moment before Jon pulled himself up the railing and then over it. Jon leaned over the side and waved a temporary goodbye to Angie. Angie disappeared around the corner to find and kill the other two guards who were patrolling separately inside the compound walls.

Jon free-climbed up to the third-floor balcony. He stopped to watch and listen. The ten-foot-tall French doors were closed but unlocked. Jon peeked through the windows and scanned the room with his NVGs. A large four-poster bed sat to his left against the far wall. The curtains attached to the upper panel were pulled closed far enough that Jon could only see the sole occupant from his feet up to his chest. Jon could hear him snoring loudly from the other side of the glass. He opened the unlocked door slowly and walked across the room. He locked the bedroom door leading to the interior of the house and then wedged a chair under the doorknob.

He walked over to the side of the bed and held up a black-and-white photo next to the man's face. Satisfied that he had found the right man he stuffed the photo back into his left cargo pocket. He slapped the man across his cheek with his left hand as he pressed his Ka-Bar knife to the man's throat. The man abruptly woke up to the pain on his face and then realized the even greater threat pressing against his jugular vein. He whispered something in Chechen that Jon didn't understand.

"I have a message to deliver. I hope you speak English. Otherwise, we'll just skip ahead to the part where you bleed to death," Jon said.

"Yes, I speak English," the man replied.

"Are you the international criminal and human trafficker, Suliman Kulayev?" Jon asked. He could see the wheels turning in Kulayev's tiny pea brain. He pressed on the blade a little harder.

Kulayev swallowed and said, "Yes."

"Thank you for your honesty," Jon said before Kulayev interrupted.

"How much do you want? I am very wealthy," Kulayev said.

Jon pressed the blade still harder into his skin, enough to draw blood. Kulayev tensed. "Don't interrupt me again. I told you I'm here to deliver a message, well several messages. Four months ago, you made a deal with Colonel Marvan Sultanovich to purchase a Catholic nun and ninety-one Ukrainian orphans. What were you going to do with them?" Jon asked.

"I was going to sell them to an adoption agency," Kulayev lied. He would answer questions all night if it gave his guards time to discover this intruder.

Jon pressed the blade deeper into his neck. Blood spurted out from under the blade in rhythm with Kulayev's heartbeat. "Try again. One last chance."

Kulayev gritted his teeth and said, "I was going to sell their organs to the highest bidder."

"There you go. It feels good to tell the truth, right? I have a message from Sister Joan and Father Del Toro. They want you to repent your sins and pledge your life to your god. Go ahead and do that. I'll give you a minute," Jon said. He watched as Kulayev mumbled something through his tears. "Are you done?" Jon asked.

Kulayev would have nodded but he was afraid the blade would go deeper. "Yes," he replied. *Where are my men!* he thought.

"Do you know Sultanovich and his men murdered the Catholic Priest, Father Del Toro?"

"Yes."

"Do you know Sultanovich raped and stabbed a little girl named Katya?"

"No." *He's going to kill me soon,* Kulayev thought.

"Then you may not know she was the granddaughter of Major General Marko Shevchenko, commanding general of the Ukrainian Rocket Artillery. He wanted to destroy Valuyki in the Belgorod Oblast with his HIMARS rocket units. That's your hometown, isn't it?"

"Yes." *How does he know that? General Gennady must be giving information to the Americans,* Kulayev thought.

"Well, I talked him out of it in exchange for your life. That's a good deal right, one miserable excuse for a human being in exchange for over 30,000 mostly innocent lives?" Jon paused a moment to let that sink in. "I was with the team that rescued the children from Sultanovich. Did you notice we killed every soldier who helped Sultanovich take the children?"

"Yes." *How can I buy this man's cooperation?* Kulayev thought.

"What does that tell you about us?" Jon asked. Kulayev was afraid to respond. "It should tell you we take a hard line with people who abuse children. Someone like you can't be trusted to be left alive. If we did, you would continue to rape, dismember, and kill little kids for money. Did you hear your old buddy Harry was found dead in his house?" Jon asked.

"Yes," Kulayev replied. *What did Harry tell him? Where are my guards? I'm running out of time!* Kulayev thought in a panic.

"Do you think he committed suicide?" Jon asked.

"No," Kulayev replied. *You must have killed him. He was too self-absorbed to kill himself,* he thought.

"Did he alert you to the rescue mission we launched to save the nun and the orphans?" Jon asked.

"Yes," Kulayev replied. *After it was too late to do any good,* he thought.

"Did you tell Sultanovich?" Jon asked.

"No," Kulayev replied. *The man was an idiot,* Kulayev thought.

"No? Why not?" Jon asked.

"I didn't think you would be crazy enough to pursue him into Russia," Kulayev said. *Where are my men?* He thought.

"Are you ready?"

"No! Wait! Let me talk! I have more information! I can help you! Please! No!" Kulayev was sobbing as he closed his eyes.

"Adios, motherfucker!" Jon said as he covered Kulayev's mouth and drove the blade into his neck. Kulayev tried to resist but he was weak from years of sitting behind a desk. Blood sprayed out of the wound around the blade soaking the bedding as Jon worked his Ka-Bar back and forth until it stopped against his spine. Within seconds the resistance ended, and the blood flow slowed to a trickle. Jon wiped his blade and hands on the bedspread and walked over to the bathroom. He silently washed his knife and hands.

He turned and headed for the balcony but stopped halfway when he saw an open briefcase sitting on the desk. He spun it around and saw it was full of banded stacks of $100 bills. "Fuck me lucky!" he said quietly to himself. He counted the stacks and stuffed them into his backpack. It totaled a little over three million. He smiled. The money would go a long way toward supporting the orphans. He stepped out onto the balcony and leaned over the side. Angie was below on one knee scanning the area with his goggles. The dogs were still snoozing. Jon free-climbed down to the second-floor balcony. He climbed over the railing and hung from the edge before dropping onto the lawn next to Angie.

"It's about bloody time, mate! Did you stop to have tea?" Angie asked.

"Kulayev asked me to wait while he made a donation to the Saint Michael's Orphan's Fund," Jon replied, sarcasm dripping from every word.

"Really? How big?" Angie asked.

"North of three mil," Jon replied, "But I'll have to hold back about ten grand to repay Gwenn for her Scottish vacation.

"I'm surprised he was so generous," Angie said.

Jon said with a sly smile, "Well, it was his dying wish." Jon felt his sat phone vibrate in his left cargo pocket. He retrieved it and read the message. "Fuck! I gotta get home! My brother's in trouble!" he said as he stepped off toward the rope on the compound wall.

"What is it, Jonny?" Angie asked as he hurried to keep up. Jon showed him the two-word message, BROKEN ARROW.

THE END

Thank you for reading ESCAPE FROM DONETSK. I sincerely hope you enjoyed it. Please, do me a huge favor and leave a review on Amazon. Indie authors, like me, struggle to get reviews for our books. I've read typically only one of 200 readers leave a review. Reviews on Amazon help move my book up in the rankings and give me a more competitive chance as I compete with more well established authors.

Also, please join my Newsletter using the link below for updates on future Jon Smith novels and short stories and I will give you a FREE copy of my Jon Smith Short Story, SMOKE SIGNALS. I promise I won't sell or share your email address with others.

Bob Asher Books Newsletter
https://BookHip.com/HXFQKLV

GLOSSARY

- **ACE** – USMC Aviation Combat Element

- **ACOG** – Advanced Combat Optical Gunsight

- **ACP** – Automatic Colt Pistol

- **AGL** – Above Ground Level

- **AIM-174B** – Long-Range Air-to-Air Missile

- **AN/PRC** – Army/Navy, Portable, Radio, Communication

- **ARG** – US Navy Amphibious Ready Group

- **BARCAP** – Barrier Combat Air Patrol

- **BMG** – Browning Machine Gun

- **BMP** – Russian Military Tracked Amphibious Infantry Fighting Vehicles

- **BTR** – Russian Military Armored Personnel Carrier

- **DDO** – Deputy Director of Operations

- **DHS** – Department of Homeland Security

- **DNI** – Director of National Intelligence

- **DOD** – Department of Defense

- **EFP** – Explosively Formed Penetrator type IED

- **EO** – Earth Observation Satellite

- **FBO** – Fixed Base Operator

- **FGM-148** – Javelin Anti-Tank Missile System

- **FLIR** – Forward Looking Infrared

- **FOB** – Forward Operating Base

- **FOV** – Field of View

- **GPNVG** – Ground Panoramic Night Vision Google

- **GRU** – Main Intelligence Directorate, Military Intelligence for the Russian Federation

- **GTFO** – Get The Fuck Out

- **HALO** – High-Altitude, Low-Opening

- **HE** – High Explosive

- **HIMARS** – M142 High Mobility Artillery Rocket System

- **HK416** – Heckler & Koch Assault Rifle Chambered in 5.56×45mm NATO

- **HMH** – Heavy Marine Helicopter Squadron

- **HMLA** – Light Attack Marine Helicopter Squadron

- **HMT** – Marine Heavy Helicopter Training Squadron

- **ICS** – Intercom System

- **IED** – Improvised Explosive Device

- **IFAK** – Individual First Aid Kit

- **IFR** – Instrument Flight Rules

- **IR** – Infrared

- **ISR** – Intelligence, Surveillance, and Reconnaissance

- **KAMPO** – Russian Military Bayonet

- **LZ** – Landing Zone

- **M-203** – 40 mm single-shot under-barrel grenade launcher

- **MANPAD** – Man-Portable Air Defense System

- **MEU** – Marine Expeditionary Unit

- **MICH** – Modular Integrated Communications Helmet

- **MRAP** – Mine Resistant Ambush Protected Vehicle

- **MRE** – Meal Read to Eat

- **MSA** – Minimum Safe Altitude

- **NATO** – North Atlantic Treaty Organization

- **NATOPS** – Naval Air Training and Operating Procedures Standardization

- **NCIS** – Naval Criminal Investigative Service

- **NVGs** – Night Vision Goggles

- **OGA** – Other Government Agency

- **PNG** – Persona Non Grata

- **POTUS** – President of the United States

- **PTT** – Push to Talk

- **QRF** – Quick Reaction Force

- **RAF** – Royal Air Force

- **RIM-66** – Medium-Range Anti-Ship Surface-to-Air Missile

- **RPG** – Rocket Propelled Grenade

- **RTB** – Return to Base

- **SAM** – Surface to Air Missile

- **SAW** – Squad Automatic Weapon

- **SEAL** – Naval Special Warfare warrior trained to conduct a wide range of special operations missions in the sea, the air, and on land.

- **SF** – Short Frame, Some Glock pistols offer a short frame model

- **SH** – Sierra Hotel, Shit Hot

- **SITREP** – Situation Report

- **SMU** – Special Mission Unit

- **SVR RF** – Foreign Intelligence Service of the Russian Federation

- **Switchblade 300** – Kamikaze drone

- **Switchblade 600** – Kamikaze drone

- **TF** – Tango Uniform, Dead or Inoperative

- **UHF** – Ultra High Frequency

- **VFR** – Visual Flight Rules

- **VS-17** – Orange and Pink Signal Panel

- **X2D** – Quadcopter drone

- **XO** – Executive Officer

- **Z** – Zulu time. Also UTC (Universal) time or GMT (Greenwich Mean Time)

NOW, PLEASE ENJOY A SNEAK

PEEK OF MY NEXT JON SMITH

NOVEL

FLASH OVERRIDE

CHAPTER 1

Jon and Angie sat next to each other in the cargo area of the L-100 cargo plane eating piping hot Zurek soup in sourdough bread bowls. They hadn't expected to eat during the flight but since they were the only passengers, their Polish flight crew shared their in-flight meal with them. They wolfed down the hearty soup and the bread bowl.

"Man, that was good. I don't know what was in it but it really hit the spot," Jon said appreciatively. He licked his MRE spoon clean and stuffed it back in his pocket. Professional soldiers always had a spoon close by just in case they came across an opportunity to eat something. The smart ones also carried a miniature bottle of Tabasco sauce.

"Yeah, it was great. It reminds me of my Ukrainian grandmother's soup. I think it's called Zurek. She made something similar when I was a kid. It was full of kielbasa, ham, boiled eggs, potatoes, and onions but this one was a lot spicier than hers," Angie replied. Angie was Jon's battle buddy, retired Warrant Officer Angus Hawkins of the Australian Special Air Service Regiment. They were in the insertion phase of their mission, a mission that started four months earlier in Ukraine when they rescued a nun and 91 Ukrainian orphans from corrupt Chechen soldiers. The soldiers were human traffickers who were selling the children to the highest bidder to be used in the sex trade or to be murdered for their vital organs. They paid for their transgressions with their lives. Jon and Angie's final target, the broker who arranged the sales of thousands of children, eluded them. In the coming days, they would finish what they started.

***

An hour later, the loadmaster's hands alternated between the bulkhead and cargo nets as he shuffled his way down the narrow path between the cargo pallets and the red nylon troop seats to talk to his only passengers. They were strapped into seats near the ramp of the white and blue Lockheed L-100 also known as a Hercules. It was a civilian version of the military C-130 tactical cargo plane. CIA Paramilitary Operations Officer Jon Smith sat with his boots crossed on top of his pack and a paperback in his hands. He had his blue LED headlamp turned on so he could read Alice York's latest Amish romance/action thriller titled *Black Hawk Down on the Farm* as the aircraft shook and shimmied its way across the foreboding sky. Angie was lying beside him in his sleeping bag, peacefully snoring the night away.

The loadmaster tapped Jon's boot to get his attention. He motioned to Angie. Jon removed one of his foam earplugs and shook Angie's shoulder. "We are on approach to Chisinau International but the ceiling and visibility are down to 700 feet and a mile and there's sleet and freezing rain in the vicinity. How badly do you need to get in there tonight?" the loadmaster asked in thickly accented English loud enough to be heard over the four Allison turboprop engines. Each was putting out 4,510 shaft horsepower.

"Not bad enough to spend my final minutes screaming in terror before I burn alive. How about you Angie?" Jon asked.

Angie looked up to the loadmaster and replied, "No thanks. I'm good with living to fight another day, and ah, thanks for the soup, mate. It was delicious." Jon nodded his agreement. Angie put his head back down in the bag.

The loadmaster smiled and threw them a thumbs up before turning to walk back the way he came.

Jon stretched and twisted his back and neck as he sat on the uncomfortable nylon bench seat. As he scanned the cabin's ceiling he noticed four olive drab parachutes hanging from the rafters. "Hey Angie, look at this," he said as he pointed to the parachutes. "That seems awfully optimistic, don't you think?"

Angie peeked out of his bag and asked, "What do you mean?"

"Well, there are four guys on the aircrew and four parachutes hanging up there. If the plane starts going down what makes them think we're going to just sit here and let them put those parachutes on?" Jon asked.

"They might get away with it if they don't wake me up," Angie replied before his head disappeared again.

Within a couple of minutes, the shaking and shimming became severe. The plane dropped abruptly like a broken elevator. If Jon and Angie weren't belted down they would have smacked into the overhead.

Suddenly, Angie wasn't sleepy anymore. His head popped out of the bag and he said, "What the hell was that, mate?"

"I don't know," Jon said as he shined his light around the cargo area and pallets in front of them.

The loadmaster hurried down the path to them again. He yelled, "Ice is building up on the wings and fuselage. We're committed to landing at Chisinau now. Stay strapped in and you'll be fine. You're in the safest seats on the airplane!" He gave them another thumbs up and rushed away toward the cockpit.

"That's funny, I don't feel safer!" Jon shouted to Angie who was now sitting up, out of his sleeping bag, with his OD green Ops-Core Fast SF High Cut helmet on.

"Why can't we fly commercial like civilized people?" Angie complained. The L-100 bucked violently.

"When have you ever been accused of being civilized?" Jon replied. He looked around, "Are we flying sideways?" His inner ear was telling him the left wing had dropped and he felt weight build up on his back as he was pressed against his nylon web seatback. Jon's eyes went wide as a heavy-duty tie-down strap holding the cargo pallet in place popped loose between his feet and flapped back and forth several feet from his face. The pallet shifted ever so slightly toward him, causing him to reflexively pull his feet back. Jon reached for the strap but his seat belt held him back. He released his seat belt just in time for the plane to return to level flight momentarily before the right wing dropped. He was thrown into the side of the pile of cargo before falling up to the ceiling and then onto the floor on the other side of the pallet. Stars danced before his eyes. The plane slowly returned to wings level.

"Are you all right, Jonny?" Angie shouted. He couldn't see Jon over the top of the cargo.

"No!" Jon replied annoyed. He blinked hard to clear the stars as he started climbing over the cargo using the cargo net for handholds. He clambered over the top and dropped down on the left side where he tried to get the cargo strap back in place. He pulled on the strap with all his strength until his arms quivered but he was still two inches short. "Angie, help me!" he yelled over the engines. Angie dropped to his knees and held the pad eye ring up. Jon quickly hooked the strap to it before ratcheting it tight. They didn't waste any time getting their seat belts back on. Then they sat anxiously waiting for the plane to disintegrate around them.

The noise level inside the cargo area lessened as the pilot throttled back on the engines to decelerate and lowered the nose to descend. Sounds they had heard hundreds of times before during their careers now sounded foreign and frightening. "What is that? Is something wrong with the engines?" Angie asked. He and Jon shared concerned looks.

"Shit! I don't know!" Jon replied. "Angie, why don't you climb up there and get a couple of those parachutes for us?" Jon asked.

"Fuck you, mate!" Angie replied.

Next, they heard electric motors activating to lower the flaps on the wings to increase the lift they provided. "Fuck! It sounds like something is scraping against the wings," Jon said.

Other motors lowered the landing gear. Jon felt a thump from behind as the left main mount locked into place. "The plane's coming apart!" He felt sick to his stomach. He grabbed an air sickness bag from the holder attached to the bulkhead behind him and spewed the yummy soup into it. Angie, being a sympathetic puker, was five seconds behind him. They had been sitting there for five minutes praying for salvation while holding their partially digested bags of Zurek when the wheels contacted the pavement of Runway 08.

The pilot reversed the pitch on the propellers to rapidly slow the plane before he turned off on the midfield taxiway and headed for the parking ramp. A follow-me truck met them and led them to their parking spot. As they came to a stop Jon saw the loadmaster climbing down the steps from the cockpit. Jon quickly said, "Take this!" and handed off his puke bag to Angie.

"Hey, hold on, mate!" Angie complained as he held the bag gingerly at arm's length like it contained Ebola.

Jon swiftly opened his pack and pulled out a two-gallon Ziplock bag with a clean change of clothes in it. He removed the clothes and stuffed them back into the pack. Jon grabbed both airsickness bags, secured them inside the Ziplock bag, and put it back in his pack right before the loadmaster stepped over their legs to get to the rear of the plane. Jon turned to Angie and said, "This never happened. If the team got wind of it they'd memorialize it somehow on the wall of shame in the team room right next to the photo you took of my naked ass in the Suburban." He was referring to an incident in Ukraine four months earlier when they came under attack while Angie was driving down the highway as Jon stood in the backseat trying to take a shit in another two-gallon Ziplock bag. The bags were extremely versatile and a favorite in the special operations community. Russian separatists in two technicals opened fire on them and Jon stood up in the open sunroof to return fire with his trousers down around his ankles. Angie took a smiling selfie with Jon's bare ass beyond Angie's right shoulder so he could share the moment with the entire fucking intelligence community.

Angie smiled and said, "What never happened?"

The loadmaster lowered the ramp and they shouldered their packs before walking down the ramp onto the pavement. The concrete was slick with a thin layer of ice. A light but steady curtain of sleet was falling as a silver Toyota Land Cruiser pulled up next to the ramp and a short man wearing a green camouflaged Gortex jacket hopped out from the front passenger side. "Jon, it's good to see you, my friend. Welcome back to Chisinau," he said with a smile.

"It's good to see you too, Cujo," Jon said as they hugged. "This is my friend, Angus Hawkins."

"It is good to meet you, Angus. I am Major Maximilian Cojocari, but please, call me Cujo," he said as they shook hands.

"Good to meet you, too, mate. You can call me Angie," he replied.

"Come. Let us get out of this miserable weather," Cujo said as they hurried to the car. Cujo's driver, his oldest son, quickly maneuvered them off the airport and onto the highway. Cujo's head was on a swivel. He had made many enemies during his twenty-five-year intel career. He alternated his attention between the highway and his guests. Cujo leaned over his seat back to talk to Jon and Angie. "The weather is too bad for you to continue your flight tonight. You will stay at my house and continue tomorrow night when the weather will be good."

"Are you sure? What about Maria?" Jon asked. Maria was Cujo's wife.

"Maria loves you. I called her. She is happy you are coming. She has a late dinner prepared. It's very good. She made a Polish soup called Zurek," Cujo reassured him.

"Great, that sounds terrific," Jon said to the back of Cujo's head as he exchanged an uneasy look with Angie.

Cujo fished some papers out of his pocket. "Have you seen these?" Cujo asked as he handed two wanted posters to Jon.

Jon studied Angie's poster and laughed at the sketch of his face. He looked like a rather mannish Catholic nun wearing Ray-ban Wayfarer sunglasses. He handed it to Angie, who cringed. "Certainly not my finest hour."

Jon looked at his own wanted poster. "This is bullshit, this looks nothing like me!" Jon complained.

Angie snatched it from his hand. "I don't know, mate. It looks accurate to me. Perhaps the eyes could be a bit beadier," he said.

"Sure, it does, in a menacing serial killer sort of way," Jon replied.

"Well, you did look quite menacing when you were driving your knife down into Sultanovich's neck and you racked up a rather spectacular body count that day. Hey, look at this," Angie said with pride as he pointed at the posters, "I'm worth twice as much as you."

"What? Let me see that!" Jon grabbed the posters. His eyes went back and forth between them. "Son of a bitch!" Angie was worth one hundred million Russian rubles which converted to a little over $1,000,000. Jon's was only fifty million.

"Maybe you need a better press agent," Angie teased.

CHAPTER 2

1200 LOCAL, THURSDAY, NOVEMBER 30, DAY 1, HIGHWAY D FARMHOUSE, ST. FRANCOIS COUNTY, MISSOURI

A red, white, and blue cement truck from A2Z Concrete drove up the gravel driveway and stopped in front of the house. The driver sent out two quick blasts from his air horn. A man stepped out from behind the house and waved the driver forward. He guided him to stop next to a 15×30 foot hole in the ground. Concrete steps ended ten feet below the ground above. What looked like a concrete foundation with a nine-foot pour was covered with a heavy-duty corrugated metal roof and a rebar matrix to reinforce it. The driver climbed out of the cab and was met by a dark-skinned man who spoke with an odd accent. "Good morning, sir. I'm Floyd Greene. What can I do for you?" he asked.

"Good morning, sir. I need a six-inch thick roof poured on top of this foundation," the man said in English. It was obvious to

Greene that the man was a highly educated foreigner from one of those countries whose names ended in stan. Four other men stood by waiting with tools and rubber boots.

"That's a lot of concrete. Are you sure the roof can support it?" Greene asked.

The man seemed perturbed. "Yes, I am quite certain. I am a civil engineer. I have done the calculations. It is more than strong enough. Please, begin the pour," he said.

Greene nodded. "Okay, sir, you got it," he said. *It'll be fun watching that roof crumple up like an empty beer can,* he thought. He started pouring and said, "Just say when."

After the proper amount of concrete was received the engineer signaled for Greene to stop and joined the others to finish the concrete roof. Greene hosed the chute clean and retrieved the clipboard that held the invoice from the cab. He set it on the rear fender while he waited for the roof to collapse, but it held. While the men worked, he decided to go down the steps and take a look inside the bunker, storm shelter, or root cellar, whatever it was. He walked down the wide stairs and stopped at a heavy gray steel commercial door. He turned the knob and pushed it open. The room was dark except for what little light made it down the stairs. He stuck his head inside and waved his cell phone light around. He found a light switch on the wall next to the door and flipped it on. Overhead fluorescent lights bathed the large room in bright blue tinted light. It was empty except for five large steel eyebolts embedded waist-high in the far wall. *Sex dungeon. Kinky,* he thought as he flipped the lights off and walked back up the stairs. He was met by the engineer who handed him the clipboard. He had already signed it. Greene peeled off his copy and gave it to him. "Here you go, sir. Let us know if you need anything else," he said.

He turned to look at the roof. "The roof looks great. You guys do good work." He climbed into the truck and drove away.

A silver Mercedes sedan passed the cement truck on the gravel driveway going in the opposite direction. The man wearing a dark gray suit parked behind the house and walked over to the bunker. "Excellent work, brothers. Soon we will be done with this God-forsaken country and we can go home," he said in Chechen. The men gathered around him.

"We may have a problem, Mukhamed," the engineer said to his brother.

"What is it, Khamza? The roof looks fine," Mukhamed asked.

"While we were distracted finishing the roof, the driver went down the stairs and looked inside. I am certain he saw the eye-bolts," Khamza said.

"I see. I realize Father put me in charge because I am the oldest but I have no experience in these matters. I will continue to rely on all of your expertise. Should we silence this man?" he asked the group.

The fourth son, a soldier, Alvi spoke up. "We cannot risk leaving him alive. He could ruin the plan before we get started. Solta, Dokka, and I will take care of it tonight. We will make it look like an accident or suicide." The others nodded their agreement.

CHAPTER 3

2300 LOCAL, DECEMBER 1, DAY 2, SKY OVER CHECHNYA

"I'm already hating this," Jon transmitted on his team radio from underneath his oxygen mask, "It's going to be minus 40°F outside when we jump." He liked jumping out of airplanes almost as much as he enjoyed long underwater ocean swims, which was not at all. There was so much that could go wrong. You could do everything right and still die horribly. He and Angie were pre-breathing 100% oxygen for 45 minutes before they jumped off the ramp of the L-100 from flight level 230 which was 7,000 meters or 23,000 ft. They were wearing insulated jumpsuits over their civilian clothes to ward off the bitter cold.

"No worries, mate. It'll all be over in a few minutes. Ground temp is a balmy 30°F," Angie teased.

"I better not break my leg before I get to kill this motherfucker," Jon whined.

"Remind me again why you became a SEAL?" Angie asked. Jon's answer was always different.

"My recruiter told me I could fly Hornets but he signed me up as a culinary specialist. No way was I going to clean tables and wash dishes for six years. My only options to get out of it in boot camp were volunteering for SEAL or EOD training. Those crazy EOD fucks jump and swim like SEALS except they get the added fun of defusing 2,000-pound bombs. Screw that," Jon replied.

"Would you prefer something smaller, say a misfired 40mm grenade?" Angie asked.

"Fuck no, I don't want to go blind or lose my hands. I would rather it be one of those big mothers. That way here one second, gone the next," Jon replied.

Angie laughed. "If you don't like jumping why do you keep doing it?" he asked.

Jon shrugged, "I guess I just like being around the type of people who like to jump. You know, crazy bastards, like you," Jon replied.

Angie laughed as the loadmaster walked past them. He motioned for them to stand up. He held up his thumb and two fingers.

Jon checked Angie's parachute and gear. He slapped him on the shoulder and said, "You're good." Jon turned around so Angie could check his.

Angie ran his hands over Jon's parachute and tactical gear and said, "I don't know Jonny; I don't think I'd jump with this parachute," Angie feigned concern.

"Ha-ha, fuck you, dickhead," Jon said as he held up his middle finger while waddling toward the ramp. Angie followed close behind. The loadmaster lowered the ramp to the level position. "Damn, that's cold!" Jon complained as the burble of frigid air came inside the cargo compartment. He lowered his GPNVGs over his clear-lensed Wiley goggles and stepped onto the ramp. The loadmaster wearing a helmet and oxygen mask of his own pointed at Jon and then turned, knelt down on one knee, and pointed off the ramp like he was a shooter or Navy catapult officer launching a Hornet off an aircraft carrier. *Everyone's a comedian,* Jon thought. He walked to the edge of the ramp and dove head-first into the dark abyss. Angie was two seconds behind him. They planned to free fall to 3,000 feet before popping their chutes.

"Gabby, please, tell me you're down there," Jon transmitted on the team radio as he reached terminal velocity, approximately 126 MPH.

"Roger that, I see you. I'm standing by," she replied.

"Is the van warmed up?" Jon asked.

"Affirmative. I even brought some hot chocolate and cookies," Gabby said.

"You know, you've always been my favorite," Jon said as he scanned the area for threats with his GPNVGs. The countryside was dark except for an occasional farmhouse. "Give us a vector."

"Steer 090° for three miles. When you get close I'll flip on my IR strobe," Gabby replied.

CHAPTER 4

The three brothers walked quietly across the field that backed up to Greene's house. He owned a two-acre lot on Highway K that was surrounded on three sides by cow pastures. The fence row was overgrown with bushes and weeds. They stopped at the fence, watched, and listened in the darkness. The fence did not continue around to the front of the house. "When Solta and I followed Greene home yesterday afternoon we did not see anyone else. We think he lives alone. The nearest house is 500 meters to the south," Alvi said.

"Does he have any dogs?" Dokka asked.

"None outside. I do not know about inside his house. Our boots are muddy. We must take them off before we go inside. Pull your masks down and keep your gloves on. He may have hidden cameras," Alvi said.

They covered their faces with ski masks and scaled the welded wire fence. They walked silently across the backyard and tried the sliding door. It opened. They sat on the edge of the small concrete patio and removed their boots. They opened the door again and Alvi turned on a dim blue LED light to help them see. They walked across the finished basement and checked the bedroom and adjacent bathroom. They were empty. Alvi led the way up the stairs. Upon opening the door on the first floor, he could hear Greene snoring on the second floor. "Clear this floor. I will go upstairs to watch Greene," Alvi whispered to his brothers. Moments later, Alvi stood in the open doorway to Greene's bedroom watching him snore. The room reeked of stale beer. He was soon joined by Solta and Dokka. Alvi readied the syringe of Propofol his older brother, the doctor provided. Mukhamed assured them it would render Greene unconscious in seconds. Solta and Dokka each held down one of Greene's arms as Alvi injected the Propofol into his neck.

"Hey, what the fuck is going on? Help! Help me!" Greene shouted into the darkness as he struggled before quickly falling silent. After a minute Solta and Dokka released their death grips on Greene's arms.

"Dokka, stay with him. Solta and I will have a look around to see what we can use for his suicide," Alvi said.

Dokka picked up Greene's cell phone off the bedside table and held it up to Greene's face to unlock it. He read through his most recent messages.

Alvi and Solta came back a few minutes later.

Dokka held up the phone. "His girlfriend broke up with him a week ago. He has been begging her to come back to him but she ignored his calls and texts. Last night he was suspended from his job for failing a drug test," Dokka said.

"Good that gives him reasons to hurt himself. There is an SKS rifle in the closet. We can use it to kill him. People in America like to kill themselves in bathtubs. It's easier to clean up. There is a bathtub in the basement. Let's take him down there. Is there a bucket in the house?" Alvi asked.

"Yes, there are several in the garage," Solta replied.

"Dokka, When we are ready. Text her that he will kill himself if she does not come to him right away. Then you and Solta watch from outside and let me know when she gets here. I'll shoot him when she gets inside so she can report hearing him shoot himself," Alvi said.

A half hour later the messages had been sent and the brothers were waiting in position. Headlights appeared a couple of miles down the highway. The car sped toward the house and slowed abruptly to pull into the driveway. "A car just arrived and a woman is running toward the front door," Solta said over his cell phone from his hidden vantage point behind the thick bushes in the fence row.

"Perhaps it would be better if this were a murder-suicide," Alvi proposed from the basement. The body was staged in the bathtub.

"Wait! A police car is coming with its emergency lights on. She must have called them before she drove here," Solta replied.

"All right, I will wait until the police are inside so they can hear the gunshot," Alvi said. He heard the woman open the unlocked front door and run upstairs to look for Floyd. Seconds later she came back to the first floor. Floyd wasn't there either. She tried the basement door and found it locked. She cried out for Floyd to unlock the door. Next Alvi heard the police knock on the front door.

CHAPTER 5

"Welcome back, Brother. How was Alabama?" Deputy Kurt Sada asked his temporary partner and trainee as they sat in the front row of tables in the St. Francois County, Missouri Sheriff's Department squad room waiting for shift change to start.

"It sucked being away from home for two months, but it wasn't all bad. The weather was warmer than it is up here and learning to fly the Black Hawk was a blast. After a couple of weeks, Patty flew down to Pensacola and we spent the weekend together. Then Patty and Danny came down to Rucker to see me over the Thanksgiving break. The extra money was nice," Deputy Zack Goodson replied. Zack had recently transferred his reserve commission from the Marine Corps to the Missouri Army National Guard and accepted orders to Fort Novosel, Alabama to go through transition training on the UH-60 Black Hawk helicopter. The Army called it the Aircraft Qualification Course. Now that he was a qualified copilot he would be working full-time as a deputy sheriff and part-time as a soldier.

"Mind if I ask how much they pay?"

"As a captain with eleven years of service with flight pay, it was a little over twenty grand before taxes for two months."

"Shit! That's six months' pay for me. I need to talk to your recruiter."

"The money's pretty good for officers, but if you sign up, you'll earn every penny. Did I miss anything interesting while I was gone?"

"A couple of weeks ago Daryl Ballard from Leadwood PD almost shot his dick off?"

"No shit! How'd he do that?"

"He was off duty having lunch at the Catfish Kettle with a friend of his. Daryl was telling him about his new Diamondback DB9 pistol. Have you ever seen one?"

Zack shook his head.

"It's a little polymer 9mm pocket gun and great for a backup because you can stick it in a pocket holster in your back pocket and it looks like a wallet. So, after they got done eating, they both went out to Daryl's truck so he could show him the pistol. They climbed in the cab and Daryl pulled the pistol out of his pocket still in the little nylon holster. He unloaded it and handed it to his buddy. He admired it for a minute and handed it back to Daryl. Daryl reloaded it and went to put it back in the holster. He was holding the holster between his legs with his left hand and began putting the pistol in the holster with his right hand when he realized his finger was in the trigger guard. He said his mind was screaming at his hand to stop, but it kept moving toward the holster. When his finger hit the edge of the holster the pistol fired and put a round through the inside of his left thigh a couple of inches from his junk. The bullet was an FMJ, so it went through the seat and stuck in the floor. People in the parking lot heard the shot and called 911. Then Daryl's buddy called 911 for an ambulance and told them Officer Ballard was shot in the leg. Dispatch put out an officer had been shot, so within five minutes ten police cars rolled into the parking lot.

"Damn, is he all right?"

"He's still on light duty walking around their station bow-legged, but yeah, he'll be okay. He does have a new nickname."

"What's that?" Zack smiled.

"Do you remember when Walter Brennan played the limping deputy in *Rio Bravo*?"

"Stumpy?"

"Yep, that's it." They both laughed.

The morning Watch Commander, Lieutenant Ike McLeod, entered the squad room and walked over to Kurt and Zack. "We already have a call. It's an attempted suicide." He handed Kurt a piece of paper with the address on it. "Get over there and see what's happening. Let me know if you need more help. Welcome back, Zack," he smiled.

***

"Central, ten-oh-five, 10-23," Zack transmitted over the cruiser's radio. 10-23 meant they had arrived at the farmhouse on Highway D.

"Ten-oh-five, 10-23, at 0549," Peggy, the Central County 911 dispatcher replied.

It was still dark as they approached the house cautiously with their Glocks held down along the sides of their legs. As they reached the porch, the front door flew open and a woman hurried outside. They could see by the porch light she had tears on her face. Before they could speak, she said, "Please, help me! He's going to kill himself!"

"Ma'am, who is he and is he armed?" Kurt asked.

"My boyfriend, Floyd locked himself in the basement. He's going to…" A gunshot thundered from inside the home. The woman screamed and yelled, "No!"

Zack and Kurt pushed past the woman with their guns aimed down the hall. Zack saw a stairway leading to the second floor. He went further down the hall and grabbed the knob on the basement door.

"The door's locked from the other side and it opens outward," Zack said. He pounded on the door with the bottom of his fist. "The door's hollow." He stepped back and kicked it. His boot went through the door and Kurt caught him before he could fall. Zack pulled his leg out of the hole and reached inside to unlock the knob. He opened the door.

Kurt stepped in front. "I'll go first." The lights were on in the basement. He called out, "Floyd, are you okay? We're here to help you! Call out if you hear me!"

Floyd's girlfriend was behind them. "Help him! He could be dying!"

"Ma'am, we're trying. Go wait by the front door. Zack, call for backup and an ambulance."

Zack made the call on his walkie.

"You have to help him. Don't just stand there." She tried to push past them. They stopped her.

"Go cuff her to the upstairs railing," Kurt said.

She refused to move so Zack picked her up around her waist and carried her back down the hall toward the front door. He handcuffed her left wrist to the cast iron railing leading upstairs and rejoined Kurt. They carefully moved down the stairs into the basement. Half of it was finished as a man cave.

"Floyd, where are you? Are you okay?" Kurt called out. There was no response. "Let's clear this room and then we'll check that bedroom back there." Kurt cleared the right side of the large room and Zack cleared the left side which included a homemade bar. They met at the bedroom doorway. They could smell blood and acrid gun smoke in the air. Kurt entered first. He could see across the room into the bathroom. "He's in the bathtub. I think he's dead." Kurt entered the bathroom with his Glock pointed at the body. He paused for a moment and holstered his pistol. "We're clear."

Zack entered behind him and they stood next to each other looking at the body. The man was wearing a gray "I Support the Right to Arm Bears" T-shirt and plaid boxers. A galvanized steel bucket was pulled down over his head. A cheap Chinese SKS rifle rested against his chest. It appeared he had stuck the barrel under his chin and pulled the trigger. The 7.62mm bullet had passed through his head and punched a hole in the bottom of the bucket. It broke one of the ceramic tiles in the wall behind him, but then the bullet ran out of energy and fell back into the tub between his legs. The bloody mess was contained within the bucket and to the top of his shirt. "I wonder why he did it. It looks like he had a nice place here," Zack wondered out loud.

"I don't know. Let's go ask her." Kurt said as he put on a pair of black nitrile gloves. They walked back upstairs.

As soon as they came into view, she asked, "Is he all right?"

"No, I'm sorry, he's not. It appears he shot himself. He's dead," Kurt replied.

She sat down on the stairs and cried.

"Zack, call Ike, on your cell phone and tell him what happened."

Zack walked outside onto the porch. "Hey, Lieutenant. It's Zack. The guy shot himself in the head right after we got here. His girlfriend is crying uncontrollably. We need the coroner and a detective out here."

"We don't have a detective right now. Mark's still on light duty rehabbing his arm, so he can't leave the station. You guys will have to handle the investigation. I'll call Les and get him heading your way," Lieutenant McLeod replied. Mark was Detective Sergeant Mark Langford. He had been shot in the left arm during an ambush about six months earlier in June by a crazed father who went on a killing spree after his daughter was found murdered. Zack had been with him during the ambush and saved his life. Les was the elected County Coroner, Lester Koplin. He also owned Koplin Funeral Home in Park Hills.

"Okay, sir. We're on it." Zack hung up and went back inside. Kurt had removed the woman's handcuffs. She was still sitting on the steps crying. "Ike said no detective today, we're it."

Kurt handed the handcuffs to Zack and nodded. "Yeah, that's what I figured." He turned back to the woman. She was beginning to regain her composure. What's your name ma'am?" Kurt asked.

"Brandy Carson."

"Do you live here?"

"No. I live with my mother in Park Hills."

Kurt wrote her name in his notebook. "What's his name?"

"Floyd Greene," she said.

"Ma'am, can you tell us why he would want to harm himself?" Kurt asked.

"I broke up with him last week and he started calling me constantly. After a few days, I stopped answering his calls. Then he started texting me. I didn't answer the texts either. About an hour ago he texted me that he was going to kill himself," she said.

"Where did he work?" Kurt asked.

"He drove a cement truck for that place, A2Z Concrete, south of Bonne Terre off Vo-Tech Road. They laid him off last night because he failed a drug test," she said.

"What was he using?" Kurt asked.

"Meth and a little weed," she said.

"Where was he getting it?" Kurt asked.

"I don't know?" she said.

"Do you use?" Kurt asked.

"No!" she feigned offense. "Is that all? Can I go now?"

"Yes, ma'am. We'll be in touch," Kurt replied.

She got up off the stairs and stomped out the front door.

"I guess you hit a nerve," Zack said as he watched her walk down the front steps.

"She probably got the drugs for him. She already has some signs of meth abuse on her face. In a year or two she'll look fifteen years older," Kurt said. "Why don't you go take some pictures and secure his rifle and that bullet."

***

An hour and a half later, Lester Koplin arrived in his van with his assistant, Timmy. They dragged their gurney across the yard and up the stairs. "Sorry, we took so long, boys. Where is he?" Koplin asked.

"He's in the basement. Follow me," Zack said.

"How was Rucker?" Timmy asked.

Zack looked up at the giant. "They changed the name. It's Novosel now. The flying was great, but I was ready to come home." He led them down the narrow basement stairs. All four of them gathered in the small bathroom.

Koplin took a minute to put on a pair of blue nitrile gloves. He looked over the body and the bucket. "This is one of the most considerate suicide victims I've ever seen. He kept the mess contained to the tub. Did you guys already take your pictures?"

"Yeah, we're good," Zack said.

Koplin leaned over to lift the bucket off the head. They heard the vacuum releasing as he raised the bucket. The bullet hole in the bottom of the bucket made it easier. As the bucket came off, the head separated in the middle and fell over on both shoulders. The brain matter slid down the front of his shirt. Zack turned away and puked all over the toilet.

Kurt was mesmerized by the grotesque headless body. "Man, that's fucked up! It smells as bad as it looks!" He leaned in next to Koplin and pointed to the left shoulder. "Is that an eyeball?" Zack hurled again as he held the toilet bowl. Kurt turned to see Zack convulsing and grinned. "You gonna be all right, Devil Dog?" Zack gave him a thumbs up and stuck his head in the sink to rinse his mouth out.

FLASH OVERRIDE Release Planned for Winter 2024

ABOUT THE AUTHOR

Bob is a retired supervisory intelligence officer with the National Geospatial-Intelligence Agency (NGA). He grew up in and around St. Louis, Missouri. By the time he was in high school he knew he wanted to do two things with his life: fly in the military and work in law enforcement. After graduating from Parks College of St. Louis University with a degree in Aeronautics he earned a commission in the USMC. He became a Naval Aviator flying the CH-53D Sea Stallion helicopter. After his active duty, he returned to the St. Louis area and worked as a police officer. When the Twin Towers were attacked, he joined the Missouri Army National Guard and flew Black Hawk helicopters in Iraq during Operation Iraqi Freedom II. While in Iraq he applied for and accepted a position with NGA. Now he and his wife live a quiet life in the country surrounded by trees.